THE LAST WITNESS - BOOK 1

K. T. ROBERTS

Novel Options
A Roberts' Imprint

DEDICATION

Dedicated to the one I love.
Without you, there is no music.

BOOKS BY K. T. ROBERTS

KENSINGTON-GERARD DETECTIVE SERIES

The Last Witness - Book 1

Elusive Justice - Book 2

Deadly Obsessions - Book 3

The Vow – Book 4

Sleeping with the Enemy - Book 5

Blind Retribution

Educating Daphne-Contemporary Romance

Strangers in the Night

Death by Stiletto – A Cape May Cozy Caper

Once Upon a Christmas – A Cape May Cozy Christmas

BOOKS BY CAROLYN HUGHEY

Dishing Up Romance – Chef's Toque Book 1

One Menu at a Time – Chef's Toque Book 2

Catering to Love – Chef's Toque Book 3

Shut up and Kiss Me

Cover Design by Carol Webb – Bella Media Management

✯ Created with Vellum

ACKNOWLEDGMENTS

As always, no book would be possible without the shared knowledge and encouragement of others throughout the process.

My heartfelt thanks to my sister, L. Jessie Esposito, a former undercover detective in the Port Authority of NY-NJ, for her knowledge and thirty-six years of expertise to make sure I was on the right track. Another thanks to the law enforcement officers at crimescenewriters, and Lee Lofland of the Writers' Police Academy who willingly answered my unending questions. On the home front, my wonderful husband, Bob, who played a significant role in helping to make this story a reality! I love you with all my heart.

PRAISE FOR K. T. ROBERTS

Praise for *The Last Witness and Elusive Justice*

"Even the ending packs a punch!"

"I'm not going to spoil anything about this book, but I will say . . . if you like James Paterson's books, you'll really enjoy this one."

"For those who got hooked on the O.J. trial, you'll enjoy the latest from K. T. Roberts."

"But perhaps my favorite character is twelve-year old Max, a kid who has to deal with the clash between conscience and curiosity. I'm ready to adopt Max."

"This mystery touches all the bases: an investigation, a villain, a dash of romance and a pinch of humanity. You'll like it. I did."

"This book really holds your attention from the very first page." "K.T. Roberts manages to weave mystery, romance and suspense all in one story. Loved it!

So much so that I started the book and could not put it down until I'd read the very last word!!"

"This is a well-structured police procedural with two sharp detectives who know how to get the job done."

CHAPTER 1

NEW YORK CITY
August 23, 2007

Run, Jessie, run! Her muscles screamed with pain and exhaustion. To stop was not an option—not now. She had to get away from whoever was chasing her.

Run, dammit, run.

White-hot pain engulfed her lungs, and the dryness in her throat made her tonsils feel swollen. She curled her tongue, squeezed her mouth to create saliva, and then swallowed. She ran up the hill, then down the other side. When the dirt shifted under her feet, she slid but stayed upright.

The wind kicked up, and Jessie coughed to expel the dust she inhaled, never letting up on her pace.

"Where the hell am I?" she screamed, unable to see what lay ahead. Her parched throat burned with every breath, yet she continued to run. She pushed the thought away.

His raspy breathing and the thunderous pounding of his feet told her he had gained on her. She must have slowed down without realizing it. The intensity of pain in her legs grew more assertive. She willed them to move faster, but they refused to cooperate. "Oh, God, please help me."

She turned her head to look over her shoulder and saw him a few feet behind her. A surge of adrenaline took over, and she sprinted forward, then tripped over the uneven terrain and fell to the ground. She tried to stand, but a sharp blow to the center of her back caused her knees to buckle and sent her sprawling forward. Pain shot through her nose when her face struck the hard surface. She squeezed her eyes shut, begging the pain to go away. Blood gushed down her face and into her mouth. The disgusting taste of copper made her gag.

She knew it was all over when his evil laughter echoed in her ears. He was going to kill her. Fear, thick as the blood running down her face, froze her to the spot. She lay helpless on the sparsely grass-covered ground and released a low, tortured sob, afraid to fight back.

He reached for her arms and pulled them behind her back. She could feel the sharpness of a rope cut into the skin on her wrists. A trickle of fluid ran down the side of her hand. Blood? Was it her blood? Or was it his sweat? The latter disgusted her and made her want to heave again.

"Oh God," she gasped, her heart hammering out of control so loudly she could feel the vibrations throughout her body. She whispered a silent prayer, hoping whatever was about to happen would be swift.

He jerked her to an upright position, whirled her around, and forced her onto a large boulder. The black hooded cape he wore concealed everything except his piercing eyes. She focused on them, trying to identify her assailant, if not for the police, for herself—so she would know who was stalking her—know who wanted her dead.

The click of the hammer echoed in the still of the night and made her cringe. If she hadn't already been sitting, her legs would have given out when he pressed the cold steel of a gun barrel against her cheek. *One last chance for someone to hear me* went through her mind, and she heard herself screaming at the top of her lungs.

Detective Tate Kensington, known as Jessie James to her peers, jerked her eyes open and forced herself to roll over onto her side to scan the room. Her muzzy thinking made her unsure of where she was. Pressing her hand against her heart, now pounding against her ribcage, she sat upright, took deep breaths, and tried to calm down, then slowly pushed herself back up against the headboard. Lowering her head into her hands, she tried to remember all the details, but as with most dreams, details never came.

When the floor creaked, she panicked. Without moving, she narrowed her eyes and peered into the darkness. It took a few minutes for them to adjust, but she needed to know whether someone was in her apartment or if it was her mind playing tricks. When heavy footsteps tromped overhead, she felt relieved that it was her neighbor and chalked it up to her paranoia.

She blew out a hefty breath of air, flopped back down on the pillows, and willed her racing heart to calm down. The sound from her ragged breathing broke the silence. Damn! If this was a dream, why did the sensation of that gun against her cheek feel so real? And why had she smelled a hint of gunpowder? Her hand instinctively reached up to touch the spot on her cheek where he'd pointed that gun. Relief washed over her when her fingertips touched the smoothness of her skin, reinforcing that it was indeed a bad dream. Still nervous, Jessie reached over, pulled open the nightstand drawer, and touched her Glock. Thank God it was still there.

The shrill ring of her phone made her jump. She raised her hand to answer it, then pulled back. The sensation of dread refused to go away. When the ringing finally stopped, she breathed a sigh of relief until it rang again a few seconds later. This time, she glanced at her phone and saw her partner's name flash across the screen. "This better be good, Gerard."

"Uh-oh, somebody's grumpy."

"What did you expect in the middle of the night? A thank you note for waking me?" She ran a hand over her face and tried to clear the cloud of fog from her head. The last thing she wanted was for her partner, or the guys in the department, to know how freaked out she'd become over a dumb dream. Not that she thought Zach Gerard would tell anyone, but men gossiped just as much as women—maybe even more. They'd been partners going on three years; they knew each other pretty well, but there were some things you didn't share. "So? What do you want?" she asked.

Gerard cleared his throat. "Are you done yet?"

"Yes."

"Good, because we have a homicide out at Central Park, specifically Bow Bridge."

She pictured his handsome face as he spoke—rugged, yet still a devilish boy inside, begging to come out when he became full of fun. And forget those damned toffee-colored eyes that seemed to look right through her. And as if that wasn't enough, the deep cleft in his chin that jutted out when he got pissed. Yeah, Zach Gerard was a gorgeous hunk of a man, but she'd told herself a million times getting involved with a playboy type was the furthest thing from her mind— at least, most of the time. His smile, his body—they did things to her mind,no other man could claim; but being dumb and foolish about getting involved with a partner, the way she had with Jack Harwell many years ago, had left a substantial scar and almost ruined her career. Although, she had to admit he sure was tempting.

"Oh man," Jessie forced her mind to listen to his words and not the sound of his sexy voice. "You mean the lieutenant couldn't give it to Santori and Paige?"

"I believe his exact words were, "no exceptions." He's expecting to see the entire team present and accounted for by the time he arrives, which no doubt will be within the hour, so get that cute little ass out of bed. I'll be outside in ten minutes." The phone went dead.

"No exceptions, huh?" Jessie clicked off the call and huffed out a breath, this time shaking her head, annoyed Jack Harwell's new assignment was in the two-one, and he was her boss.

Swinging her legs over the side of the bed, she leaned forward and flipped on the lamp. The light flooded the room with a soft amber glow.

She had ten years on the force, three of those in the two-one. When her peers started treating her differently, she knew word was out that she'd dated Harwell. The problem was they thought it was current events and not a thing of the past. And then it started. Threatening notes began to appear. Though Jessie wasn't sure, she was convinced the guys were sending those notes, hoping she'd quit. They resented that she always seemed to get the good cases.

Things had been fine in the department until Harwell had accepted the promotion. Jessie couldn't help but feel resentful. She realized she could have transferred out, but leaving Gerard and getting another partner she might not get along with was not an option. She shrugged, telling herself everything was a trade-off and she'd just have to make the best of it.

Jessie crossed the room and entered the bathroom, turning on the faucet to brush her teeth. Squeezing paste onto her toothbrush, she did the deed, then ran a brush through her long auburn locks, pulling her hair into a ponytail with a scrunchie she'd found on the messy counter.

She groaned when she glanced at her reflection in the mirror. A pair of bloodshot eyes that resembled a roadmap stared back at her. And the bags underneath her eyes were definitely from lack of sleep and did not do much for her appearance. But then, this wasn't a beauty pageant but a homicide in the middle of the freakin' night.

Her fingertips pushed on the skin as if the pressure would release the puffiness and decrease the swelling. Vanity was evident even at 3:50 in the morning. Still groggy, Jessie walked to the nightstand, removed her Glock from the drawer, and checked the chamber to see if she'd remembered to load it last night. Last night? It had only been a few hours since she'd gone to bed. She released another grumble of displeasure, then reached for her shoulder holster draped over her bedpost. Before snapping the holster, she checked the ammo carrier and snapped the stays around her belt. Her eyes took one last scan around her apartment to ensure she hadn't forgotten anything, and she was out the door.

A warm breeze brushed against her face when she hit the outdoors, and she wished for colder weather. August in New York City was always the worst summer month with its hazy, hot, and humid days.

Gerard's lean body rested against the unmarked car, one ankle crossed over the other, a smirk spread across his face, and a large container of coffee in his outstretched hand. She accepted the coffee as she passed by him on her way to the passenger's side of the vehicle.

The tight T-shirt he wore stretched across his chest deserved a second glance. But so did his other attributes, like his thick, dark, wavy hair that rested on his collar, the stubble on his chin against his bronzed tan, and his piercing eyes that made her shudder every time he gazed into hers. Yeah, those eyes were something all right. They made her feel like he was digging into the very core of her soul.

Jessie pushed her mind back to the real world and reminded herself if history had taught her anything, it was never to repeat mistakes. Zach Gerard was mighty fine all right, but getting involved with another partner wasn't worth the aggravation. Of course, there was no harm in dreaming.

"Glad to see you made it, Jessie James."

She sipped the coffee. Hearing Gerard call her Jessie James always made her smile and reminded her of how she'd gained the moniker early in her career when she was a uniformed cop. Anxious to prove she was one of the guys in the male-dominated precinct, the opportunity presented itself during a night watch at the Lincoln Tunnel when two guys, armed with double-barreled sawed-off shotguns, ran across the Plaza and into the tower behind her. Scared to death, Jessie knew if she was going to make her mark in the department, she had to do something heroic. She remembered sneaking up behind them, weapon drawn; she held them at bay until backup arrived. Ever since then, everyone knew her as the gun-slinging Jesse James.

"Thanks."

"Want to drive?" he asked.

"Not unless you want to get into an accident," Jessie rolled her eyes, as she opened the passenger's door and slid across the seat, while holding her container of coffee.

"I figured I'd better bring you some peace offering after interrupting your beauty rest." His devilish grin accentuated the deep dimples in his cheeks, and his eyes sparkled like gemstones.

"Yeah, I can see the tears running down your cheeks." She shook her head and changed the subject. "Who called in the homicide?"

"Your favorite law enforcer, Tip Jackson. He was first on the scene after dispatch got the call from a biker going through the park."

"A biker in Central Park at this hour of the morning?" Her eyebrows creased. "What? Is he training for the Olympics? And how long did Jackson wait before contacting us?" She fired one question after another like it was an interrogation. When he didn't respond immediately and sat staring at her, she tossed her hand. "What?"

"I believe it was right away," Gerard said.

"And how the hell did the biker see a dead body in the dark? Was it under a street light?"

"Whoa, slow down, Jessie," he said, reaching over to pat the top of her hand. "You're getting yourself all fired up over there. Two witnesses were in the park and found the body. They didn't have a cell phone, so they did the next best thing—flagged down a biker and asked him to call 911." He gave her a side glance; his eyebrows rose high on his forehead. "What's the matter? I'm not talking fast enough for you?" He laughed. "I know your head's not in the same place as mine right now, but I'll get to it if you give me a chance."

"Only nut jobs," she scowled, "would visit the park at this hour?"

"Dispatch said the couple, who claim they were out watching the stars, fell over the body."

"Who doesn't carry a cell phone with them today?"

"Uh, Jess -- you need to get out more. At that hour of the morning, these people weren't going for a stroll. I think they were screwing in the bushes." Gerard shook his head at her impatience. "You're a piece of work this morning." He stared into the distance as though he had something on his mind. "You know, that's how I want my marriage to be, out watching the stars or in the bushes with my wife. Mmm," his hand tapped the steering wheel, "Yep, that's what I want."

"Are you kidding me? You? Married? You're in and out of too many beds to settle down with one woman." She twisted her mouth to the side when she recounted how many women he'd mentioned over the last month.

"I don't tell tales out of school."

"I wasn't asking, hotshot," she countered and downed a swig of coffee.

"Lighten up, will you?" His eyes narrowed in a frown. "What's biting you?"

"Nothing, Gerard. You woke me up out of a sound sleep."

"This isn't the first time you've gotten a call in the middle of the night. What's the big deal?"

She eased off and took a deep breath. Gerard was right; she did need to lighten up.

When Jessie didn't respond, Gerard flipped the switch for the siren and remained silent until they reached the crime scene. He pulled over to the side of the road, jammed the gearshift into park, and they swiftly exited the vehicle. Pulling out his flashlight, he beamed it onto the ground, lighting a path. Jessie grabbed the flashlight from the car and walked over to the paramedics as they lifted someone into the cavity of the EMS vehicle. She checked the time, noting it was four thirty-five AM. She jotted the time down in her notebook.

"Who is this person?" she asked.

In the background, the older of the two paramedics was talking to the hospital, giving the victim's stats. "A female in her mid to late thir-ties," the young man reported. He didn't look old enough to drive, let alone be an EMT.

"Wait, I'm confused," Jessie frowned, wondering why they hadn't received a second call from dispatch confirming another casualty. "I thought we had a dead male."

"You do," he nodded toward the crime scene. "He's back by Bow Bridge waiting for the coroner to arrive."

"And is that where you found her?"

"We found her in the area of the Ramble, passed out on the edge of the rock slab. One false move, and she might have rolled down those cascading rocks right into the lake and drowned." He wrote something down on the clipboard he held in his hand. "She has some bruising under her eyes, probably from the airbag's impact, some abrasions about the face, a large gash on her back thigh, and she's drowsy.

Maybe a concussion, or maybe she's on something." He shrugged. "We've already asked the hospital to do a Tox screen to be sure."

Jessie entered the vehicle to take a closer look at the woman. She was pretty. Her long dark hair was slightly matted. Examining her fingers, Jessie noticed her perfectly manicured nails. Her brows rose at the size of the diamond ring and wedding band on her left hand. Dried blood was caked under her nose and on her cheek.

"Unless she has internal bleeding, Detective, I'd say she's not critically injured," the paramedic added, "but we'll let the hospital make that determination."

Jessie watched the other paramedic insert an IV into the woman's vein. Her eyes flipped open from the prick of the needle. The woman's breathing increased as she glanced from one person to the next.

"You're going to be okay, ma'am," Jessie said, patting her hand. "I'm Detective Kensington from the two-one precinct." She gently brushed a strand of hair stuck to the woman's cheek. "Can you tell me what happened?"

"A man, a man," she mumbled through swollen lips.

"What, man?"

"A man," she said, then slowly drifted back to an unconscious state. Her yellow paisley print dress was torn and stained with blood in several places. Jessie exited the vehicle and stood on the sidelines, watching the senior paramedic close the doors.

He nodded as he slid behind the steering wheel, flipped the switch for the siren, and sped out of the area toward Lenox Hill Medical Hospital.

"Who was that?" Gerard asked, walking up beside her after checking the path for evidence.

"It seems we have two victims," she said as they walked side-by-side to the crime scene. "The paramedic told me we have a male victim out by Bow Bridge and this young woman."

"Did you talk to her?"

"Yes, very briefly. The woman was unconscious until the paramedic pricked her with a needle, then she blinked her eyes open."

"Is she going to be alright?" he asked.

"From what the paramedic said, he thought she would be, but he's not a doctor."

"Did she tell you what happened?"

Jessie shrugged. "I asked her. She said something about a man, but not enough to give me an idea who he was."

"Yeah. Maybe it's the dead man at the crime scene," Gerard pointed out.

"What? You think he turned the gun on himself after he did a number on her?"

"His wounds will tell the story."

"Okay, partner, we'll see." She glanced at him, "You've been known to be wrong before." She grinned.

"Gee, thanks. I can always count on you to remind me of my flaws."

"By the way, they found her near the Ramble, several feet from the auto. Sounds like she was trying to get away."

Gerard hurried along the path, with Jessie quickening her pace to keep up. Sergeant Jackson greeted them with a wave when they reached the scene. In the distance, the muffled sound of a helicopter's rotor echoed against the trees as it neared the crime scene. The pair walked toward the body on the ground. Sgt. Jackson stood by the sidelines with the witnesses, his flashlight aimed and illuminating the body on the ground. The detectives did the same and noted the victim's bent legs were a sign he tried to escape his assailant. The victim was face down on the grassy knoll. His skull was ripped apart by a bullet to the back of his head. A mass of flies buzzed at the site of the wound. "I guess we can rule out suicide," Gerard said.

Jessie's stomach coiled. She tasted bile in the back of her throat and inhaled deeply to avoid losing the coffee she'd had earlier. She turned her eyes away, unable to continue listening to the flies feasting on the open wound. "What a disgusting sight." She shuddered. "I don't think I'll ever get used to it."

Gerard acknowledged with a nod, then turned his attention toward the sergeant. "Whatcha got for us, Jackson?"

"As you can see, we have a few witnesses, although they claim they only saw shadows before they fell over the top of the body." He flashed his light in their direction. "And we have a vehicle hung up on the cast iron rail of Bow Bridge."

Jessie remembered that bridge all too well.

When the helicopter arrived and hovered over the crime scene, it was as though Mother Nature had taken control and forced daylight when the pilot flipped on the light switch. Gerard squatted down next to the body and examined the wound more closely. All but one fly took off with a vengeance, giving him a chance to secure it in an evidence bag.

"Good catch, Detective," the investigator said while continuing to click his camera in rapid succession as he photographed every angle of the body.

"Has the ME been called?" Gerard asked Jackson.

"Yes. Clara had another murder across town but is on her way." He no sooner finished his sentence when the medical examiner arrived carrying her large kit. Clara was a strict, no-nonsense, military-trained examiner. She knelt next to the body and went to work. "I'll take it from here, Detectives," she said.

Gerard backed off but stayed close by and waited for Clara to say something.

"I don't think he's been here very long. Look at his skin. It's purple and waxy looking." She checked the victim's fingernails. "His nails are almost white." She looked up at the investigator. "Did you get all the pictures you need for the initial scene?"

"I did. Thanks."

Clara flipped the body over. Jessie was the first to recognize him. "Oh man," she said with disgust. "That's Lenny Scerbo," she mumbled under her breath.

"You know this guy?" Clara asked.

"Yep," Jessie nodded. "I do."

"Well, it's looking like he royally pissed somebody off. This wound isn't the work of someone mildly annoyed."

"What's your best guesstimate for the time of death?" Gerard asked.

"Stop back and see me later. Off the top of my head, though, I'd say a few hours, tops. But don't hold me to that."

"Let's question the witnesses," Gerard said and approached them.

Jackson had already marked the perimeter with yellow tape and acted as gatekeeper, allowing no one to enter or leave unless authorized by the detectives.

The thought of losing another confidential informant made Jessie's mouth curl in disappointment. "Dammit," she said in a low voice, "another CI. What's going on here?"

"Hey," Gerard answered, "that's all part of the deal, Jess." He shrugged. "What are you going to do? There's always Tony Ricci."

"Yeah, but we asked Lenny to take the job at the chop shop because he was the more reliable of the two."

Gerard shrugged. "It works if Tony gives us a lead to a mole in the department and the real name of this Sonny guy who owns the chop shop." He looked back at Lenny's lifeless body. "You want to call it Jessie."

"I'm calling it a jealous husband, or his assailant knew he was working with us."

"Could be," he shrugged. "But judging from what you told me about the woman, do you think they were involved with one another? Of course, he was a widower."

"We've seen stranger things," Jessie said, "but I can't imagine Lenny and this woman—at least, I don't think so. What little I saw of her toned body told me she took good care of herself. I'd say our victim was a runner, and judging from the size of the rock on her finger, I'd say the woman has money and lots of it. Involvement with one another?" she shook her head. "Good lord, he's in his fifties. What would a pretty little thing like her be doing with an overweight, filthy man like him?"

"Maybe he's her father," Gerard said with a shrug.

They crossed over the path on their way to see Jackson and the witnesses. Gerard glanced over to the sidelines at a couple wrapped in a blanket. "Are these our witnesses?"

Jackson nodded in the affirmative. "That would be them."

"Are they cold?" Jessie inquired. "Is that why they're huddled inside a blanket?" she pointed.

"Ah, no. They're naked." Jackson chuckled.

"Oh crap, another image I need to erase from my mind," Jessie grumbled. "I guess I blocked that information out on the way over here." She sighed. "Just freakin' disgusting."

"Now, don't be a prude," Gerard told her. "Did they ruin anything by falling on the body?" He asked Jackson.

Jackson raised his palms in the air. "I have no clue." He shrugged.

Gerard watched his partner's reaction and grinned.

"Take your pick, Gerard. Which one do you want to question?" she asked.

He headed toward the woman, and she wasn't surprised.

CHAPTER 2

*L*ieutenant Jack Harwell pulled into Central Park, eased his vehicle to the side of the road, and stepped out into the hot, humid air that lingered above his head like a water balloon ready to burst.

The screeching sound of a siren wailed past him en route to the hospital.

He smiled when he saw the helicopter hovering above, lighting the way for the investigators. A sense of satisfaction washed over him from his progress since coming to the two-one precinct as a lieutenant. He'd managed to wade through the bureaucracy and obtain updated equipment.

Seeing a CSI measuring skid marks along the path, Harwell stopped to speak to him. The officer looked up when Harwell approached.

"And what do we have here?" Harwell asked.

"A suspicious set of skid marks that don't match the vehicle involved in the accident."

"How many vehicles were involved?"

"Unless there's another in the water, this is it, Lieutenant. It looks like the killer rammed the victim's car from behind into this ravine."

"Who found the bodies?"

"That couple talking to Detectives Kensington and Gerard found the dead male, although the first officers discovered the woman."

Noticing the young guy dressed in racing gear and looking annoyed, Harwell asked about him. "And the biker? What's up with him?"

"Beats me, Lieutenant."

"Okay, make sure you get a good mold of those skid marks for the lab, son," he said.

"Yes, sir."

Harwell stood upright and continued toward the wrecked car. When he reached the vehicle, he looked at his detectives, who were still questioning the witnesses.

The 1997 Volvo station wagon, the hood jammed up against the bottom of the bridge, was nestled in mud covering the wheels. Harwell made his way closer to the wreck to see the damage. The windshield, the side window on the driver's side, and the rear window shattered.

Detective Gerard noticed his boss and left the witnesses with Jessie and another officer, who handed the male witness another blanket.

"What the hell is that all about?" Harwell asked.

"They were getting it on when they stumbled . . . or I should say fell on the victim," he grinned.

"And what happened to their clothing?" Harwell's eyebrows rose in a questionable frown, "where the hell is that?"

"At the hotel," Gerard smiled.

"You know, these idiots never cease to amaze me," he said, shaking his head, "just when you think you've seen it all, something like this happens." Harwell cleared his throat. "What else do you have for me?"

"We don't have a clear picture yet. Fortunately, the female victim is still alive and on her way to the hospital. She had no ID, so we have no idea about her identity. DOA is Lenny Scerbo, who was shot in the back of his head. His body was fifty feet from the car we believe was driven by the female. Clara estimates Lenny's been dead for a few hours, but she won't confirm that until she finishes the examination. That means the accident, if the two are related, occurred in the wee hours this morning."

"As for Lenny," Harwell said, "it was only a matter of time. Maybe someone from the chop shop found out he was working for us."

Gerard motioned for the Lieutenant to move closer to the vehicle.

"Where are the license plates?" the Lieutenant asked.

"No plates or registration anywhere. Nada, zip, nothing!" Gerard said, "But Jackson is following up on the VIN and registration."

"Do you think Lenny was driving the vehicle?" Harwell asked.

"Not according to Paige. He said he lifted three sets of prints, but two were smudged. As I said, all indications point to the woman as the driver because the smaller prints were the most prominent. Who knows if we'll get anything from the smudged prints? He wasn't in that car unless we can get some of those prints to match Lenny's."

"Then how the hell did he get here?"

"Another car, I suspect. One of the technicians was taking a mold of some tire tracks."

"Yeah, I spoke to him on my way over to the scene," Harwell said. "he mentioned they were suspicious."

Gerard walked over to the broken window on the passenger's side of the vehicle. "Fortunately for the driver, the airbag deployed. That's what saved her life. Earlier, I found a piece of bloody flesh and some bloody fabric on the jagged edge of this window, so I'm assuming this is how she escaped. The fabric had little flowers on it."

"You mean a paisley print." Detective Kensington said when she joined them.

"Yeah, whatever," Gerard said.

She released a humorous chuckle. "Hi, Lieutenant."

"You look like shit, Kensington," Harwell said, the deep frown lines creasing his forehead. "Aren't you getting any sleep?"

"It's good to see you, too, Lieutenant."

* * *

The trio turned when a flatbed truck pulled up near the vehicle. The driver, a stocky man wearing an NYPD baseball cap and a lit cigar hanging out from the corner of his mouth, jumped down from the cab and walked to where they stood conversing.

"Phew, Lieutenant," Gerard said, pretending to wipe the sweat from his brows, "I think this man saved us from Jessie's wrath." He winked.

"Hilarious, Gerard," she said, twisting her mouth. She tossed her hand and walked back to interview the cyclist.

The truck driver interrupted their conversation. "Is this vehicle ready for transport?"

"Yes, sir."

He handed them a receipt for the vehicle, returned to his truck and backed it up as close as possible, hooked the cable to the undercarriage, and pulled the damaged car onto the tray. Harwell and Gerard moved over to the side and slightly waved as he drove away from the scene.

"You know, Lieutenant," Gerard said, "I can't imagine Lenny's connection to the woman. We're wondering if these are two unrelated incidents. Hopefully, our Jane Doe can shed some light on this when she regains consciousness." He wiped the sweat from his forehead with the back of his hand. "It's clear the vehicle was hit multiple times from the rear . . . and it looks like whoever was pushing her vehicle gave an extra shove for good measure to make sure the vehicle rammed into the bridge. I'd bet money on it that whoever did this thinks the woman is dead."

"Well, let's hope the asshole comes back to check."

Gerard nodded. "Judging from the location of the dents, I'd say the mystery vehicle is an SUV or a Hummer." Gerard waited for Harwell to comment, and when he didn't, the detective looked his way. Harwell was checking the ground. Frowning, Gerard addressed him. "Sir?" Gerard stared at him, waiting for a response.

"No purse on this woman, huh?" Harwell asked.

"What are you looking for, Lieutenant?"

"I thought I might find something."

Gerard released a sigh and shook his head. "I can assure you, Lieutenant. We've combed every inch of this crime scene."

"I have no doubt, Gerard. Just checking, that's all."

Gerard cleared his throat, slightly amused, slightly annoyed by Harwell's lack of confidence in his ability.

Harwell grinned. "Listen, Gerard, if you miss something, it's my ass in the sling, and if mine is in the sling, so is yours."

"I think my reputation speaks for itself, don't you?" Gerard asked.

Harwell's eyebrows rose. "But there's always a first time. So is that it?"

Gerard knew he was wasting his time saying anything to Harwell about continuing his ground search, but he wished it wasn't taking him so long to figure out Gerard was no rookie. The fact was, Harwell hadn't been a lieutenant that long. Gerard brushed it off and continued. "Other than a VIN, that's it. Divers should be here soon to drag the lake. Maybe that's where we'll find her purse," Gerard said, but Harwell was still checking the ground. Gerard tried to ignore him and continued. "I can't imagine any woman leaving the house without a purse, especially one about to drive. Christ, their purses are like chains around their necks," Gerard said without looking at Harwell.

"Very true, but a woman who's running to get away from someone chasing her wouldn't stop for her purse," Harwell said with arched brows. Removing his cap, he ran his hand over his closely cropped hair. "All she wants to do is get the hell away."

"You're right," Gerard said. "Jess spoke briefly with the victim before the paramedics left for the hospital. She said the woman seemed confused and affluent."

"Oh? And how did she know this?"

Gerard relayed what Jess had told him.

"Well, hell, that makes it easier." Harwell joked. "That only leaves us with about half the population of the city who are loaded."

"Right," he snickered. "By the way," Gerard said, "I hear Bradshaw's already over at Lenox Hill. Can he look in on Jane Doe until we get there?"

"Sure." Harwell started to walk away but stopped. "Who did you say was checking on the VIN?"

"Jackson."

"And he was first on the scene?" Harwell twisted his mouth into a smirk.

"Yes, sir."

"That's fucking terrific." Harwell blew out a steady stream of air. "I wonder which of his men will screw up this time."

"Lieutenant," Gerard said with a sigh, "you can't judge all his guys based on that one schmuck who got caught screwing a prostitute while on duty. Besides, Internal Affairs expelled him. I think that was a loud message to the rest of the troops. Don't you?"

"Yeah, I guess. But some people never learn. I know Jackson tampered with that evidence. I need to find a way to prove it." Noticing Gerard had turned a deaf ear, the Lieutenant gave a nonchalant wave and walked toward the path, "You know where I'll be."

* * *

"What'd you get when you ran the VIN?" Harwell asked when he approached Jackson. It was apparent by Jackson's expression that he resented Harwell.

Jackson held up his finger, indicating he wanted his superiors to wait, removed his cap from his head, exposing his full head of dark curly hair, and used his shoulder to wipe the sweat running down his cheek. Harwell's imposing height made him feel like an ant looking at the mighty grasshopper. He finally responded.

"It came back to a guy named John Graham."

"Her husband, maybe?"

"We're checking that out now."

"Okay, keep me posted. I want to know the minute you have something." Harwell headed toward the Medical Examiner and stopped when he heard Jackson calling out to him. He turned around to see Jackson on his cell phone, who was motioning for Harwell to join him.

"Lieutenant," Jackson said, "my guys met with Graham, and he's not married. Graham said he was dropping his date off, left his vehicle double-parked with the engine running, and the woman ran down the street and jumped into his car."

"He left the engine running?" Harwell screeched. "Where did he leave his car double-parked?"

"West 87th."

"Oh, I guess this bonehead figured high-class area, no one would take his car." Harwell looked bewildered. "Doesn't he know where the muggers and burglars go first?"

"I guess not, Lieutenant."

"Asshole," Harwell said with hostility. "I want to know how he got through the city without plates on his car?" Harwell shook his head, "And what the fuck were our guys doing that they didn't see him?" He scuffed a hand over his face. "Do we know how long he's been driving the car that way?"

"The kid said he took possession of the vehicle yesterday. He went to the DMV to register it, received a pile of stuff from the clerk, including the placard, and then rushed home to shower for his date. He was running late, and it never occurred to him until later that he hadn't affixed the placard to the windshield. He figured he'd take care of it today."

"How old is this bozo?"

"Eighteen."

"That figures. I hope the kid has a good job so he can pay the hefty fine the department will slap on him."

"I guess he's going to learn the hard way."

"Yeah. There's a lot of that going around." Harwell's hands went to his hips. "Did he report the car missing to the Auto Crime Unit?"

"Yes, they do have a record of the theft."

"What time was that?"

"I don't have the answer to that yet."

"What a jerk," Harwell said. "Just think," he said with a disgusted shake of his head, "this kid is old enough to vote. It's pretty scary stuff if you ask me. What's interesting, though, is that the kid knew enough to call to report his car missing but wasn't the least bit worried about driving around without plates." He tossed his hands in the air and turned to leave, stopping mid-step. "Get Graham's fingerprints and his whereabouts. I want to know every place this kid went."

"With all due respect, sir. I have an excellent team of officers who know the procedures well."

"That's news to me," Harwell said over his shoulder. "You and I know what some of these guys are like on the force. If they're not wasting time by talking to some babe, they're sitting around eating donuts and drinking coffee or screwing some prostitute while on duty. And when they finish that, they're performing illegal searches and screwing up our cases." Jackson's mouth clamped shut.

Harwell strolled down the path toward the medical examiner, enjoying the expression on Jackson's face after reminding him he hadn't forgotten.

* * *

Sgt. Tip Jackson pounded his feet down the path toward his men, annoyed at himself for allowing Harwell to get to him. He resented how his superior spoke to him, but he didn't have to like it—the man was his boss. Besides, he was thankful this job gave him the outlets he needed for the extra cash he used to support his gambling habit.

His pace quickened when he saw two divers in wet suits walking toward the river. "It's about time you guys got here. I only called you two hours ago."

The larger of the two divers cocked his head to the side and, in a thick Brooklyn accent, shot back, full of sarcasm, "Gee, Sarge, we're sorry to keep you waiting."

Jackson assured himself pulling rank on this jerk wasn't worth the effort, especially since he'd just mouthed off to his superior officer. "I want you guys to do a thorough search. Whatever you can find."

The aggressive one saluted him, "Tell me, Sarge, is there any other kind?" The guy didn't wait long enough to hear Jackson's retort because he swiftly dove into the water while the other diver walked further down to search a different lake area.

Suddenly realizing the sun was up and the helicopter was gone, Jackson was surprised he hadn't noticed it sooner. But then, he'd been so busy that he didn't have time to pay attention to such things. A team member approached and handed him a bottle of cold water.

Jackson nodded a thank you and took a swig, allowing the cold water to linger on his tongue for a while.

"Hey, am I going to see you later?" Rory asked.

"Absolutely."

"Thanks for the water."

"Six-thirty tonight, right?" Rory asked.

"Yes, sir."

Jackson rolled the cold bottle over his cheek to feel the coolness against his skin, wiped the moisture from his thick black mustache with his fingertips, then wiped his fingers on his pants. He removed the lid from his water and took another long swig, then checked his watch for the time and smiled, knowing his workday was almost over.

Excitement filled him just thinking about the big poker game he'd managed to get in on tonight—and tomorrow promised to be even better. Just the thought of the big race at Aqueduct sent a shiver through his body and caused his heart to race. He could almost visualize those horses running around that track, and his choice, Danny's Desire, was in the lead.

CHAPTER 3

*M*ax Harwell tiptoed into the darkened vestibule of St. Catherine's Roman Catholic Church and dipped his finger into the holy water to bless himself. His nerves spiked, knowing he didn't have much time to hide the voice-activated microphone to record the confessions before Father McKinley's associate arrived to hear them.

Excitement welled inside him at the prospect of being the only twelve-year-old amateur detective to do something so daring by using the surveillance equipment that belonged to his father's precinct. He wasn't expecting to hear anything exciting. It would not be exciting if his recorded material were like his confessions. But that was okay; it was the experience that mattered most, the first of many he'd have during his lifelong career.

He scanned the nave to make sure he was alone. The familiar smell of musty old wood and incense filled his nostrils as he tiptoed down the aisle to the confessional when the floorboards released a loud creaking noise beneath his feet. Max's pulse shot up as he looked around the nave, checking to see if the noise he'd just made had alerted the priests, who might already be vested in the Sacristy. Max panicked. A recollection of Father McKinley chastising him for past indiscretions made him duck into the first pew and hunch down low.

The longer he remained there, the more anxious he became. He had to get into that confessional and fast. He'd waited too long to set this up and couldn't afford to let his nerves get twisted into a tightwad. Max sucked in a deep breath and held it for a while before blowing it out. He couldn't believe how shaky his hands were. This covert stuff was exciting, but it sure was scary.

The church's silence remained absolute except for the hum of the air conditioning. After a few seconds, convinced he was alone, Max edged out, slowly tiptoeing to the confessional. He slowly twisted the doorknob, opened the door, and entered total darkness in the confining cubicle. He squatted down onto his knees, and when he heard the loud clunk, he knew the microphone had fallen from his breast pocket. His hand clutched his chest. He immediately chastised himself for being so careless and not holding the microphone in his hand. Nervous tension ached in his neck and made his head pound. Why was he so tense? He'd planned his covert operation for weeks, and he sure didn't need anything else to go wrong before he could get the job done.

He slid his hands across the floor, trying to find the microphone, but he couldn't feel anything. Where could it have gone? More panic shot through him. Was there a hole in the floor? Had the microphone dropped through to the basement of the church?

After serving as an altar boy for a year, he thought he knew every inch of the church, but now he was questioning himself. He sighed. The darn thing had to be in that tiny cubicle. He filled his cheeks with air, willing his pulse to calm down, but it did little to compensate for his slight dizziness. He suddenly became aware he was hyperventilating, something he'd warned himself against earlier. Losing control was out of the question and a guarantee for making costly mistakes.

He braced his hands on the floor to navigate the confined quarters. He was relieved when his fingers felt the microphone tip lodged between the wall and the kneeler. Now, he could finish the job and get the hell out of there. He picked up the microphone, kissed it, and positioned it where he'd get the best recording.

Max was proud of his accomplishment after finishing his first mission. That is until the sudden creak of the heavy wooden entry doors opened. His eyes widened in surprise as he mouthed a silent scream when the loud noise of the doors closing bounced off the walls and slammed to the closed position. His breath caught in the back of his throat while his heart pounded in his chest, afraid someone would see what he was up to and tell his father. Making the sign of the cross, he kissed his thumb and tossed it up to God the way he'd seen one of the older women do, as though sending a kiss to God. Lightheadedness took over, and he feared he'd pass out. Heavy footsteps told him someone had entered the church. He gasped, his hand reaching up to cover his mouth to muffle the sound. He practiced controlling his breathing—willing himself to calm down because getting caught would ruin everything after he'd worked so hard. His breath slowly tapered off into a more natural state enough that he could return to rational thinking.

Why was this person inside the church so early anyway? Had he made an appointment with Father ahead of time? Or had he wasted too much time trying to plant the microphone, and confessions were about to begin? Fear as thick as jam washed over him at the thought of this person walking into his side of the confessional. But then, he didn't know if the man was there for confession. Maybe he wasn't. That thought made him feel better, and he planned his escape.

He peered through the door's crack; it was still dark inside, which meant he still had time. But how could he crawl on his knees and exit through the side door without being noticed?

The muffled sound of a cell phone's keypad beeped seven digits in the distance, and a man's angry voice echoed through the church. Max jerked back, startled. He listened, trying to understand the conversation, but the man was so angry he made little sense. Max did feel sorry for this poor Vito guy, though, who seemed to be the target of all the vicious shouting. That's when Max convinced himself to stay clear of this person.

Who knew what the guy would do to him if he realized Max was listening? Maybe this was his time to run for it while the man was preoccupied with his conversation. He tried to convince himself that the stranger wouldn't see him if he crawled out and made a beeline for the side door of the church, which would make noise, but then he'd be outside and could make a run for it.

Confident with his plan, Max snuck out of the confessional on all fours. His foot inadvertently clipped the door in haste, causing it to creak. His hands, now clammy, were shaking from the adrenaline pulsating through his veins. Sweat rolled down the sides of his face and dropped to the floor. He used his shoulder to dry the moisture, and for a second, there was complete silence until the man's gruff voice cut through the silence.

"Hello? Who's there?" A brief silence passed. "Who's there, dammit?"

Max froze, his heart pounding wildly in his ears; he wondered if the loud hammering was audible to the man. He had to get out of there. Deep wrinkles clustered on his forehead as he contemplated his next move. The man's voice faded in a sudden twist of fate, and the heavy door opened and closed again. He blew out a hefty breath of air, thankful the man was gone. Or was this a trick to make him think the man had left the church?

Max knew he was overthinking and decided, either way; he had to take the chance. He'd already taken a risk by planting the microphone; he could do this, too. Max prided himself on being a risk-taker. With some self-coaching, he stood upright and ran from the building, dive-bombing behind a bush to watch for the man. He remained there longer than he intended but wanted to ensure the coast was clear.

Thoughts of his friend Ritchie came to mind. Ritchie was supposed to be waiting for him behind some large boulders at the top of the hill. Max had no doubt the excitement of what was happening had Ritchie crapping in his pants. His friend wasn't as adventuresome as he and often freaked out over the most minor things. Max could only imagine how frantic the boy had gotten when he saw the man enter the church, knowing Max was working hard inside.

A rush of excitement flowed through him, and the terror he felt earlier faded with satisfaction, knowing his plan would come to fruition.

When a few seconds passed, and nothing happened, he made a beeline up the hill toward Ritchie when he noticed a black Mercedes in the parking lot and figured it had to belong to the angry man. Being cautious, he scanned the surrounding area with his eyes. His dad always told him police officers had to have eyes in the back of their heads to survive and, most of all, be ready for combat because they never knew when someone would attack.

Satisfied he was free to run to where Ritchie was waiting, he ran up the hill to find his friend.

"Where have you been?" Ritchie blurted out when he saw Max.

"Setting up," Max said in a snarky tone when he saw Ritchie was spazzing out.

"Did you know a man went inside the church while you were there?"

"Relax, Rich," he replied, faking a nonchalant air, "It's not a big deal." Max had a reputation to uphold, and the last thing he wanted was for Ritchie to know how scared he'd been. "Besides, he walked back outside before he ever saw me." Max gave his friend the thumbs-up signal. Ritchie rolled his eyes. "Did you notice if he went back inside the church?" Max asked.

Ritchie was shaking his head, a disconcerted expression on his face. His hands flung into the air. "Yeah, he did, but you're lucky you didn't get caught because he was furious at someone." Ritchie frowned. "I was scared to death, thinking he was shouting at you."

CHAPTER 4

*B*less me, Father, for I have sinned," the man said, releasing a heavy sigh.

"How can I help you, my son?"

"I killed my wife."

Father McKinley recognized his confessor's voice and spun around to face him instead of remaining in the traditional position. Max flinched when his stomach cramped. The terror he experienced went deep into his core and reminded him of another time a parishioner confessed he'd killed someone. He was much younger then, fresh out of the seminary in Ireland, naïve and unprepared to handle a situation that almost cost him his life.

A queasy feeling of anxiety erupted in the old priest's stomach. He knew this man and his wife. An unfathomable image of the dead woman flashed through his mind. He'd seen her only recently preparing the altar for the weekend Masses, exchanging the dead flowers with fresh ones. Now, it appeared she was as dead as those flowers. His eyes welled with tears over the loss of his friend. He instinctively reached for the cross hanging from his waist, gripped it tightly, and prayed for guidance.

The priest's silence brought an edge of fury to the man's voice. "Are you listening to me, Father?"

The man's aggressive personality change concerned the priest deeply, rendering a momentary silence. His belly filled with heat from the anger and intense disappointment he felt. He'd become friends with this family--broken bread with them in their home. He had no idea anything was wrong with their marriage. The man's impatient tapping on the screen interrupted his thoughts.

"Why aren't you speaking?" he growled. "Is this some ploy of yours to trick me?"

"No. I'm trying to absorb the magnitude of what you've just told me."

The Father knew a more priest-like response was required, but his mind was running a marathon of thoughts, and that was all he could muster up. Perspiration had collected on his upper lip and began trickling down the sides of his mouth. He wiped it with his hand. The dim light overhead in the confessional gave his confessor a clear visual of him. He reminded himself to be careful about overreacting. He sucked in his breath.

"Why would you do such a thing?"

"She wouldn't give me what I wanted."

"And what was that?"

"It doesn't matter now. She wouldn't give it to me, and because of it, she forced my hand, and now she's paid the price." He laughed. "You should have seen how scared she was when she ran and jumped into a car in the middle of the road. But I followed her in my car. And the stupid bitch drove right into Central Park at that hour." He laughed again. "She made it easy for me. The park was closed, and that's when I nailed her up against Bow Bridge. The way I rammed into the back of the car she'd stolen," he snickered, "let's just say she's history. Talk about a lucky break. And the best part was saying goodbye, bitch before I pulled away."

Squinting to see the man's face to read his silent reactions was difficult, but the priest could see a partial. The man leaned back on his heels again, apparently deciding this was a good position for him; his face, now fully exposed, was a mask of smugness.

Father McKinley inhaled. "Tell me you went back to check on her."

"Yeah, I did. With Lenny. The guy who was too nosey for his good, so he got what he deserved, too."

"Are you saying you killed him too?"

"Exactly, Padre!" he said. "Now you're catching on."

"And what have you done with their bodies?"

"That's no concern of yours, Father. They'll find both of them soon enough. They may already have." He began rocking back and forth.

"I can't believe you are the same man I've known for all these years. Your mother would be appalled at your behavior."

"You leave my mother out of this."

"I'm begging you. Please confess your sins to the police."

"No! The only concession I'm making is to you. Once you absolve me of my sin, I'm home free."

Father McKinley's lips tightened into a thin line. He shook his head in despair. "So you think that's all there is to it?"

"Absolutely. No one can say I didn't confess."

"Do you feel any guilt for your actions?"

"Uh," the man rubbed his chin, a slight smirk on his face. "No!"

"Then there's no way I can absolve you from your sins without it. What you've told me is not considered a sacramental confession."

"Listen, Father. Your job is to hear my confession, not judge me."

"I hear your confession, but it is my job to counsel you as well. If you won't repent for your sins, confessing it to me is only a temporary respite. Running away from your responsibilities isn't the answer, and you are intelligent enough to know that."

"I have only one responsibility, and you know what that is, Padre."

The man's arrogance sent chills down the priest's spine, and he feared for himself and others. "You have to know your life will be one lie after another -- a path of destruction." He exhaled, trying to hide his labored breathing. "I'm begging you now. Please do the right thing."

"No," he said, raising his voice louder, "they won't understand that I did the right thing. I was justified." The man had changed positions again, causing Father McKinley to lean in closer.

Sensing what he was doing, the man pressed his face against the screen. "There, does that help? Can you see my expression now? Don't think I don't know what you're trying to do. You want to see if anything you've said has me feeling remorseful." He laughed. "Let me save you the trouble. I'm not."

Recognizing he wasn't getting through to the man, the priest tried another approach. "You know, I've always thought of you as a devout Catholic, and I'm shocked you have disobeyed the church's laws and broken one of the Ten Commandments."

"Fooled ya, didn't I?"

"You certainly did. Shouldn't you be punished for breaking the laws of the church?"

"Why should I? I told you a few minutes ago. She drove me to it — like self-defense."

"Are you saying she attempted to kill you too?"

"No," he covered his hand over his mouth to stifle his laughter.

"This is all very amusing to you, eh?"

"It is. I'm finally free to move forward with my plans. That's the way it works. When you don't get what you want, you take it! Plain and simple."

"Two wrongs never make a right. Maybe the police won't understand, but you need help badly. They can give it to you. If you confess now, they'll go much easier on you than if you hide from the truth."

"Oh, yeah, they'll help me all right. The police will hold my hand and walk me to my cell."

"Stop it. You know what I mean."

"Look, I'm confessing my sin to you. You're the only one who knows the truth, but I know you won't tell anyone. Isn't that right, Padre?"

"Please don't waste your time trying to intimidate me. It will not work."

The man laughed into the screen again, and for the first time, Father McKinley could smell liquor on his breath. The priest sat still, only staring back at him. "You've been drinking again, haven't you?"

"Hell, yeah. I've been celebrating."

The old priest closed his eyes and sighed. The man must have sensed his disapproval because he backed off and waited for the priest to continue.

"I think you know very well the seal of confession cannot be broken without repercussions. But understand one thing: I cannot help you save your soul if you don't help yourself. I ask you to remember that one day, you will have to answer to the Lord, our God. How does that make you feel?" He watched the man's body stiffen from the challenge.

"I will continue this façade until the cloud of her death blows over — and it will blow over. Trust me on that one."

The man's shoulders slumped as he lowered his head to his hands and began to rock back and forth.

The priest smiled, inwardly sensing he was getting through to him. Father McKinley cleared his throat to get the man's attention, "Is that remorse I'm detecting, after all?"

"No, I told you, I don't regret anything."

"I'm sorry, but I think you do, and it's eating away at you a wee bit at a time."

"Nice try, Padre," he answered in a rush of words.

The fear the priest felt earlier vanished, only to leave him with a feeling of despair. He needed to try something different--something to get his attention. A sudden thought occurred to him, and he raised his arm to slide the screen across the track to shut him out, hoping to scare him. "I can't help you . . . please leave my confessional."

The man's voice rose as he slammed his fist against the wall, "You wait just a damn minute. I'm not done!"

"Then say something that makes sense," the priest fired back as he sank deeper into his seat.

"She was a bitch, and she got what she deserved." The man pressed his nose on the partially opened screen, trying to see the priest with one eye.

Father McKinley opened the screen the rest of the way. "Do not swear in God's house." He watched as the man's hands balled into fists.

His face flushed with anger. "I came to you to confess my—"

The priest cut him off. "Because you wanted me to tell you it was okay?" He shook his head, baffled by his behavior. "Penance is not psychotherapy. Contrition is willful regret for your sins. It isn't a matter of feeling comfortable, but acknowledging the evil of your sin and the resolution to sin no more."

The man laughed. "I don't intend to do anything like this again," a smirk planted on his face. "There, now that solves your problem, doesn't it?"

"What problem is that?"

"You wanted to hear me say I won't do this again."

"You're not listening to me. I want to hear you say you're sorry for your sins because, without repentance, your confession is not valid." He swallowed hard. "I'm going to ask you one more time. Do you regret—"

The melody of a popular ringtone cut the priest off. Annoyed by the intrusion, Father McKinley watched the man check his cell phone screen and then jump to his feet.

"I have to leave, Padre," and he was out the door before the priest could say another word.

    * * *

Pulling a cap out of his back pocket, the tall, bulky man dressed in all black covered his head, adjusted the brim of his hat down lower to hide his face, and walked out the door. The thick, humid air hit him as if he'd just entered a sauna, causing his sinuses to swell, making breathing more difficult. He hated humid days like this because it made him feel clammy, like he hadn't showered.

In the distance, a flash of lightning snaked across the sky, beckoning the threat of rain. The man hurried toward his car, parked at the end of the lot in a secluded area. He developed a sudden paranoia along the walkway as though someone was watching him. His chest heaved in and out as he gulped in deep breaths of air to defray the illusion of a chain being tightened around his midsection, cutting off

K. T. ROBERTS

the circulation. He coughed, trying to rid himself of the feeling, and looked around the area with a suspicious eye. He half-smiled, remembering how silly he'd been earlier thinking someone was in the church. It wasn't until the wind kicked up that he decided his mind was playing tricks on him and convinced himself that paranoia would ruin everything he'd been working toward if he didn't nip it in the bud.

CHAPTER 5

*R*itchie's chubby fingers latched onto Max's arm, "Dive," he warned.

"Wha . . . what . . . dive?"

"The man is back," he whispered.

"I know, Rich. I can see for myself."

The boys flattened their bodies onto the velvety knoll. Ritchie lay as flat as a pancake, but his feet jiggled nervously. Max gently kicked him on the side of his leg.

"Move closer to the bush," he whispered in the boy's ear.

"Okay, okay."

Max looked over his shoulder to check on Ritchie to ensure he had all his body parts concealed. Not an easy thing to do for an overweight boy. Noticing that Ritchie's feet still jutted out in plain view, he elbowed a warning to him and nodded in that direction, signaling for him to move them up. Ritchie tucked himself into the fetal position while Max held onto the lower branches of the bush to pull himself in closer to get a better view of the stranger.

As the man's footsteps grew heavier, Ritchie began hyperventilating, and Max was furious, wishing he hadn't pressured Ritchie into being his sidekick. He gave an anxious tug on his arm and leaned in close to his friend. "I can hear you breathing."

In the distance, another flash of lightning skittered across the sky and then crackled into a loud bang. Max covered the recorder with his backpack, knowing the rain would pour down any minute, and recalled the last time he and Ritchie were in a lightning storm. Ritchie had freaked out with fear. He looked at him now and noticed Ritchie's head buried inside the well of his crossed arms. Frightened, Ritchie's body continued to shake uncontrollably. Seeing Ritchie's distress, Max felt sympathy and draped his arm across Ritchie's back to let him know he wasn't alone. As the man got closer, Max felt another adrenaline rush. Being an amateur detective was so much fun.

The man's footsteps became rushed and more pronounced. Curious, Max moved in closer to the bush, pulling on the undergrowth this time, causing the brush to rustle. The tension in Max's body stiffened when the man stopped again, surveying the area with wariness. When a sudden gust of wind kicked up, Max blew out a breath of air, relieved God helped him out again. The man's face creased into a smirk, and he quickly jogged past the boys.

A flicker of apprehension shot through Max, wondering if the man saw them when he passed. But wouldn't he have stopped? Max brushed off the thought but not without saying a silent prayer first.

Despite the large sleet-like drops pelting against his body, he could not leave his post. When the rain increased, Max readjusted himself over the recorder. A non-functional recorder with water spots would be a dead giveaway when his father picked up the equipment from the house. Max turned his attention back to the man and watched him click on his key fob to unlock the car doors, then scoot behind the steering wheel in one quick shot. As soon as he started the engine, the windows fogged within seconds. Refusing to take his eyes off him, Max watched as the driver's side window suddenly lowered. The rain came down more forcefully a few minutes later, but Max was determined to tough it out.

When the man's car was out of sight, Max opened the back of the recorder to see if he'd recorded anything and smiled when he saw the reel was thicker on the recording side. Satisfied, he jumped to his feet, frantically shoved the recorder into his backpack, and zipped it back up. "C'mon, Rich, let's get out of here."

"Why are you acting so scared all of a sudden?" Ritchie asked wide-eyed. "You think he saw us, don't you?" the boy demanded, his voice climbing to a higher pitch.

"I'm not scared," he said casually and ignored Ritchie's question about the man seeing them. "All I know is I'm soaking wet." Ritchie watched as Max pulled his T-shirt over his head, twisted it to squeeze the water out, and then used it as a towel to wipe his head. After squeezing the rainwater out of the shirt again, he slipped it back on.

"Do you think he saw us?" Ritchie asked again, his red hair tightly curled around his face, his freckled nose, and deep blue eyes now bug-eyed with fear.

"I have no clue," Max answered calmly, but that didn't mean he wasn't scared. He was just better at hiding it. "Stop worrying. If he had seen us, he would have stopped. Maybe even offered us a ride."

"Yeah, right." Rich shook his head

"You didn't look up, did you?"

"No."

"Okay, then we're fine." Max puffed his cheeks up with air and blew it out in one steady stream. He didn't have the heart to tell Ritchie he had looked up, and the man did look in his direction. Maybe the man saw his face. Or maybe he was just paranoid. "C'mon, let's get out of here," Max said.

"Hey, you have to go back in and get the microphone."

"Forget it. Dad will figure he misplaced it."

"Now, you know he's going to blame you."

"Crap, Ritchie, you sound just like him."

Ritchie ignored Max's sarcasm and launched back into questioning. "Did that man look familiar to you?"

"Yes, but I can't figure out how or where I've seen him."

"Oh, crap," Ritchie said in a shaky voice, "that scares me even more." He jiggled nervously in place.

"What difference does it make?" Max shouted impatiently. "He doesn't know who we are anyway. Besides, he zipped past us too fast to even get a look."

"Are you sure?" Ritchie stood wide-eyed. "I'm scared."

"Scared of what? The man? Or getting caught?"

"Both . . . I guess." Ritchie kicked a stray stone on the sidewalk with the tip of his sneaker. When the rain stopped abruptly, both boys sighed simultaneously.

"But it's too late to be thinking about that now." Max grabbed the end of his T-shirt and wiped the raindrops running down the sides of his face. "We better get home before it rains again, Rich."

"But you have to get the microphone."

"Nuh-uh," Max shook his head emphatically. "That means I'll have to confess some bogus sin if I get caught in the confessional. I just went to confession last week. Why don't you go for me, and if Father opens the screen, you confess your sins?"

"I'm not Catholic, you bonehead."

"Oh, yeah. Well, I could tell you how to do it." Max could see by the expression on Ritchie's face he wasn't about to budge. Max scratched his head, disappointed his friend wouldn't do it for him. He stepped back and tried to figure out how to return to the confessional for the microphone without being noticed. He rubbed a hand over his chin as he thought about it. "I guess I could just go back in and make something up."

"Won't you go to hell if you do that?"

"If I lie, you mean?" Max asked.

"Yeah, if you lie. Doesn't God keep a list of your lies?"

"Why are you asking me such stupid questions? I don't know."

Ritchie pointed his finger in Max's face. "If you're worried about having something to confess, you can always tell the priest how you stole the precinct's surveillance equipment after your father already told you to leave it alone."

"Hilarious, Richie," Max smirked. "C'mon, man," Max begged, "go for me."

Max stared at Ritchie. He scrunched his face and pouted, hoping his friend would change his mind, but Ritchie ignored his request.

What kind of friend was Ritchie? Max sighed dramatically, realizing no amount of begging would work–Ritchie wouldn't help him out no matter how much he begged.

Max groaned in frustration. "Okay, I guess I'll just go and get it over with." His stomach somersaulted, dreading a return to the confessional. "You wait by the bikes," Max ordered. "Hold my back-pack until I return, and be ready to take off as soon as I come out."

Ritchie nodded in agreement.

Max was drawn toward the parking lot when he heard tires crunching over the stones. He began to run down the hill so fast he lost his footing and slid on the wet grass. Max jerked to break his fall. A sharp pain shot up his leg, and he stopped to rub the muscle, hoping to relieve the ache. Cars pulling into the parking lot meant confessions were underway. He groaned and continued his trek toward the church.

The sidewalks steamed like the busy streets in Manhattan. Steamy roads in the winter were good, but not much during the summer when the humidity was as high as the temperature. He knew it was only a matter of time before it would encase his body and make him feel worse than he already did. He entered the vestibule, walked through the opened double doors, and dipped his finger into the holy water. A fleeting thought gave him comfort, knowing he'd blessed himself twice. Maybe he wouldn't go to hell after all. He made his way down the aisle toward the confessional. His wet sneakers squeaked and sloshed in concert with the creaking old floors and drew the attention of a few parishioners sitting in the pews, waiting to confess their sins.

Max remembered being surprised at Mass when Father McKinley announced he was expanding the days and hours of confession. Seeing how many people were in the pews helped him understand the priest's expansion. He hadn't realized there were so many sinners in New York. He wasn't nervous when he recognized a few familiar faces. If they told his parents he was in church, they'd probably cele-brate, thinking he'd seen the error of his ways.

The light above the confessional glowed red, indicating the booth was in use.

He eased himself into a pew, knelt, and began reciting every prayer he ever knew, one after the other. He prayed for any sign from above that his father wouldn't find out he'd used the surveillance equipment. He panicked and prayed harder when nothing unusual happened to let him know God was listening. Nevertheless, he wasn't sorry he'd recorded what he'd hoped would be some confessions. At least he had something on tape, which was good.

The green light above the confessional flicked on, and the door opened. Max stepped out of the pew ahead of a parishioner who shot him an irritated expression but nodded agreement when she eyed his wet clothes. He mouthed a thank you, and she smiled. Stepping back to allow the person exiting the confessional more room, Max was surprised when the man turned out to be Mr. Cullen, a local merchant. The man immediately recognized Max and gave him the thumbs-up sign, but he frowned at his wet clothing. Max grinned slightly and shrugged. He patted Max on the shoulder.

Over the last several months, during Father McKinley's Homily, the priest had been pushing for the young parishioners of St. Catherine's to confess their sins every week. The priest thought it would help make them more aware of their behavior outside the church.

Then, when Father McKinley extended catechism throughout the summer, Max knew his parents would insist he attend it along with summer school for failing English literature. Over the last six weeks, he'd felt like a sequestered Carmelite Monk who prayed most of the day, but now his summer break was almost over. Today was the most fun he'd had because regardless of his sins or shortcomings, being an amateur detective took precedence over everything else. Nevertheless, he still hoped to get in and out of the confessional without speaking.

He walked into the confining room and knelt. He could hear the low whisper of voices from the other side.

For a brief moment, Max's mind relaxed, reminding him that if he moved fast enough, he wouldn't have to confess a bogus sin to the priest. Besides, it didn't feel right to lie to a man of the cloth. Lying to his parents or a friend was one thing, but lying to a priest? That wasn't cool. He pictured the devil rubbing his hands together with a gleeful expression.

He shook off the image and crouched low in the darkness, quickly sliding his hand toward the microphone's location. Doing something he wasn't supposed to always made him break into a cold sweat, especially with the air conditioning blowing against his wet shirt. He shivered while his heart hammered out of control, banging against his rib cage like a jackhammer cutting through the pavement. A heart attack seemed unrealistic for a twelve-year-old, but it didn't stop him from wondering if he might croak right there.

When his hand located the microphone, he shoved it into his pocket, reminding himself how it had dropped out. This time, he'd hold onto his pocket when he made his beeline exit. Excited, the task moved quickly; he stood upright and left the confessional just as the priest slid the screen open. He closed the door behind him and bolted down the aisle like the church was in flames.

Once outside, he sighed heavily, relieved he and Ritchie could head home.

As instructed, Ritchie was straddled over his bike, ready to take off. Max unzipped his backpack from Ritchie and shoved the microphone inside. He hoisted it over his shoulder, sliding one arm, then the other through the loops, adjusting the straps so it would sit evenly on his back. He jumped on his bike and pedaled as fast as he could out of the church parking lot, the wet road spraying more water over his socks and sneakers.

Thoughts raced through his mind as he pedaled toward home, unaware his legs were working harder than ever. Sweat trickled down inside his T-shirt. The breeze circled his body as he pedaled faster, making him feel calmer. The fact that his home was a short distance from St. Catherine's church gave him solace because he could put the equipment back where his father left it, and no one would be the wiser.

* * *

The boys pedaled across the Upper West Side of the city and made the final left onto 95th Street, right into Harwell's driveway. Nausea waved through Max's body when he saw his father's police car parked in the driveway.

"Oh God," he shrieked, "Dad's here. Damn Ritchie, how will I get the equipment back in the basement before he notices?" He shivered from a cold sweat and looked over at his friend. "I'm scared," he finally revealed to his friend.

"You should have thought of that before, Max," Ritchie said coldly. "Listen, I'm heading back to my house."

"You mean you're not going to stand by me?"

"Nope. I told you not to do this." Ritchie wiped the sweat from his upper lip. "See you around," he waved and continued down the driveway.

The door opened, and Jack Harwell waved to his son. "Hey, Max."

Max relaxed a bit, hearing his father's upbeat greeting, and sensed things were still okay in the life of Max Harwell, the Upper West Side's amateur detective.

"Hey, Dad. What are you doing home so early?"

"I'm here to pick up the surveillance equipment."

Max's heart kicked up its pace. He swallowed hard just as his legs turned to jelly at the mention of the equipment and lost control of his bike. He jumped off his bike and let it fall to the ground.

"Are you all right, Max?" his father asked, rushing onto the porch.

"Yeah, I wasn't paying attention." Max squeezed his shirt, and a small amount of water ran down his leg.

"You're soaked to the gills, son. You got caught in that downpour, huh?"

"Yeah," he squeaked out of his mouth. Max held his breath as he walked up the steps. His father's mood confused him. Did he know what Max had been up to this afternoon? He pushed the thought from his mind, sure it was his guilty conscience working overtime. He released his pent-up anxiety and walked up the steps to the porch, waiting for an introduction to the young man standing next to his father.

"Max, I'd like you to meet Ryan O'Reilly. He's enrolled in the Police

Academy for its next session. We're giving him a ride-along so he can see what it's like to be a cop." Max watched his dad lean over toward Ryan and whisper something. He knew what he'd said to the young man—the same thing he told everyone.

Ryan smiled. "The Lieutenant tells me you want to be a law enforcer too."

"Yeah, someday, maybe," he answered on his way to greet him. Before extending his hand to Ryan, Max wiped his clammy palm on his damp shorts. He thrust his trembling hand toward him and prayed his father wouldn't notice his nervousness.

Max looked at his father. "I need to go to the bathroom, Dad. Bad," he announced and ran down the hall to the wake of laughter.

He slammed the door, removed the backpack weighing heavily on his shoulders, and rested his back against the door. He closed his eyes as if in pain and wished he'd listened to Ritchie's warning. He said a quick prayer and promised God he'd never touch the surveillance equipment again if he'd help him out of this jam.

He placed his ear flush against the door and strained to hear his father's conversation. He mentally urged his father to stay outside a little longer so he could make a fast trip down to the basement and return the equipment. Instead, their voices sounded closer.

His heart was pounding like a machine gun in battle from worry about his father and Ryan being right on the other side of the door. How would he get downstairs to the basement if they went before him? His heart accelerated when he heard the basement door open. God, he was in so much trouble.

Waves of nausea made his stomach feel like he had a bad case of seasickness. He ran to the sink and turned on the water, cupping his hands underneath. He filled them with the liquid, brought it to his mouth, and swallowed, wiping the remaining moisture with a hand towel. He resumed his post, straining harder to hear the conversation when he heard Ryan asking for something. Startled by a sharp rap on the bathroom door, Max jumped.

"Are you all right in there, son?"

"Yeah, Dad, I'm okay." His voice cracked.

"Did you eat something that didn't agree with you, son?"

"I guess so."

"Okay, call me if you need anything. Otherwise, join us in the kitchen. Ryan and I are going to have a cold drink."

Max caught a glimpse of his surprised facial expression in the mirror. "I'll be out in a little while." Before resuming his position on his stomach, he looked skyward and said a prayer, thankful when he saw the shadow of his father's feet disappear from underneath the doorframe. Satisfied they were gone, he gingerly opened the door and peeked out. When the coast was clear, Max lifted his backpack off the floor and slowly tiptoed toward the basement door, reminding himself there were no second chances on this one.

He slowly opened the basement door, praying it wouldn't creak and alert his father. Grateful he got his wish, he walked down the stairs, taking slow, deliberate steps to avoid making unnecessary noise. With four steps from the bottom, he heard footsteps overhead and rushed to the bottom. Hoisting his heavy backpack onto the table, he unzipped the bag and removed the equipment, placing it in the same spot when the recorded confessions came to mind. He flipped the lid open, pulled out the tiny cassette, and slipped it into his pocket.

The light flicked on, and he could see his father's feet as he descended each step. His first thought was to hide behind the furnace, but he ruled it out, figuring if he got caught, he'd be in a boatload of trouble—trouble his father knew nothing about—at least not yet. And, he'd never be able to step outside the house again except to attend school and church.

His stomach was cramped with severe pains that felt like someone had just punched him in the gut. Max convinced himself to walk back up the steps like a man and face whatever happened. He was exhausted from the morning's events, and all he wanted to do was go to bed and pretend it never happened.

"Max?" Jack Harwell said quizzically. "What are you doing down here in the dark?"

Man, he was screwing up royally today. "Dad," he pointed toward the window. "It's bright enough outside," he said. "I can see everything just fine." He turned and smiled as he began to mount the steps, surprised he'd come up with an answer so quickly.

"Oh, that's right," his father grinned. "How could I have forgotten your eyes glow in the dark?"

"Hilarious, Dad," he said over his shoulder.

"I guess this means you're okay?"

"Yeah, Dad. I'm fine."

"So, what are you doing down here? I thought you were joining us in the kitchen."

"Well," Max stammered to come up with a logical explanation. "I wanted to return the hammer I borrowed from your toolbox. Me and Ritchie are building a treehouse over at his place." He chastised himself for the tall tale.

"Ritchie and I," his father corrected.

"Yeah, that's what I meant. Ritchie and I."

"Terrific. I'm sure your mother will be proud of you." He gave a hearty chuckle. "Education in using tools is good, especially since I'm not handy around here." He turned to Ryan, "My wife keeps buying me all these tools," his hand swayed to the pegboard. "She thinks it will incentivize me to learn, but I have two left hands regarding repairs."

Ryan laughed. "My mom has the same thing on her wish list."

"So, Max, is Mr. Jones teaching you how to build the treehouse?"

"Yeah."

Father McKinley's last sermon about the effects of telling lies flashed through his mind. The waves of nausea returned and danced in the pit of his stomach.

"Please, make sure you do that with any tools you borrow. I don't want your mother thinking she needs to replace them with more tools." He snickered.

"I won't."

By the time Max reached the top step, he felt much better. The equipment was back where it belonged, and all was good.

He looked up at the ceiling and said another silent prayer, thanking God for the big favor, grateful he wouldn't have to deal with his father's fierce temper.

He gave a dramatic exhale, relieved he'd returned the recorder until his father's voice reverberated off the walls. He closed his eyes for a brief second.

"Max, damn it," he shouted. "You did it again, didn't—" his voice trailed off when his two-way radio squawked. He grabbed Ryan's arm, "Let's go, O'Reilly."

The two men rushed past him. "We'll discuss this later, young man," Jack Harwell said, his finger pointed in his son's face.

CHAPTER 6

*P*atrick Sawyer sat in his car with the engine running, waiting for Jane Clayton to drop his daughter Gabi off after a two-day sleepover with her best friend, Marti, and he couldn't wait for her to arrive. Taking another slug of beer, he could feel the excitement surging through his body, knowing he had finally achieved the long-anticipated desire he lived for, and now he could enjoy the fruits of his labor. Patrick knew Gabi would be upset when she heard her mother had already left on vacation with her friends without saying goodbye first, but he hoped the afternoon he'd planned would help her deal with the disappointment.

Patrick finished the last of his beer and flung the bottle out the window into a neighbor's yard, knowing they weren't home, then pushed the window control button to shut out the heat. The window slid into place with a smooth finish, silencing any outside noise. Sweat ran down his neck. He adjusted the temperature and turned the fan higher.

Drinking always made him sweat, just as it did with his father. "Dammit," he said, slamming his fist against the steering wheel. His deceased father was the last person he ever wanted to think about. He hated the bastard. Wiping more sweat that accumulated, a sharp pain hit his gut. He feared it was his father punishing him for what he'd done. He'd take that pain any day of the week, knowing he'd never have to face that bastard again. He didn't want to be anything like him. He tried to push the thoughts away, but his mind wouldn't shut down.

Most men thought of their fathers with fond memories, but not him. All he remembered were the many times he and his mother suffered at the hands of the drunken old man who'd used them as punching bags to show his prowess. Tears collected on his lashes when he pictured his mother's face. She was the only woman he'd ever loved, and now realizing how many beatings she'd taken in his place caused those tears to roll down his cheeks. He swiped at them.

"God rest your soul, Mama," he murmured the words and punched his fist into his opened hand. His vivid thoughts of the night the old man died brought a wide grin as he relived the excitement he'd felt watching Clifford J. Sawyer take his last breath after he'd pushed him. Patrick smiled, remembering the expression on his face when he hit his head on the fieldstone fireplace. That was the happiest day of his life. That's when his mother cautioned him never to tell anyone what happened, and he never did.

* * *

A loud thud to the side of the car caught him off guard. He smiled when he realized Gabi was pressing her nose against the window. He rolled down the window. "You goof," he said. She giggled, waved to her friends, and got inside the car.

"Why are you using the Maybach?" she asked.

"You said you wanted to ride in it when you saw it on the lot, right?" Gabi nodded. "Okay, so here it is."

"Can we keep it?"

"We'll see."

"Where's mommy?" she asked.

"Well."

"What, Daddy? Where is she?" Gabi said with concern.

"Mommy got a phone call this morning from her friends in Ohio asking if she'd join them for a fun get-together. She didn't want to leave without saying goodbye to you first, but I told her she deserved some fun with her friends, so she decided I was right and packed her bags."

"Without saying goodbye to me?" Gabi's voice rose.

"She had to take the only available flight early this morning. She promised to call later." Gabi pouted. Patrick reached for her hand. "Aww, come on now. Mom is always doing stuff for us. We can't be selfish about this. Doesn't she deserve to have fun too?"

"I guess so," Gabi pouted.

Patrick chuckled and poked his finger into her ribs. Gabi giggled.

"Okay," she said, elongating the letters.

"Good girl. Well, are you ready for a surprise?" he asked, noticing that Jane hadn't driven away. He lowered the window again so she could see it was him. They exchanged a wave, and she drove off.

Gabi snapped her seat belt into place. "What surprise?" she asked wide-eyed.

"Well," he said, glancing at her while easing the car onto the road-way. "We're going to have a lot of fun while Mom is away. I have lots of things planned."

"Like what?"

"For starters, I'm taking you to see *The Lion King*."

She gasped with surprise. "Oh my gosh, Daddy. Really?"

"Yes."

"But isn't Mommy going to be sad because she's not here with us?"

"No. Mommy is the one who suggested it because she knew how sad you were going to be because she'd left before you got home."

"Aww, that was nice of her." Seemingly satisfied, Gabi turned the radio on and began singing at the top of her lungs to a Taylor Swift song.

Watching her facial expressions brought such warmth to his center. This little girl was born the day after his mother died, making him sure his mother sent her as her replacement. The love he felt for this child was beyond belief. What an accomplishment! And to think, he'd made her, and now he got to see this little angel with the cherub face and the turned-up nose every day. He didn't like that she was growing up so quickly, but there wasn't much he could do about that.

Could she be entering the fourth grade already? Patrick shook his head, reached for her hand, and squeezed it.

Gabi looked at him with an open smile without missing a beat of the song, her two missing front teeth making her more adorable than ever. He tugged gently on one of her brunette ringlets, framing her face. She hated those ringlets. She'd always said they made her look like a baby, but he didn't care. It kept her young in his mind, not all grown up. He dreaded the thought of her one day getting involved with some guy when he'd have to take a backseat in her life. He didn't relish the idea of playing second fiddle. He told himself to stop thinking of such idiotic rubbish and enjoy his cute date. The humidity always made her hair curlier. She was moving to the beat of the music, her ponytail in a long curl swaying like a puppy's tail. She filled him with pride. She was beautiful!

The song ended, and she looked at him. "You know, Dad, I'm going to be so sad when Mufasa dies."

"Who's Mufasa?"

"Geez, Dad. He's Simba's father. Mufasa's brother Scar lures the two of them into a stampede of beasts hoping to get him killed so he can take over the throne, but the only one who dies is Mufasa."

"Hey, if you know all of this, why are we going to see it?"

"Because," Gabi said, her hand on her hip, "all my friends saw it. I'm the only one who hasn't."

"Well, now, we can't have that. Okay, so I guess I should continue down Broadway, right?" Gabi released a hefty sigh. "You want to know the next surprise?" he asked.

"What?"

"You're going to meet my cousin, Maria, after the show." Frowning, Gabi looked at him quizzically.

"How come I've never met her before?"

"Because we had a silly argument years ago and haven't spoken to each other in a long time."

"Oh. Does Maria have kids?"

"No, I'm afraid not. She can't have children."

"She could adopt or pay someone to be a surrogate mother."

Patrick frowned. "What do you know about surrogacy?"

"Well, I only know a little. My friend, Stephanie's mom, will have a baby, and I asked her about her bump. She told me what the baby's sex was and even let me rub her tummy, and then she told me she got paid for having babies."

"What's Stephanie's last name?"

"Winters."

"That bitch!"

"Daddy. That wasn't very nice. She's a nice lady."

"I don't care how nice you think she is. I don't want you anywhere near Stephanie or her mother."

Gabi huffed and stared out the window. Seeing he'd ruined her excitement, he softened his approach.

"Listen, I'm sorry. I don't like people feeding you grown-up stuff like that. You could have asked Mom or me about surrogacy."

"I didn't know what it was until she told me. Do I have to stop being friends with Stephanie?" she whined.

"No. How about we forget this conversation for now and have fun? Okay?"

"Okay." Gabi grinned. "Does she like children?"

"Absolutely. Maria loves them."

"Then I feel sorry for her. Is she married?"

"She was, but her husband just died."

"Aww, then I'm glad we'll see her."

"Yes. I want to offer my support and make up for our years apart."

"Does Mommy know her?"

"No, but when she returns, I'll introduce them." Patrick pulled into the parking garage, and the attendant left his office. "Do you have a special place for my car so I don't have to worry someone will run into or steal it?"

"Yes, sir, but it will cost you more."

* * *

"Well, this has certainly been an interesting morning," Jessie told her partner as they watched the Stuarts walk away.

"To say the least." He shook his head. "Hopefully, the Stuarts will be more useful once they're dressed and down at headquarters."

"You thought she was pretty nice, huh, Gerard?" A tiny surge of jealousy tugged at her heart as she waited for his response.

"Are you kidding me? She's not my type of woman. Not that I'm knocking her choice of sex games." He turned to her and released a loud whoop. "What do you think, Jessie? Are you going to be that kind of woman when you get married?"

"Probably not, because I'm never getting married."

"Yes, you are. You're going to marry me." He winked, and she thought her heart would jump out of her chest. The heat from the blush colored her cheeks.

"Only in your dreams, Bud."

Gerard grinned. "Then why the blush?"

"Well, I'm embarrassed for Mrs. Stuart," she lied. "Now, everyone knows about their fetish."

"Hell, she wasn't embarrassed. Didn't you see the look on her face? She loved every minute of the attention. I wouldn't be surprised if they don't use this as one of their future fantasies and hire actors to play the cops." He flung his hand in the air. "Speaking of which, didn't I tell you they were getting it on? You didn't believe me."

Jessie rolled her eyes. "All you men ever think about is women on their backs?" Gerard waggled his eyebrows. "You're pathetic, you know that?" she said with an eye roll. "I, on the other hand, could care less about what people do in private."

"Liar."

"Why do you say that?"

"Because most women would say the same thing. But deep inside, they're dying to know every detail so they can live vicariously through them. Why do you think they read those bodice ripper books?"

Jessie snickered. "And you know this, how?" she asked.

"Because I know women."

"Of course you do, Don Juan."

Her thoughts drifted back to the kind of woman he wanted for a wife, and it gave her a warm fuzzy feeling. She wasn't sure she even knew what a good marriage was. She'd never met anyone who was happily married. How could she? Growing up in a dysfunctional household while playing nursemaid to a mother who turned to the bottle after her husband walked out and the slew of men who paraded in and out of their lives left her somewhat disillusioned. Remembering those years gave her a sick feeling inside. A sudden sadness crept up and made her eyes water. Gerard noticed.

"Hey, Jessie," he latched onto her arm and stopped her. His eyes scanned her face as his hand cupped under her chin, "why the tears?"

His gentle touch caused her pulse to increase. Instead of rushing into his arms, she brushed his hand aside and continued staring ahead.

"Talk to me," he called after her. "What's wrong?"

"Nothing, Gerard." She wiped the tears with her forefinger a few feet away from him. "One of those tiny gnats flew into my eye, you knucklehead," she said, looking back at him over her shoulder. "C'mon, let's get out of here."

"You're so full of it! But, if that's how you want to play it." Giving her a side glance, he changed the subject. "I guess the Stuarts' little rendezvous didn't turn out to be so private after all!" Gerard said.

"I guess not." she shrugged, "but I'll bet they never expected to stumble over a dead body."

Gerard snickered. "That's for sure."

"You know, though," Jess said, "what has me puzzled is the significance of leaving their clothing at the hotel. Like seriously, what was the point?"

Gerard lowered his head and shook it in disbelief. "Jessie, Jessie, Jessie. It's called passion." A light chuckle spilled from his mouth. "C'mon, let's go get some food. My stomach is talking back to me. I haven't eaten since last night's dinner at ten o'clock." He checked the time. "Christ, that was twelve hours ago."

"Ooh, how could you even think of food after inhaling the stink on our bodies? We need showers first, hotshot. I'm not sitting across from you and eating a hamburger." She brought her arm up close to her nose and smelled her skin. "I'm disgusting. And if you didn't stink just as bad, I'd be embarrassed.

"Moi stinks?"

"Oh yeah," she said with a wide-eyed nod. "Big time."

"Hey, thanks for the compliment."

"Ah, that wasn't meant as a compliment."

"No shit, Dick Tracy," he said. "That was meant sarcastically."

She rolled her eyes and gave him a fake smile. "Drop me off at my place so I can shower, will you? I can't go to the precinct dressed in these clothes anyway."

"Didn't you bring a change of clothes with you?"

"No, I didn't. Did you see me carrying anything out this morning?"

"Uh . . . I don't know. I guess I had my mind on other things."

She ignored his innuendo and continued talking. "Besides, I was half asleep and not thinking clearly, for God's sake."

"Well, you could always parade around like our witnesses," he teased. He placed his hands on his hips. "What do you think?" She twisted her mouth to the side at his comment. "Not such a good idea, huh?"

"No."

"And by the way, just for the record," he said, "I have my clothes in the trunk," he boasted. "I can't believe you forgot to bring a change of clothes. All good detectives have an extra suitcase packed at all times."

"I never repacked my overnight bag from the last time we pulled an all-nighter."

Several strands of hair had managed to loosen from the scrunchie, securing her long locks. She removed the band and smoothed her auburn hair back with both hands, then pulled the scrunchie off her wrist and pulled it over her thick ponytail. Gerard gave her ponytail a playful tug.

* * *

By the way, Bradshaw is already at the hospital and will check in on our Jane Doe until we arrive."

"I know, Jess. I was the one who asked the lieutenant to have Bradshaw check on Jane." Jess's palms rose in the air. He grinned. "Food . . . now, okay?"

"No," she pinched the sides of her nose with her fingers. "Showers first . . . Then food. We're sticky from sweating and drenched from that downpour. I can't imagine walking into a restaurant—fast food or otherwise in this shape." She rushed to the driver's side door. "I'll drive this time." Gerard pulled the keys from his pocket, unlocked the doors, and tossed them to her. Inside the hot car, they looked at one another simultaneously, grimaced, and rolled down all the windows.

"You're right," he said, pinching his nose. "We stink! Can I shower at your place too?"

Jessie pulled away from the curb. Now that it was mid-morning, there was a lot more traffic, and the ride promised to take much longer than they anticipated.

"Sure. What do you say," Jessie said, her hand on the switch, "we let the siren wail so we can hurry and eat faster?"

"I say, go for it." He waggled his brows again. It sounds like you're anxious to get me into your apartment, Jess." He flashed a toothy grin, and the dimples in his cheeks seemed even more profound. "You do know," he said devilishly, "I can't be trusted."

"Oh, really?" she teased right back. "Well then, I should warn you, Sherlock, I'm tired, suffering from PMS, and carrying a gun. Any questions?"

"Nope," he shook his head. "None whatsoever."

CHAPTER 7

*P*hillip Bradshaw, the burly Detective mumbled to the desk nurse and slipped his shield back inside his pocket. "I'm here to see Jane Doe." He sucked in a deep breath, tired from a long, arduous night, wishing he had shut his phone off before Harwell's call came in, asking him to check on another victim.

A rush of panic broke out and distracted the nurse checking the patient database for him.

A staff member shouted to everyone in the room, "Bus accident, all hands on deck," Bradshaw turned just as a team of medical doctors and nurses rushed outside to meet the ESU vehicles. The red lights flashing against the building resembled the flames of a dancing fire.

"I have to go," the nurse said, dashing past him.

Bradshaw moved aside and watched a caravan of gurneys rush through the entrance. Pained cries echoed through the area like a bad dream. Two security guards handled the area to prevent curious bystanders from getting in the way. The air reeked of blood—a rusty iron smell that the Detective remembered all too well.

He swallowed hard when he saw a female victim on a gurney passing by him. She looked directly into his eyes, an expression of horror on her face that he knew all too well. He shuddered and turned away, unable to deal with the agony, and forced himself into a chair. The memory of his wife's suicide rushed to the forefront of his mind. She'd had that same fearful expression, dying only minutes after he'd arrived. He forced the thoughts away and stood upright.

There had to be someone who could help him. He entered the ER through the double doors and began checking inside the curtained rooms.

"Hey," a man shouted from behind, "What are you doing?"

He flashed his shield. "I'm trying to find someone to help me locate Jane Doe."

"We have one who arrived tonight, who was in a car accident? Is that yours?" he asked.

"Sounds like her. I'm handling this for one of the other detectives since I was here anyway." Bradshaw turned to see what the commotion was behind him. A few seconds later, he turned back only to see the curtain being closed on a cubicle behind him; the voice of the man he'd just spoken to faded into the background.

Bradshaw heaved a hefty sigh and noticed a nurse unlocking a drug cabinet. "I'm looking for Jane Doe," he said, rushing up to her.

"She's on a gurney down the overflow hallway," she pointed. "I believe she was one of the patients who didn't require immediate attention." She shook her head from side to side. "We're having difficulty keeping up with these patients tonight since the bus accident." She walked briskly into a curtained stall and drew the drapes to the closed position.

"Thanks," he mumbled, but she was already gone. He walked down the hallway. Gurneys lined up against the wall. Family members surrounded the stretchers, except one at the end of the row, which had no one around it. Detective Bradshaw decided this had to be his Jane Doe. With a glance at her chart, Bradshaw blew out a frustrated breath because the only thing done for Jane was a change of clothing. A residue of blood remained along the crevice of her nose. She was sleeping or unconscious—he wasn't sure which. A technician rolled a piece of equipment past. Bradshaw stopped him to ask a question.

"When will this patient get some attention?" he asked.

"We're waiting for someone to get her to run tests. Are you a relative?"

"No. I'm Detective Bradshaw of the two-one."

She glanced at Jane's chart and then returned it under the mattress. "Yeah, that's what we're waiting on, Detective. As you can see from this chaos, it may be a while. We've got every available staff member here helping out." A second later, she disappeared. Bradshaw leaned over the side rails and took a closer look at Jane. She had two black circles under her eyes, probably from the impact from the vehicle's airbag. She seemed to be resting comfortably. He wondered what was going through her mind as he watched the rise and fall of her chest. Suddenly, her breathing increased, and her face distorted into a painful expression. He rubbed her forearm, and her expression returned to normal.

She looked so peaceful—angelic-like and not nearly as bad as he'd anticipated. The daunting expression from the woman he'd seen earlier flashed through his mind again and reminded him of his wife. A tear rolled down his cheek. Riddled with guilt, he blinked back the tears. If only he had listened to her. If only he'd noticed her depression, she might never have taken her own life. A sinking feeling waved through his stomach.

He reached for Jane's hand and held it between his. He knew it was improper for him to show emotion, but from what he'd heard from Harwell, someone wanted this woman dead. He wanted her to know she wasn't alone.

A young woman in scrubs called out to him, "Can I get you a chair?"

He released a breath. "Please." He bent his leg back and forth a few times. "These arthritic knees are mighty tired."

She slid a plastic chair over to him, and he exhaled as he eased himself down onto the seat, using the side rails of the gurney for support. He relaxed his shoulders and sighed of exhaustion, relieved to be sitting. He would have liked something more comfortable, but he assured himself this was no time to ask. "Do you know how soon they'll take Jane for testing?"

"I'm afraid not, sir. As you can see, we're in chaos with the massive bus accident. Tack on the huge amount of cutbacks, and it's pretty much anybody's guess as to how soon she'll have the tests."

"Okay, I can understand that, but has anyone checked her vitals, pressed on her stomach to check for internal bleeding?"

"Yes, sir, we have. A while ago, before you arrived."

"What happened to her clothing?"

"It's probably in a brown paper bag. Check the curtained rack. The staff might have put it there for safekeeping."

He stood and moved the curtain aside, seeing a brown bag tucked in among the bedding, gowns, medical supplies, and scrubs. He left the bag where it was for safekeeping and eased himself back down into the chair. He was tired. He closed his eyes, his hand still tightly clasped over Jane's.

A sudden jerk awakened him. He couldn't believe he'd fallen asleep, but it couldn't have been more than minutes. His eyes flew open, temporarily unaware of his surroundings. He cleared his throat and straightened his body to an upright position.

Jane was sitting up in bed, her two black eyes reminding him of a raccoon, her lips so swollen it tilted her mouth into a crooked smile. Bradshaw rubbed a hand over his face trying to wake up, then pushed himself back into the chair.

"Who are you?" she asked, her voice garbled by her swollen mouth. She glanced at Bradshaw's hand, still latched onto hers. It caused him a sudden self-consciousness, and he pulled it away.

"My name is Phillip Bradshaw . . . Detective in the two-one."

"The two-one?" she asked, her eyes wide with fear.

"The two-one Precinct, NYPD."

She swallowed hard. "Am I under arrest? Did I do something wrong?"

"No. You're not under arrest." He patted the top of her hand. He couldn't shake the paternal instinct he felt for her. She looked like a lost soul—just like him.

"Why am I in a hospital?"

"Do you remember anything about the accident?"

She gasped. "I had an accident? Is that why I'm so sore?" Jane's beautiful blue eyes against the backdrop of bruising filled with fear— her pupils speckled with tiny dots. He wanted to reach out and hold her, to let her know it would be all right, but he knew better. He was a lonely old man.

"It's okay, Jane, we can wait. You know, until you're feeling up to it."

"Is that my name?"

"I don't know, but that's what I'm going to call you—if that's okay." Jane gave a slight nod of her head. "Unless, of course, you know your name." Jane stared into space. Confused, she shook her head from side to side.

"That's okay," he patted her hand. "As soon as all your tests return, we will take you to a state facility and nurse you back to health. You'll be safe, get three squares daily, and a team of around-the-clock doctors and nurses. So don't worry about a thing. I'm sure someone out there is looking for you." He smiled. "I promise; we'll take good care of you." Bradshaw stopped talking when his cell phone rang. He flipped it open, checked the screen, held his finger up, and mouthed, "I'll be with you in a minute."

It was Detective Gerard checking in on their victim. Bradshaw noticed Jane straining to hear his side of the conversation. He saw no reason to add to her anxiety and pointed toward the sofa at the end of the hall to let her know he was leaving. She nodded and gave him a slight wave as he strode past the other gurneys down the aisle.

Fifteen minutes later, Bradshaw ended his call and shuffled back down the hallway toward Jane's bed. She was gone! A sudden panicked feeling tugged at his heart. He blew out a hefty breath of air, trying to convince himself not to jump to conclusions. Had they taken her for testing? But wouldn't he have seen them take her away from where he sat? Was he even watching? Panic tied his stomach in knots. He must have looked elsewhere. Bradshaw closed his eyes, tired from a long night and desperately trying to remember if he'd had Jane in sight the entire time. And then he remembered -- he'd struck up a conversation with a beautiful woman who sat next to him after he'd disconnected his call with Gerard. Besieged with guilt, he had to admit he'd been on the job too long, and the panic returned. What was he going to do? *Think clearly*, his mind shouted. He had to ask someone before he jumped to any more conclusions. But who? Everyone was busy.

Bradshaw turned around in circles looking for someone to ask. The medicinal smell of the ER made him cough uncontrollably. He rushed to the water fountain, drank, and returned down the hallway. Maybe one of the relatives of the other patients waiting saw where Jane went. A door opened from one of the rooms in the hall, and a nurse walked out, pushing her drug cart. He rushed up to her. "Did you see the woman on this gurney?" he asked, pointing to the empty bed.

"Sir," she sighed heavily, "I honestly couldn't tell you."

He rushed into the ER and spotted the nurse he'd spoken to earlier walking out from a curtained exam room.

"Where is my Jane Doe? Did they take her for testing?"

"I don't know, Detective. I'm up to my eyeballs with my patients."

"Listen, dammit," spilled from his mouth, "I need some help here."

"I'd like to help you, Detective, but I must tend to another patient. Check with the Hospital Administrator sitting at the desk over there," she pointed. "She should be able to tell you."

Why hadn't he thought of the administrator? Retiring at the end of the week couldn't come soon enough for him. He rushed over to the woman. "I'm Detective Bradshaw," he flashed his shield. "Jane Doe," he pointed down toward the hallway where she'd been. "She's gone."

"Which one is your Jane Doe, Detective?"

"She was brought in early this morning, a car accident—"

"Oh her. Yeah, I just passed by her a little while ago," she said, interrupting him, "when I walked back from the restroom."

"Well, she's not there now," his head wagged in disbelief. "Did she go for testing?" he asked.

The administrator held up her finger. "Hold on a minute," she said, calling out to the young girl passing. "Jackie, please take over for me. I need to help this Detective." The young girl sat down and took the next patient waiting in line while the administrator moved to another computer.

"I'm not sure, but I can tell you, these accident victims have top priority." Her name tag identified her as *Linda Tanners*. She clicked on another screen.

"Would they have transferred her to another hospital?"

"I didn't do any transfer paperwork for her."

Bradshaw closed the gap between them, watching over her shoulder as she flashed through various screens on the computer. He inhaled the sweet rose scent of her perfume, a welcomed odor compared to what he'd been inhaling. Linda scrolled down a list of names. "No, Detective, she's not on this list. But let me make a quick call to the department."

Bradshaw followed her to the phone. "Hi, Sandy. Yeah, this is Linda. I'm checking on a patient to see if she's in your area." Linda's head nodded. "I understand. I did check the computer, but her name isn't in the lineup." Her eyebrows inched up. "Listen, Sandy, we're all busy. Just check, okay?" Linda stood, drumming her fingers on the top of the metal filing cabinet. "You're sure?" she shook her head. "Okay, thanks." Linda looked exasperated when she turned to Bradshaw. "Sorry, Detective. She's not there. Hmm," her finger went up again, "let me check with the head nurse to see if she knows anything." She began to walk away.

Bradshaw stood by Jane Doe's gurney and spotted the tie from a hospital nightgown under the blanket. "I think she's left the building," he said.

"Why would you say that?"

He pulled the gown free and held it up. "This is Jane's gown."

"Detective, we can't be sure that gown was the one she wore."

"But it's on the gurney."

Linda's cheeks blazed with color. She increased her pace, almost to a jog. "I'll be right back," she said over her shoulder and entered the ER.

Bile rose to the back of his throat. He coughed and rushed to the water fountain for another drink. What was he going to do? What was he going to tell the detectives? That he hadn't been paying attention? His stomach recoiled again like he was riding on a roller coaster. He'd wait for Linda to return, but it looked like he'd have to make that dreaded call to Gerard. He shook his head in disbelief. Bradshaw and Gerard had had a few run-ins, mostly over territorial crap, but hard feelings had lingered. Maybe he should call Detective Kensington instead and let her break it to her partner. She was a good egg. He paced back and forth, his legs aching from standing on his feet too long, and watched for Linda's return. He found a chair and eased himself down when he saw Linda rushing back to him.

"No one has seen her," Linda said, breathless from rushing around. "I can't believe this," her hand went to her forehead as if holding her head in place. "Oh God," she rolled her eyes, "I just started this job. They'll throw me out the door if I don't find this woman." She called out to an aide who passed by the door. "Karen, come here for a minute. I need to ask you something." Linda and Bradshaw met the woman halfway.

"Did you see the patients in the auxiliary hallway?"

She nodded. "Yeah, I was down that hallway a short while ago, refilling the rack for the interns. Why do you ask?"

"Because we have a patient missing," the woman said.

"No. That can't be right," Karen said. Then a sudden look of fright washed over her face. "Oh no," she squealed and took off like a shot toward the linen rack. She pulled the draped curtain aside and counted the scrubs. "I always keep sets of six on this shelf for the staff – there's only five left. An orderly replaced the laundry bin less than five minutes ago. Let me check to see what's in there." She entered the room, lifted the large bin lid, and peered inside. "No, nothing in here. What did your patient look like?" she asked.

Bradshaw closed his eyes and released an exasperated sigh. "She'd be hard to miss . . . two black eyes, a few abrasions on her face, and a bandage on the left side of her forehead."

"She's a nurse, right?"

"Not to my knowledge. Why?"

"A woman in blue scrubs resembling your description passed me in the hallway."

"I don't know what she was wearing. We found her hospital gown on the empty gurney."

"Detective," Linda said, "we don't know if that was her gown." She sighed. "Look, while you two are talking, I'll call Security. I'll be right back." Bradshaw nodded. Linda took off at a fast clip toward the nurse's station, leaving Bradshaw and Karen in the middle of the hallway.

"Karen, when you saw this woman, why wouldn't you have questioned how she looked? Black eyes and all?"

She sighed. Her head swayed back and forth. "Detective," she paused to exhale, "we've been bombarded with patients tonight. We've had cutbacks like crazy. With the bus accident, it seemed logical that the hospital would try to get as many people on the floor as possible to assist. They've even called me to come in when I've been on vacation, so—"

"So, you're saying you didn't ask her?" Bradshaw asked.

"No." She blinked her eyes shut. "We just passed in the hall."

"What went through your mind when you saw the black eyes?"

"That she'd had a nose job. That's what I looked like after I had mine." Her breathing increased in short rapid spurts.

"Did you see anyone walking with her?" Bradshaw asked the aide.

"Many people were walking behind her, but I can't be sure they were with her. We get a lot of foot traffic down these halls. It's hard to keep track of visitors." She paced. Geez, it wasn't that long ago when I saw her."

Hearing her say that made him think Jane couldn't have gotten too far. Linda was speaking to someone on the phone. He strained to listen to what she was saying. "This is Linda Tanners, the administrator in the ER. We're missing a patient." Bradshaw watched her facial expression as she spoke into the phone. "No, sir, this is not a joke." She shook her head while listening to the man and disconnected briefly. She returned to where the Detective stood and briefed him on her conversation.

"What do you mean there's no surveillance footage available for the front or rear exits of the hospital?" he asked.

"The captain said they've been working on setting up a new system."

"What? No backup cameras?" Bradshaw's voice grew louder.

"Oh, I don't know, Detective." Linda's hands rose in the air. "He also said patients do this all the time. They become impatient and just walk out."

"But she isn't just anybody. She might have the answers to another homicide we're working on."

"I'm so sorry."

"But they do have footage from the halls, right?"

"Yes, they do. The captain said he'd notify his guards to check the entire facility thoroughly. I gave him a detailed description, and he suggested we check the footage of the halls first."

Thoughts raced through Bradshaw's mind, and a picture of Jane Doe's assailant returning to finish the job encroached. Things had gone downhill in a matter of minutes. Dread filled him, knowing he had to make the inevitable phone call to the two young detectives. The tense ache punching in the mid-section of his stomach caused him to wince. He pressed his hands against the pain, took a deep breath, and shuffled his feet across the polished floors. He still couldn't believe she'd vanished a few feet away. "Wait!" he shouted. "The brown bag with her clothing. Where's the bag with her clothing? We need it to test her DNA. I need that bag."

"Then you'd better get the gown you think she wore, just in case there's something on it," Linda nodded toward the gurney.

"Good idea." Bradshaw turned and noticed an orderly tearing the bed apart and shoving everything into a bin. He ran over to him and flashed his badge. "Wait, I need that gown."

He watched the orderly rummage through the bin and realized the gown had already come into contact with the other dirty laundry. He sighed and blinked his eyes shut. "Never mind. It's already contaminated."

"I'm sorry, sir. I'm just doing my job."

65

"I know, son." Bradshaw turned and noticed Karen heading toward him slowly, her palms in the air and a mass of confusion covering her face.

"Oh God, this whole thing is just too bizarre." Her body shook.

"Let's go to security, Detective," Linda repeated.

"I need to call my precinct first."

Bradshaw shuffled to a chair in the lounge to call Gerard. He could almost feel his blood pressure rising. Thirsty, he pulled a cup from the dispenser and filled it with water, took a long swig, then sat down and reluctantly punched in Gerard's number. He was thankful when he heard Gerard's voicemail because it gave him time to regroup before speaking to the Detective.

* * *

"Have the Stuarts arrived from this morning's crime scene?" Jessie asked, stopping in front of the desk sergeant.

"Yes, ma'am." He gave her a lopsided grin. "The woman is in Interview Room Three. The man is behind door number two."

Gerard came up beside her and leaned over the high desk. "I'll bet that beautiful woman just made your day, Sarge?" he whispered.

The balding, middle-aged sergeant nodded. "You bet, Detective."

Jessie shook her head at the two men. "I think you should take Mrs. Stuart, Gerard."

"No. I think you should take Mrs. Stuart."

"Nope. You said you're the expert on women, so here's your chance, hotshot. Just throw some masculine charm on her, and you'll have her eating out of your hand." She turned on her heels. "Tootles," she waved her hand in the air and went down the hall.

"Detectives," the desk sergeant said, "please don't fight over who should take the woman. I'd be happy to take her off your hands."

Gerard snorted. "No, Sarge, I think I can handle it." Gerard watched the sway of Jessie's hips as she swaggered down the hall, her long red hair swinging in step with her movement. He liked watching her but forced himself back to reality to focus on the job. "When do you want to notify Lenny's daughter?" he called after her.

"Right now."

"I thought we were interviewing the Stuarts?"

"You can get started. I'll start my interview after I make this call."

His face formed into a frown. "You're calling Lenny's daughter instead of going to the house?"

"Yeah, bozo," she sighed, "his daughter lives in Ohio. I'm calling the OPD to ask them to inform her."

"Oh, well, see, I didn't know that."

"Yeah, well, that's probably because . . . oh, never mind."

"Okay, carry on," he said with a wink.

"Gee, thanks, hotshot," she saluted. "Now, do you mind if I get to work?"

"Not at all." He sighed and entered the interview room.

Mrs. Stuart, a woman in her early thirties, sat staring at her bent fingers, checking out her manicure. Dressed in tight-fitting jeans and a short T-shirt, exposing the creamy color of her midriff, she looked better than she did earlier. Her long dark hair was pulled back with a large barrette on the nape of her neck.

"Mrs. Stuart, thank you for coming to the station house."

"You are most welcome," she flirted enthusiastically. "I'm always happy to help—especially the good-looking ones."

Gerard cleared his throat to sidetrack her comment. "Now, before we get started, I'm going to read you your rights and record our conversation."

She jerked her head in surprise. "Whatever for?"

"For our mutual protection."

"Am I under arrest, Detective?" she fluttered her lashes at him.

"No, ma'am. It's for everyone's protection. This way, you know what you said, and I know what you said. It's all on tape."

"If you must."

"Okay, let's get started. Tell me about your evening—everything that led up to the moment of contact with the dead body."

She giggled like a teenager. "You want to know every little detail?"

"Every." Gerard did all he could to contain himself from laughing. She was attractive but not a beauty queen by any stretch of the imagination. He wondered if Mr. Stuart realized his wife tried to come on to other men. Grateful the interview was being recorded and viewed by Harwell, Gerard wasn't the least worried she'd file sexual harassment charges against him when he ignored her advances.

* * *

Jessie entered the interview room and found Mr. Stuart pacing back and forth. He was a distinguished-looking man with a full head of white hair and quite a bit older than his wife. He wore a grey silk business suit that complimented his hair color.

"Thanks for coming down, sir. I'll try not to take up too much of your time."

"That's good, Detective Kensington because I have a flight to catch later this afternoon."

"Oh, sir, I'm not sure you'll be on that flight. We may need to question you again."

John Stuart released a loud groan. "I have to be on that flight." His face tensed; a muscle flickered on the side of his jaw.

"Let's get down to business and see where we are when we finish." She watched his body language with interest. It was no secret; he was the type of man who needed to feel like he was in control. She spoke softly and smiled. "Mr. Stuart, please give me a detailed account of your evening last night."

He grinned. "Catherine and I finished dinner at about ten-thirty, then returned to our hotel room for the night. We watched a movie on cable, then Catherine and I decided to partake in a little more excitement, so we—"

Jessie interrupted. "You can take it from the time you fell over the body. I don't need to know why or how you decided to go to Central Park. However, before we go any further, the home address you gave me earlier is local. Is that correct?" she asked, slightly confused about why they were at a hotel. She opened the file on the table to view her notes and verify the information. An uneasy feeling erupted in her stomach. Was she the only woman in the world who hadn't considered a rendezvous?

John Stuart shifted uncomfortably. "Uh, detective, can I count on your discretion?"

"Well, that depends." John Stuart's blue eyes never left Jessie's face. "Okay, let's hear it." His expression gave him away. "You're having an affair, and she's not your wife." He nodded in the affirmative. "Swell." She shook her head. "Do either of you live here in New York?"

"Yes, we both do."

"Can you give me her last name?"

"You have the correct name for her. It's Catherine Stuart." He gave her a sheepish grin.

"And, she's spelling it the same as yours? S-t-u-a-r-t?"

"Yes. Catherine is my sister-in-law," he answered without an ounce of remorse. "She's married to my brother."

Jessie swallowed hard and forced herself not to react. She felt sick and could only imagine how she would have felt if it had been her relative. "Okay, then give me a run-down of the chain of events."

"Well, we decided to have some emotionally charged sex and figured Central Park would be a fun place -- and had we . . . well, you know."

"So, you arrived at what time?"

"It was about two o'clock in the morning or maybe two-thirty."

"At what time did you discover the bodies?"

"You mean body. We never saw the other one, the woman who was alive. That didn't happen until later when Catherine heard a loud painful moan shortly after the officer arrived. As for time, I'm not sure, Detective. We were so involved." He released nervous laughter.

"Yeah, right. Okay, so why did you leave your clothes at the hotel?"

"I told you before. Because it was an emotional high to drive over there, to see Catherine—"

"Naked?" She finished the sentence for him. She scratched her head. "That blanket couldn't have been large enough to be wrapped around the both of you while you were driving?"

"That was the whole point, Detective." He grinned. "You've never done anything naughty, have you?"

Jessie cleared her throat. "I'm the one asking the questions here, Mr. Stuart."

"Yes, ma'am."

"Excuse me, Mr. Stuart, I need to check with the lab," she said, rushing out of the room before she smacked him silly. He was a smug bastard, and she loathed his type. Screw trying to make him think he was in control. Outside, she keyed in the lab's number on her cell phone. "Do you have any results for me on that blanket?" She looked through the door window and watched him pace back and forth. "Yeah, okay. Will you have someone call me the minute those results are in?" When Jessie returned to the room, Mr. Stuart was pacing faster than before. She pointed to the chair. "Please sit, sir."

"Detective, you can't honestly believe we killed those people."

"I never said that, sir. Everyone near or around a crime scene is an automatic suspect until proven otherwise. If you allow me to rule you and your lady out, you can be on your way."

"Oh, that's just great," he griped. "If the media gets a hold of this, we'll be in the newspapers." He stood and began pacing again. "My wife is going to kill me if she finds out." Jessie stared at him and prayed his brother would find out. It would serve him right.

"Please sit down, Mr. Stuart. A few more questions."

"Well, what exactly are you looking for?"

"Do you own a pistol, sir?"

"No. Of course not," Stuart shot back. "I'm a civilized community member and greatly respected lawyer."

Jessie chuckled and wondered if "civilized" included cheating on one's spouse. A rap on the door interrupted her thoughts. One of the technicians from the lab handed her the results. She nodded a thank you, viewed the paper, and read it aloud. "The results show semen, gun residue, and the victim's blood on the blanket."

Mr. Stuart released a heavy sigh of frustration.

Detective Kensington reached down into her case and removed a light. "Please hold out your hands."

"You can't be serious," his voice filled with irritation. "I've seen enough CSI episodes to know what you're thinking. You're being absurd."

"Sir, did you shower when the officer drove you back to your hotel?"

"Are you kidding? He barely gave us enough time to get dressed."

"Okay, then hold out your hands, please." She flashed the light over his hands. "They're clean."

"Big surprise there, Detective."

"Mr. Stuart," she said, "I've already told you. When I'm satisfied, you're telling the truth; you can leave and return to your life. The more you protest, the longer you'll be here."

He twisted his mouth into a sour grin without commenting, then sat down in the chair and crossed his arms against his chest.

Jess stood. "Please excuse me for a moment, Mr. Stuart. I need to confer with my partner." She walked down the hall to Gerard's room, knocked on the door, then walked inside. "Can I see you for a minute, Gerard?"

"Sure." He followed her into the hallway.

"What's up?"

"The blanket only shows Lenny's blood. No residue was found on his hands. I think their alibi checks out, so we can release these scum bags."

"I agree. Those two were oblivious until they tripped and fell on the body."

"By the way," she snorted, "did she tell you she's Stuart's sister-in-law?"

"No," his brows pulled together. "You shittin' me?"

"No. I'm not. At first, I thought you might be right about them having a reckless adventure to freshen their marriage, and I even warmed up to the idea, but when he revealed the truth, I wanted to puke. How's that for brotherly love?"

"Pretty pathetic. Okay, let's get these two out of here. Mrs. Stuart's been coming onto me for the last half hour."

"I thought you enjoyed that?" Jessie quipped.

"It depends on who it is." He headed back inside the interview room. "Hey," he called after her. "By the way, I'm happy you warmed up to the idea." His wink gave her a tingle.

When Jessie returned to John Stuart, he was now sitting, his crossed leg bouncing in a mechanical motion.

"Okay, Mr. Stuart. We're releasing you and Mrs. Stuart." He stood upright. "Make sure you're available in case we need to contact you again," she said.

"How will you get in touch with us?" he asked.

"We'll call your office or the cell number you provided."

They exited the room together and walked toward the lobby to wait for Catherine to join him. A few minutes later, he and Catherine left the building holding hands.

"So much for frolicking in the woods, huh, Gerard?" Jessie said.

"Uh-huh." He shook his head in disgust. "How'd you make out with OPD?"

"Good. The captain said they would bring the local priest when they visited the residence." Jessie rushed past him toward her desk.

Gerard eased himself down in his desk chair and listened to his voicemail. A few seconds into the playback, his hand slammed down on the desk when he heard Detective Bradshaw's message.

CHAPTER 8

*D*etective Zach Gerard parked the car in the hospital parking lot and exited simultaneously with Jessie. Both rushed over to Bradshaw, who's expression was grim, was waiting by the door of the ER.

"What the hell happened here, Bradshaw?" Gerard demanded without so much as an acknowledgment. "Where did she go? Did anyone see her leave?"

It was apparent Bradshaw was miserable about what had happened—it was written all over his face. He sat down on the bench. "Look, I waited with her for a long time. Every available staff member cared for the victims of the big bus accident downtown. When all Hell broke loose, the staff was running every which way. It was like a friggin' zoo in this place. Gurneys all in a row like a brigade in the waiting rooms, the hallways. You name it." Jessie listened intently without comment. "Those patients had first dibs, and the ones who could wait for treatment were rolled into the adjoining hallways of the ER. Our Jane Doe was one of them." Bradshaw scrubbed his hand over his face. "When you called, I didn't think Jane Doe needed to hear our conversation—she was already scared to death, so I left her side and walked down to the end of the hall. When I finished the call with you, I found the nightgown she'd worn on the bed tucked between the sheets. I ran down the hall looking for her, and when I didn't see her, I figured they'd taken her to the labs for testing," his hands raised in anguish, "but she hadn't."

"What about the surveillance tapes?" Jessie asked.

"Nothing on the tapes."

"Nothing from the footage from the entrance or exits?" she asked.

"There is no footage from the entrance or exits."

"Because?" Jessie inquired.

"The hospital just switched to a new system, and the installation is still in progress."

"Are you shittin' me? Today?" Gerard snapped. "They had to do that today?"

"I'm afraid so," Bradshaw confirmed.

"And what did you see on the hall footage?" Jessie asked.

"Nothing. The only conclusion I can draw is the assailant found out she was still alive and abducted her from the hospital to finish the job." Bradshaw sighed. "And the bastard knew exactly how to avoid the hall cameras."

"What did she wear out of here? The ragged dress she arrived in?" Jessie asked.

"No," Bradshaw responded, shaking his head. "The aide thinks she stole a set of blue scrubs."

"How can she be sure of that?" Gerard asked.

"Because the girl had just replenished the rack, and when she saw Jane, she later realized the one missing set of scrubs was most likely what Jane was wearing."

Gerard's head jerked back. "She saw Jane and didn't stop her?"

"No, she didn't," Gerard interrupted, but Bradshaw held his hand up, "because they were short-handed, and when she saw Jane's black eyes, she figured she'd been called into work from sick leave."

"Really?" Gerard frowned. "And what did she think those black eyes represented? Domestic violence?"

"No, she thought Jane had recently had a nose job."

"Un-fucking-believable." Gerard's words were sharply curt.

"Gerard," Jessie scolded. "Stop this right now." He clamped his mouth shut. "Where is her dress?" Jessie asked. "Do you know?"

"The bag is gone," Bradshaw huffed out a breath. "It was on the same rack with the scrubs and bedding stuff when I arrived. Since we were in the hallway, I left it on the rack for safekeeping, figuring Jane would either be released or moved to a room after the doctors took care of her. When the administrator, the aide, and I scoured the place, I asked about the bag, but it too was missing."

 "What about security?" Gerard asked, his voice much calmer.

Bradshaw shrugged. "They've checked every floor, every nook, and cranny of this building, without a sign of her anywhere. But as you know, it's not unusual for patients to leave the ER if they've been waiting a long time."

"Okay, then, let's head on down to security." Jessie stared at Gerard and Bradshaw, waiting for them to move toward the walkway.

"Fine," Gerard noticed the expression on Jessie's face and shooed her on, "Go!"

They trailed behind her quickened steps, exiting through the double doors down the long hallway. A robust medicinal smell attacked Jessie's nose. She held her breath, trying to avoid inhaling the sickening sweet, disinfectant-like scent reminding her of when her mother was in the hospital after an automobile accident. The blood-soaked bandages decaying in the wastebaskets until an orderly could remove the trash didn't help.

"What did security say about their apparent lapse in vigilance?" Gerard asked Bradshaw.

He scoffed. "The same thing we'd say. How do you prevent something like this from happening when there's complete chaos?" Bradshaw turned to face him. "The other issue is the newly minted interns infiltrating the ER. Let's face it; they focus on saving lives, not playing guard dog."

Gerard shook his head. A young intern passed looking tired, as though he hadn't slept in weeks. He nodded an acknowledgment.

"Security is right down here to the right," Bradshaw directed.

Jessie, who was already several feet ahead of them, disappeared behind the door.

"You mentioned Jane was conscious."

"She was," Bradshaw said, "but she was confused. She didn't know her name, what happened, or where she was. She couldn't tell me anything." He rubbed his eyes. "I've seen enough of these cases during my career to know she was traumatized." Bradshaw coughed. "I think she may even have a touch of amnesia."

"Great!" Gerard said, "We have a victim who doesn't know who she is roaming the streets, or was possibly kidnapped by our mystery assailant . . . or worse yet, maybe dead."

"While we waited together," Bradshaw added, "I told her as soon as her wounds were tended to, someone from the NYPD would take her to a state facility until we learned her identity because I was sure someone was looking for her."

"You told her all that?"

"Well, yeah. I didn't want to lie to her. She was looking for some answers."

"Geez, Bradshaw. You were so worried about her listening in on our conversation because she was scared. Did it ever occur to you that you startled her even more again by telling her the truth." he criticized.

"I thought I was helping her." Bradshaw glared at Gerard. "Stop treating me like I'm a rookie. I've been doing this job for forty-five years—longer than you've been out of diapers. I sure as hell don't need you treating me like a moron."

A muscle flickered in Gerard's jaw from frustration by the insufficient evidence they had. He was angry with Bradshaw for leaving their victim in a hallway along with other patients and his overall disregard for Jane Doe. He tightened his lips in a thin line. "Okay, okay. I'm sorry," Gerard said. "I'm frustrated we have no leads, and the one lead we did have, is gone." The pair entered the small security office. Jessie was already in a deep conversation with one of the guards. The man looked up when the detectives stood and watched them.

Jessie pointed to the two men. "They're with me."

"What's up, Jess?" Gerard asked.

"Exactly as Detective Bradshaw informed us. Nada." She rolled her eyes and sighed. "At least we have her DNA from the skin you found on the window that we can match to the nightgown she wore."

"Uh, no. The orderly had thrown the gown into the receptacle before I had returned to Jane Doe's gurney in the hall."

Gerard threw his hands up in the air. "Goddammit! And the bad news is if she's not in the system, there's no way to track her anyway."

The trio left the security office and walked back through the tunnel.

"We'll check the missing person database to see if we can find a match," Gerard said, turning to Jess. "Let's pay a little visit to Tony. He and Lenny were best friends. He must know something."

She turned to Bradshaw. "Thanks for helping us out."

"I'm sorry I couldn't be more help, Jessie," Bradshaw said.

"It's all right, Detective. Shit happens. As much as we'd like to think we have everything under control, it doesn't always work out that way."

"Thanks, Jess." He smiled at her and glanced off at Gerard. "I'll see you at headquarters." He nodded a farewell to Gerard and walked up ahead.

"See you at headquarters," she called after him. "Get some rest tonight." He waved his hand in the air and continued.

Gerard fixed her with an angry stare when he was out of earshot. "Why are you giving this guy a free pass? He lost our victim."

"I'm not giving him a free pass, Gerard. This shit happens to us on an ongoing basis. And, it seems to me I remember a certain someone, who—"

He cut her off, suddenly defensive. "Fine! I don't need a rundown of my mistakes on the job. Point taken."

* * *

"Tony should be at his old hangout by now." Together, they walked to the car. Cranking up the engine, he eased the car into the traffic congestion.

"I'll be interested in finding out what he knows." She studied Gerard's profile for a short while. She could see how his mouth formed in irritation; Gerard had something on his mind. "Okay, hotshot, besides the no leads, what else is bothering you?"

His jaw flickered. A few minutes of silence passed between them before he spoke. "Do you have something you want to tell me, Jess?"

"My life is an open book for chrissake. There isn't anything you don't already know about me."

He reached into his shirt pocket and pulled out a folded paper. "Oh? Then what's this?"

Recognizing it as one of the three threatening notes she'd received, she snatched the paper from his hand. "Where did you get this?"

"It fell out of your pocket when you went to the restroom at Lizzie's Diner. So now, do you want to tell me about this?"

"It's no big deal, Gerard. It's a prank. The new boss is here, and the guys think I'm getting special treatment. It's a test, that's all."

"And why would you be receiving special treatment?" his eyebrows rose.

"I don't know. Because I'm cute?" Jessie chuckled.

"You're not that cute."

"I'm not?" she grinned.

"Listen up, smartass. Are you saying you think this is from someone in the department?"

"Well, yeah."

"What makes you think it's not a criminal threatening your life? Suppose he was released and wants to get even with you. Or maybe it's a member of his family who's getting even?" His finger hit the dashboard, trying to drive his point home. "How do you know?"

Her stomach clenched. "I guess I don't. But no one has tried to break into my apartment or tried to attack me on the street." She rubbed her hands on her slacks to dry her clammy palms.

"Are you just going to dismiss this? Is that it?"

"Pretty much," she nodded.

"How many of these have you received?" he inquired.

She fell silent, but the heat of his ardent stare told her she'd better answer. "Okay. It's the third one."

"The third one?" he was nodding with pursed lips. "And when were you planning to tell me . . . your partner?"

She could see he was pissed. "Look, Gerard. I can handle this myself, even if it isn't someone from the department. I'm a big girl now—I know how to use a gun."

He snorted. "You slay me. You're always so busy trying to prove how tough you are. The funny thing is you lose sight of what's real and what's not. We all know you can take care of yourself on the job, but you're just as vulnerable as the rest of us. If you think it's someone in the department, fine, then I'm going to ask around, and when I do find out which asshole is playing games here, I'll string the bastard up by his balls—"

His voice faded into the background as a barrage of dreamy thoughts attacked her mind. His penchant for wanting to protect her stoked a warm glow inside her. She blew out a breath of pent-up air. This whole thing was messing with her head. If she didn't want a relationship, why did she have these thoughts throughout the day? Jess shook her head in disbelief, disgusted with herself for not making up her mind one way or the other. She pushed the unanswered question from her mind and focused on what he was saying.

". . . . but I have to say I have serious doubts about any of the guys being so dumb. Do you think anyone of them would risk their career to play a prank on you?"

"It's possible if they thought they wouldn't get caught. What about all the politicians who cheat on their wives convinced no one will ever find out?"

"Oh, Jess, get real, will you? You're not worth losing a job over."

She was taken aback; the sting of his comment hit like a sucker punch to the gut. "Okay, I apologize. I should have told you."

"Damn straight. You should have. And, while we're on the subject, when had you planned to tell me you dated Harwell? Is that why you thought the guys might think you're getting special treatment?"

"Who told you that?" she snarled.

"It doesn't matter. I heard it, okay?" He paused briefly. "Is anything going on between the two of you now? Because, man, if you think I want to partner with the boss' girlfriend, we're finished."

"Are you out of your freakin' mind? I don't date married men." She shook her head in disgust. "That was a long time ago. I was a foolish young girl."

"So, why is the rumor still following you?"

"How should I know?" His question hit a nerve. Her nostrils flared, and she snapped back. "So then, my theory isn't all that far-fetched after all. Is it?"

"Perhaps. I doubt anyone would want to get in the middle of that. A newly ordained lieutenant screwing his subordinate?" His hand flew in the air. "Now, that's asking for trouble."

She turned away from him and stared out the window. Under normal circumstances, she loved to people-watch, but this time, she only saw red.

"How long ago did these notes start?" he asked.

"Recently -- within the last two weeks. Okay?"

"What are WE going to do about them?"

"WE?"

"Yeah, you heard me right. WE!"

They exchanged glances, and a sudden awkward moment passed between them. Jessie had never seen him so angry, and for that matter, he'd never made her this angry either.

"So what, now you're my Guardian Angel?" she gaped.

"You bet your sweet ass I am. As partners, we need to know what's going on with each other. Something like this on your mind could make you careless -- take unnecessary chances. I cover your ass. You cover mine. That's how it works."

"Oh, stop. I don't take chances."

"You just did, Tate."

She knew he was mad. He rarely, if ever, called her by her first name. She released a sigh and held up her hand. "Okay, enough." She gazed out the window again and noticed Tony. "There he is. He's in front of Cutter's Bar with his cronies."

Gerard parked the car. When Tony saw them, he took off in the opposite direction. The pair raced after him and caught up in an alley. Tony was about to climb over a chain-link fence until Gerard latched onto him and threw him to the ground. He snapped the cuffs on his wrists and pulled him upright. Tony sat on the pavement, his back leaning against the wall, while the two detectives bent over, their hands holding onto their knees, trying to catch their breath.

"Who are you running from, Tony?" Jessie asked.

"I don't know anythin'."

"You don't know what?" Gerard asked. "Who killed Lenny?"

"I didn't do it," he said. A painful distortion crossed his face when Jessie reached behind him and gave his cuffs another hard tug.

"Hey Gerard," she scolded, "Tony said he doesn't know anything."

It was evident whatever Tony knew shook him up. His eyes blinked like he was tapping out the Morse code.

"Tony, why are you so nervous?" Gerard asked and pulled the man to his feet. He turned to face his partner. "I think we should take Tony down to the precinct for questioning."

The twitch on Tony's jawline increased, and he started to jump around. "No. Please don't. I can't let anyone see me with you." Tears filled his eyes. "I'll come down to the station by myself."

"Seen by whom? Who are you afraid of?"

"I have a family. I can't," he shook his head. "I can't."

Gerard looked at his partner. "What do you think?"

"Okay, Tony," she said. "Here's the deal. You have a half-hour to get to the station. If you're not there in thirty minutes, we'll find you, and you know we will," she nodded as she spoke, "then we're going to cart your ass off to jail. You got that?" She removed the cuffs from his wrists, "thirty minutes, Tony." She checked her watch. "T-h-i-r-t-y minutes," she spelled out, then glanced at her watch again, nodding her head with the movement of the second hand, "tick-tock, tick-tock, and now, you have twenty-nine minutes." Tony took off like a shot, rounding the corner like someone was chasing him.

"Whoa," Gerard said, "he's terrified." He shook his head. "I can't believe how much he's aged since we last saw him."

"Yeah, he does look a lot older. He has dark circles under his eyes. Did you notice that?"

"I did. Maybe Tony's wife is keeping him up at night." Gerard winked at her.

"Well, something keeps him up at night, but I don't think it's his wife. He knows something about Lenny's death."

"Okay," Gerard said, "let's get back in the car and wait for him, out of sight, down the street. I have my doubts about him coming to the station house."

"He'll be there," Jessie assured.

They returned to their vehicle without comment. Gerard eased the car away from the curb and turned in her direction. "You like that bad cop shit, don't you?"

"I do," she said with conviction. "That's to show the creeps I'm no pushover."

He chuckled. "You like to make these guys toe the line."

"Yes, sir. That's my lot in life. You'd better watch out—you might be next." She was happy the air had cleared. At least his humor was back. Having friction between them made for a long uncomfortable day.

Stuck in the gridlock, Jessie spotted Tony heading down the subway steps to the train.

"See, Gerard; I told you he'd come. Ye of little faith."

"Okay, you win," he said, cocking his head. "Now that Tony's on his way, we still have some unfinished business to discuss," he inched the car up a length.

"No, we don't. That conversation is over."

"Oh no, it's not." He shot her a stern look. "I swear," he pointed his finger in her direction, "I'll go directly to the lieutenant if you don't start talking."

"You wouldn't dare."

"You don't want to test me, do—" He stopped talking when he saw Tony walk back up the stairs. "See," he pointed, "that little bastard never intended to head downtown. Now, who has little faith?"

Jessie jumped out of the car and darted through the gridlocked traffic until she reached Tony. Holding her badge up for bystanders, they cleared a path and watched as she flipped Tony around and the cuffs on his wrists so fast he jerked back in shock. Cheers and jeers from the crowd made Tony tense, but Jessie tugged on the cuffs and guided him toward the car.

"What were you thinking, Tony?" she asked when she held his head down to help him into the backseat. "You made a liar out of me. I just told Detective Gerard to have more faith in you—that you would show up at the precinct just like you promised. You keep this up, shit-head, and I'll throw your ass in jail so fast your head will spin. You got that?"

Tony remained silent, his body shaking.

"Yeah, Tony," Gerard said, looking at him through the rearview mirror, "you're developing a bad track record. What was that all about?"

"I ain't never done that to you before." Tony's words came out intermittently. "I'm scared, that's all."

"What are you scared of, Tony?" Jess asked. Tony slumped in the seat and remained silent until they reached the precinct.

Exiting the vehicle, Jessie opened the back door, grabbed Tony's bent elbows, and helped him through the opened precinct door. "Why are you so scared?" Tony shrugged and continued down the hall until they entered the interrogation room.

"You giving me a reward for being here?" Tony asked. Jessie swung him around and pushed him into a chair.

Gerard gave a hearty chuckle. "You're scared about someone seeing you, yet you're asking for a reward?" Gerard stared at him with a deadpan expression. "Why? Would you be more forthcoming if we paid you?"

"Forthcoming?" Tony asked.

"Yeah. In other words, would money help your memory?"

"Maybe."

"Listen, scumbag," Jessie said, "Your reward is staying out of the slammer. Let me remind you there are still those drug charges pending against you, but if you'd rather do your time, we can arrange that."

"No. No. I was asking. I can barely feed my eight kids in this economy. I just thought—"

"Yeah, I know what you thought," Gerard said. "You thought you could squeeze a little more out of the department. Well, forget it. You're not the only one feeling it. We're all feeling it." Gerard grabbed water from the small refrigerator in the room and passed one to Tony. "Okay, the party's over; down to business. Lenny was living with you and the family. Is that right?" he asked.

"Yes. Lenny has been living with us since his wife died." Tears welled in Tony's eyes, but he remained speechless, fidgeting nervously in his chair, his feet tapping against the floor.

Gerard hammered at him. "Who killed your friend?"

"I . . . I . . . I don't know nuttin', Detective."

"We think you do. Was it this Sonny guy who owns the garage you're watching for us? Or was Lenny being too friendly? Maybe asking too many questions?"

"I ain't ever seen this, Sonny guy." Tony's bottom jaw jutted out, a clear indication he was lying.

Jessie interrupted. "Then why are you so afraid?"

"Because Vito tells us he's a badass and not to mess around with him." He rubbed the side of his face with his shoulder. "Listen, the only reason Lenny and I agreed to work at the chop shop was for you guys, but Vito's warnings scared us."

"First of all, Tony," Gerard said, "you weren't doing this for us; you were doing it to keep that fat ass of yours out of jail."

Jessie intervened. "Tony, you claim you've never seen this Sonny guy, so he doesn't know who you are anyway."

"Oh yes, he does," Tony shook his head up and down, his eyes wide as saucers. "Vito took our pictures and pinned them on the bulletin board."

"Look, we're going to protect you and your family."

"No one can protect us from him. Vito says he has eyes and ears everywhere."

"When was the last time you were at the chop shop?" Gerard asked.

"Friday."

"Didn't you work today?"

"No, Detective. It's my day off."

"And you just decided to hang out with your friends instead of your wife and kids?"

"The wife is cooking, and the kids—well, I don't know what the kids are doin'."

"We think you know who killed Lenny."

"I told ya, I don't know nuttin'." Tony rubbed his eyes with his fingertips, then twisted the cap off the water and slugged back more than a mouthful.

Detective Kensington reached inside the small refrigerator and handed him another bottle. "Relax, Tony. No one saw you come into the precinct." Tony's eyes blinked like a stuttered dial tone. "Tell us what you know, Tony?"

"Nuttin'. But, I promise, the minute I know something, I'll get in touch with you."

Gerard's cell phone rang. "I'll be right there," he told the caller before disconnecting. He looked toward his partner, "Continue without me, Jess." He brushed past her and inhaled the familiar scent of her body. He couldn't remember what she'd told him the last time he'd asked, but he seemed to recall her saying something about vegetables and fruit. A bizarre combination, but whatever it was, he loved the clean smell. "That was the Lieutenant."

He watched her face form into a panicked expression. He smiled to himself. She was worried he would follow through with his threat. Hell, he had no intention of telling the boss, but he figured he'd scared her enough that from now on, she'd be filling him in on the details of any new threats she was receiving. Gerard grinned, pleased that his threat worked like a charm.

* * *

Lieutenant Harwell gestured him into the viewing room. "I just wanted to let you know that Paige and Santori are staking out the chop shop. Let's hope we catch this bastard when he checks in on his assets. I guess we'll have to provide around-the-clock surveillance to catch the bastard, or do you think Tony's smart enough to set up the surveillance equipment for us?"

"Are you kidding?" Gerard snorted. "We're lucky if the guy knows his name." He laughed. "No, Lieutenant, he's not bright enough to pull that off."

"Hell, my twelve-year-old kid knows how to operate the equipment. Okay," Harwell shrugged. "Just thought I'd ask. Where'd you find him?"

"He was hanging out with his buddies at Cutter's Bar. When he saw us, he took off like a shot. We chased him down, and he's been jumpy ever since—he's afraid someone saw him."

"Did he say anything about the Sonny guy or Lenny?"

"Nothing of value, just that Vito told them Sonny was a badass. It's still early in the game. We reminded him of his obligations, so we'll see how soon he spills his guts. If he doesn't open up soon, we'll let his ass sit in jail for a while to see how he likes it."

"He must be feeling pretty bad about Lenny," Harwell said. "He's the one who recommended him."

"He is," Gerard agreed. "But hey, he's the one who said Lenny was tougher than him. We asked Tony if he thought that's what happened to Lenny, but he didn't answer. As for Sonny, Tony claims he's never seen the guy, but Vito scared the shit out of them, and this Sonny guy knows what all his employees look like. Tony's afraid he'll be next."

Gerard threw his hands up in disgust. "How does this Sonny guy get in and out of the shop without being seen?"

Harwell huffed out a frustrated breath. "If Tony doesn't give you something soon," Harwell said, "let him serve his time because he sure isn't good to us."

"Just a little more time, Lieutenant." Gerard scowled. "He insists he doesn't know anything."

"Okay, keep me posted," Harwell said, turning toward his office.

Jess looked up when Gerard walked back into the interrogation room and gave him a quizzical look, but he never gave her any indication about his discussion with Harwell. She continued asking questions while he looked on.

"Tony, did Lenny have a girlfriend?"

"No," he dragged the letters out. "He was still in a funk from his wife dying." Tony frowned. "Why are you asking me?"

"Because we found a woman in the same vicinity."

"Was she killed too?" he asked nervously.

"No. But we suspect that was the intent." Gerard rubbed his hand over the stubble on his jawline. "Are you sure he wasn't seeing someone?"

"Not that I know of."

"We know he has a daughter out of state, but does he have another here in New York?"

"No, just the one daughter."

"Okay, so tell us what happened to scare you?" Tony released a heavy sigh. "Look, don't you want to help us find Lenny's killer?" Tony nodded in agreement. "We're here to protect you from anything bad happening."

"No, you're not," he screeched. "You're gonna get me killed." His shaky hand wiped the condensation off the water bottle while avoiding eye contact. When his hands began to shake more vigorously, he hid them under the table.

"Relax, Tony," Jess said.

"I told you, I have nothing to say, so don't try to put words in my mouth. You're just lookin' for a scapegoat—someone to take the heat off you—so the Lieutenant thinks you're doin' your job."

"Tony," Gerard interrupted. "Have we ever done that to you?"

"Well, I don't know. You could have."

"Listen, you and Lenny were our best confidential informants, and for that information, we gave you a free pass, and you avoided jail time. If you'd prefer, you can do time." Tony aggressively shook his head from side to side. "We think someone came into the shop, Tony, maybe this Sonny guy who owns the chop shop . . . maybe Lenny acted too interested, and that's what got him killed." Tony's facial expression gave him away. "How am I doing, Tony?"

"I ain't got nuttin' to say."

"What's Sonny's real name, Tony?"

"I don't know. Vito only calls him Sonny."

"So then, you have seen him."

"No. I meant when Vito talks about him. Can I go now?" He stood to leave.

"Not so fast, cowboy," Jessie said, rushing to the door to block his exit. Tony's hand rested on the doorknob, ready to dash. "Tony, don't make me cuff you again," she warned. He rubbed his wrists as though remembering the sting of the cuffs, then shoved his hands inside the pockets of his trousers. Gerard signaled to Jess that he wanted to take over.

"Tony, why are you making this so difficult?" He touched the man's forearm for contact and edged him back to the table. "We've noticed how good you've been." Gerard thought he'd try a more positive approach with him to see if it worked.

"Yeah, my old lady, she's givin' me a hard time. She says the kids miss me when I'm in jail." Tony took a long swig of water.

"Okay, Tony, if you want to leave now, you can." Gerard placed his hand on the man's shoulder. "You know, you're our lead CI now that Lenny's gone, so if you say you don't have anything to share, then we believe you."

Gerard pulled out a money clip and waved a hundred-dollar bill in front of his face. "Of course, if you remember something after you leave here, I'll give you this." He could see he'd hit the magic button from the expression on Tony's face. "It would help with your eight kids, wouldn't it?" Tony didn't respond, but his eyes never moved away from the bill. "Hey," Gerard grinned, "who knows. You might even get lucky with that old lady of yours," he smiled. "Maybe take her out for a nice evening on the town."

"The money would help my family, Detective—but like I said, if I knew something. But I don't have nuttin' for you. If I happen to hear something through the grapevine, though, I'll letcha know."

Jessie opened the back door and stepped outside to look around to make sure everything was clear. Satisfied, she motioned for Tony to exit. He did so and took off down the street as fast as his feet would carry him.

* * *

Patrick brushed Gabi's hair away from her face as she slept on the ride to Maria's house. She'd had a full day, too much junk food, and she'd become overtired and fell asleep, but it felt good, allowing her to step over the line occasionally. He couldn't help but smile when he pictured Gabi singing all the songs to the *Lion King* during the stage performance. He couldn't believe she knew all the words. A warmth encased his heart. It wasn't long before he was pulling into Maria's driveway. He watched as she opened the door and rushed down the stairs, almost tripping, trying to get to them quickly. Patrick stared at her for a moment. Her long black hair over her shoulder made her even more gorgeous than he remembered. He'd been so anxious to see her, to make up for the lost time, that it brought a smile to his face. She was one of the few people who made him happy. He was glad Gabi was meeting her. He knew Maria would love her instantly.

* * *

Maria knew Gabi had fallen asleep because he'd texted her a few blocks away. Gabi stirred when the door opened. She sat up briefly, looked around, then flopped back down.

"Somebody's a sleepyhead," Patrick said with a tickle to her ribs. Maria couldn't stop smiling when she looked at Gabi. The first words from her mouth were what Patrick expected, "She's beautiful!"

Patrick rubbed Gabi's arms to wake her. "C'mon, munchkin, I want you to meet Maria."

Gabi opened her eyes. "Did Mommy call?"

"Yes, sweetie. I'll let you listen to the message when we get inside."

"No, Daddy, I want to hear Mommy's voice now."

"Gabrielle," her father said sternly, "Let's not be rude."

Gabi sat upright. "I'm sorry," she said, extending her hand as she'd no doubt seen her mother do during introductions, "it's nice to meet you." Those words were no sooner out than she was asking about her mother again. "Did Mommy say where she was?"

"Yes, Gabi, she did. Now, please go ahead inside with Maria while I get the luggage. We'll talk then. Okay?"

"Yes, Daddy," she said with a nod and took Maria's hand.

"I'm happy to meet you, Gabi." The child nodded without saying anything, but she sniffed when they entered the kitchen.

"Your house smells like dessert."

Maria laughed. "That's because I made you chocolate chip cookies." She led Gabi into the kitchen and watched as she climbed onto the breakfast bar's high stool." Would you like one now?"

Gabi shook her head. "No, thank you. My Mommy bakes when she knows we'll have company too."

"We do that so our guests feel special." Seeing her father, Gabi slid off the stool and ran to him, clutching her stomach.

"Uh-oh, looks like somebody's got a tummy ache." Gabi blinked her eyes and nodded.

"Then we'd better get her into bed, Sonny. I have her room already," Maria said.

Gabi didn't like her comment. "No!" shot from her mouth. Maria jerked back with surprise.

"Gabrielle!" Patrick chastised, "Don't be rude. Now, you say you're sorry."

Gabi's head lowered, unable to make eye contact with either of them. Patrick jerked her arm. "Apologize now," he said.

"I'm sorry," came out in a low voice just before the avalanche of tears erupted. Patrick bent down and scooped her up into his arms. "I want Mommy."

"I know, sweetie. Do you want to listen to her message now?" Gabi nodded. "But can I hug Maria before you listen to it?" he asked the child. Gabi nodded. Seeing Maria again made his heart sing with delight. He remembered she'd always looked beautiful, but tonight she was stunning. He pulled the woman into his arms and held her close to him. "It's great to see you."

"You too, Sonny," she said casually.

Patrick turned to Gabi. "Okay, let's get that message." He sat down on the stool and pulled out his phone. He tapped the screen to access his messages.

Noticing his panic, Gabi became concerned. "What's wrong, Dad?"

"I don't know what happened to your mother's message." He kept scrolling the screen up, and nothing. "Oh, Gabi, I don't know what I did." He showed her the phone, and she pulled it from his hands.

"Daddy," her frustrated voice stretched the letters in disappointment. "Doesn't your phone have a trash can like the computer?" she asked.

Tapping the trashcan on the screen, he made a face. "Dammit," he said, "there's nothing in it." Patrick sighed. "I swear, sweetie, I don't know what happened. Maybe I automatically deleted it."

"Can't you call her back on her phone?"

"Well, no." Patrick's face contorted into embarrassment. "In mom's haste this morning, she left her cell phone behind."

"Oh, Daddy." Her hands rose, "what do we do now?"

"Relax, honey. We'll figure this out."

"Do you remember what her message said?" Maria inquired.

"Yes. Mommy told me she was in Ohio with Aunt Sissy and her friends. She was tired after the flight, but before disconnecting, she wanted me to apologize to you because she left without saying good-bye." He winked at Gabi. "She said she loves you to the moon and back." Gabi's mouth curled into a slight smile.

"Do you know what her friends' names are?" Gabi asked.

"Boy, I wish I did, Gab." Patrick twisted his mouth to the side. "I know it was a Jessica something," He scratched his neck while staring into the distance, deep in thought. "Geez, I was so involved in a nego-tiation at the time, I didn't hear the whole thing."

"You always do that, Dad."

"I'm so sorry, baby. I promise we'll figure this out tomorrow after she buys a new phone. She'll call us again."

"Call Aunt Sissy." He was staring at Maria. Gabi tapped his leg to get his attention. "Call Aunt Sissy, Dad."

Patrick was silent for a few minutes, his mouth twisting into a sour look. "Gab," he paused and inhaled, "I don't have Aunt Sissy's phone number in my phone. Mom always took care of calling her, so she's not on my list of contacts."

"How about Gram's phone number?" Patrick shook his head. "Can't you just ask the operator for their numbers?"

"I'm afraid not. Those numbers are not in the phone directory."

"Well, let's go home. Mom has them both in the little flowered book in the drawer under the phone table."

"Gabi, please, I'm exhausted. I'm not going back to the house tonight. Mom's probably sleeping anyway. She said she was tired." Patrick felt terrible for her, but it would have to wait until the morning.

She ignored her father and spoke to Maria. "Can I go to bed now?" she asked.

"Yes, you can. Do you want something for that tummy ache first?"

"No, it's gone. I want to go to bed now."

Maria led Gabi into the hallway and up the long winding stairway. "Your room is right at the top of the stairs to the right." Gabi could hear her father's footsteps right behind her. He was carrying her suitcase. Maria pushed on the door, and Gabi smiled because when she walked inside the room, and saw it decorated in various shades of lavender with a royal princess-style mosquito net that hung from the ceiling and draped over the entire length of the bed.

Gabi stood wide-eyed. "This is a pretty room."

"I'm glad you like it."

"Do you have a daughter?" Gabi asked, forgetting Maria couldn't have children.

"No, I don't. I had hoped I would someday, but that never happened, so I'm happy you're the first to sleep in the room." Gabi's eyes widened with surprise.

"Thank you." Gabi was suddenly feeling sadder for Maria than herself. She liked her.

The women watched Patrick open the suitcase on one of the chairs and pull out her favorite nightgown. "Okay. Dad, you can leave now," she said dryly.

He laughed lowly and handed her the gown before leaving the room.

"I'm sorry you didn't get to talk to your mommy tonight,"

Maria said, "But I know she's thinking about you."

"How do you know?"

"Because all moms think about their children all the time." Gabi smiled and hopped into bed. Maria pulled the covers up, tucked her in, and leaned over and kissed her forehead. "Goodnight, sweetie," Maria said and turned to leave. "Pleasant dreams."

"Can I ask you a question?" Gabi asked. Maria stopped and turned back to her.

"Sure."

"Why do you call my dad Sonny?"

Maria grinned, "Because, when we were kids, he always tried to make me laugh. Because of it, I thought he had a sunny disposition, so I called him Sonny, and the name stuck." Maria brushed Gabi's hair back. "Good night, Twinkle Toes," she said, kissing Gabi's forehead again.

"Good night, Maria. Thank you for letting me stay in this pretty room."

"It's my pleasure." She threw Gabi a kiss and walked out of the room.

Gabi slipped out from under the covers and knelt next to the bed and said her prayers as soon as Maria was gone, asking God to watch over her mother. Finished, she crawled back under the covers, and closed her eyes, but sleep wouldn't come. She kept tossing and turning for what seemed like a long time. Deciding she was thirsty, she got out of bed and opened her bedroom door. It was dark downstairs with only a nightlight at the bottom of the stairs. Knowing everyone was sleeping, she crept down the stairs one at a time until she finally got to the bottom and headed for the kitchen for her drink when she noticed her father's cell phone sitting on the counter, the charger plugged into the socket. Filling a glass with water, she drank it all the while contemplating calling Marti. She could tell her where the house key was and how to find her mother's directory for Aunt Sissy's phone number.

Gabi unplugged the phone and carried it into the downstairs bathroom. Turning on the light, she closed the door and keyed in Marti's cell number. It was late, but Gabi knew Marti wouldn't mind. She answered on the first ring.

"Marti, it's me."

"How's the cruise?"

"What cruise? We're not on a cruise," Gabi said, perplexed.

"Mom and I were shopping, and we saw Mrs. Simon, who said your dad called to say you were going to miss the beginning of school because you were going on a cruise."

"Dad's been giving me many surprises today, but my mom's away in Ohio with my Aunt Sissy. Maybe we're going when she gets back."

"Then, where are you?"

"At my dad's cousin's house. Her name is Maria."

"I was mad that you didn't tell me."

"You know I tell you everything." Gabi rubbed her eyes. "I need you to do me a favor."

"Okay. What?"

"I need you to go to my house and—"

"What the hell are you doing, young lady," Patrick's voice boomed like a volcano until the phone went dead.

CHAPTER 9

Detective Kensington strode down the corridor in search of Bradshaw, a loud clicking sound echoing through the narrow hall as the heels from her shoes hit against the tiled floors.

The door from the men's locker room opened, and she wrinkled her nose as a whiff of sweat permeated the air. One of the new cadets, freshly showered, walked past her, his worn gym bag hanging off his shoulder. He nodded, acknowledging her presence.

She returned his nod with a smile. Continuing her search, she stopped to peek into the first interrogation room where Phillip Bradshaw stood in front of the viewing window listening to the conversation between a detective and a young man.

"Hey, Detective," she said. "What's going on in there?"

"Santori is questioning a slime bag about a rash of recent burglaries: the same MO for all of them—families out of town on vacation."

"We need to get the word out to the residents to ensure they contact us when leaving town."

"That's part of the problem. These residents did."

"Uh-oh, heads are going to fly on this one. Whose department is this?"

He made a face. "Jackson." Jessie blinked her eyes shut in disgust but remained silent. "Did you want me for something?" he asked.

"I did. Since you spent more time with Jane than anyone else, the sketch artist is waiting for you."

"Okay. Did Jane Doe's DNA come back yet?" he asked.

"No. The lab said they'd put a rush on it, but you know how that goes. It could take months, maybe a year, before we know anything. I checked with the bureau to see if anyone filed a missing person report, but nothing yet." She shrugged. "Maybe her family isn't aware she's missing." Bradshaw agreed with a slow nod. "So, we keep plugging along until they do." She sighed.

He gave her a warm smile. "You know, you're a lot like I was at your age," his voice sounded determined. "The guys had a hard time with me in those days, too, just like they do with you, but that's their problem, not yours. You make them work harder." He smirked. "And Kensington," his facial expression grew more serious. She sensed what he was about to say. "I don't care if you dated Harwell or not. What you did, or are doing in your personal life, is of no concern to me whatsoever."

Jessie jerked her head back in surprise. "You said something?" A long strand of hair escaped her barrette and tickled her face. She removed the barrette, held it between her teeth, smoothed her hair back with both hands then clipped it together again. "I hear you're an avid fisherman," she said, changing the subject.

"Yeah," he said. "I have a lakefront cabin in the Adirondacks. Do you fish, Detective?"

"No. I'm like you. I work too much to enjoy any hobbies."

She'd always had a soft spot for Bradshaw. He was the perfect father image; a big old teddy bear whose lap a child could crawl upon and know the depth of his love from his affectionate hug. A fleeting thought of her father passed through her mind, and she wondered if he looked anything like Bradshaw. The only image she could muster was his face as he walked out the door when she was seven. She shook off the sentimental feeling and continued her exchange with the

Detective. "So, tomorrow's your last day. I'll bet you're chomping at the bit to bait that hook?"

"Oh," he gave a dismissive wave of his hand. "I've decided to stick around for a while to lend a hand on your case. I won't be on the force to work in full capacity, but I'll be working on the sidelines."

"Why?" An anxious feeling erupted inside her. "We'll solve the case." She eyed his expression and felt sad for him. He'd been depressed for a long time after his wife died, but a noticeable difference had occurred when he'd decided to retire.

"Please don't do that, Phil." She reached for his arm. "You've more than earned a rest after all the years you've been on the force."

His eyes lowered to the floor. "I feel slightly responsible for Jane's disappearance." He mumbled in an apologetic voice. "It's a loose end I must help resolve before leaving the city."

She touched his arm again. "Please don't take responsibility for her disappearance, Phil. It could have happened to any one of us."

"But maybe you can use the help from this old man." An anxious smile crossed his face. "I know your partner doesn't like me, but I'll try to stay out of his way and work in the background."

"Oh, don't pay any attention to him. He's always uptight."

"Are you coming tomorrow night?" He asked.

"To your retirement party?" He nodded. "I wouldn't miss it."

"Good, I'll look forward to seeing you." He held up his hand, "Well, I'd better go. I don't want to keep the artist waiting."

"Thanks, Phil. I think a sketch of Jane Doe is our first step to finding her."

As Jessie meandered down the corridor, she replayed the comment Bradshaw made about the guys in the department. It gave her relief knowing she'd been right after all.

"Have a good night, Jessie," Bradshaw said, pulling the door open; he stopped and looked at her. "I think you're pretty cool; you know that?"

His comment warmed her heart and brought a smile to her face. "Thanks, Phil. I think you're pretty cool yourself." She turned and headed back down the hall to her office with a sudden spring in her step after hearing his compliment.

* * *

"What's up, Jess?" Gerard asked.

"Bradshaw is meeting with the sketch artist. Let's hope this helps."

"Who's in there?" he nodded toward the interrogation room.

"There has been a shitload of B&Es in our jurisdiction."

"Yeah, I heard one of the guys talking about that in the locker room earlier. You know whose unit handles that, don't you?" Jess smirked.

"Oh, yeah. My favorite person."

"He can't help himself, can he?" Jessie shrugged. "By the way, you smell good."

"Thanks," she chuckled. "A lot better than when we left the crime scene a few days ago."

"That's for sure." She gave him a playful jab. "Hey, do you know what time it is?"

"No."

"It's almost time to leave. Let's get out of here and grab a bite to eat."

She wrinkled her nose. "I think I'll pass. Thanks for the invitation, though." She covered her mouth with her hand to stifle a yawn. "Cereal for dinner and curling up with a good book sounds like a win-win."

He arched his brow. "Yeah, no. We still have a little matter we need to discuss." His voice bordered on the side of edgy. "And since it's too difficult to discuss the matter while we work, a quiet dinner should give you plenty of uninterrupted time to tell me about it."

Gerard watched her face morph into a fake smile. That was one of the things he loved about her. He loved watching her animated facial expressions that always gave her away. She looked lovely today in her beige tailored pants suit. The rust background of her floral blouse complimented her hair and brought out the green in her eyes that sparkled when she smiled. The prospect of being alone with her sent his pulse sailing.

His six-foot-three frame, a full six inches taller than hers, was imposing to those who didn't know him.

"I'm waiting," he said, tapping his foot.

She released an exasperated sigh. "You're a freakin' pain in the ass."

The corners of his mouth curled into a wide grin. "It's a date, then?"

"No. This is not a date, bud. It's to get you off my back." Her voice was firm.

He was excited she'd agreed and convinced himself he was well on his way to a relationship with her. "I knew you'd see it my way."

They walked down the hallway side by side. Jessie stopped short.

"Maybe we should wait for the artist's sketch, so we can start hanging Jane Doe's picture around town."

"Nice try, Jess. No. The beat cops will take care of that. I called the newspaper before I came here, figuring you would ask Bradshaw to see the artist."

"Oh, now you're reading my mind?"

He gave her a sexy side glance. "If only that were true."

She stopped to grab her handbag before they walked outside to hail a cab. As usual, the traffic backed up as far as the eye could see. Impatient drivers leaned on their horns, trying to intimidate those ahead to move forward. Gerard made a face when he inhaled the smell of exhaust fumes from the massive line-up of vehicles. She noticed.

"An ongoing issue of living in the city," she reminded him.

"Yeah, but it doesn't mean I have to like it. I tolerate it," Gerard said, swiping at the sweat running down the side of his face with the hanky he'd pulled from his back pocket.

"Okay, so if I have to do this, where are we having dinner?" The tone of her voice was much lighter now.

"I'm in the mood for a big fat juicy steak, a baked potato with lots of sour cream, and a side salad," he said, drooling when he pictured the image of a steak, the juice running out with each slice of the knife. "Are you okay with that?"

"Sure. It works just fine."

The sound of shuffling footsteps behind startled Jessie, and she latched onto Gerard's arm with a firm grip. He watched her shoulders tremble as he glanced her way. "What's wrong?" he whispered.

"Good job today," Harwell said on his way past them.

"Ooh. Lieutenant," Jessie exhaled and stepped back, her hand clutched to her chest. "You startled me."

"Sorry." He gave Gerard a questionable glance. "Where are you two going?"

"Jessie's helping me pick out a gift for my brother," he lied.

"Sounds like a good deal. We guys don't know much about gift-giving. Well, don't stay up too late, Kensington . . . you need to get some sleep tonight."

"Yes, sir," she saluted. "I will if you'll promise not to call me in the wee hours of the morning."

Harwell shrugged his broad shoulders. "Hey, when duty calls, I call."

Gerard and Harwell both hailed cabs. Seconds later, two taxis pulled up to the curb.

Harwell gave a wave and jumped into the first taxi.

"Oh, man," she exclaimed, "He'll be calling one of us into his office tomorrow for a chastising."

Gerard snorted. "Seriously? He can't very well say much to you with his history," his eyebrows rose, "now can he?"

"Yeah, but things are different now that he's the boss."

"Does this mean romance *is* on your mind after all?" He winked.

Jess gave him an eye roll. The second cabbie pulled up and stopped. Gerard opened the car door for her.

"My, my," she said, with a slight tilt of her head, "and he's a gentleman too."

"Why? Don't you deserve to be treated like a lady?"

"I do, and thank you for recognizing that."

Gerard got into the taxi and slid a few inches away from Jessie.

"So," she teased, "does this mean you'll start being gallant during work hours too?"

"Hey, when we're working, you're one of the guys. Isn't that how you want me to treat you?" He glanced her way.

"That's definitely what I want." She leaned over and squeezed his arm. "Thank you, Gerard. I like that chivalry isn't dead."

Gerard patted her hand and changed the subject. He wanted her to know his genuine gestures and not some weak excuse to get her into the sack. Although, if he were being honest, he wouldn't mind that at all.

When the taxi pulled away from the curb, the figure in the far corner of the building stepped out and watched. "We'll see about that, bitch. By the time I'm finished with you, you won't need to worry about the boss making any demands on you."

* * *

The cab stopped in front of Wolfgang Puck's Steakhouse. Exiting the vehicle, Jessie ran her hands down the front of her slacks to smooth any newly acquired wrinkles when she looked up and noticed Gerard giving her an approving glance. He smiled when he realized she'd caught him, and her heart skipped a beat. God, he was gorgeous. Jessie couldn't recall the last time anyone had complimented her. She'd forgotten how good it felt, yet she reminded herself not to read too much into it. He was a player. Even so, she couldn't help but let the internal giddiness linger a little longer.

She watched him from the corner of her eye. The lights from passing cars illuminated his handsome face like a neon light. Falling for him would be so easy -- and so wrong. Once a playboy, always a playboy, Jessie reminded herself. And then there was that thing about getting involved with her partner.

"What?" tripped off the tip of his tongue. "You're staring at me."

A crimson blush colored her cheeks and caused her stomach to do a flip-flop. "I'm sorry. I didn't realize I was staring."

"That's okay because you had a smile on your face." He gave her a playful nudge with his elbow. "You were thinking about us, weren't you?"

"I hate to disappoint you," she lied, "there was no 'us' on my mind."

"I think you're lying."

"And I think you're a little too confident."

"Never hurts to try."

Inside the entry of the restaurant, large groups of people sat on benches waiting for a table. The low carved ceilings with stone arches gave the place a warm and friendly atmosphere but did nothing to buffer the loud noise of clanking dishes and enthusiastic conversations. Jessie waited while Gerard gave his name to the receptionist. Seeing the large trays of hot steaming food delivered to nearby tables had her salivating.

"Mmm, it smells way too good in here. And now, I'm starving."

He frowned, "I'm afraid we're in for a long wait. We could go somewhere else."

"Are you kidding me? After luring me into having a steak with you, there's no way I'm leaving this place without one."

He winked. "Ooh, baby, I like the way you think." He latched onto her elbow and steered her toward the lounge to a newly vacated table. He quickly eased into the seat before anyone else could take it.

"Are you ready to order?" the cocktail waitress asked while setting down a dish of nuts.

"What'll you have, Jessie James?" He popped a nut into his mouth.

"I'll have a double martini on the rocks."

"And I'll have a beer on draft," Gerard said, reaching for another handful of nuts.

"Thank you. I'll be back in a few minutes." The waitress walked away.

"Let's talk about Jane Doe's disappearance," Jessie said.

"No, Jess," he said forcefully, "we're here to discuss the notes."

"I'd much rather discuss our case."

"And I'd much rather discuss the notes."

"Okay, okay." She flung her hand in the air. "Go ahead. Let's put this to rest before I scream."

"Finally!" He cleared his throat. "Tonight, when you heard footsteps behind us, you were afraid. Now you can pretend all you want. You can tell me until you're blue in the face that you're not scared, but tonight's panicked look when Harwell came up behind us told me something else."

"Oh, stop already."

He shot her a stern look. "Start talking."

"The footsteps startled me; that's all. No need to read anything into it." His brow quirked. "What?" she said. "You never get startled?"

"On occasion, but even you must admit that reaction is unusual for you. Shit like that never bothered you before these notes started."

"Okay," she admitted, "maybe I am a little shaken up. Once I find out which one of the guys is doing this, it'll all be over, and we can get back to life as we know it."

"Like I said earlier, how do you know it's the guys at work?"

"Bradshaw all but confirmed my suspicions tonight."

"Oh, like he's the authority on the scuttlebutt in the precinct?" He gave her a wary look. "What exactly did he say?"

"He told me they resented me and added he didn't care who I'd dated, then or now. That's enough lead for me to feel better about suspecting them. The only other proof I need is to catch the person in the act."

"Okay, then tomorrow morning, I will take care of this matter."

"Oh, no, you're not. I'm not a damsel in distress waiting for my prince charming to rescue me. I don't need you or anyone else taking care of anything. I'm a big girl now; this is my problem, not yours."

The waitress returned and placed Jessie's martini down in front of her. She took a sip.

"Yeah, so you've said." He took a swig of beer. "Will you tell me again how the notes started?"

"Look, I appreciate your concern, but I'll be fine."

He rubbed a smudge of mascara off her cheek with his thumb. "Jessie, how did you receive the three notes?"

The tone of his voice told her he wasn't kidding. "On the windshield of my car in the parking garage."

"Do you rent a garage for your car?"

"No, I mean at the precinct."

"But you don't drive to work. How did your car get into the garage?"

"I drive when I go to the precinct during sleepless nights." A chill skittered down her spine as she remembered her initial reaction to receiving that first note, the cut-out letters pasted to a notecard spelling out the words *she'd better watch out*. She remembered shaking so vigorously that the note slipped from her hands and fell to the cement floor. Before stooping down to retrieve it, she'd done a quick scan of the area, her hand firmly planted on her Glock, ready to draw it if necessary.

"Hello," Gerard said, waving his hand before her eyes, "Where are you, Jessie?"

"I was just trying to remember the first time."

"You were scared, weren't you?"

"Sure, a little. But it's old hat to me now."

"Old hat, huh?" He leaned back against the leather seat, his eyes never leaving her face. "How often do you return to the office late at night?"

"Oh, I don't know. Maybe, once, twice a week." She sipped her martini.

"And what time do you usually leave?"

"Two, maybe three o'clock in the morning." She shrugged, "Sometimes later."

"You go out at that hour . . . by yourself?" Gerard asked, surprised. "Are you crazy?"

"Well, what should I do when I can't sleep? Twiddle my thumbs? Besides, plenty of people are working the night shift, so I'm not alone at the precinct, and I carry a gun."

"So you've reminded me a few hundred times." He closed his eyes and inhaled. "Have all the notes appeared during these late-night returns to the precinct?"

"Two did."

"And where did the third one show up?"

"I found it in my inbox when we returned to the precinct after meeting Tony and Lenny for a status report."

His eyes widened in surprise. "Okay. Maybe you are right about it being someone in the precinct. Have you watched the video from the garage surveillance for those days?"

"Yes."

"And?" his hand gestured impatiently, "What did you see?"

"Nothing except the usual people going in and out. Let's face it; everyone knows where the hidden cameras are."

"That's right. We do." He shook his head in disbelief. "Those sons of bitches. We'll get to the bottom of this. And so, help me God," he flung his hand in the air, "when I find out who's doing this, I'll kill the bastard."

"Ah-ha! Then you do agree with me?"

"In theory, but not in practice. I don't think we can rule out the possibility of a former criminal trying to get even. Nor can we rule out the scumbag's family. Have you considered the possibility that someone on the inside is pissed at you for being the boss's former girlfriend, and he's fronting for the criminal?" He paused when she rolled her eyes. "Look, I know you want me to believe you're tough as nails and can handle this all by yourself, but I'm not letting you go through this alone, and I don't care what you say."

She smiled, warmed by his concern. Yet she felt a tinge of guilt for not having trusted her partner enough to tell him.

"I'd like to know which one of those assholes is stupid enough to pull crap like this." His face formed into a concerned frown. "I want you to promise me you'll stop going to the precinct in the middle of the night. If you can't sleep, read a book, buy a computer, and play a game. Please don't return to the precinct. You're setting yourself up—especially with a stalker on the loose."

"Gerard, that's all well and good, but how am I supposed to find out who's doing this?"

"Whoever this is, he's bound to mess up sooner or later. If it is someone in the department, you can be sure he won't kill you. His mission is most likely to scare the crap out of you. But I still think you need to take every precaution to avoid the other more logical questions. Since you found the note in your inbox, it takes the heat off of an outsider doing it -- but only for the time being."

"Thanks, Gerard. I appreciate your compassion." A tender moment passed between them, and her heart rate surged. He was so hot. Jumping into the sack with him would be way too easy. She reached for her drink and tilted the glass to her lips, spilling the last few swallows into her lap. The effect was like taking a cold shower, snapping her back to reality. "Dammit," she said, jumping up. She grabbed the napkin from the table and tried to blot the liquid. "Christ, I've made a mess."

"I see that."

"I need a club soda."

He motioned for the waitress. "Can you bring a glass of club soda and an extra napkin for my date?"

The waitress nodded and headed back to the bar.

"Since when did this become a date?"

"Well, you know what I mean. It's not, but I see no reason to explain it to the waitress."

"Fair enough."

When the waitress returned with the club soda, Jessie excused herself. "I'll be back." On her way to the restroom, she convinced herself that her thoughts of becoming intimate with him were the byproduct of ambiance and alcohol—mostly alcohol. When she returned ten minutes later, he picked up the conversation right where they'd left off.

"So, will you promise me you'll stay away from the precinct in the wee hours of the morning?"

"I'll consider it. Now, please stop worrying."

"Well, someone has to worry. You're certainly not."

Jessie swallowed hard. She wanted to believe it was the guys in the department, but what if it wasn't? She couldn't let Gerard know, she questioned herself. It would make her look weak.

Fingers snapped in front of her eyes. "Hello, Jessie. You keep drifting off into la-la land. What's going on?"

"I think the alcohol has gone to my head. I need food."

"Then it's good that the hostess is on her way here to take us to our table. No more alcohol for you." They stood and followed the waitress. "Tell me you won't go to the precinct again in the middle of the night."

"You don't give up, do you?"

"I should think after three years of partnering, you'd know better than anyone that I don't give up easily. So, does that mean you'll promise?"

"I swear, I promise, I won't do it again." She held her hand up. "I'll buy a computer and play games, read gossip columns, and let my ass get as big as a house. Now, will you please stop?"

"I'll check with the guys tomorrow."

"Gerard, no, dammit. I don't need protection. I can handle this."

"You mean like you already have?"

"Whoa, that's a low blow," she tapped a balled fist against her heart.

"I'm sorry, but even the lieutenant has noticed something is wrong."

"How do you know that? Did he say something to you?"

"No, but he's already told you to get some sleep. He can see you have something on your mind."

"Are you going to spend the rest of your life joined at my hip?"

"Hmm, now that wouldn't be such a bad idea," he said with a twinkle in his eye.

She shook her head. "Get serious, Gerard."

"I am serious." He reached over and grasped her hand. Surprised, she jerked it back. "Whoa . . . excuse me."

"I'm not your type of woman."

"Type? I have a type?" he chuckled. "Geez, you make it sound like I'm a playboy."

"Well?" Her brows rose, daring him to deny it.

He jerked his head back. "Hey, I can't help it if the women chase after me."

"Careful, your ego is showing."

"I don't have an ego."

"Yeah, right," she snorted.

"I'm so misunderstood." He threw his hands in the air and shrugged. "Okay, just one more question."

"What now?"

He stared at her straight on. "Are you and Harwell still involved?"

She smacked her hands against her thighs. "I can't believe you asked me that again. No—and you know me better than that. I answered this question before. Didn't you believe me?"

"Relax. I just wanted to be sure I'm not treading on anyone else's turf. I'm sorry." He gave her a weak smile and reached for her hand again. This time, she didn't pull back and enjoyed the pleasure of his thumb caressing her knuckles. "I believe you." He stopped and leaned back in his chair, but his eyes remained steady on her face.

"What?" she asked. "Why are you staring at me like that?"

"I just thought about how great it would be to do this regularly -- like make it more of a permanent relationship." Her hand shot up like a stop sign. "And this comes as a shock?" He scratched his head.

"Oh, Gerard, I can't risk it again."

"Does that mean you've considered it?"

"I'd be a liar if I told you I hadn't, but it's never going to happen, and you know it."

He leaned forward and caressed her cheek with the back of his hand. Her heart revved up. She bit her lip to stop letting him see the pleasure it brought her.

"I'll be careful about not letting anyone see us," he whispered, "I'll even leave the department."

She shook her head. "Stop being silly. You love working in the two-one."

"But not enough to keep us apart."

"It's never going to happen." Her mouth was saying no, but her heart was saying yes. "For the three years we've worked together, I can't remember when we've run into each other off-duty that you didn't have some gorgeous creature hanging off your arm." She swallowed hard, stunned she'd vocalized that she'd noticed.

His face softened into a smile. "Did that make you jealous?"

Damn right, it made her jealous. "Good Lord, no," she lied and took another sip of water. "You're. . . you're having too much fun playing the field." There. It was out. Now he knew the long line of beauties hanging off his arm bothered her. A tinge of remorse attacked her stomach, and it tightened into a knot. She shouldn't have revealed so much to him. Damn the alcohol. It was like a truth serum for her. She shouldn't have had anything to drink because she didn't know enough to keep her mouth shut. But it was too late; he was already grinning like a schoolboy with his first crush. God, he was gorgeous.

"What if I told you I don't want any other woman but you?"

Jessie's fingers ached to reach over and pull him forward and kiss him. But she stopped herself, grabbed her glass of water, and gulped it down. "I'd say you were full of it."

His eyes filled with determination. "Did Harwell hurt you so badly that you won't allow yourself the pleasure of a relationship with me? Is that what this is all about? Or are you punishing yourself like you think the guys are for falsely accusing you of having a relationship with someone now our boss?"

"That's ludicrous." She took in a deep breath and exhaled. "Harwell wasn't married when I dated him." The mention of Harwell's name caused her lighthearted mood to fade.

"Is that why he came to our precinct—to compensate for the pain he caused you?"

"My God, you're making up your own story as you go along."

"Then talk to me, Jessie. Please. Help me understand what you've been through so I know how to act around you."

"Okay," she said. Seeing the waitress, she held up her empty martini glass for another. "I'll tell you. When Harwell came on board six months ago, word got out that we'd dated. Cripes, that was over ten years ago. I would have thought by now, no one would even remember. Someone from the old precinct probably felt resentful about his promotion because I can almost pinpoint when they found out. All the banter between the guys and me came to a screeching halt. No more silly pranks, nothing, nada—all gone." She waved her hand. "I told myself I imagined things, that the guys I'd had the most fun with were having a bad day. But I knew better. This rumor mill crap happened at the old job, too. And he was single then until he dumped me and got married soon after." Jessie played with the edge of the paper napkin under her water glass.

"You didn't answer my question. What caused the break-up?"

"I'd rather not say. Harwell is our boss. If the real reason ever got out, it would only come back to haunt me. I have enough problems as it is."

"You have to know I'd never repeat anything you tell me."

"I know you wouldn't mean to, but it does happen. And, if you knew, you wouldn't treat him the same either." Jessie rubbed her long fingers through the ends of her hair. "So now," she continued, "the guys act as if they're on a tightrope around me, afraid to say anything for fear; I'll report it back to the boss."

"You believe they're sending you the threatening notes, don't you?"

"I do, Gerard. That's why I'm not as concerned as you think I should be."

"Well, I guess I can understand why you feel that way, especially after how they've treated you. I had no idea this was going on. I'm sorry."

"Thank you. I know the guys would like me to leave the precinct, and to tell you the truth, I've considered it, but that would be the easy way out." A rush of sadness ached inside her chest, and a feeling of emptiness encompassed her.

The waitress returned with her drink and took their food order. Gerard's hand reached across the table for her again, and she relished the feel of his touch. She was having trouble focusing, suddenly feeling like putty in his hands. His face brightened, but he never moved his eyes from hers. She couldn't believe how much she enjoyed his company regardless of the questions he'd asked. She knew he worried about her. That was a first. A warm glow settled inside her chest like a cup of hot chocolate on a windy day, and she was happy she'd accepted his offer to have dinner.

The food, the ambiance, Gerard—it was building to a perfect evening.

"Tell me why it's so important for you to prove to everyone that you're tough." He set his drink down, waiting for her response.

"You've never had to prove yourself, have you, Gerard"

"I've had to prove myself every day of my life." He tightened his lips into a thin line. "The only problem is, the person whose approval I've sought for most of my life has never acknowledged me. I stopped caring a long time ago about what other people think."

"And, who would that be?"

"My old man. Nothing I've ever done was good enough for him. He's an attorney who thought I should follow in his footsteps, regardless of what I wanted. When I wasn't interested in living the life he'd planned for me or marrying the woman he'd chosen to be my wife, he turned his back on me and said I'd never amount to anything without his help."

"Ooh, how awful. I'm so sorry to hear that."

"Yeah, me too. But that's how the cookie crumbles."

"Your father wouldn't be Alan Gerard, the high-profile attorney I've been reading about in the newspapers, would it?"

"That's him."

"But you still see your mother, don't you?"

"I wish. My mother died five years ago." He became silent. "How about we change the subject?"

She could tell from the expression on his face; the subject made him uncomfortable. "Sounds like a good idea."

* * *

Finished with dinner, they waited outside for the taxi to pull up in front of the restaurant. Holding the door open on the cab, Jessie slid across the seat, and he squeezed in beside her, his hand wrapped around hers. She tossed her head back against the cushion and closed her eyes. Gerard moved closer and gently pulled her head down onto his shoulder. She hadn't remembered feeling such contentment. When the cab pulled up in front of her apartment building, she wished the night wouldn't end. Gerard helped her out and walked her to the door. She released a contented sigh as they walked up the stairs, their arms wrapped around each other's waist. Words could not express the emotions surging through her body. An awkward moment passed between them, and she thought she might burst if she didn't unlock the door to her apartment building and go inside. She broke the silence. "Thank you. It's been a wonderful evening." She turned and shoved her key into the lock, and pushed the door open.

"Me too, Jess. I hope this evening is the first of many more to come."

She smiled as she walked through the opened door and stopped halfway to glance back at him. That's when he pulled her outside and devoured her mouth. His kiss was urgent and hungry. She felt the fire erupt inside her body as though she was in the middle of a million fireworks on the fourth of July. She stood stunned, wrapped in his tight embrace, unable to speak, and listened to the thunder of his heart. He pulled back and stared into her eyes.

"Are you sure you want to call it a night?"

CHAPTER 10

The early morning sunlight stirred Jessie from a sound sleep. She moaned in pain from a throbbing headache—the result of too many martinis. She rubbed her temples, willing the sledge-hammer pounding against her skull to subside, and wished she'd listened to Gerard about not having another drink.

"Oh God," tripped off her tongue. The memory of last night rushed to the front of her mind. Her hand instinctively reached over to the opposite side of the bed and patted the mattress. It was empty. She blew out a steady stream of air, relieved the alcohol hadn't clouded her thinking. Thank God, she hadn't slept with Gerard. Squinting her eyes from the sunlight coming through the window, she grabbed the extra pillow and covered her face. That's when she smelled his cologne. She gasped. "Dammit," she said, fisting her hands. She'd done it. Broken her own Cardinal Rule and slept with Zach Gerard

Her stomach tightened. How could she have been so stupid? Yeah, he was hot. Yeah, she'd even dreamt about him . . . fantasized about them being together, but she hadn't planned to act out her fantasy. She rolled onto her stomach, the pillow now tight against the back of her head. She growled into the mattress. Why did she agree to have dinner with him in the first place? Her feet angrily banged against the bed. The jostle only made the pain worse. Blowing out a frustrated breath, she told herself it was too late for regrets now. . . the damage was already done.

Her mind flashed to the guys at work and what they'd say about them sleeping together? It would make her life a living hell. Suddenly remembering this was a work day, she peeked out from the pillow's corner to check the clock. Jessie groaned when she realized she didn't have much time before she had to be at the precinct. By comparison, though, that was the easy part. What wouldn't be so easy was facing Gerard. She groaned and promised herself she would handle it before it worsened. She rolled over onto her back, clutching her head with her two hands, determination took over, and she forced herself to get out of bed. The room spun around like a top. She closed her eyes and flopped back down onto the pillow. The pounding of pain intensified. Dread encompassed her body. Why did she drink so much? Why? Why? Why?

Counting to three, she made another attempt to sit up. Nausea worked its way up into her throat, and she bolted out of bed, threw the toilet seat lid up, and leaned over the bowl. Finished, she attempted to stand, but her body wasn't ready to move. Instead, she hugged the bowl and closed her eyes. The sour aftertaste of vomit lingering in her mouth.

A few minutes later, she held onto the cabinet for leverage and stood, quickly turning on the faucet, dipped her head under the stream of cold water. Turning from side to side, she took in a gulp of water to rinse her mouth. Without drying her hair, she bent down and pulled the bottle of ibuprofen from the cabinet and dropped three capsules into her hand, caring not that the water was everywhere, including dripping down her body. She washed down the capsules with the water from her cupped hand praying for relief.

The silence in the apartment was almost deafening until she heard the turn of a key in the lock. She panicked wondering who had a key to her apartment? Could she make it to her bedroom for the Glock? Probably not. Her fuzzy mind played out scenarios about saving herself, but before she got too deeply into thought, she heard his voice.

"Hey, Hotshot, are you all right in there?" Gerard asked.

Her heart sunk. What had she done? She crawled to the bathroom door, peeked around the corner, and groaned when she saw him looking so chipper. Catching her reflection in the mirror, she slumped to the floor, hoping he'd go away.

She didn't have enough time to kick the door shut when she heard him heading in her direction. He stood by the opened door inching his arm inside with a bag of food. The smell from the bag sent her spiraling back to the bowl. She hated having him see her like this, but as far as she was concerned, after today, she was never going to see him again anyway.

Zach walked away, seemingly giving her privacy, but seeing him set a florist box on the counter made her smile. Had he bought her flowers? Jessie shut her mind down and crawled into the shower, pulling the shower curtain to the closed position. Bracing her hands against the wall, she stood under the steady water flow. It cleared her head somewhat. She cringed when she heard him speak.

"Hey, sweetheart, you don't need to hide from me. I've seen worse."

Christ, she thought, now he's calling me sweetheart. She'd broken her rule and succumbed to her partner. Holding her head, she couldn't believe what she'd done. She looked and felt like shit.

If she'd learned anything, it was to avoid drinking around her partner. The ache of regret filled her chest with anxiety. Zach even told her no more alcohol last night, but did she listen? No, not this strong, independent woman. Jessie sighed deeply and stepped back into the shower, praying the headache would disappear and take Gerard with it. A short while later, he reentered the bathroom and pulled the curtain aside.

"Hey, are you ever coming out of this shower?"

"Go away."

"Now, that's not what you said last night." She watched him stoop down and wipe the water off the floor with a towel from the rack.

"Forget about last night. Forget about me. I'll be out of the department by the end of the week."

He laughed. "Oh, stop it, for God's sake. We're not children. We're consenting adults."

"Don't remind me."

He smiled and headed back out to the kitchen. "You're even beautiful when you're barfing."

"Oh, shut up."

When she heard the door close, she stepped out of the shower and reached for an oversized towel in the linen closet, wrapping it tightly around her body. She stood before the mirror and eyed the reflection staring back at her. The long red locks she'd always taken great pains to showcase were now a tangled mess. She brushed out the knots and shuffled into the kitchen.

"You're beautiful!"

"Shut up," she said.

"Uh-oh, somebody's grumpy." He was clean-shaven and dressed in dark brown dress slacks, a striped, brown, black, and white shirt, and tasseled loafers. She looked away. She didn't need to see him looking so hot, but the masculine scent of his cologne only reminded her of the foolish mistake she'd made.

He held a container out to her. "Here, drink this, Ms. Martini Girl. It will make you feel better." He smirked. "How's that head this morning?" She didn't respond. "That bad, huh?"

She grimaced and slowly removed the lid from the container, and took a swig.

"Yep, that bad." He pointed to the florist's box. "These were at your front door when I returned. Have you been keeping something from me?"

"No. I have no clue who sent the flowers." She gave him a quizzical glance.

"It wasn't me."

She walked to the cupboard, reached inside for a vase, filled it with water, and returned to untie the ribbon around the box. Unable to release the knot, she got a pair of scissors to cut the ribbon. Disturbed by her current state of mind, she couldn't believe a minute ago, she was dreading that she'd slept with him, yet now, the flowers caused her heart to palpitate. What was wrong with her? Even though Gerard had denied it, she was sure he'd bought the flowers but was too embarrassed to admit it. This was a side of him she'd never seen. Jessie racked her brain, trying to remember whether she'd enjoyed the sex. He must have enjoyed it. He hadn't stopped smiling since he'd returned with breakfast. The idea of being courted by him appealed to her senses. She smiled—he was a smooth operator.

With the tie undone, she sighed and lifted the lid, only to gasp, paralyzed in place as she viewed the contents. They were roses, all right, but not the kind she'd expected. She shoved the floral box onto the floor, afraid to touch them. Crumbled pieces of dried, black roses scattered over the floor tiles.

"What the hell?" Gerard said.

Seeing the notecard, Jessie bent over to pick it up. Gerard jumped to his feet and grabbed the note from her hand. Insecurity overcame her and made her wonder if Gerard was doing this to her. Was it possible? A slight flashback of what she remembered about their evening gave her pause. Was he trying to trick her into thinking he wanted a relationship to drive her out of the department? Had the guys at work put him up to this? He gave her a sympathetic glance, and the guilt of wondering how she could even think such a thing took over.

"Are you all right?" He said, wrapping his arms around her. She pushed him away. "Are you okay?" He stood looking at her, a deep crease in his forehead. "Jess?"

"I'm fine."

"Yeah, I can see that."

She bent down to clean up the mess she'd made.

"Don't touch anything," Gerard commanded. "You know better than that." He pulled her hand back, then called headquarters. "Send a crew over to Detective Kensington's apartment. Yes, the address is . . ."

"No, dammit." She shot him an angry look. "Now, I'll never find out which asshole is doing this."

CHAPTER 11

*J*essie walked into headquarters at a fast clip leaving Gerard several paces behind, and headed to her desk. Lieutenant Harwell noticed her from his windowed office and walked out.

"Are you okay?" he asked.

"I'm fine." She pulled a file from her drawer and lowered her head to check the contents, blocking out the questions the lieutenant was sure to ask. She tried to ignore the dull ache that remained in her head.

"Kensington, in my office, please."

Jessie deliberately ignored him. Her attention focused on the report she was pretending to read.

"That wasn't a request, Detective Kensington. That was a direct order. Now!" he said firmly, catching the attention of her peers.

Annoyed by his order, she begrudgingly pushed her chair back, and walked to his office. He shut the door behind her. "Sit!" he pointed. Tension tightened in her chest. "You want to tell me what the fuck is going on?"

"That's just what I'd like to know." Jessie sucked in her lips. "I'm furious with my partner. I had this! But now that the world knows, my chances of finding the culprit are shot to hell."

"That's some attitude, Detective."

Refusing to look at him, she fiddled with the loose fabric on her chino slacks. "I'd like to know how long you've kept this from me."

"It isn't anything I can't handle," she said.

"You let me be the judge of that." Her lips pursed. "Yeah, I know how tough you are. Answer the question. How long has this been going on?" He moved papers from his desktop into the inbox, a feeble attempt to tidy up.

"For two weeks."

"Let me see if I have this straight. You've received three notes in two weeks and black roses today with another note, and you've kept this to yourself?" He pursed his lips. "Unbelievable, Kensington. Even for you."

"If I thought it was serious, Lieutenant, I would have come to you. Honest." Her shoulders relaxed. "I think it's from one of the assholes in the department." She looked directly into his honey-colored eyes. "They know about us. Did you know that?"

"You're shittin' me, right?" His eyes opened wide. "You mean that crap is still making headlines after all this time?"

"Exactly. The guys seem to think we're still involved."

"Do they now?" He shook his head in disgust. "Interesting. So, how does that tie into what's happening with these black roses?"

"It's Friday the thirteenth. It's supposed to be a scary day. Bad things happen. Think about the connection with the guys for a minute. Let's face it, Lieutenant, you came here after your promotion. We had a previous relationship, and now you're my boss. Since your arrival, the guys treat me differently. They're afraid to talk to me anymore. They nod when they pass by. I know they're worried that I'll tell you something they've said. I can see it on their faces."

"How can you possibly know this? Did someone tell you?"

"No. Wouldn't you feel the same way?"

"Speculation doesn't solve crimes." He stood and paced, his hands planted on his hips. When he noticed several officers watching him through the glass window, he pulled the shade down. "Okay, so who do you think is doing this?"

"I have no idea. That's why I didn't want it reported. But of course, my jackass partner had to get involved."

"For Chrissake, Jessie, he's concerned about you. Besides, he's your partner. He needs to know what's going on with you, just as you do with him. You know that better than anyone."

"Oh yeah, and I'm just thrilled." She rolled her eyes.

Harwell shook his head. "Look, I'm having a hard time believing the guys in this department would do something like this, but, hey, I'll check it out—"

"But—"

"Discreetly," he raised his finger in the air as though he was disciplining a child, his voice lowered to a gruff pitch. Jessie slumped back into the chair, her hands folded and resting in her lap. "As a place to start, I want a complete list of every case and every criminal you've arrested in the last three years . . . and, if you think it's one of the guys, then you'd better include those names too."

She huffed out a breath, stood to leave, and flung her hand in the air on her way to the door.

"I haven't dismissed you yet," he said abruptly, pointing to the chair.

She slumped back down in the chair. "Sorry."

"And I want those on my desk," his finger tapped on the surface, "by the end of the week."

She shot him a look, her mouth twisted in irritation, but his warning look told her not to mess with him.

"What if it turns out to be a waste of time?" she asked.

"If nothing turns up, I'll call the crew and tell them what's happening." He brushed the dust off the end of his desk. "Alright, Detective, get out there," he pointed, "focus on Lenny's killer and your Jane Doe. To make this clear, I'll handle your problem myself. I do not want you involved in this whatsoever. You can't be objective about it, and you can't focus on your job." She stood to leave. "If you receive any more notes, dead flowers . . . anything of any kind, you are to report it to me immediately." She didn't respond. "Am I making myself clear?"

"Yes, sir."

"Can you push this aside?" he asked. "Or do I need to take your shield and firearm away?"

"No. Please," Jessie begged. "Let me do my job. I'll go crazy at home wondering what's happening with my Jane Doe case."

"Fine. Then get the hell out of here and do some work." She exited without comment.

Passing by her desk, she saw Gerard was on the telephone. He gave her a weak smile; she gave him a dirty look and continued down the hall to the records department. He flung his hands in the air as he watched her steadfast steps, sure he'd never understand women, especially this red-headed spitfire.

CHAPTER 12

*L*ieutenant Jack Harwell leaned back in his chair, hands tightly clasped behind his head, his feet resting on the top of his desk, and wondered about Kensington and the threatening notes.

If her suspicions were correct, and those notes were coming from someone on the inside, he'd make the bastard pay—big time. If it hadn't been for Gerard calling the precinct when the roses showed up, he would never have known—until she got killed or had a shootout. He shook his head in despair. He'd lost her all those years ago because of a drunken one-night stand that changed his life forever. The thought of losing her again would devastate him. Not in a romantic sense, but if someone wanted her dead, it would kill him too. The biggest obstacle facing him was being discreet with his investigation. But when he found out, he'd put the bastard's ass behind bars. He wouldn't rest until he did. He owed her that much.

A recap of Jessie's expression when he'd told her they were breaking up, sent a ripple of anxiety to settle in the pit of his stomach. It had haunted him since the day it happened and would continue to haunt him for the rest of his life. He had to right the wrong somehow, and although finding the stalker would help, it certainly couldn't erase the pain he'd caused.

His fist clenched and came down on the desk with a vengeance as the resentment tightened in his chest; angry Jess had to go through this—upset, it caused her more pain.

Reaching for the frame sitting on his desk with Max's picture, he admitted his son was the only good thing that had come out of his reckless one night of passion with Ginny. Although he did not love her when they married, it was the right thing to do. Over the years, he'd learned to accept that this was his fate. He shuddered and forced himself to shake off the thought and focus on Jessie's dilemma. Was the person doing this trying to get even with them? It was certain his list of enemies far outweighed his friends. The most logical suspect on his list was Sergeant Tip Jackson. It was no secret the two men despised one another. If the rumor mill talked about his prior relationship with Jessie, he could almost guarantee Jackson was the ringleader.

He flicked on the intercom. "Pauline, are Kensington and Gerard still in the precinct?"

"Yes, Lieutenant, I saw them walking into the lab." She paused. "Did you want me to call them?"

"Yes."

* * *

Ten minutes later, the pair entered Harwell's office. "Have a seat," he said. "I need more information from you, Jessie."

"Regarding?" Jessie asked.

"To figure out who would be dumb enough to send threatening notes to one of my detectives." His hand swept back and forth over the top of his closely cropped hair, a nervous habit he'd had for as long as she'd known him. "So, I've come up with the answer."

"Okay," she said.

"If it is anyone in this department, it's Jackson, but we have to check out every possibility and not just focus on one person. We're going to treat this like any other case we work on and go with the assumption that it might be someone you've likely put in the slammer, and he's out on parole and looking for revenge." Gerard was nodding in agreement.

She looked from Harwell to Gerard. "I wish you'd both stop and let me handle my problem." She threw her hands up impatiently.

"Jessie, you know better than to have tunnel vision," Gerard said. "Stop thinking about this personally and begin to consider all the possibilities."

She shook her head and watched her partner's face break into a toothy grin. He sure as hell wasn't helping her cause. She eyed the two of them again and was swept away with unease at having slept with both men. What had she been thinking? But that was just it—she hadn't thought. She'd allowed her emotions and the alcohol to cloud her judgment. Now, she had to tell Gerard she'd made a colossal mistake. But how could she tell him when that damn smile of his had become a permanent fixture on his handsome face? Getting involved with Harwell had been a stupid rookie mistake, but at the time, she'd been lonely and so desperately in need of being loved it seemed a natural choice. But what was her excuse this time? Gerard's knee bumped against hers when he crossed his legs and sent a jolt through her. She hoped it wasn't obvious.

"Are you working on your list of cases, Detective?"

"No. I have other, more important cases that need my attention."

"Is that a fact?" His face flushed. "Then let me repeat this directive. This isn't a request. It's a direct order." His jaw jutted out. "I told you two days ago I want that list on my desk by Friday, and you only have three days left to get it to me." He glared at her as if daring her to decline to obey his order. "I'm going to find out one way or another, Jessie, so you might as well be the one to tell me."

"Look, Lieutenant," she said, "these guys and I have been through thick and thin together, supported each other when we've been down, and congratulated each other for a job well done. Giving you a list of names is like being Serpico. The last thing I want is to cause an uproar in the department."

"In fairness to Jess, Lieutenant," Gerard interrupted. "It could be because of . . ." He stopped short.

"Because of our previous affiliation," Harwell finished his sentence, his finger swayed back and forth between the two of them.

"Uh, yeah."

A sudden hush came over the room for what seemed like an eternity to Jessie. She squirmed uncomfortably in her seat, wishing they weren't having this discussion. Annoyed, she broke the silence. "Please, Lieutenant, do we need to air our dirty laundry with Gerard here?" She was astounded he'd even broached the subject. "If I wanted my personal life aired, I would have shared it with everyone myself."

"Hey," Harwell said, "I have nothing to hide—do you?"

"Well, no." She tilted her head to the side. "But it's my private life we're discussing here. I should be able to decide whether or not I want people to know."

"Yeah, and now it's coming back to bite you in the ass." Harwell's voice elevated. "He's your partner, Jessie. Do you want to keep him in the dark? What if this is more serious than you think? He needs to know what's going on."

"But our relationship is ancient history."

"Yes, it is, but the longer this goes on, the more it becomes current events in the eyes of the stalker. So why don't we get this crap out in the open, so we can all move on."

"Well, I'm not happy about it." She sighed.

"Yeah, well, that's too bad. Get over yourself." Harwell's sharp rebuttal brought back a host of memories. It was like the sting of a bee. "Okay. Are we all on the same page now?" the Lieutenant asked.

Gerard nodded, a little too vigorously, she thought, wishing she could wipe the smirk off his face.

"As a matter of fact, I was thinking about another scenario after our first discussion, and since I know Jessie's going to drag her feet on this, I want both of you to make the list." Jessie's brows rose. "Hey, who knows, this person could be someone who dislikes Gerard and sending you the letters is their way of getting back at him." Gerard nodded.

"I hadn't thought of that," Gerard said, "but you could be right."

"Start with the precinct first." Jessie's head angled in disbelief. "He may think of someone you don't."

"I do that, and I'll be labeled a whiny bit . . ."

"I want," his finger rose in the air, ignoring her comment, "the list to include anyone you've had words with, any uncomfortable encounters, anyone who's made you feel the least bit suspicious—and I don't care who it is, just put the damn name on the list." His finger pounded on the desk. "I'll deal with it later."

"Like you, Lieutenant, the first one on my list would be Jackson," Gerard said.

Jessie's mouth started to open to say something, but she reluctantly sighed and sat back.

"Jessie, I'm not going to tell you this again. Do you get me?" Harwell said.

"Okay, fine." She flung her hand in the air, disgusted and tired of fighting. "I guess -- yes, he's on my list too. If he's spreading the rumors, he may try to get back at you through me, especially if he thinks we're still an item."

"Now that's the first sensible thing you've said." Harwell's head shook in bafflement. "I find it hard to believe he'd be so foolish . . . especially given our history."

"I don't trust him to tell you the truth," Gerard said. "And it's not because of what he did for Officer Ramirez, but he keeps showing up in the most unexpected places."

"Oh? Then make sure you put those occurrences on the list next to his name. Okay, is there anyone else that comes to mind?"

The office door opened, and everyone turned to see who was entering. "Sorry to interrupt, Detectives," Harwell's secretary said as she entered the office. "Lieutenant, I think you should take this call."

"Pauline, can't you see we're busy?"

"Yes, Lieutenant. I can see that. But Sara Milligan says the sketch of the unidentified woman posted around the borough is her sister."

Gerard stood. "Sit," Harwell said. "We'll all listen to the call." He pushed the speaker button. "This is Lieutenant Harwell."

"I'm sorry, Lieutenant, but I specifically asked for Detective Gerard."

"I'm right here, Sara," Gerard said.

"Oh, thank God. I'm so glad I got through to you."

Jessie did not acknowledge her presence. She'd played bad cop during a few encounters with the woman and didn't want to stifle what information Sara had for them.

"What can I do for you, Sara?" he asked.

"That sketch hanging all over the city," her voice cracked, "it's my sister."

"What makes you say it's your sister?"

"It's a good likeness of her. She was supposed to meet me on Wednesday and never showed."

"Maybe she had something else to do and forgot to call you. Did you check your voicemail?"

"That's hilarious, Detective Gerard."

"Sara, you've told me so many lies in the past; how do I know you're telling me the truth now?"

"I'm telling you, Detective, the sketch . . . that's my sister's face." She became silent.

"Alright. Come in to talk to us. I'll tell the desk sergeant you have an appointment." They disconnected.

"What's the story with Sara Milligan?" Harwell asked.

"She's been in and out of drug rehab several times, got involved hooking for her dealer, and various other felonies. Do you know who her brother-in-law is?"

"I don't believe I do."

"Patrick Sawyer."

"No kidding," Harwell's eyes opened wide with surprise.

Knowing Harwell, Jessie could tell the wheels were turning in his mind over the possibilities of information Sara might have on his archenemy.

"I vaguely remember the last time she was at the precinct," Harwell said, "but I didn't know there was a connection between her and

Sawyer." He puffed his lips out. "Has she ever mentioned him during those visits?"

"She has," Gerard confirmed, "but nothing has ever materialized."

"What makes you think the information she provides today will be any more valuable."

"We don't, but I didn't notice any slurring of her words this time. Did you, Jessie?"

"No, I didn't," she said.

"Neither did I," Harwell agreed. "How many times has she been in rehab?"

"I've lost count," he offered. "The last occurrence was . . ." he looked to Jess for an answer. "Two, three months ago?"

"Yeah, I think it was two months ago. Even so, Sara's brain is fried after all those years on crack."

Gerard tapped his pencil on his notebook. "But we'll listen to what she says and weed through the crap. It's our responsibility to check them all out."

"Of course, we will," Harwell said.

"Want to join us in the interrogation room, Lieutenant?"

"I think I will."

"Just so you'll know, Lieutenant," Jessie said, "Sara hates me with a passion."

"Maybe she has something to do with those threatening notes."

"Nah. Sara's not bright enough to pull off something like that."

"So, why doesn't she like you?"

"I was the tough interrogator." She pointed to her partner, "Gerard, over here, charms the hell right out of her."

Gerard stood to leave, a smirk firmly planted on his face. "Okay, I'll call you as soon as she arrives." He stopped in front of Harwell's desk. "You want both our lists on Friday?" he asked with a grin.

"I wanted it this afternoon," he said, looking over at Jessie, who was rolling her eyes. He winked at Gerard, "The end of the week is okay."

Seeing Gerard's smirk out of the corner of her eye, she shot him a dirty look. He snickered. "And you thought you were off the hook, didn't you?" She increased her pace. "Hey, want to have dinner with me tonight?" he called after her.

Her stomach clenched. She hadn't been able to stop thinking about their romantic interlude, but this meeting between them convinced her getting involved with another partner was a bad idea. The words barreled out of her mouth. "Not a good idea!"

"Oh yeah? Why is that?"

"Because you're already bordering on the edge of possessiveness—like you think you own me."

His mouth twisted to the side. "Is that a fact? It's only dinner; it's not like I asked you to marry me."

His words stabbed at her heart, confirming she'd made the right decision.

* * *

Gerard disconnected his cell and pushed his chair away from his desk. "Milligan is waiting in interview room three."

"Oh goody," Jessie said, standing upright. "I can hardly wait to see her again. I wonder how much bullshit she has in store for us today." She shrugged.

"You never know, Jess, she may give us something useful this time." He grinned.

"Want me to let Harwell know we're ready?"

A tinge of jealousy waved through his stomach. He chalked it up to being insecure . . . a feeling he's never had before. "Go ahead. I'll wait for you." He knew he was acting like a lovesick teenage boy in high school waiting to walk his girl to her next class, but he couldn't help himself . . . he was falling head over heels in love with her. He shook his head in disbelief. When had the roles reversed? Women always chased after him, but this one had him eating out of the palm of her hand.

A few minutes later, Jessie joined him. He shook his head as they walked down the hall in silence. Christ, he was supposed to be thinking about the meeting with Sara Milligan, but remembering their night of passion was much nicer. He released a lovesick sigh and watched her profile as she spoke. He'd known from the moment he'd met Jessie that she was something special. She'd given him a challenge that kept him awake at night, trying to devise ways to convince her they should date. He chuckled aloud. She had no idea how persistent he could be.

"What's so funny?" she asked.

"Nothing."

She flashed a skeptical frown and tapped on the interview room door, waiting to enter.

"I'm not expecting too much from this interview," he said before entering the room. "Unless Sara's life has changed for the better. In which case, I'd be all wet. But there's still that shred of hope."

When they entered, Sara's back was to the door. She turned toward them and smiled. Jessie's wide-eyed expression gave her away.

Sara's scowl was noticeable when she glanced off Jess and smiled at Gerard. "Hi, Detective Gerard."

"Hi, Sara," Jessie said. "It's nice to see you looking so well." Sara did not acknowledge her greeting.

"Good to see you, Sara," Gerard said. He couldn't believe his eyes. The woman had cleaned herself up this time. A faint aroma of lavender filled the air. At least this Sara smelled clean, instead of the usual stench of urine and sweat. Seconds later, Harwell entered the room.

"Sara, I'd like you to meet our new lieutenant." Gerard gestured his hand toward his boss. "Jack Harwell." They exchanged greetings.

Harwell made his way over to one of the chairs across from Sara's table. The detectives joined him. Jessie sat next to the recorder, ready to push the button. Gerard sat down at the head of the table.

"As soon as you're ready, Sara," Jessie said, "I'll be recording this session."

"Why?" She turned toward Gerard. "Gerard, I thought I was going to see you alone. I feel uncomfortable with an audience."

"Sara, my partner, and I will work on this interview."

"But you told me to come to see you anytime I needed help."

"Yes, I did, Sara, and that's exactly what I'm doing. When I say *me*, it means both of *us*. We're a team." Sara looked disgusted and crossed her arms, leaning them against her chest.

Harwell intervened. "If you're concerned about your sister, tell my detectives what you know. Otherwise, you're wasting our time."

"Okay. But why is this being recorded?"

"To be sure we don't miss anything important," Jessie said. "We don't want to walk away from the session wondering whether you said the sky was green or blue."

"Why? Are you too lazy to take notes?" Sara snapped at her.

Gerard stood. "Okay, let's forget this interview?" They all stood to leave. He winked at Jessie as they headed toward the door. "We have too much work to do to waste time on this."

"No. Wait," Sara reacted. "I'm sorry" Her shoulders sagged. "I'm just not myself these days," she said, directing her conversation to Harwell. "I'm doing this all alone, you know, after my parents disowned me several years ago." She shrugged. "I can't blame them, considering all the trouble I've caused. Anyway, I did call my mother to tell her about the artist's sketch and that I thought it was Amanda . . . that's my sister's name, but she hung up on me." She looked down at her hands for a few seconds. "Is recording these sessions something new, Detective Gerard?" she asked.

"No, Sara, we've been doing this for a long time—you were always too strung out to know the difference." He eyed her, trying to read her question. "Is there a reason the recorder upsets you?"

"Well, no. But I know how you guys operate." She rolled up her sleeves, exposing her veins. "Look for yourselves. I'm clean, and I have been for two months." Gerard examined her arms. There were several scars but no evidence of fresh marks.

"Congratulations, Sara. I hope you'll continue to stay clean."

"Look, I know you don't trust me. This is the last place I want to be right now, but I'm worried about Amanda, and I'd do anything for her." She paused, looking from one detective to the other. "Are you going to help me or not?"

"We'll do our best," Gerard said. "Go ahead."

Jessie reclined in a resting position leaning against the back of the chair while her partner began the interview.

"Today is August 28th, 2007 – 4:07 PM. I'm Detective Zach Gerard, and present with me is my partner, Detective Jessie Kensington, and my supervisor, Lieutenant Jack Harwell. On this date, we are interviewing Sara Milligan. My partner and I will be conducting the interview." Gerard looked directly at Sara. "For the record, would you please state your name, address, place of employment, and phone numbers for residence and work?"

"My name is Sara Jane Milligan, and I don't have a permanent address or phone number—I've been staying with different friends for the last two months."

"Are you working, Sara?" Jessie asked.

"Is that a trick question?" Sara blinked her eyes. "Unless you know of someone who hires former junkies, I doubt I'll get a job."

"How will we get in touch with you then?" Jessie asked

"You won't. But I'll keep in touch. I want my sister back."

"Okay, Sara, tell me about your sister. How do you know she's missing?" Gerard asked.

"Because I haven't heard from her in over a week. We met at the park every Wednesday, and she didn't show up this week. I figured she was blowing me off, but the more I thought about it, the more I realized she wouldn't do that to me." Tears brimmed on her lashes. "Then I saw this sketch around the city," she said, holding the paper up and pointing to the sketch. "I know it's her." She wiped her eyes.

"What makes you think she's missing just because she didn't show up? Couldn't she have had something else to do instead?"

"No. Even if Amanda did have something else to do, she would have gotten word to me. Unlike me, she's as reliable as the day is long."

"Sara, you just told us you're unreliable," Jessie said. "So, why should we believe you today?"

"Because I'm telling you. My sister is missing," she said, raising her voice.

"Okay, Sara, calm down," Gerard said. "We just need to be sure your information is factual before we begin an all-out investigation."

"You're giving me a hard time because of my priors. I knew you wouldn't believe me," she said in a rush of words. "With all the time you're wasting, my sister could be dead by now."

Harwell intervened. "Sara." She looked his way. "We have to do this. I know you're upset, so give us what we need to begin our investigation."

"My sister was the only one who cared enough to stick by me, and I owe her a lot. She's been giving me money for food."

"Are you out of money? Is that why you came here today?" Harwell asked.

Sara gave him a daggered look. "No, damn it!" Her fist balled. "I came here because I want you to find my sister."

"Have you been to your sister's house recently?"

"No. The big man won't allow me to be around my niece."

"I assume you're referring to Patrick Sawyer," Harwell said. "And where is he?"

"Yeah, I'm referring to that douchebag. It wouldn't surprise me if Patrick had something to do with her disappearance. I wanted to go over to the house and snoop around, but I couldn't get anyone to give me a ride, and I didn't have the cab fare."

"Okay, give us her address, and we'll check it out."

"They live on W 87th Street, Upper West Side, with all the muckety- mucks."

"What information do you have about Mr. Sawyer?" Harwell asked with interest. "And, what makes you think he had anything to do with this?"

"Because he's an asshole. He's been smacking Amanda around for a long time. I don't know why she put up with it for this long, but they have a kid."

"Have you tried to reach your brother-in-law to find out?" Gerard asked.

"I just told you he won't allow me in the house, so what makes you think he'll talk to me?" Her foot tapped the floor like she was keeping in time with the music.

"Would you be willing to give us a DNA sample?" Jessie asked.

"Why?"

"Because it would help us with our investigation to match things up in case we find your sister."

"DNA is just for relatives, though, isn't it?"

"Yeah," Jessie said, "she is your sister, isn't she?"

"Well, in name only. The Milligans adopted me."

CHAPTER 13

Two law enforcement vehicles followed behind the two detectives to the Sawyer residence at 634 W 87th Street.

"Boy, I wouldn't mind living in this neighborhood," Jessie said when they pulled up in front of the mansion. "We're obviously in the wrong field."

"That's for sure."

"How about we pool our money and go into the car dealership business?" Jess suggested.

Gerard laughed. "I might have enough to get a chop shop going, but that's about it." He turned to Jessie. "Hey, does that mean we're a thing?"

"Not a chance, my friend. We aren't anything."

"Are you saying the other night was just a try-out?"

"No. The other night was a mistake." There. It was out. She'd finally said it.

"Yeah, I guess I have to agree with you," Gerard said, smiling. He liked giving her a dose of her own medicine and wondered if it would affect her. He gave her a side glance to check her reaction, and she didn't disappoint. She clamped her mouth shut and exited the vehicle. He smiled at her body language. It was just the reaction he was hoping to see. A rush of confidence flowed through him, knowing it was her nature to fight a relationship with him until the bitter end, but he was a patient man. He sensed she felt awkward by the way she averted her eyes from his. He tapped her on the arm, anxious to break the ice.

"What?" she said.

"You ready to go inside?"

"You bet."

"I'm praying Mr. Milligan didn't compromise our evidence, but I guess we'll find out soon enough," Gerard said. "Do you think Sawyer had anything to do with the fire in this place? If what Sara said about him batting his wife around, it's a good possibility."

"That thought crossed my mind too," Jess said, "but we'll keep that information to ourselves right now and take one thing at a time before we look for more. We've already got a full plate."

Gerard groaned. "You're telling me!" He nodded, "Agreed." He unlocked the door, realizing Jessie was still admiring the residence, he commented. "Are you going to get in here and do some work, or are you going to stand there and ogle the place all day?"

Jess gave him a raspberry. "I want to live here," she said, "This place looks like the Taj Mahal, for chrissake."

"I don't think you'd want this kind of life. Not all wealthy people have a good life. They only have the monetary means to buy what they want. Having expensive things doesn't define who they are—how they treat people does."

Jessie smirked. "Well, listen to you. Thanks for the dissertation, Professor Gerard."

The exterior was the classic Beaux-Arts structure, with a light brick and limestone facade extending the entire length of the dwelling. There was no question about it; the house was beautiful.

Just as Gerard was about to enter the home, he turned around to see if she was behind him. "Anytime, Detective." Hearing voices in the distance, he lingered a minute longer. A few seconds later, the woman was on her cell phone, and he could hear her telling someone about their presence.

"It won't be long before the entire friggin' neighborhood is camping out here," Gerard said sarcastically.

"Fascination," Jessie responded. "Pure fascination."

The man called out to the detectives. "Is everything all right in there?" he pointed toward the Sawyer house.

"Nothing to be alarmed about, sir. We're merely doing an investigation." The man stepped forward, encroaching on Gerard's space. Gerard's hand automatically rose in a stop gesture causing the small white dog to bark incessantly. "Sir, please step back."

The woman bent down, scooped the dog off the pavement, and cradled him in her arms, rocking him like a baby. The dog continued to growl despite the woman's attempt to control his behavior.

"Uh, sure." The man stepped back, glancing at the woman standing next to him. "But if there's something we need to be concerned about, you'll be sure to notify everyone in the neighborhood, right?"

"The operative word here, sir, is *if*. Now, please let us do our jobs."

As Gerard suspected, a parade of neighbors made their way down the sidewalk headed toward the scene.

Gerard turned to one of the two officers who'd trailed behind him. "You guys have crowd control." They both nodded their agreement, and one held up a reel of yellow tape. Gerard nodded in agreement. The tape would be an excellent barrier to keep people away.

Jessie began examining the frame around the front door. "There doesn't appear to be any point of forced entry, but let's not be hasty." With guns drawn, they entered the home, each going in different directions, one after the other, shouting "Clear." Shortly after, the team convened in the entryway to divvy the floors to check for evidence.

Jessie's mouth gaped at the statues adorning the gothic columns. Large planters housed trees. She walked over and touched a leaf. "Holy shit, these are real!" She gasped and walked around, shaking her head. "Talk about luxury? Oh, my God." She scanned the room slowly, taking it all in. "I've always wondered what this place looked like inside."

"Yeah," Gerard said, shaking his head, "but now I'm wondering where the money came from."

"How can you say that? If he has a successful dealership, he can afford all these luxuries, and besides, we can't convict on what he owns. But if all this stuff is the byproduct of ripping off the public, that's a different story."

"Yeah, but you've forgotten his dealership is in financial trouble."

"So maybe he bought this stuff when times were good."

"Okay, okay," he gave a one-shoulder shrug, "maybe you're right. I'll give him the benefit of the doubt." She grinned and walked into the living room.

Jessie's eyes opened wide when she saw the furniture. Her hand slid over the arm of an upholstered chair decorated in 18th Century French provincial. "Not necessarily my taste, but beautiful," she mumbled aloud to anyone listening.

The theme continued into the dining room with a light-colored sideboard. International antique dishes were held up by a groove on the shelf and rested against the back. The room had a long oval table with wooden chairs and thick yellow cushions on the seat. Overhead, a large elegant chandelier hung from the ceiling.

"What do you think this place is worth?" she asked her partner.

"Oh, probably a mere fifteen to twenty Mil . . . without the furnishings, maybe more."

"My God, I've never been in a home worth so much money. I only thought movie stars and sports icons lived in places like this — not car dealers." She picked up speed and walked into the kitchen, shouting a question to him along the way. "So how many people do you think live in this—" She never finished her sentence because the disgusting smell of sour milk and garbage took her breath away. The investigator snapping pictures, made a face and nodded.

"It does stink in here," he said, scrunching his nose.

Jessie called out to Gerard, who was out of sight. "Hey, Gerard. Come see this kitchen." She heard him barrel down the stairs and waited for him by the door, still holding her nose when he finally entered.

"One of the investigators just found blood on the bedroom carpet," he exclaimed before she'd had a chance to point out the mess in the kitchen.

"How much blood?"

"A drop or two, and no signs of an attempted clean up."

"Listen, if Sawyer is responsible for his wife's disappearance, would he have been foolish enough to leave so many pieces of evidence around, hoping we'd find them?" She pointed to what she'd found. "This is even worse than what the Milligans described. Shriveled pieces of fruit with cereal strewn over the counter that spilled down onto the lower cabinets now covered with caked-on milk." She covered her nose and mouth with her hand. "Would he?" she asked.

"Yeah, Sawyer's dumb like a fox," Gerard said. "He could have been in a hurry to get out of here, or he could have figured we'd never suspect him of being so careless. I'm sure they had a live-in maid. Wouldn't you think so?"

"I would think so," Jess shrugged, "but you never know. I have a feeling he's the type who didn't want any witnesses who'd tell the world what he's been doing."

Gerard eyed the room suspiciously. "You know, this could be the thing that tips the scales and blows up his entire enterprise. You and I both know that, sooner or later, these assholes screw up. He can't outsmart us forever." His eyes continued to scan the area. "If he isn't doing something illegal, our department has wasted a lot of taxpayers' money keeping the radar on him."

Unconsciously moving closer to Gerard while she checked out further, she heard him inhale deeply. Turning toward him, the sexy grin on his face told her she was standing too close. She moved away. "Oh, I'm sorry."

"Oh, trust me," he said, holding his hand, "It's okay; you smell good," he flashed another sexy smile. "It beats smelling that curdled milk on the counter." Jess didn't comment, but she sure wished she didn't feel the way she did about dating her partner. He was everything and more. She stopped her mind from wandering and changed the subject.

"You know," she said, pushing a loose curl away from her eyes, tucking it behind her ear, "we're pointing the finger at Sawyer, but what if they kidnapped him too? It's also possible someone broke into their house and wore rubber gloves. It's not uncommon for thugs to break into a vacant home and eat when they're hungry. Especially if they knew the Sawyers were away, and they wouldn't get caught."

"You're forgetting there's no forced entry, and even if they had managed to get in without a key, the alarm would have gone off?"

"Gerard, Gerard, Gerard. You're not thinking today. You want to catch Sawyer so badly you forget how easy it is for someone in the know to disarm an alarm."

"And that's why we'll check out every avenue to prove me wrong. But I don't think I am."

They both exited the kitchen leaving the investigator to continue his search for evidence, and resumed their search.

Returning to the living room, Jessie admired the beautiful fireplace at the far end with its original wood mantel. Looking around the room, she smiled at the furnishings because it made for a perfect old-time Christmas, with its tufted sofa, loveseat, and two high-back chairs. A corner curio cabinet housed a variety of porcelain flowers and several tiny teacups.

A melancholy feeling punched in the pit of her stomach as she remembered the last holiday she'd spent with her mother and father as a family. Christmas no longer held the same excitement it once had. She pictured a Christmas tree from the ceiling to the floor covered with real candles, although she wasn't sure what they used for lights during that era. She imagined the tree covered with red velvet bows and ornaments. She even pictured stockings hanging from the mantle. Curious, she crossed the room to check for nail holes in the front of the thick wood. She smiled when she ran her hand across the front and allowed her fingers to stop at each hole when she spotted more blood on the carpet.

She called out to her partner again. He walked down the stairs and into the room.

"What did you find in here?" he asked.

She headed out of the room just as Gerard's phone rang.

"Detective Gerard here." His head nodded in the affirmative. "Good job, Dave. That's what I've been suspecting." He nodded again. "Yep. Thanks." He turned to his partner, apparently hearing her footsteps. "I think we're winning this one, Jessie."

"What's happening?"

"I think we got him." She watched him key in a number. "Yeah, Lieutenant, Gerard here. We have enough evidence to suspect Sawyer. I sent officers out to canvas the neighbors to find out what they know about the Sawyers, and a woman by the name of Jane Clayton, who lives down the other end of the block, said her daughter Marti and Sawyer's daughter are best friends. The last time she saw Sawyer was when she'd dropped Gabi off after lunch the next day, and Sawyer was waiting in his car with the engine running. The wife wasn't in the car, and she said Sawyer seemed preoccupied, looked terrible, like he hadn't slept in a while. Jane had expected him to initiate a conversation, but he drove off when Gabi was in the car. She didn't have anything else to add but said she'd call us as soon as she spoke to her daughter or if she thought of anything else. Jess and I also found blood on the carpets. One spot upstairs in the bedroom, one in the living room."

Gerard walked over to his partner while he spoke to Harwell so that she could hear the conversation. He tapped her shoulder and mouthed Harwell's name. "We have a large crowd of neighbors outside, asking questions. We'll let the investigators finish here while Jessie and I head back to the dealership to see what we can find out about his whereabouts." He gave Jessie the thumbs-up sign and flashed another smile. "Yep. I want this bastard as much as you do. We'll keep you posted."

CHAPTER 14

It was dark outside when Lieutenant Jack Harwell parked his car in front of his home. Exhausted from a long day, he exited the vehicle. A cool rush of air breezed against his face, reminding him winter was just around the corner. He loved the cool nights and the warm Indian summer days they'd been having. September had always been his favorite time of year when the leaves began to change color like a vivid oil painting.

He stopped to admire the maze of brilliant colors the leaves show-cased in the soft glow hosted by the streetlights. Warm thoughts flooded his mind and brought him back to the happy memories of his childhood.

The lingering smell of burnt leaves captured his senses, like comfort food. He drew in the pleasant odor and remembered how he and his brother used to jump into the giant mound of leaves raked up by his father, causing the pile to deflate into a brown carpet across the lawn. He pictured his father, who would pretend to be upset, sneak up behind the two of them, and tackle his sons to the ground. He subconsciously brushed his sleeve as though removing the leaves his dad threw over the top of them. A wave of sadness washed over him, making him wish he had that time to spend with his son. He wondered how his father, a homicide detective in NYPD, had found the time to do it.

The distinctive smell of meatloaf escaped when he opened the front door to his home, and his mouth salivated. He could hear his wife banging pots in the kitchen. She turned to face him when he came through the door. "Dinner's almost ready, Jack."

He leaned over and kissed her hello. "Mmm, it smells pretty good in here. I'm hungry."

"Good," she said, "I made meatloaf."

"I know. That smell hit me the minute I opened the door." He smiled. "Where's Max?"

"He's holed up in his room with a ton of homework."

"How was your day, Hon?" he asked.

"My day?" She made a face. "Well, let's see. I had a pile of laundry to do, grocery shopping at the market, and then I came home and cleaned and made dinner. That's how my day was," she answered, disgruntled.

Jack recognized her mood and backed off. He reached for the stack of mail on the counter and leafed through the pile. Jack wasn't in any mood to argue tonight. He was tired and hungry; all he wanted to do was put his feet up and read the newspaper.

"So, how was your day?" she asked.

"Uneventful," he said while tearing the edge of an envelope.

"That doesn't sound good. What happened? No bad guys out there today?" He gave a dismissive shrug of his shoulder and continued to open the mail. "I guess that means you can't talk about it." She stared at him impatiently, waiting for a response.

He placed the mail on the counter and rubbed his eyes with his hand. "It's been a very long day, Ginny."

"How's the old girlfriend working out?"

"For chrissake, Ginny. I'm tired of hearing this shit when I walk through the door every night. I don't even want to come home anymore. It was a long time ago -- long before we had a relationship."

"Well, actually not. You decided to screw me while you were dating her. Remember? Only I got pregnant." Her lips curled at the sides.

"Once a cheater, always a cheater. I'll bet seeing her again brings back lots of memories. I have no doubt you're doing the same thing to me. Gives you goosebumps, doesn't it, Jack?" she sneered.

"Yeah, it sends chills down my spine," he shot back.

"Did you know she was at this precinct when you accepted the job?" She leered. "I don't understand why you had to transfer to the precinct where she worked."

He exhaled and headed upstairs toward Max's room. "And I'm sure you never will."

"Dinner's ready in five minutes," she said caustically. She pulled plates from the cupboard and banged them onto the counter.

He shuddered from the loud noise and wondered if she'd broken the dishes. He knew better than to ask. The woman couldn't help herself. She always found a way to ruin a family evening for him. He reached the top of the stairs, knocked on Max's bedroom door, and stuck his head in without permission. "Max, it's time for dinner."

Max seemed startled by the intrusion. "Oh, okay, Dad."

"Can I come in?"

"Sure, Dad."

Jack walked inside, sat on his son's bed, and patted his hand on the surface, motioning for Max to sit beside him. On his way home, Jack decided to ask Max, in a non-accusatory manner, about the missing cassette from the surveillance equipment. Lord knew he'd been privy to all kinds of accusations from his wife. He didn't want Max to experience that feeling. Jack leaned over and gave Max a hug when his son sat down next to him. "How was school today, champ?"

"Boring." He groaned. "I've got a ton of homework . . . but I'm almost finished."

"Need any help?"

"Thanks, but I'm okay."

"All right." Jack pursed his lips. "Hey, Max, before we go downstairs, can I ask you something?"

"Sure, Dad. What?"

"Well, we never finished our conversation about the missing cassette. I could have sworn there was one in the machine when I brought it home, but I can't be positive." He fixed his eyes on his son's face to gauge his reaction.

"Gee, I don't know, Dad," Max's hand tapped the bed nervously.

"Max? You weren't using the equipment again, were you?"

Max jumped off the bed and stood. "No, Dad, but I did show Richie how it worked . . . I didn't take it off the table, though," he said nervously. "Don't you have more blank cassettes?"

"Of course I do, but I'm trying to determine if the officer who used the equipment last followed protocol. My staff has been instructed to remove the cassette from their session if it has a recording on it and replace it with a new one." He shrugged. "We need to safeguard those recordings. Can you imagine what would happen to evidence on the cassette if the officer forgot to replace it with a new one, and the next guy taped over it?"

Jack glanced over at his son, whose eyes were fixed straight ahead. He knew Max was lying because he feared what would happen to him. Jack had to admit he'd been pretty hard on the boy the last time he used the equipment without permission. He decided to let it go for now. Jack remembered being as curious as Max when he was his age. He smiled to himself at the similarities between them.

"I'm sorry, Dad. I wish I could help."

"Okay, Max, I guess I was mistaken."

The two walked downstairs and took their places at the table. Ginny brought the steaming hot food to the table, filled their plates, and placed the dishes in front of each.

Dinner in the Harwell dining room was tranquil except for the clicking of utensils against the plates. Max loved his mother's meatloaf and mashed potatoes smothered in gravy. It was his favorite meal. He cleaned his plate and added a second helping. His parents barely said a word throughout the meal. He didn't understand why things had changed since his father had taken this new job, but his mother's behavior toward his father had become nightmarish in their household. When Max swallowed the last fork full of food, he asked to be excused from the dinner table.

"Yes, Max," Ginny said. "Don't forget to take your plate into the kitchen."

"Okay, Mom." Max rushed into the kitchen, placed his dish and silverware inside the dishwasher, and then walked back into the dining room.

"Is it okay if I return to my room and finish my homework?" he asked his parents.

"Sure." Jack also stood and removed his plate and utensils from the table, leaving his wife alone. Max watched him enter the kitchen, then cross the room toward his office and close the door without saying a word. When the lock clicked into place, Max looked at his mother's expression, and he shared the sadness she felt.

He walked over to her and kissed her on the cheek. "Dinner was awesome, Mom. Thanks." She nodded and remained silent. He bolted for the stairs and closed his bedroom door when he reached the top.

He didn't like telling his father lies, but this time was necessary. A guilty feeling tightened his stomach muscles, and the first thing he thought about was a trip to the confessional to tell Father McKinley he'd lied to his dad. His mind raced, figuring out how to make it right without getting caught. If he put the cassette on the floor somewhere in the basement, his father would assume he dropped it, and things would be back to normal. His stomach tightened again just thinking about it. He keyed in Ritchie's number.

"Ritchie, my dad's asking a lot of questions."

"Questions about what?"

"The missing cassette."

"I told you. Why don't you just tell your father the truth?"

"I can't, Ritchie . . . Especially since I lied again tonight." Max sighed and wondered why he'd called Ritchie for support. He'd never been supportive in situations like this. "Okay, I'd better get back to my homework. I just thought you might have an answer for me."

"Yeah, I do. Tell your dad the truth and face the music."

"I just told you, Rich, I can't do that."

"Well, have you listened to the recording? Maybe there's a bunch of nonsense on the cassette, and you can erase it."

"I have nothing I can use to listen to the cassette. Dad took the equipment back to the precinct."

"Well, you'd better pray he brings it home again." The boy paused. "I hate to say it, Maxie, but you really should have thought—"

Ritchie's comment stung like an arrow to the heart. He interrupted his friend, vowing to conduct his future investigative work by himself. "Yeah, thanks, Richie," he said sarcastically.

"I know you don't like to hear this stuff, Max, but just because your dad is a cop and you want to be one doesn't mean you should play detective. You could wind up getting killed or something."

"Yeah, right. I have a better chance of getting killed by my father." He shook his head and chastised himself again for calling Ritchie.

"But, you're just asking for trouble."

"When did you take on the role of my self-proclaimed Guardian Angel?" Max could hear Ritchie sigh. "Geez, Ritchie. I called you for support. I should have known better." He rubbed his hand through his hair. "I have to go." He started to flip his phone shut when Ritchie's voice rang out.

"Hey, want to come over tomorrow after school? Mom says I have to babysit my sister so she can go to the store. We can watch a movie or something."

"No. I've gotta go."

"Wait. Don't hang up. I'm sorry, Max. I shouldn't be such a jerk."

"Right. You shouldn't. I have to go. See you at school." Max clicked off the call and sat on the edge of his bed when the smell of rich buttery pie crust filled the air. He knew his mother had made his favorite--cherry pie. He remembered the last time she'd made it, the feel of the crust crunching between his teeth, the release of sweet liquid when he bit into the plump cherries. It made his mouth water. But tonight, he had to pass on his favorite dessert. It would kill him, but he needed to avoid his father or risk another onslaught of questions. He wasn't sure how long he could keep up this charade.

Opening his closet door, Max pushed his clothes aside. Holding onto the doorframe with one hand, he braced himself enough to reach inside his secret hiding place for the cassette and pulled it out. Max tossed the cassette on the bed and remembered his old recorder. The one he used to listen to Dr. Seuss tapes and prayed the mini-cassette would fit. Rummaging through his old toy chest, Max was hopeful he'd find the small Sony when he heard his father's voice call him from downstairs. He ran to the door before his father could walk up the steps.

"Yeah, Dad," he said, sticking his head out the door.

"C'mon down. Mom made your favorite dessert."

"Uh, Dad, I'm not done with my homework yet. Maybe later."

"You can't be serious. You're passing on your mother's homemade cherry pie and ice cream?"

"Save me a piece, will you?" Max shut the door and continued rummaging through his toy chest. A sudden series of thuds on the stairs made him panic—his father was on his way up to his room. He quickly closed the toy chest, grabbed the first thing closest to him to make his father think he was studying, and jumped on his bed, making sure to sit on the cassette just as his bedroom door creaked open. His heart was pounding furiously. He took a deep breath, afraid his father would notice his nervousness.

"Are you okay, son?" Jack asked. "I can't believe you're passing on cherry pie."

"It's okay, Dad."

"All right. If you're sure." His father turned around and started to walk away.

"Oh, Dad," he called after him, remembering he had a little matter to clear up. His father stopped and turned to face him.

"What, son?"

"I do remember something about the recorder. I don't know why I didn't think of this when you asked me, but there wasn't any cassette in the recorder. As I said, Dad, I was trying to show Ritchie how it worked, and without the cassette, I couldn't show him anything." He shrugged, "so I just told him how to set it up."

"Oh, okay, son, I guess that makes sense. That's just what I was worried about." He nodded. "All right, I'll take this up with the last person who used the equipment. There'll be hell to pay tomorrow."

When he left the room, Max exhaled a sigh of relief that he was gone, but his stomach felt like someone was continuously punching him. Maybe his dad wouldn't be so hard on the officer. He waited a few more minutes until he could no longer hear his father's footsteps. He quickly jumped off the bed and rummaged through his toy chest again but gave up when he didn't see the recorder. He walked to his closet to return the cassette to its secret hiding place and continued doing his homework, trying not to think about the officer he'd just gotten into trouble or the cherry pie he'd just passed on.

CHAPTER 15

*J*essie walked to her desk with a container of coffee. Her partner was already at his desk, his feet propped up on top, eating a powdered donut.

"You're going to get fat from all those trans-fatty foods you're consuming, hotshot."

"Yeah, my mother used to tell me the same thing, but I work out, so I can eat all I want." He waved the box past her nose. "Want one?"

"No, thanks. I've already had breakfast." Her cell phone chimed its melodic ringtone.

"Detective Kensington." She poked him in the arm so he'd pay attention and pointed to her phone. "Yes, Mrs. Clayton." He sat upright, leaning in to hear above the noisy office. She rested her hip against his desk, automatically wiping a dot of white powder off the corner of his mouth with her fingers. He gave an appreciative grin.

"She did?" Jessie said and gave him the thumbs-up signal. "Okay, terrific. When would be a good time for us to meet with Marti?" She smiled excitedly. "Wonderful. Thank you, Mrs. Clayton. This is the first positive news we've received so far. Detective Gerard and I will be there by ten-thirty this morning." She disconnected the call.

"Sounds like good news," Gerard said.

"It was. Jane Clayton said after our cold canvas, she thought about her daughter Marti and wondered if the kid had communicated with Gabrielle since they'd last seen each other. Marti is visiting with her grandmother today, but after talking to her daughter, she said Marti confirmed she heard from the Sawyer girl and agreed to talk to us -- at her parent's insistence."

"Finally! Did she say where the Sawyer kid was calling from?"

"Mrs. Clayton didn't go into detail. She said Marti was reluctant to discuss it with her, fearing she'd get the Sawyer kid in trouble, but they assured her she'd be helping her friend. Mrs. Clayton picked up Marti from her grandmother's and is home today. Hopefully, she'll give us something to help build this case." He gave her a sexy smile. "What?" she said.

"Thank you for taking care of me." He squeezed her arm.

"Oh, Christ, don't get all syrupy on me just because I wiped your mouth. I didn't want sugar falling onto the report." He winked, and she thought her heart would jump out of her chest. Damn it. She was furious at herself for continuing to react to him as she did. He stared at her with a slight grin, almost as if reading her thoughts. She cleared her throat. "After we talk to her, she'll return to her grandmother's house for the rest of the week, so it's probably prudent for us to make up a list of questions we want to ask her before going to the house. Mrs. Clayton said she doesn't mind being cooperative but doesn't want to freak her daughter out. So, let's get as much as possible while the fire's hot."

* * *

Gerard pulled up in front of the Clayton residence at the end of West 87th Street, several doors down from the Sawyers. Jessie rang the bell.

"You should be the one to interview the young girl," he said, "I think she'll relate a lot better to you than to me."

"I agree."

"Who is it?" a woman's voice rang out through the intercom.

"Detectives Kensington and Gerard, NYPD."

The door opened. "Please come inside. The Claytons are expecting you."

"Detectives," Jane Clayton said, walking toward them. She extended her hand in greeting. "We're all in the den."

Jane was an attractive woman. Her dress and short trendy hairstyle complimented her features. They followed behind and saw a young child curled up on a chair; her face flooded with conflicting emotions. "This is Marti." Jessie smiled and nodded a greeting. "Please have a seat," Mrs. Clayton said, gesturing to the sofa across from the child.

Jessie pointed to the ottoman in front of the young girl so she'd be closer to Marti, and Jane shook her head in agreement.

"Hi Marti, I'm Detective Kensington. Thank you for agreeing to talk to us about your friend, Gabi. I'm sure you're worried about her safety, and I want to put your mind at ease assuring you we will do whatever we can to find her."

The young girl's mouth creased into a half-smile. Gerard reached inside his briefcase and removed the recorder from the case, placing it on the coffee table in preparation for the interview. It was evident Marti felt anxious.

Robert Clayton stood and walked over to his daughter, squatting on the floor before her. "Marti, don't be nervous. These detectives will ask you some questions about your conversation with Gabi. Okay, sweetie?" She gave him a blank stare. "And you're not going to get into trouble, so take a deep breath, and answer whatever they ask. Okay?"

"Yes, Dad," she said with a slight smirk.

"Are you ready?" Gerard asked before turning on the recorder.

Marti nodded, then turned her attention toward Jessie. "I'm really scared for Gabi," she said.

"Why are you scared for her, Marti?" Jessie asked. "Did she say something that made you worry?"

"No. But Gabi's dad came into the room and yelled at her."

"Dads do that sometimes."

"I know," she said, glancing at her father. "But not like this. His voice sounded mean—like he was going to hurt her." Tears welled in the child's eyes.

Jane Clayton made her way over to comfort her daughter. "It's okay, sweetie. You're doing a good thing for Gabi, so don't worry." She brushed away a stray hair from her daughter's eyes.

Jessie changed the subject to take the pressure off Marti. "So, what grade are you in, Marti?"

"I'm in the fifth grade at St. Catherine's."

"Oh?" Marti nodded. "I know someone who goes there, and I think he may even be in the fifth grade. His name is Max Harwell. Do you know him?"

"Really?" She grinned. "I know, Max." She smiled. "He's in the seventh grade, though. I know his friend, Ritchie too. Gabi's got a crush on Max." She gasped, then quickly covered her mouth with both hands, seemingly embarrassed about revealing her friend's secret.

"Not to worry," Jessie placed her hand on her heart. "Your secret is safe with me." Marti smiled, obviously feeling better about the detective. "Do you have to take the subway to St. Catherine's?"

"Yeah, Gabi and I both do. Most of the kids do because we all live so far away."

"It's an outstanding school," Jane Clayton added. She smiled at her daughter.

"Will you tell me about the conversation you and Gabi had?"

"We didn't talk that long."

"That's okay. Whatever you can remember will be very helpful. And, even after we leave here, you can always call me if you think of something else." Jessie handed Marti her business card. "You keep this card, and whenever you want to talk to me, you can reach me at this number. Okay?" She nodded again. "Okay, do you remember what day she called?"

"I think it was on Friday. No, wait." She looked over at her mother. "Mommy, is that the day we shopped?"

"No, sweetie, we shopped on Thursday."

"Right. That's the night she called." Her face flushed. "Sorry. I'm a little nervous."

Jessie reassured the child one more time. "Sweetheart, you don't need to be. Gabi would be pleased if she knew how much you cared

THE LAST WITNESS - BOOK 1

about her." Jessie held her hand. "Honest, and one day you'll look back on this and know you did the right thing."

"I hope so. I don't want Gabi to get mad at me."

"Did she call you on your cell or house phone?"

Marti pulled her cell phone out of her jeans pocket and held it in the air. "She called me on my cell." Her fingers flipped through the screens with speed. "Gabi called me Thursday night at ten-thirty."

"Can I have the phone number she called you from?"

"Of course, but I don't think it works anymore." Her eyes watered again. "That's why her father yelled. She was using his cell phone."

"Gabi doesn't have her cell phone?"

"No. Patrick won't let her have one," Jane said.

Jessie tried to hide her surprise. Most kids Gabi's age were most likely on their second phones. "Was he very strict with her?"

"No." Her eyes opened wide. "And that's why I'm worried. He never yells at her . . . and not like this."

"Why won't he let her have a cell phone?"

"He doesn't want her to become a spoiled brat."

"Oh." Jessie gave her partner a brief look. That was probably the first sensible thing Patrick Sawyer had ever done. "But was Gabi allowed to use her father's cell phone?" she asked.

"No."

"Do you think that's why he yelled? Did she take the phone without asking for permission?"

"I think so." Another tear ran down her cheek. "I should have stopped asking her questions. She wanted me to do something for her."

"Maybe she'll call back."

"I hope so . . . cause I'm going to be scared until she does."

"Can you tell me what you discussed before her father entered?"

"Well, I was surprised she called because Mommy and I saw Mrs. Simon at the mall. She's the school secretary at St. Catherine's and asked me if Gabi was having a good time on her cruise." Her eyes widened. "Mrs. Simon knows we're friends." Marti stopped talking and took in a deep breath.

"It's okay, Marti. Take your time."

"Thank you." She swallowed hard. "I mean, Gabi and I tell each other everything, so I was a little mad that she didn't even tell me she was going on a cruise when she'd slept over at my house for two days before her dad picked her up. You know, like, how could she forget to tell me something so exciting?"

"Do you think her dad was trying to surprise her?"

"Um, well, she did say that after I asked. She thought her father was waiting for her mom to return before they left. Oh, and then she said her dad was acting different since her mom was away . . . like he was giving her a lot of surprises."

"How different?"

"She didn't say."

"Okay, so you asked her how the cruise was, and she said?"

Marti seemed more relaxed now. "She said they weren't on a cruise . . . they were at her dad's cousin's house." She touched her chin. "I think she said her name was Maria."

"Did Gabi say where Maria lived?"

"No, we didn't get that far."

"Okay, did she say anything else about her mom?"

"That was why she was calling. She told me her mother was in Ohio with her Aunt Sissy, and her dad didn't have her aunt's phone number in his new phone. That's why she couldn't talk to her."

"Doesn't her mom have a cell phone?"

"Yeah," Marti nodded, "she does. But maybe it wasn't working?" Marti shrugged again. "She wanted me to do something for her." Marti hunched her shoulders. "I don't know what it was though, but that's when her father walked into the room and shouted—" Marti stopped talking and looked at her parents as if waiting for their approval before continuing.

"Go ahead, Marti," Mrs. Clayton said. "It's okay for you to repeat the exact words Mr. Sawyer used."

Marti took in another breath. "He shouted, 'What the hell are you doing?'. . . then the phone went dead." She shrugged.

"That's good information, Marti. And you've never heard Mr. Sawyer raise his voice like that to Gabi?"

"No . . . That's why I'm scared for her. She only wanted to talk to her mom."

"It sounds that way. Well, is there anything else you'd like to add?"

"No. That's all I know." The young girl looked over at her parents. "Mommy, can I go back to Grandma's now?"

"As soon as we finish with the detectives. You run along to your room. Daddy and I have a few more things to discuss."

"Okay."

"Marti," Detective Kensington said, "Thank you for all your help. You did a great job today." The young girl smiled back and took off like a shot in the opposite direction.

"Marti," her father called after her. "Please leave your cell phone here so the detectives can take the phone number Gabi called from."

"Oh, yeah," she gave a weak giggle. "Sorry," she said, hesitantly handing her phone to the detective.

Jessie sensed her reluctance and reassured her. "I'll tell you what. If you stand right here, I'll return it to you as soon as I write the number down. Okay?" The young girl nodded. "Oh, and Marti, one more thing," Jessie added, "Please don't discuss this conversation with any of your friends."

"I won't." She took her phone and left the room.

Gerard stopped the recorder. "Thanks, Marti," he said, barely catching her before she was bounding up the steps, taking two at a time. Gerard smiled and turned to the parents. "Thank you very much for allowing us to talk with your daughter," he said. "The information she provided brings us closer to solving this mystery. Do you mind if we ask you a few questions?"

"Not at all. We're happy to help."

"I'm going to turn the recorder back on," Gerard said.

"That's fine, Detective," Mr. Clayton responded.

"How well did you know the Sawyers?" Gerard asked.

"We weren't close friends, if that's what you're asking. Patrick has always been very nice around us. We've attended several of their new car launching parties, but so do a lot of other people."

"New car launching parties?" Jessie asked.

"Yes, mostly," the wife added. "Patrick always made it sound as though he wanted us to be the first to see the new cars, but what he wanted was for his guests to buy one." She chuckled. "I have no doubt that was why we got the invitation." Glancing at her husband, she continued. "Don't you think?"

"Of course. I mean, it's not like we socialized with the Sawyers. The best way to describe our relationship with him was at the acquaintance level."

"Do you know who their closest friends are?"

"Uh, seriously? I don't think they have any," he said with a tilt of his head.

Jane nodded in agreement. "Although I have to say, Amanda and I were much closer. We've shopped together a few times. We were developing a nice friendship, then something happened, and we lost contact."

"You don't know what that was?"

"No. I don't know. Maybe Amanda was too busy. I shouldn't be saying things I'm not sure about."

"Do you remember what happened the last time you saw her? Did she have any bruising on her body?"

Jane jerked her head back in surprise. "Why? Do you suspect him of being a wife-beater?"

"We don't know. We're checking out every possibility. We know we haven't been able to prove the Sawyers are on a cruise."

"Oh my God," Jane said, turning her head away. Lines of deep concentration gathered on her forehead. "I should have realized something was wrong several weeks ago when we tried on clothes at Neiman Marcus." Both detectives sat a little straighter. "She had a long bruise that ran the length of her thigh."

"Did you ask her about it?" Jessie asked.

"I did."

"How did she explain the mark?"

"She told me she was walking down to the basement of her home and felt faint. When she came to, she found herself on the basement floor." Jane shook her head in bafflement. "Amanda said they'd been hoping for another child. You see, Patrick is an only child, and Amanda, in particular, didn't want Gabi to grow up without the experience of a sibling. She didn't even care that Gabi was ten or that she was in her forties; she still wanted more. Patrick, too, for that matter. She told me he wanted a house full of kids, but the poor thing couldn't seem to carry full term. She miscarried several times."

Jessie nodded. "That's what we've heard."

Jane shook her head in despair while staring into space, deep in thought. She finally turned toward Jessie. "Amanda was hoping the cause of her passing out meant she was pregnant. She planned to see her doctor, but I never heard anything beyond that." She paused. "I guess that was around the time when we stopped seeing each other." Jane's brows rose as she released a sigh. "I've been curious, even going so far as to ask Gabi how her mother was doing, hoping she'd tell me Amanda was pregnant, but Gabi tells me she's fine. Since I haven't heard anything, I can only presume she wasn't."

Jessie smiled, but that didn't stop her mind from buzzing with speculation as she wondered if Sawyer was the one who prevented his wife from seeing Jane, afraid she'd find out his secret. "You wouldn't happen to know her doctor's name, would you?"

"Sorry. I don't. I last saw Amanda two months ago, just in passing. As for Patrick, the last time I saw him was when he picked Gabi up in his fancy new car with the engine running."

"How did you know the engine was running? Mercedes' are very quiet." Jessie asked.

"I didn't even realize it was him because he was in a different car. Not until I saw Gabi pressing her nose against the window. I wanted to be sure she wasn't getting into some stranger's car, so I waited. Patrick finally rolled down the window. I'm sure he saw the concerned look on my face." She shrugged.

"Okay, I think we have enough information for now. If we have more questions, I hope you won't mind if we come back to you."

"Not at all. We're happy to help."

* * *

Jessie pulled her cell phone out of her pocket on her way back to the car and punched in Sawyer's phone number. "Humph," she said, "Marti was right. Sawyer's phone is disconnected." Her face formed into a scowl.

"A disconnected phone number. Why would Sawyer do that?" The scowl deepened. "Especially if his wife is away and doesn't have her phone. This whole thing sounds fishy -- like he's trying to hide something."

"That's for sure."

"Okay, let's see what our computer analyst can learn about Sawyer's family tree." Jessie put the phone on speaker and gave Gerard a devilish grin. "I think you should talk to her. You know how much she loves you."

"Oh yeah, I'd forgotten how much," he winked. His mouth creased into a smile when Crystal answered. "Hey, pretty lady, Gerard here."

"Ooh, sexy man," she purred. Gerard glanced over at Jessie and stifled his laughter. "I've been waiting for your call. Whatcha got for me."

"Check out Patrick Sawyer, West 87th Street, his dealership, and any other place his name appears to see if you can find someone named Maria in his life. We don't have a last name for her, but we think she's a relative, so see what you can find."

"I'm on it." She hummed as she worked. "I haven't heard from you in a while. Where have you been?"

"My partner has me busting my ass over here, sweetness. Why? Did you miss me?" he flirted.

"You know it, baby." He glanced over at his partner, who was now rolling her eyes.

"Let's see. Hmm, I don't see a Maria on the family tree here. Not anywhere on this list. Do you know where she lives?"

"Crystal . . . seriously, would I have called you if I knew the address?"

"Oh yeah—right." She giggled like a teenager.

"How many Marias have purchased cars from his dealership in the last six months? Get back to me as soon as possible, sweetheart, okay?"

"Ooh, you called me sweetheart . . . is that a proposal?"

He laughed. "No. Jessie James over here says I'm not the marrying kind."

"You're not? Oh, I'm so disappointed." She sighed. "Okay," she said in a business-like manner, "let me work my magic. I'll get back to you."

"Thank you." He flipped the phone shut and pulled away from the curb, easing into the stagnated traffic. Gerard glanced over at Jessie and nodded. "I know you're jealous!"

"You wish."

He nodded his head in the affirmative. "Yep, you're jealous! I can see it on your face."

"Don't flatter yourself, Gerard."

"Ooh, I love it when you're mean to me." Every time he glanced her way to check her facial expressions, he found himself winking at her. "Yeah, you're jealous," he said.

"Pay attention to your driving."

"Yes, yes, yes," he said, raising his fist, "there is a God. The foxy redhead sitting next to me is falling in love with me." He dipped his head down and looked up toward the sky, "Now God, if you could help her admit it, I'd sure appreciate it." He turned toward her and kissed the air.

"You are so pathetic!"

Gerard's cell phone rang. He pressed the speaker button and laid the phone on the seat between them. "Okay, Crystal. What have you got for me?"

"I found two Marias connected to Sawyer in the database. One is Maria Watson. The other is Maria Alexander."

"Well, that certainly makes life easier." He frowned. How can there only be two? In all of New York?"

She chuckled. "There are more, but this is a good place to start. So, being the efficient employee I am, I dug a little deeper, and there are one-hundred twenty-one Maria Watsons and sixty-one Maria

Alexanders in New York. After I give you the addresses for these two women, I'll check on the other one hundred seventy-nine to see if Sawyer is in the picture."

"That's my girl."

She giggled again. "So, write this down—" A loud ear-popping sound paused the conversation.

"What the hell was that?"

"Sorry, I'm chewing bubble gum, and—"

"Right," he interrupted, "and you blew a face-smacking bubble."

"Well, yeah. Sort of."

"Crystal," he said in a firm voice, "this is important."

"I'm sorry." She cleared her throat. "Okay, Maria Watson purchased a CLK convertible from the dealership in February of this year, and . . . Maria Alexander purchased an SL500. Hmm, and it looks like she also worked for the dealership."

"Which one?"

"Maria Alexander."

"In what capacity?" Gerard asked.

"It doesn't tell me, but here are the addresses."

"Hold on a second." He turned to Jessie, "You ready?" She nodded and keyed the information into her cell phone. "Okay, Crystal, we'll catch up with you later," Gerard said. "Thanks for your help."

Looking at his profile, Jess wanted to scream that he was right. She was jealous of any woman who paid attention to him regardless of whether or not she had the right to feel that way. Falling for him would be so easy. Hell, who was she kidding? She was crazy about him, dammit. She couldn't even remember their love-making, but something was different between them—a special bond. The thought squeezed her heart. She sighed. What the hell was she doing to herself? She tried to distract herself by glancing at the crowded side-walk from the side window. She couldn't stop the emotional attachment she felt for him. Maybe considering another assignment was the thing to do. That thought made her head jerk back.

Gerard noticed. "Hey, what's going on over there?"

"What do you mean?"

"You were sighing and nodding your head over there." He grinned, and the sparkle in his eyes had her heart beating faster. "You're thinking about us, aren't you?"

"Gerard," she said, "you must stop talking to Crystal. She inflates your ego way too much. She has you thinking everyone wants you. Get a grip, will you?"

He threw his head back and laughed. "Is that what you think?" She nodded. "You're full of it. I see you peeking at me when you don't think I know." His face cracked into a wide grin. "You're wondering if you should give in to it, right?"

Jess rolled her eyes. Was he reading her mind? Were her thoughts that transparent? "In your dreams, bud."

"You are in my dreams," Gerard said.

"Yeah, you're in mine too, only they're nightmares."

"Is that a fact?"

"That's a fact." A bemused smile curled the corners of her mouth. Oh, he'd been in her dreams, alright—every night. He was all she could think about these days. Maybe she should give in to it? Jess blew out a breath. Cripes, that meant getting used to another partner—the last thing she wanted. She enjoyed working with him. Zach Gerard was easy on the eyes and fun to be around when he wasn't a jerk. And there was the banter between them—she'd miss that, but would dating him ruin their relationship? Jess swallowed hard, trying to stop her mind from working overtime. She was the one who needed to get a grip. Daydreaming about a relationship with Gerard was far better than getting involved with him. He glanced her way when she changed the subject.

"How do you think Harwell will take the news about the prospects of putting Patrick Sawyer away?"

"Are you kidding? We'll have him dancing down the halls of the precinct."

"Harwell? Dancing down the halls? Unemotional, Harwell? Now that would be a hoot." She snickered. "What a visual. Can't you just picture Harwell as the dancing baby from the Ally McBeal show?" They burst out laughing.

"Okay," he said between bouts of laughter, "maybe that was stretching it a bit, but you get the point."

"I do."

He reached across the seat and grabbed her hand, and squeezed it. His touch was like an electric current charging through her body. When her heart skipped a beat, she pulled back instead of allowing herself to enjoy it. He gave her a blank stare. "Why do you make this so difficult?" he asked.

"I was young and naïve when I got involved with Harwell. I should have known better, but I convinced myself we were in love. Now, look where it's gotten me. Threatening notes, a reputation that has followed me from one job to the next, and now I'm working for the man who dumped me on my ass. Do you think I want to risk more of that shit?"

"What you're saying is if we didn't work on the same force, we could have a relationship? Wow!" He stopped talking and glanced at her with a blank expression. "I told you before; I don't have a problem asking for a transfer."

"Stop." She held her hand up. "You're killing me over here." He was just too damn sexy for his own

good.

"By the way, how's that list of people coming along?" he asked.

"Geez, I feel like I've stepped into a cold shower."

"Hey, we can still talk about getting together."

"No, let's leave it where it was—on the back burner. I haven't gotten very far with the list." She shrugged. "I can't stop thinking about this case; quite frankly, this is more important."

"The lieutenant will be all over your ass if you don't provide him with that list."

"I don't know how many ways I can say this to you, Gerard, but this case is more important."

"More important than your life?"

"Let's solve the case first, then we'll worry about my life," she said. "Besides, I haven't received any notes for a while."

"Yeah, what has it been . . . seven whole days since the last one?"

CHAPTER 16

*D*etective Gerard pressed the doorbell to the home of Maria Watson. He could see her silhouette through the front door sidelights as she walked toward them.

"I'll keep her occupied," Gerard said, "but you do the bathroom thing so you can see if there are any signs of Sawyer being here." She nodded.

Ms. Watson opened the door as far as the chain would allow and peered out.

"Can I help you?" she asked.

"Mrs. Watson, we're Detectives Kensington and Gerard from the two-one precinct, NYPD. We want to ask you a few questions about your interaction with the Sawyer Mercedes dealership on Broadway. Your name was on the list as having purchased a car within the last six months. Can we speak to you for a moment?"

"Sure." When the woman opened the door, the frown on her face softened into a sexy smile when she caught a glimpse of Gerard. "It's Miss."

"Sorry," he responded. "We're investigating an Identity Theft," he lied.

"Whose identity—mine or Mr. Sawyer's?" she asked.

"His ma'am. Can we come inside so we can ask you a few questions?"

"Certainly." She moved aside to allow their entry. Jessie looked around before she led them into a small garden room filled with large plants. She gestured toward a light blue wicker sofa covered with billowy flowered pillows. "Please have a seat." They both sat down. "Can I offer you a cold drink?"

"No, thank you," Jessie declined, "but, may I please use your bathroom?"

"Of course, dear." The woman stood and pointed. "It's down the hall and to the left."

"Thank you."

Maria Watson eased herself back down on the chair across from Gerard. She crossed her legs, her short skirt revealing more than Gerard wanted to see from a woman who appeared to be in her late sixties. "So, how can I help?"

"When was the last time you saw Mr. Sawyer?"

"This is a little embarrassing, but I don't mind telling you." She laughed. "I have a convertible and was having difficulty getting the top down. You know, it stopped halfway and wouldn't go any further no matter what I did." She made a face as she shrugged. "I drove to the dealership, hoping he was still open. Fortunately, he was. Other than that, I've never had real contact with him." Her eyebrows knitted together in confusion. "Is Mr. Sawyer in trouble with his dealership now because of identity theft?"

"No," Gerard said, "not at all, ma'am. We're just checking everyone on the list."

"That has to be a lot of people."

"It is, but other members of the precinct are helping out, so it shouldn't be bad."

Jessie returned and gave Gerard a nod to let him know she hadn't found anything."

"I wish I could be more help," the woman said. "He's such a lovely man. I'd hate to think of anyone trying to hurt him." She smiled slightly. "But I know the NYPD will take care of him."

"That's for sure," Gerard said as he stood. "Thank you for speaking with us today. If you think of anything, here's my card."

"I will do that," Miss Watson said, shoving Gerard's card into her bra.

Jessie couldn't help but laugh at Gerard's reaction. "You have a lovely home," Jess said.

"Thank you, dear. I've lived here for several years by myself. I'm not complaining, you understand, but I thought I'd have a husband, children, and grandchildren by now, but I guess it just wasn't in the cards for me." She smiled broadly at Gerard. "Of course, I'm always looking for that special someone." She smiled at Gerard. "Are you married, Detective?"

Gerard's face colored slightly. "No, ma'am, I'm not." A few awkward seconds passed between then until Gerard's hand hit his leg to close out the conversation. "Okay," he looked at Jessie, "I think we have all we need." He nodded to the woman. "Thank you again."

"You're very welcome. I hope Mr. Sawyer fares well on whatever is going on at his dealership. Please let me know if there's anything else I can do for you." She gave Gerard another sexy smile. He glanced at his partner, who was struggling to maintain her calm. He rolled his eyes on his way to the door, exited the home, and walked toward their vehicle at a fast pace anxious to get inside his car. Jessie rushed to get in on the passenger's side. As soon as Jess shut the door, she burst into uncontrollable laughter.

"Ooh, Don Juan. She was hitting on you."

"No, kidding. She's like a hundred and ninety years old, for chrissake."

"Hey, don't discount that old broad. She might just teach you a trick or two," she teased.

"Please, spare me the advice." He cleared his throat and started the engine, pulling into the traffic. "Did you find anything?" he asked.

"Nothing. There were no prescriptions in the medicine chest or male clothing anywhere that would indicate Sawyer was or had been there. How about you?"

"Nothing from me either," he shrugged dismissively. "This is like looking for a needle in a haystack. Okay, we're off to the next one. Let me have the address again." Jessie viewed the screen of her phone and repeated the street address.

"I don't know about you, but I'm starving, Jessie James. Let's grab a bite before we go to the next house?"

"Pizza?" she asked.

"Hey, works for me."

Gridlock slowed to a standstill while impatient drivers honked their horns like an orchestra tuning up before a performance. In the middle of the street stood two people shouting at one another.

"Shouldn't we stop?"

"No. Let the flatfoots handle it." His hand reached up and flipped on the siren. "There's more than one way to skin a cat."

"I guess there is."

* * *

Exiting Ray's Pizzeria, Jessie held her hand out for the car keys, and Gerard didn't object, tossing them in the air for her to catch. "Okay, what is the next address?"

"Make a right on West 116th Street and head for Tribeca. She's on Duane Street. Number 935, to be exact."

Jessie parked on the street in front of house. "This is a beautiful neighborhood," Jess said, admiring the maple trees lining both sides. It was an upper-class neighborhood. The home was a single-family residence with a two-car garage. The house was brick with white trim. The front picture window bowed out, and Jess imagined it had a window seat with cushions. The pair mounted the stairs leading up to the white windowed front door with a brass knocker.

"Not too shabby," Jess commented.

"I'll say." Pressing on the doorbell, Jess could see a woman heading their way through the sheer curtain covering the window panes. A tall, slender woman with high cheekbones and dark brown hair opened the door. Wisps of hair fell onto her cheeks. She brushed it aside.

"Can I help you?" she asked.

"Good afternoon. We're Detectives Kensington and Gerard, NYPD, and we're looking for Maria Alexander?"

"You've found her." Dressed in red shorts with a matching striped halter top. "What can I do for you?" she asked.

"We'd like to ask you some questions about Patrick Sawyer."

"What about him?"

"Is he here?"

"No. Why would he be here?"

"Do you know him, ma'am?"

"Yes, I know him. I used to work for him at the Mercedes dealership. Has something happened to him?" she asked with concern.

"No, ma'am. We're just trying to locate him." "We have an urgent matter we need to discuss with him." Gerard watched her reaction. He could tell by the expression on her face that she was lying. There was no question in his mind. "You are related to him?"

"Goodness, no. We're just good friends."

"Would you mind if we came inside for a few minutes to ask some questions? It's scorching out here," he said when he noticed a small child crouched down at the top of the stairs, staring at them with interest through the balusters.

"Do you know where Mr. Sawyer is, ma'am?" Jessie asked again.

"Daddy's at the store," the girl yelled before the woman could respond. Seconds later, she was on her feet and galloping down the stairs toward the detectives. "Did something happen to my dad?"

"I'm sorry, Detectives," Maria apologized, her face flushed, embarrassed about being caught in a lie. "She's right. He's picking up some groceries." She shifted with unease from one foot to the other. "I'm sure you can imagine how many people want to see Mr. Sawyer. I try to guard his privacy."

"Do you still work for Mr. Sawyer?"

"No. But we've remained good friends over the years," she mouthed in a low voice, frequently glancing at the young girl. "Please come inside." She shut the door with her foot.

Maria shot Gabi a dirty look when they walked past her. The home was nicely appointed with black lacquered, hand-carved oriental furnishings that were expensive-looking. Oriental area rugs covered the floors. "Please, sit in the living room," she gestured. "This is Gabi Sawyer," she told the detectives.

Gabi stood and stared wide-eyed at the detectives. "What's wrong?"

"What makes you think there's something wrong?" Jess asked the child.

"Because you wouldn't be here, and because Daddy is out, and I haven't heard from Mommy," she exclaimed.

"Gabi," Maria said, reaching for the child's hand, "why don't you wait in your room upstairs so the adults can talk."

Gabi yanked her hand back. "No. I'm staying right here."

"Is something wrong here, Ms. Alexander?" Gerard asked.

"No," she shook her head. "Nothing—"

The hum of the garage door raising drew the child's attention. She darted for the door. "Daddy, the cops are here."

"What's going on here?" Patrick Sawyer asked, loaded with two bags of groceries in his arms.

"Sir, we're Detectives Gerard and Kensington from the two-one precinct. We want to talk to you. Is there a place where we can speak in private?"

"Sure. What's this about? Your boss wouldn't be trying to give me more grief, would he?" He closed his eyes in disgust. "We can go outside." He handed the grocery bags to Maria and turned to his daughter. "It's fine, munchkin. Get that worried look off your face."

"I'm scared, Daddy."

He smoothed her hair back with his hand. "Don't be scared, Gabi. We don't even know why the detectives are here. You stay here with Maria while I find out what they want. Okay?"

"Why can't I listen too?"

"Gabrielle," he pointed toward the other room. "Now!"

Gabi turned on her heels and stomped out of the room. Sawyer was a tall, imposing man who stood as straight as an arrow. He had a trim build; he walked with authority onto the porch and sat on the black bench. Sawyer was known to have an edgy personality that became even worse when the agency questioned him—regardless of the subject. The problem stemmed from a long, drawn-out history of dislike between him and Harwell regarding his dealership. Although Harwell didn't air his dirty laundry publicly, the discord between the parties was no secret.

Sawyer's face flushed with anger. "If this is another of your boss's ploys to get my goat, he'll wish he hadn't bothered."

"Mr. Sawyer," Gerard said firmly, "Is that a threat?"

"No, Detective. But it's a promise that I'll go directly to the mayor over his harassment. You might want to think twice about your reason for being here."

"I can assure you, sir, in these strained economic times, the city doesn't have money to throw away on harassing its residents." Gerard's brow arched. "Now, may I tell you why we're here?"

"Yes. Enlighten me, will you?"

"We came to discuss your wife, Amanda."

"What about Amanda?" he said, a curious expression on his face.

"We have reason to believe she's missing, sir."

"No, she's not," he guffawed. "Where did you get that silly notion?"

"Her parents have filed a Missing Persons."

"A what? Why would they do that? She's with her sister in Ohio."

"Well, we know she's not with her sister because she's the one who initiated this investigation."

Sawyer snorted. "She finally blew her sister off, huh? I've been waiting for her to get her head out of that sand."

Gerard sidestepped his comment. "Mr. Sawyer. We're telling you we think your wife is missing," Gerard's muscles tensed, "and you will focus on your sister-in-law's issues. Aren't you the least bit concerned your wife might be missing?"

"I told you, Amanda is with her friends in Ohio."

"Okay, that's fine. Give us a number to reach your wife, and we'll be on our way."

"Unfortunately, I don't have a number. Amanda and her sister -- I mean, Amanda went to Ohio to visit old school chums—a girlfriend's get-together, and believe it or not, she left her cell phone at home."

"Have you had contact with your wife since she left?"

"Just once. That was two days after Amanda left. Gabi and I were in the theatre then and couldn't talk to her, but she left a message."

"Good. Can we listen to that message?"

"I'm afraid I don't have the message or the phone anymore, Detectives. Once Gabi listened to it, I erased it." Sawyer gave the detectives a curious frown. "Should I be calling my attorney?"

"Do you think you need one, Mr. Sawyer?" Jessie asked.

"Is that a trick question, Detective?"

"When was the last time you were in your home, Mr. Sawyer?" Gerard asked.

"Oh, geez," he shifted in place. "It's been at least a week. Why? Is something wrong with my house?"

"We have reason to believe there's been foul play," Gerard said. "That's why the Milligans filed a missing person report."

"Go on."

"We've been to your home, and it looks like a crime scene," Gerard added.

Sawyer's mouth gaped while he stared at them. "Crime scene? What do you mean, a crime scene?" His body began to shake. When Sawyer noticed his daughter standing at the window, her nose pressed against the pane, he moved slightly from her view. "What do you mean a crime scene?" he said calmly, his eyes settling on the detectives. "You didn't do any damage getting into my home, did you?"

Jessie's face scrunched in disbelief. "No," she said. "After we obtained a warrant, we used the keys your in-laws have in their possession."

"Really? I didn't even know they had a key." He raised his shoulder dismissively. "Well, I guess it's a good thing under the circumstances. Can you take me there?"

"I'm afraid not, Mr. Sawyer. The area is taped off until we finish our investigation."

He scuffed his hand over his face. "What does this break-in have to do with my wife?"

"Mr. Sawyer, we'd like to continue this conversation downtown?"

"Sure. Just let me tell Maria to keep an eye on Gabi." They followed him back into the residence. Gabi rushed up to him.

"What's wrong, Dad?"

"Nothing, sweetheart. These nice detectives would like to talk to me about something at the car dealership, so I must go with them. Okay, munchkin?" Gabi made a face. "Maria will be fixing dinner soon, so will you give her a hand?" Sawyer seemed to ignore his daughter's reaction. "I'll see you guys later." He began walking toward the front door when Gabi called out.

"Wait, Dad. I'm going with you." Gabi made a beeline across the floor. "I'll get my stuff," she said over her shoulder just before she hit the steps.

"Gabi, sweetie," Sawyer said calmly, "not this time. We can discuss this when I return."

"But, Dad. I want to go home."

"Gabrielle," he said in a firm voice, pointing toward the kitchen, "I'm going back to the city with these two detectives. When I return, we will discuss it."

The expression on the young girl's face echoed the discord she was feeling. She whipped around and stomped her feet again, exiting the room. Upon hearing the commotion, Maria entered the living room and frowned at Gabi, who passed by her.

"Is something wrong?" Maria asked inquisitively.

In a low whisper, Sawyer told her what they wanted. "These detectives say Amanda is missing, and my home looks like a crime scene."

"Oh no," she gasped, her hand covering her mouth. "What happened?"

"I don't know yet."

"Look, you go take care of business; I'll take care of Gabi."

Gerard glanced at his partner to see if her facial expression echoed what he thought when Sawyer communicated with the woman. Maria's expression of adornment was like a neon sign. Suddenly, a plausible motive surfed through his mind.

"Thank you." He reached into his pocket, pulled money from his billfold, and handed it to her. "I'll see you later." He turned back to the detectives. "Okay, I'm ready."

Gerard and Jessie sandwiched Sawyer between them when they exited the house. "Thank you for not blowing my story in front of my daughter. She'd be devastated if anything happened to her mother."

"How about you, Mr. Sawyer?" Jessie asked.

"What a ridiculous question, Detective. Of course, I'd be upset."

CHAPTER 17

"*P*lease have a seat, Mr. Sawyer," Jessie said when they entered the interrogation room.

"Why couldn't you have questioned me at the house?"

"Because your daughter doesn't need to hear any of this."

"You actually think I would do something to hurt my wife? My God, who do you think I am?"

"Relax, Mr. Sawyer. No one is accusing you of anything," she said. "It's just a formality. We're collecting information to complete this investigation and find your wife."

He exhaled dramatically, while his shoulders sagged like a tire deflating. "I'm sorry. I'm just so shocked by the news. Based on the investigation you conducted at my house, do you have proof Amanda is missing? Or is there blood or something in my house that makes you think something happened to her?"

"We can't discuss any of that with you, Mr. Sawyer. I'm sure you can understand." Gerard rubbed a hand over his mouth. "But it is an odd thing for you to ask."

"It seems like a logical question." He shook his head. "If my house looks like a crime scene, it must be a break-in."

"That's what's so interesting. There was no break-in. No marks on any of the doors. Just a massive mess."

"Well, if my in-laws had a key, maybe the crackhead had one too and brought her friends in to trash the home. That bitch and I hate each other."

Jess could see a muscle quiver in his jaw. "Tell us about the last time you saw your wife. We want a detailed description of what transpired before she left," Jessie said.

"Fine," he said in a gruff voice. "We got up early. I showered and went into the kitchen for breakfast. Amanda was on the phone at the time. I sat down to eat my toast. When she ended her call, she was pretty excited. She told me it was her friend," he paused, thinking, "Oh hell, a Jessica something," his palms rose in the air. Sawyer huffed out a breath at the same time. "I can't remember her last name, but she's a former classmate of Amanda's. . . anyway, she wanted the two sisters to fly out that morning to Ohio for a weeklong get-together." He gave an eye roll. "I guess the gossip hadn't reached her that Sara was a crackhead."

Gerard ignored his comment. "Just like that? A spur-of-the-moment decision without any prior planning?" Gerard shot back.

"Yes. It's called spontaneity." His head nodded in agreement, "Yep, just like that." A wry grin curled at the corners of Sawyer's mouth.

"Didn't that seem a little odd to you?"

"Hell, no! Nothing Amanda does is ever odd. Amanda has a mind of her own, no matter what I suggest."

"I'm sensing a slight irritation in your voice, Mr. Sawyer," Jessie added. "Were you and Mrs. Sawyer having marital problems?"

"No more than other couples," he responded coolly. "We don't agree on everything, but—" He stopped talking and crossed his arms, slamming them against his chest like a belligerent child. "Detectives, I don't see the value in these questions. You're wasting time."

"Mr. Sawyer, we're just collecting the facts. The only thing we do know for sure is that something happened in your home. What time did your wife leave the house?"

"I guess around nine forty-five in the morning." His response was more subdued.

"Did you drive her to the airport?"

"No. Amanda called a cab."

"What airline?"

"I believe it was American, but you can check with the airlines."

"I'll do that. Do you recall what your wife was wearing the morning she left?"

He chuckled. "Are you kidding me? She has a closet full of clothes and usually changes at least five times before she's satisfied with what she has on."

"Okay, so how about shoes? Do you know what shoes she was wearing?" Gerard asked.

He shook his head and snickered. "No. If you were at my house and looked in her closet, you know the answer to that question." He smirked.

"Mr. Sawyer," Jessie said, "what time did you leave the house that morning?"

"I left right after Amanda did."

"Did you see the car drive down the road?"

"Yes, I stood at the curb and waved."

"What taxi company did she use?"

"It was a yellow cab. That's all I can tell you. I was anxious to get going and only half paying attention."

"And what time did you say that was?" Jessie paced back and forth.

"I already told you. It was about nine forty-five in the morning."

"And you're certain of that?"

"Yes, because I looked at my watch. I met at the dealership at eleven o'clock, and I know I wasn't late."

"Mr. Sawyer, your dealership is across town. How did you make it through the gridlock for an eleven o'clock meeting?"

"I can't be sure because I didn't check my watch again, but maybe I was late for my meeting and didn't realize it. The guy said nothing, so I guess it wasn't objectionable."

"Who were you meeting?"

"A customer."

"What was that customer's name?"

He sucked in his lips. "I'm embarrassed to say I don't remember." His face flushed.

"Wouldn't the customer's name be listed on your calendar?" Gerard fired back.

"Normally, I would have added it, but this was a last-minute walk-in. My secretary called and informed me."

"If you called her right now, wouldn't she know the customer's name?"

"That would be the shock of the century."

Gerard could see Jess was getting pissed. "You know, Mr. Sawyer, this is beginning to sound like a well-rehearsed script," she said, her foot subconsciously tapping against the floor. "You don't know exactly where your wife is, you don't know the last name of the friend she's visiting, and you don't have a phone number. You had a meeting with a customer, but you can't remember who you met. What is this, a game to you?"

Sawyer held his hand up. "I know how this must all sound to you, but I swear, I'm telling you the truth."

"That's good, Mr. Sawyer because we will find out."

"I should hope so, Detectives."

Jessie continued, her hands firmly planted on her hips now. "And where did you go after the meeting with the customer, whose name you can't remember?"

"I went out to the lot—where else would I go?"

"Can anyone verify that?"

"Does anyone need to?" He answered irritably. "Look, I want to know what you're doing about my wife. What proof do you have that she's missing?"

"Your sister-in-law, Sara. The one you said was with Mrs. Sawyer," Jessie said matter-of-factly. "She told us Amanda picks her up every Wednesday, and she didn't show up last Wednesday."

He snorted. "And that's what you're basing your investigation on? Something a drug addict tells you. Are you kidding me?"

"Well, Mr. Sawyer, you don't seem to be able to give us much to work with here. Do you have the cell phone containing your wife's voicemail?"

"I told you before," he argued. "After Gabi listened to the message, I deleted the message, then tossed the phone and purchased another prepaid phone."

"Why would a businessman do that? That can't be very cost-effective."

"For chrissake, the minutes ran out. That's why, and . . . and, because "complaining customers continually hound me."

"You mean all those commercials on television with you boasting about being number one in customer satisfaction is a lie?"

"No. Of course not."

"So why the disposable phones?" Gerard asked.

"It's just easier."

Gerard was shaking his head, then checked his notes. "Tell us about this cruise that everyone thinks you're on.

"The cruise?"

"Yeah, the cruise you supposedly told Mrs. Simon, the school secretary, that you'd be on and why Gabi would be missing the beginning of the new school year. Funny, we've checked the cruise logs, and your name did not appear on any of the rosters. Care to explain that?" Jessie was losing patience with his responses.

"I was planning a surprise for Amanda and Gabi, but when Amanda decided to visit with her friends instead, I didn't have the heart to ruin her excitement about seeing them, so I canceled it."

"You canceled it?" Gerard asked.

"Yes," he said, with a dismissive shoulder raise.

"Which cruise line was this? We want to check it out."

"Why? Because you think I'm lying?" He shot up out of his chair. "I'm out of here. Call me when you have something concrete to tell me. Don't waste my time on your fishing expedition."

"Mr. Sawyer, I know you're upset, but if you don't sit down this second, I'll put you in a holding cell until I get my answers. I can hold you for seventy-two hours." Jessie gave him a defiant stare.

"I know the laws, Detective."

"That's good, Mr. Sawyer, because refusing to cooperate sends a strong message you're lying."

Sawyer gave her an empty stare, took a deep breath to settle himself as if reconsidering his hostility, and eased back into the chair. "I'd like to know about my wife and what the police are doing to find her."

"Did you make the arrangements or have someone do it for you?" Gerard persisted.

"Travel agent. I think it was a Carnival cruise. Call my travel agent, Barry Shackle—Around the World Travel Agency on Broadway."

"Did you use a fictitious name when you booked the travel arrangements, Mr. Sawyer?"

"Barry doesn't usually . . . although he knew I wanted to spend uninterrupted time with my family."

"So, just to be clear, Mr. Sawyer, you used your real name when you made the arrangements for the cruise?"

"Unless Shackle made one up. Check with him if you don't believe me."

"We will. Now about that tossed phone. Where did you dispose of it?" Gerard fired back. He was doing his best to wear down Sawyer's defenses, especially since he'd already made a judgment call regarding his guilt based on the house and his reactions to his wife's disappearance. If the man thought his performance was convincing, he had another thought coming. Gerard was even more determined to put the guy away. "Your hesitation in answering leads us to believe you have something to hide."

"I can't remember where I disposed of it, to tell you the truth."

"What did her message say?"

"That she was sorry she left without saying goodbye."

"Whoa, whoa. Wait a minute. You told us you saw your wife in the morning. You even waved goodbye to her."

"The message," he huffed, "Detective Gerard, was for our daughter, Gabi. Amanda left before Gabi came home from her friend's house, and she was apologizing for not waiting."

"Why couldn't she wait?"

"She wanted an early start due to her flight ahead."

"Are you having financial problems?"

"Not at the moment, but we're doing what everyone else is doing—cutting back."

"Does cutting back include throwing your disposable phone in a public trash can?" Jessie asked.

"I never told you I tossed it in a public trashcan," he said with a twinge of forced calmness. "What is it you want to know, Detectives? I've told you I will give you whatever information you require."

"Good," Jessie shoved a pad and pen over to him. "You said your daughter was at her girlfriend's house for a sleepover. Is that correct?"

"Yes."

"How many days did she spend with her friend?"

"Two, three days. I don't know, Detectives. I don't keep track of that stuff."

"Please list your whereabouts since your wife left."

Sawyer's jaw jutted out in anger. His pen moved down the pad, occasionally staring at the wall.

"We'll be right outside the door," Gerard said. "I'd like to confer with my partner."

"Fine," he said without looking up.

They entered the viewing room where the Lieutenant waited.

"Turn him loose. You don't have anything to keep him here," Harwell said.

"Okay, but I want to ask him a few more questions."

"Be my guest. But unless you have something solid . . . turn him loose."

When Jessie reentered the interview room, Patrick sat in a resting position.

"Thank you, Mr. Sawyer." Jessie picked up the pad and eyed the list.

"Did you tell me Mrs. Sawyer forgot her phone?"

"Yes."

"Where is that phone?"

"It has to be in the house somewhere. Maybe one of your investigators found it."

"Can you tell us the number Mrs. Sawyer called you from?"

"It's on the list, Detective Kensington. It's a public telephone."

"How do you know that?"

"A stranger answered when I called and told me so."

Jessie's finger moved down the list. "Right, okay, I see it right here. Are you saying you memorized that number?"

Yeah, I've called the damn thing so many times!"

"Thank you. That's very helpful."

"Until then, you didn't know it was a public telephone?"

"How would I have known that, Detective?" Signs of irritation crossed his face. "I still don't see how this information will help you find my, as you say, missing wife. I want you working on this and not on me."

Gerard reentered the room and responded to Sawyer's demand. "We have a team of investigators working on this case. I've just contacted the Ohio PD and requested an all-points- bulletin. Tell me, do you have a photograph of your wife?"

"Not on me. Do you have fingerprints from whoever broke into my house?"

"That's a good question, Mr. Sawyer. We've matched your wife's and daughter's prints to those in residence, and the only other prints are yours."

"How did you match Amanda's and Gabi's prints?"

"Your in-laws provided copies of those."

"Huh?" he frowned. "What are they doing with a set of prints?"

"I asked that same question and was told, as a responsible parent, your wife gave them a set of Gabi's." Gerard's brow arched. "Now, why would she have given them a set of hers? Could it have been that she was trying to warn them about something?" Gerard asked. "It wouldn't have anything to do with your behavior toward your wife, right?"

"And what behavior is that?" Sawyer asked, somewhat miffed. "Is someone making up lies about my marriage?"

"I never said that, Mr. Sawyer." Now it was Gerard who was pacing.

"Do you know anyone who would want to harm your wife?" Jessie asked.

"No. I don't. I'm having a difficult time trying to process this." He sat and stared out in a daze. "Amanda was such a loving and caring woman." His voice cracked. "I can't even imagine it."

Gerard paused for a moment. "Mr. Sawyer. You spoke of your wife in the past tense. Is there something you want to tell us?"

"Oh, for chrissake. It was a figure of speech." He shook his head. "I'd like to see photos of my home . . . or the crime scene, as you call it."

"Okay." Jessie pulled the photos from the file and fanned them on the table.

He picked each one up and shook his head in bewilderment. "I can't believe the mess my house is in."

"Do you remember what the kitchen looked like when you left?"

"It was spotless. Amanda is a compulsive cleaner. She never leaves a thing out of place."

"That's what your in-laws said."

"Well, at least that's one thing we agree on."

"Don't you get along with the Milligans?" Gerard asked.

"They're okay."

"Have you ever had words with them, Mr. Sawyer?"

"No," his voice increased in volume, clearly annoyed by the question.

"Have they done something to make you dislike them?"

"Amanda and her parents are very close, so she listens to them more than me."

Jessie stood behind Sawyer and flashed two fingers in the air. Gerard nodded in agreement that it was a second motive. He continued to watch Sawyer's body language.

"Sounds like a power struggle going on," Jessie's brows furrowed. She studied him more closely. "That must have been a bone of contention in your marriage."

"Detectives, I find your behavior degrading and mean-spirited. Is this how Harwell told you to treat me?"

"Nice try, Mr. Sawyer," Jess said. "What I'm finding so interesting is that you don't seem to be taking any of this very seriously," Jessie smirked. "Why is that?"

"Because I think you'll find Amanda, and this is all for naught. As for the break-in, or whatever you're calling it, I'd better call my insurance company. We have a lot of money invested in that house. Or should I wait for you to finish your investigation?"

"With all due respect, Mr. Sawyer, this seems to be the only thing you're concerned about." Jessie shot back.

"That's absurd. I'm concerned, but I think you're spinning your wheels and wasting taxpayer money on an investigation for a woman on vacation with her friends. I still can't believe you're taking the word of a known drug addict. Sara has to be the most unreliable person on the planet, especially when she's higher than a kite. Amanda probably left Sara behind on purpose, and now it seems her parents are falling into her trap again."

"No. Not this time," Jessie said. "She was an addict, but she's cleaned herself up."

"For how long?" he smirked.

"Mr. Sawyer, we're not here to defend or discuss the plausibility of Sara's sobriety. Do you have a hidden key somewhere in case you forget yours?" Gerard inquired.

"Yes. But no one would be able to find it unless they knew where to look."

"Do you use a cleaning service?" Jessie asked.

"Yes. We have a woman who comes in, but what does that have to do with it?"

"Does she have a key to your house?"

He crossed his arms abruptly. "No. Amanda and I talked about this, and I told her not. Of course, that's not to say she didn't give it to the woman behind my back. As I mentioned earlier, Amanda has a mind of her own."

"What is your cleaning woman's name and address?"

"Rosarita Alvarez. I don't know where she lives, but if you let me into my house, I can look it up in our phone directory."

"I've already told you there's no entry into your home until our investigation is complete. I'll let you know when that is. Tell us where to look for the directory. We'll have one of our investigators get the number."

"Amanda kept it in the middle drawer of the desk in the kitchen."

"Okay, we'll check there." Jessie jotted down the information. "Tell me, Mr. Sawyer. Do you have a life insurance policy for your wife? A prenuptial agreement?"

"What?" Sawyer's expression darkened. "You people are unbelievable."

"We're doing our job, sir. Just like you would in your—"

He interrupted her. "You said my in-laws filed a Missing Persons."

"Yes, they did."

"Why didn't they call me?"

"They did try to reach you, Mr. Sawyer, by using the same numbers we had."

Patrick Sawyer's expression turned to a mask of stone. "They could have contacted me through my secretary at the dealership."

"Nope. I'm afraid not. The Milligans have been there, done that, and so have we. And Mrs. Simon gave us the same information she told your in-laws; you were on a cruise and unreachable. Why would she tell us that?"

Sawyer lowered his head into his hands. "Christ. First off, the girl is new. Look, I get so many damn phone calls when I'm out of the office, from employees to customers. I've told my secretary, outside of death, I do not want to be disturbed."

"But we told her it was an emergency. Did you call in to check messages?"

"No. I did not."

"Wouldn't you think she'd be smart enough to inform you the police wanted to speak to you?"

"Now that's the sixty-four-thousand-dollar question. Do you know how hard it is to find good help these days? I guess I just wasn't clear enough in my instructions."

"Did she have the new cell phone number? Or did you toss it before you gave her the new number?"

"I can't remember. I—I guess I thought I gave it to her." He blew out a breath of air.

"How interesting. Let me get this straight," Gerard said. "Every time you're away, you purchase a new phone?"

"I purchase disposable phones exclusively."

"How do the people who matter get in touch with you?"

"They call my main number at the shop."

"What shop is that, Mr. Sawyer?" Gerard continued.

"The dealership." He lowered his voice; his expression was a picture of confusion. "What other shop would there be?"

"I don't know, Mr. Sawyer. You tell me."

"I don't have the money for more than one dealership." He shook his head again. "This economy is killing me."

Jessie locked her eyes on her partner. They knew each other so well that reading each other's expressions was easy. She smiled at him, and he nodded to let her know he understood.

"Sir, we have just one more question for today."

"What is that?"

"Why don't you have any family pictures in your home?"

Sawyer shrugged. "I don't know. I guess we're just not photogenic."

"Do you have a photograph of your wife in your office?"

"No. There are a lot of strangers who prance in and out of my office. Having photographs of my family for everyone to see is too risky."

"While that may be true, not having any hasn't made your family safer. Especially your wife." Sawyer shrugged. "How about your daughter, Mr. Sawyer? Do you have a picture of her in your wallet?"

Sawyer reached into his back pocket, pulled his wallet out, and instantly produced a photo of his daughter Gabrielle. "I always have pictures of my little girl."

"Why her and not your wife?" Jessie's chest tightened. "Don't you love your wife as much as your daughter?" She knew the answer to that question.

"I think it's obvious that I love my wife and daughter differently." He checked his watch. "I have to get back. Are we done here?"

"Sir, we're talking about your missing wife here. We're talking about possible foul play at your house, and you're anxious to get out of here?"

Sawyer released a heavy breath. "Don't you dare try to do this to me? I'm very concerned about my wife and her safety, but you haven't told me anything substantive about what you're calling a disappearance or what the NYPD is doing to find her."

"Mr. Sawyer," Gerard said. "We don't have much to go on here. That's why we asked you to come in to answer some questions. The problem is that you haven't told us much of anything we already know."

"Mr. Sawyer," Jessie asked, "what kind of car do you drive?"

"I drive a Maybach."

"How long have you had that vehicle?"

"About a week."

"What did you drive before that?"

"I drove a Mercedes ML550."

"That's an SUV, isn't it?"

"Yes, it is."

"And what color was that car?"

"Black." Sawyer's brows knitted together. "Why do you ask?"

"And how long did you have the black SUV?"

"I don't even know to tell you the truth." His palms rose in the air. "I have a dealership, Detectives; I can drive a different car every day if I want, and most of the time, I do. It's hard to sell a car without trying it out."

"One last thing before we end this session, Mr. Sawyer." Jessie pulled the sketch from her folder and held it up for him to see. "Do you recognize the person in this sketch?"

Sawyer focused on the face. He held it up in the distance, then placed it on the table. "Is this supposed to be my wife?"

"Well, your sister-in-law seems to think it's your wife."

He rolled his eyes. "There's nothing about this sketch that resembles my wife. Sara must be smoking something if she thinks this is Amanda."

"Mrs. Milligan thought the same thing," Jessie said.

"Did she? And how about Charles?" Sawyer's tone edged on the side of sarcasm. "Did he think so too?"

"He thought it resembled Amanda but wasn't convinced."

"Where can we get a photograph of your wife if we can't find one in the desk you suggested, Mr. Sawyer?"

"I'm sure her parents have one. They seem to have everything else. But there's got to be an album somewhere in my house." He eyed the drawing again. "Who is this woman, anyway?"

"It was a sketch of someone else, and when Sara saw it posted throughout the Borough, she called the precinct and stopped here to discuss it."

"And you believed her?" Sawyer asked.

"We have nothing else to go on, so until we see your wife, we have to assume Sara is correct."

"Is this woman also missing?" his finger snapped against the paper.

"We can't discuss an ongoing investigation with you, Mr. Sawyer."

Sawyer stood to leave. "I trust you'll keep me apprised of your findings."

"Mr. Sawyer," Jessie said. "I have another question for you. Can you elaborate on the fire at your home?"

Sawyer frowned. "What fire is that?"

"The fire that burned your wife's face."

"Christ. I can't believe I forgot about that fire. Yes. I was on my way home from my dealership. Gabi had stayed overnight at her friend's because Amanda hadn't been feeling well after having miscarried another baby." He shook his head. "Thank God one of the neighbors saw the flames and called the fire department because Amanda was in a deep sleep and didn't even realize what was happening until the firemen arrived. She was trapped and screaming. I was shocked when I drove down our street and saw trucks lined up in front of my house. I panicked until I saw Amanda lying on the gurney."

"Did you set that fire, Mr. Sawyer?"

"Are you fucking crazy?" He shot her a look. "Why would I do that?"

"Just asking." Jess could see Sawyer's jaw quiver by her directness, but she didn't care. He was a jerk.

"Let me call one of our guys to drive you home," Gerard said.

"No thanks," he shot Jess a dirty look, "I'll take a cab."

"Mr. Sawyer," Jessie cautioned when she escorted him to the door, "do not leave the city."

"And where is it you think I'm going?"

"I have no idea, Mr. Sawyer."

He gave the bar on the door a hard push and exited.

Gerard approached from behind and startled her—she wasn't expecting him. "The Lieutenant wants to see us."

"Did he watch the rest of the questioning?"

"Apparently."

When they entered, Harwell was biting into a jelly donut, his mouth covered in white powder. For a brief second, Gerard felt a tinge of jealousy, wondering if Jessie would wipe the powder off Harwell's mouth like she'd done his a few days ago. Instead, she turned her attention to her partner and smiled, sensing he was watching her.

Harwell placed the unfinished donut on his desk and rubbed his mouth with a napkin. "You both worked him over pretty good," he said with his mouth full.

"He's one shrewd sonofabitch," Gerard said wryly.

Jessie nodded. "He is Gerard, but his arrogance couldn't mask his frustration and lies. What did you think, Lieutenant?"

"He's had a lot of practice. But there's no doubt that something is happening with him."

"Can we get one of the guys to check with the cab companies to find out if they had a pick-up at the Sawyer residence on the date in question?" Gerard asked. "And, while they're at it, check all those other details about the travel agent, the cruise line, and airline travel must also be verified."

"Absolutely."

"The other thing I was thinking about," Jess said, "is whether or not there are any security cameras in the neighborhood that might have recorded what happened. I can't imagine that upscale neighborhood leaving security to chance."

"Good point," Harwell said, "I'll have the guys check that out too." Harwell took another bite of his donut. "I'm sorry for eating before you, but I've been dying for this damned donut." He wiped the powder off before continuing. "I think there's enough of a motive, just not the proof. But maybe the cameras recorded just what we need." He leaned back in his chair. "We'll catch this bastard one way or another." Harwell's hand hit the desk. "Someone's telling him we're watching, and that's why we can't catch him at the shop. If what we're thinking about his wife's disappearance is true, I think his over-anxiousness will do him in—we need to be patient."

"And I'm betting the farm on his involvement in a money-laundering scheme," Gerard said. He stopped mid-way. "I spoke to the prosecutor earlier and requested a warrant for a Forensic Accountant to check Sawyer's books at the dealership and his accounts."

"And I have Santini and Paige checking on the insurance angle," Harwell said.

"His mention of the economy hurting his dealership said a lot." Gerard counted on his fingers. "One, financial trouble; two, marital issues; three, his missing wife and four, a possible girlfriend."

"You mean his cousin?" Jess said.

Gerard chuckled. "If you believe she's his cousin, then I've got some swampland in Florida I'd like to sell you."

"I just find it hard to believe someone with such a precious little daughter would do something so evil."

"You sound like a rookie, Jess," Harwell said.

"I suppose I do. It's been a long day."

"How's that list coming along," Harwell asked while Gerard was talking on his phone."

Jess felt the anger pinching her nerves. "Lieutenant, I'm up to my friggin' eyeballs with this case, and you want me to stop to make a list?"

"Jessie, it's for your protection! There's someone out there who's trying to hurt you. I want to stop them in their tracks." A troubled frown capped his face. "Okay, how about we do this? Can you spare ten minutes to sit with my secretary?"

"To do what?"

"Tell her the names and let her type it up for me."

"That would work much better. As for the chronological list of my cases, maybe she can run through the database for that too?"

"Good idea. Okay, you're off the hook, but schedule some time with her."

"Yes, sir." She felt relieved. "Thank you." Jess blew out a breath. "I'm curious how Lenny fits into all of this. Did it have to do with the chop shop, Sawyer's wife, or did he do something else?"

Harwell shrugged. "There could be a million reasons why Lenny's dead and a million people who wanted him dead. He had a lot of enemies."

"Well, maybe Tony can tell us something. I'll call and tell him we need to see him now," Jessie said.

"Yeah, this is the last time," Harwell said. "No holding back, or his ass is in jail."

Jessie pressed in the numbers. His voicemail played. "Tony, Detective Kensington here. Gerard and I are on our way over to see you. We can do this one of two ways. We can come into the warehouse or wait for you in the alley behind the building." She snapped her phone shut and shook her head from side to side. "He's not answering his cell."

"Call his house phone," Gerard suggested.

She checked the file and keyed in the phone number. "Okay, something's rotten in Denmark. There's no answer at the house either. What do you want to do?"

"Go over to his house."

Jessie looked at her partner. "Are you thinking the same thing I am?"

"I'm afraid so, Jess."

* * *

Jessie vaguely remembered Tony and his family lived in an apartment over top of a restaurant on Mulberry Street in New York's Little Italy. Driving slowly down the road, she pointed out the address. "Here's 127 Mulberry."

"How convenient that Tony lives close to Central Booking." He chuckled. "I'll park in the lot, and we'll walk back." Gerard found a space, then exited the car. "Damn, that Italian food is making me hungry. It feels like I haven't eaten in weeks," Gerard said.

"We always say that," Jessie said.

"That's because it's true. We don't eat during the day. Who the hell has time?" he asked."Then it's a date, right? We'll come here for dinner."

"Gerard," she warned, "focus on Tony."

"Yes, ma'am," he said with a salute.

"I'll take the fire escape; you take the stairs. I don't want this weasel going out the window when Tony sees you at the door."

"Yep, I'm on it." Jessie pulled the door open. The smell of Italian sauce hit her in the face. She inhaled deeply and tried to ignore the aroma making her stomach growl. She took the stairs two at a time to the apartment door and rang the bell. There was no answer. Checking the door, she suddenly noticed it was slightly ajar. Jessie gave a push and entered. The apartment was bare; no furniture, no residents, no nothing. Just as she turned around to leave, Gerard opened the bottom door and stood with his hands on his hips.

"Do you believe this?"

"I guess he wasn't kidding when he said he was scared." Gerard pounded the wall with his fist. "We're never going to solve this friggin' case."

Tension throbbed at her temples. She rubbed them in a circular motion hoping to relieve the pain, then removed her cell phone from her pocket and called dispatch. "Detective Kensington here, badge number 107; I need an APB out on Tony Ricci."

CHAPTER 18

"*D*ammit!" Gerard said on their way back to the vehicle. "No, Lenny, no Tony, and I'll bet Vito's trailing close behind," He released a frustrated breath. "I'm stopping at the drive-through for a burger," he bellowed. "I'm starving."

"What time do you think Vito quits work at the shop?"

"Forget it! I'm telling you, he's gone too," he insisted.

"You're becoming a real pain in the ass with your negative attitude. You know it?" she said, entering the vehicle.

"I'm just saying." Gerard slipped in behind the steering wheel. "Do you want to drive?"

"Do I look like I want to drive?" she barked.

"What's your problem?" Gerard asked. "What's going on?"

"Well, maybe Vito is gone, but unlike you, I'm not ready to give up on finding the truth, dammit. Somebody out there knows something, and we'll find out who does." He slowed the car down, ready to turn right into McDonald's.

"And as for food, I'm not having another burger smothered in grease. We'll go to Lizzie's and get a table to see when Vito walks down the hill. If you want a greasy burger, you can get it there. At least I have an option of what I want to eat."

He shot her a look. "Yes, ma'am," he saluted again. "So, I guess that means you don't have any plans for tonight. Is that right?"

"Does eating lunch at Lizzie's have anything to do with whether I have plans for tonight? And what if I did?"

"You'd cancel them for me, right?" he said, trying to lighten her mood.

"Of course, Gerard," she snapped back. "You know I'm only here to please you."

"Yeah, that's kinda what I thought." He reached for her hand. "I'm sorry I've been such a prick. I want to catch this guy so bad, and I'm frustrated there are no good leads."

"Like I'm not?"

"I know. Let's leave it at I'm sorry."

"Okay."

"Even though I get angry with you," he said, "I appreciate it when you set me straight."

"Yeah, I can tell."

Tip Jackson sat at the counter drinking coffee and flirting with the waitress when they entered Lizzie's Diner. The waitress handed him a piece of paper, and he shoved it into his breast pocket.

"I'm amazed he's all over town and not where he's supposed to be. What do you think was on that piece of paper Blondie just handed him?" Jessie asked.

"Oh," Gerard said and gently shoved her toward the other side of the diner, away from Jackson's range of view. "Maybe it's a good thing he is here. He hasn't seen us yet, and I hope to catch him in the act."

"Act of what? Flirting?"

"No. I can't shake the feeling that Jackson's up to no good. I don't have a good grasp on it yet. He does seem to show up where he's not supposed to be. It just doesn't add up, Jessie. Maybe he's waiting for Vito too."

The food no sooner arrived than Vito strolled down the street and headed toward the subway. "There he is, Jessie," Gerard said, tossing the car keys on the table. "I'm going to catch up to him." He took off like a bolt of lightning toward the subway. Jessie summoned the waitress, requested the food in take-out containers, paid the bill, and headed to the car. Jackson never looked up. Her cell phone rang.

"No luck; Vito made me and took the first train that pulled up."

Jessie sighed, shaking her head from side to side. "Okay, not much we can do about it except stake out the shop. I wouldn't be a bit surprised if Vito abandons the place. Of course, he's not thinking about his fingerprints being all over the joint." She placed the containers in the back seat, got behind the steering wheel, and headed toward Gerard.

Jessie spotted Gerard, who gestured when he saw her and stopped to wait for her to catch up. He was panting from the unexpected run.

"You okay?" she asked.

"Yeah. I want to tell you I'm breathing like this because of you, but I'm getting old."

"You're out of shape, hotshot. I think you need to start joining me at the gym."

"Mmm, is that an invitation?"

"No. It's a necessity." She grinned. "Your food is in the back seat."

"Bless you. Thanks." He twisted on his side and tried unsuccessfully stretching his arm to reach for the containers. Temporarily releasing his seat belt, he turned and knelt on the seat, grabbed both boxes, then slid around and strapped himself in before popping the lids. He carefully placed her food on the seat near his leg, hoping that her hand would touch his when she picked up the container, then took a massive bite like he hadn't eaten in days.

Jessie shoved a handful of fries in her mouth. He gave her a surprised side glance.

"What?"

"I thought you didn't want a high-caloric lunch today. What do you think those fries are worth in calories?"

"These were ready when you called, so I changed my order. I guess one more day isn't going to matter."

Gerard resumed eating his burger. A drop of ketchup fell from his roll onto his white shirt. He reached for the napkin and tried wiping it. "Damn it. Now, I look like one of those fat, flat-footed cops who spill all kinds of shit on themselves."

Jessie laughed. "Reach inside my case. There's one of those bleaching pens."

"You're shitin' me, right?"

"No."

"How about that? She's 'Little Miss Domestication.' I like that."

CHAPTER 19

*J*essie barreled down the hall toward Gerard and Harwell. "You are not going to believe who just called," she said breathlessly.

"Try us," Harwell said.

"Vito Lorenzano."

"And?" Harwell said, his hand twirling in a circular motion, "What did he say?"

"He wants to talk."

"Hot damn!" Gerard said with effervescence. "Chalk another one up for our team. Where are we meeting him?"

"He wants us to meet him by the Vincent van Gogh exhibit in the Metropolitan Museum of Art at six o'clock."

"Where?" Gerard's voice raised an octave.

"You heard me right."

"You've got to be kidding."

"No. And it was Vito's idea. How about that?"

"I guess that's the last place anyone would ever suspect he'd be."

"I think that's the whole idea."

"Good," Harwell said, "get out of here and get his story."

"Did you check the museum's hours of operation?" Gerard asked. "I think they close at five-thirty tonight."

"No, they're open until nine on Fridays and Saturdays."

"Oh crap," Gerard snapped his fingers. "I forgot it was Friday. I have a heavy date." His mouth curled into disappointment. "I guess I can reschedule it for tomorrow."

Jessie looked away; a sudden sinking feeling attacked her insides. She wasn't sure she liked the idea of him having a date. But then, they weren't exclusive. She did tell him to forget about her.

"Are you okay?" Gerard asked.

"Why wouldn't I be?" Jessie responded sharply and exited out the back door of the precinct. She gave him a brief side-glance and noticed a grin on his face. Resentment flooded through her like a wind-swept fire in a forest.

* * *

The detectives entered the museum and meandered toward the van Gogh exhibit, where Vito said he'd meet them.

Gerard scanned the area with his eyes, sure Vito would blow them off as Tony did. "I don't see him, Jess." A large faction circled the docent to listen to her well-rehearsed account of van Gogh's life.

Gerard's impatience got the best of him. "I think we have another Tony on our hands," Gerard barked.

"Here you go again with the negativity." She shook her head, baffled by his attitude. "He'll be here," she insisted.

Gerard removed his wallet from his back pocket, pulled out a twenty-dollar bill, and waved it in her face. "Twenty bucks says he bailed."

"You still haven't learned, huh, hotshot? You'll see."

Gerard made a grunting noise and walked up to a painting, pretending to be interested, except the expression on his face was not.

Eyeing everyone around the exhibit, Jessie noticed a tall woman with long dark hair dressed in jeans and a sweater, viewing one of the famous artist's works in the following display. The woman gradually made her way over beside Jessie, carelessly whacking Jessie's arm with an oversized handbag hanging off her shoulder when she turned. The corners of Jessie's mouth curled into annoyance, and she countered with sarcasm.

"You should watch where you're going with that lethal weapon," she snapped. The woman glared at her with an unwavering stare until Jessie realized it was Vito. She acknowledged him with a nod and snatched the twenty-dollar bill out of Gerard's hand. "Next time, hotshot, you'll trust my judgment."

CHAPTER 20

"You can pull up right in front of this house," Patrick Sawyer said to the cab driver. He paid his fare and slowly walked to Maria's house. With his hand on the knob, he swallowed hard and pushed the door open, hoping he would be able to console his daughter when she heard the news about her mother.

When he entered the living room where the women sat, Gabi jumped to her feet. "Daddy, you were gone a long time," she said. He squatted down to her level and hugged her.

"You know Daddy loves you more than anything in the whole world, don't you?"

"Of course, I do, silly. I love you too." She stopped talking and stared at him. Her face a picture of questions. "What's wrong, Dad?" Patrick stared at her with a blank expression. "You're scaring me."

"I have something I need to tell you, pumpkin."

"What?"

"It's about your mother."

"Yeah."

"Your mother is missing, sweetheart."

"Yeah, she's in Ohio?"

He shook his head. "No, sweetie. No one knows where she is right now."

Gabi began to wail and scream. "Then, where is she, Daddy? Is that why those detectives were here?"

"Yes, sweetie. I didn't want to tell you until I was sure they were telling me the truth."

Gabi jumped off the chair and grabbed his hand. "Daddy, let's go home. Mommy won't know where we are when she comes home."

"The police won't let us go home yet. The police have to do an investigation first."

"Why?" A mass of confusion covered her face. "Do they think Mommy's there?" Tears rolled down her cheeks.

"No, they already checked there."

"But what if she comes home? She won't know where we are."

"Don't worry, Gabi," he said, wiping the tears from her left cheek, "If Mommy comes home, a police officer will be at the house to tell her where we are."

"Maybe she's at Gram's house, Daddy," she said frantically. "Let's call her."

Maria moved closer and bent down to dry Gabi's tears with her thumb. She held her while the child sobbed into her shoulder.

"What happened?" Maria mouthed.

He shrugged and made a face. "The police say Amanda's missing, and right now, they don't have any leads." He smoothed his hand over Gabi's shoulder while still embraced in Maria's arms. She sobbed more vigorously, the tears rolling down her cheeks like an avalanche. He mouthed the words. "They think someone broke into the house and did something to her." He shrugged.

"But you saw her leave, didn't you?" Maria mouthed back.

"Let me get her a drink," he tipped his head to the side, gesturing for Maria to follow him.

Maria put the child down on the chair. "I'll be right back, sweetie." She walked toward Patrick, who was waiting in the hallway. "What happened?" Maria whispered.

"I'm guessing whoever did this forced her to return home. The police said no signs of forced entry existed, but the house was a mess. Amanda would never have left the house like that—she was a "neat freak." He glanced toward his daughter. "I can't believe this."

Gabi's sobbing increased in volume. "I'll get the water; you go to her."

He nodded in agreement. He'd expected Gabi to be upset, but this felt worse than he'd imagined—it was like a stake was driven through his chest, and the life was being sucked right out of him. Patrick knelt in front of his daughter and whispered words of encouragement, but she pushed against him.

"This is all your fault, Dad." She pounded her fists against his chest. He wrapped his arms around the child to console her, which only caused her anger to flare. "You never should have let Mommy go. I hate you, and I'm never going to forgive you." She ran for the stairs and raced up to her room.

Maria placed the glass on the end table to go after her, but Patrick pulled her back.

"It's okay. Gabi will get over it. Let her have a good cry. She'll be okay."

* * *

Gabi rushed into the bedroom and slammed the door. She threw herself on the bed and cried into the bedspread. She would never believe her mother wasn't coming back for her. She just couldn't.

"Mommy, you have to come back home," she shouted as though her mother could hear.

She lay in the center of the bed, trembling with fear, wondering what would happen to her. Gabi wasn't sure she loved her father anymore. "No," she shouted, "I hate him. This is all Daddy's fault." A few seconds later, she slid down off the bed and got on bended knees to pray. "Please, God, let Mommy be okay." Her stomach hurt. Her heart ached, and she was scared. "God, if I vow never to eat ice cream for the rest of my life or ride my bike again, will you promise to bring Mommy back?" Hot tears seared her cheeks. She knew she wished for a miracle, but surely God would answer her prayers if she prayed hard enough. She wished she had her rosary beads, but Gabi didn't need to hold them in her hands because she knew the order of the prayers since Sister Mary Catherine made the class recite them every day.

Closing her eyes, Gabi pictured the rosary beads and began to say the prayers associated with each group of beads, but an image of her mother begging for help flashed through her mind. She felt like someone was trying to yank her heart out of her chest. She rolled over into a sitting position, placed her face in her hands, and sobbed. Bitterness welled inside her chest, aimed at her father. She'd never forgive her father if her mother didn't come home. Her T-shirt was wet from crying, but she didn't care and wiped her nose on it anyway. She had to finish the rosary to show God she was serious. She couldn't give up hope.

* * *

"Are you okay, Sonny?" Maria asked.

"I don't know, Maria. I don't know how I'm going to deal with Gabi's grief. I guess I'll have to call Amanda's parents. I'm sure they're pretty upset too."

"You should go to them, Sonny. They're your family." She gave him a sympathetic glance. "Can I make you a cup of soup or tea?"

"No. I'm not hungry." His facial expression changed. "I'd like a Bourbon on the rocks, though." Maria stood to leave. Patrick reached for her hand. "You might just become a mother, after all." He looked lovingly into her eyes. "Would you like that?"

Maria stared at him with astonishment and pulled back. "Sonny. Stop talking crazy stuff. I know you're upset, but be careful about what you say. You don't want Gabi hearing you write her mother off so quickly."

"But if you could take care of her, would you?"

"Of course, I would," she shot back. "You know that." Maria swallowed hard. "You know how much I've always wanted children. I'd welcome her with open arms," Maria said as she rubbed her hands up and down her crossed arms. "But, let's not discuss this right now. We'll cross that bridge when we come to it."

He leaned in and kissed her passionately. A sick feeling erupted in her stomach. Maria shoved him away, unable to comprehend what was going through his mind at a time like this. "My God, what are you doing?"

He held his strong hands tightly around her body. "You know I love you. I've always loved you."

"Please, stop this right now. Gabi should be your first concern, not me." Maria jerked away from him and rushed to the kitchen, her heart pounding from his erratic behavior. She questioned his kiss so soon after he'd learned his wife was missing. Sure, they'd wanted to be together for a long time, but not this way. She inhaled and exhaled a few times to control her racing heart, then convinced herself he needed her understanding. She'd never thought this day would come, but now that it was here, it scared her. She persuaded herself to over-look the kiss and chalked it up to his emotional state of mind over Amanda's disappearance. But was he that upset? Sure, he seemed sincere, but he didn't act upset except when consoling Gabi.

Maria filled a glass with Bourbon and chugged it down, hoping to calm her nerves. The liquor burned as it eased its way down her throat. She stood for a long while and stared out the window; a mixture of emotions rushed through her mind clouding her thoughts. Sonny needed her support right now. She reached for his drink and headed back to the living room.

Her hands smoothed her skirt down as she headed for the door, then something made her stop mid-way. She wasn't ready to return to the room and face Sonny—she needed more time to clear her head. He wasn't thinking clearly, and now it was up to her to help him, and Gabi deal with their loss. Maybe Amanda wasn't missing. Perhaps she was hiding out somewhere. But leaving Gabi? From all the things he'd told her about Gabi and Amanda's close relationship, hearing she'd left without her daughter didn't make sense.

Maria was no stranger to Patrick's broken promises. It had been that way for years and she didn't see it changing anytime soon. Like most women, she'd talked herself into believing that having him part-time was better than not. On occasion, handling the second fiddle part had gotten to her, but Maria had accepted she'd never have him around for special holidays or more than a week at a time, often pushing her patience to the limit. That's when she'd started nagging him about moving faster. God. Was she the reason his wife was missing? Did she push him into doing something to Amanda?

Maria checked the clock and realized she'd been in the kitchen longer than she'd intended. She reached for the bottle of Bourbon again, refilled the glass half full, and then headed out to him.

"You took a long time," he said. "What happened?"

"I couldn't remember where I'd put the Bourbon," she lied. He reached out for the glass and guzzled it down in one gulp.

"What did the police say to you?" she asked.

"They think . . . I had something to do with it."

She gasped. "Oh, my God. Did you do something to her?"

"No, but I don't know how to prove it."

"What do you mean? Don't you have an alibi?"

"Not an ironclad one. Gabi was at her friend's house, and Amanda and I were the only ones there. The next morning, Amanda received a phone call from her friend and left. Unless they find her, I'm the one they're coming after."

"Oh, no. You have to hire the best lawyer in New York."

"I will, but I don't know what to do if they charge me." He rubbed a hand over his face. "How am I going to prove I'm innocent?"

"Sonny, tell me the truth. Did you have anything to do with her disappearance? Did my nagging push you into this?"

"Of course not. What kind of monster do you think I am? Christ, if you don't believe me, no one will."

Guilt washed over her for doubting him, and she reached out to him. "I believe you, honey." She wanted to assure him everything would be all right, that she'd stand by him, no matter what, but the words would not come out of her mouth. The thought of him in jail for a crime he didn't commit was too much to bear. She rubbed his cheek with the back of her hand to comfort him, to let him know she was on his side even after all that had happened. "What can I do to help?"

He reached for her again. This time his hands slid over the mounds of her breasts and down between her thighs. A low throaty moan escaped from her mouth, and any previous doubts she'd had vanished by her need for a more profound ecstasy. She willingly gave in to his demands. "Take me," she whispered.

When he scooped her into his arms and mounted the stairs, she was overwhelmed with passion, telling herself he needed comfort—it would be okay. He carried her into the bedroom, gently kicking the door shut with his foot, and placed her on the bed.

Gabi quickly ducked back inside the bedroom when she saw her father carrying Maria up the stairs. She couldn't believe her eyes— Maria was his cousin. He was disgusting. How could he do this to her mother? She reached for her backpack sitting on the chair next to her bed. She wasn't staying in this house another minute.

Stomach cramps attacked her insides, and she thought she would throw up listening to the moaning from Maria's bedroom. She had to escape, and Marti was the only person who could help her now. Gabi sat down on the steps, sliding down them one by one, praying the old wood wouldn't creak and give her away. She couldn't believe how much she hated her father.

Gabi's head throbbed whenever she thought about her mother and where she might be. Her imagination ran wild, and she couldn't help but picture bad things happening to her by someone with an evil face. She clutched her stomach, pressing her hands firmly against it, hoping to stop the cramping. On the last step, she stood and tiptoed to the kitchen, grabbed the flashlight and cordless phone. She opened the door leading into the garage, gingerly opened the car door, slid behind the steering wheel, and called Marti's cell phone. The girl answered on the second ring.

"Marti," she said, sobbing, "I need to talk to you. I'm so scared."

"Gabi," she screamed, "is that you?"

"Yes. You have to help me."

"What's wrong? I've been so worried about you," she said excitedly. "The other night, I was scared when you hung up so quickly. I wanted to call you back, but my mother came into the room, and I hid the phone so she wouldn't yell at me."

"No. I'm not okay. My mother is missing, and they don't know where she is. Someone broke into our house, and they think—" Gabi's sobbing increased.

"Ooh, Gabi. I heard the news and wanted to call but feared you'd get in trouble again. Who told you?"

"My father. The detectives came here and told him." Gabi dried her tears on her arm. "Marti!" she wailed.

"Yeah?"

"My father is upstairs having sex with his cousin." Gabi started hyperventilating, unable to catch her breath.

"Eww, that's sick. How disgusting."

"I don't know what to do." Gabi found a box of tissues on the seat and wiped her nose. "What should I do?"

"Tell me where you are, Gabi."

When a bright light flashed into Gabi's eyes, she knew her father had caught her again. Anger seared his face. Pulling the door open, he yanked her out of the car swiftly. "I've had it with your bad behavior. What the hell do you think you're doing?" He grabbed the phone from her hands and clicked it off. "Who were you talking to?" he demanded. Tears rolled down Gabi's cheeks. She couldn't believe her father had turned into a monster. "Answer me, Gabrielle. Who were you talking to?"

"Marti."

He twirled her around and spanked her backside up every step back to her bedroom. "You stay in that room until I tell you it's all right to come out. Do you understand me?"

CHAPTER 21

"*A*re you sure you won't have dinner with me?" Gerard asked
when he pulled up in front of Jessie's apartment building.

"No, thanks. I think I'm just going to have cereal for dinner and
watch a little television."

"Okay," he said, disappointed. "If you change your mind, call me."
He blew her a kiss as she exited the car.

She smiled, shut the door, and walked up the stairs to her front
door. The door clicked open as soon as she entered the code. As she
watched Gerard edge his way into the traffic, a loving feeling
warmed her center. The anger she'd felt after last week's black rose
incident had subsided. She was no longer suspicious and even felt
guilty for thinking such a thing. Everything about him told her he
was sincere.

Inside, her elderly neighbor was struggling with a plastic bag of
garbage. Jessie rushed over and took the bag from her.

"I'll take that for you, Mrs. Curly," she said. "You go back inside
your apartment and stay cool." Jessie wiped the sweat from her upper
lip. "We're sure having an Indian summer this year," she said. "I can
hardly wait for winter."

"Me too, but then we'll be saying the same thing wishing it was summer." Mrs. Curly smiled, her wrinkled face gathering together like an accordion. "Thanks for helping out an old lady. You're my angel."

She chuckled. "There are several people who'd dispute that with you."

"That's because they're all criminals." She smiled and walked back inside her apartment, waving as she closed the door.

Jessie reached for the bag and shoved it down the chute, then raced up the stairs to her apartment, ready for that bowl of cereal. She flipped on the light switch and saw a small envelope on the floor when she entered the apartment. She groaned when she noticed it was the same type and color as all the others.

"Shit!" Jessie said and tossed the note on the counter, deciding to ignore it. "Just leave me the fuck alone," she growled. It had been a while since she'd received a threatening note. It made her think whoever was doing this had become bored and moved on. Her stomach quivered with anxiety. She sighed while walking to the cupboard and removed a bowl, filling it with granola from the box on the counter where she'd left it the day before. Trying to ignore the envelope, she caught a glimpse of it in her peripheral vision, and curiosity got the best of her. She tore the edge off and removed the folded card.

The note bore the exact resemblance as the others—cut-out letters from a magazine to form words pasted to a card. "Let's see what your feeble brain came up with this time," Jessie said, reading the note.

Your presence has drowned me in my boat of life,
You have taken my joy and given me strife,
Leave us alone—go back to where you're from,
Or you'll wish you'd listened to the beat of my drum.

Jessie's cell phone rang, and she jumped. The words *blocked call* flashed across the screen. Annoyed, she accepted the call only to hear the wail of a cat crying out in pain. The sound caused her to shudder and sent a chill down her spine. She quickly disconnected the call, closed her eyes, and inhaled, trying to block out the cry replaying in her brain. A few seconds later, her phone rang again. This time, she clicked on it without reservation. She was going to give the caller a piece of her mind. This time, though, it was the sound of sinister laughter channeling through the receiver.

"Go to hell," she shouted into the mouthpiece. "Your little game is starting to piss me off." She slammed her cell phone on the counter, shaking from the intrusion. Immediate remorse overcame her—she'd given the creep precisely what he wanted—to scare her. Why was she allowing this person to get to her? Had she given up the notion that it was someone within the department? She released a ragged breath and forced herself to be strong.

An image of her mother entered her mind. She shuddered as she visualized her playing the victim role her entire life and the familiar loathsome feeling constricted in her stomach. Her mother was weak —she was not, and to prove it, she calmly sat down in the chair and stared out the window. A chill skittered down her spine, stopping at each vertebra before going to the next. Her breathing became labored. Maybe she wasn't as brave as she thought. Air, she needed air. She pushed the slider open to her balcony, her breath catching in her throat, shocked by what she saw. Two vases of dead black roses sat on the small balcony. Sinister laughter from below caused her to run back inside her apartment. She slammed and locked the door shut.

Calling for help wasn't about her being weak anymore. Gerard was right; she needed to pay attention to these threats. Whoever was doing this was out to get her. And they were getting too close for comfort.

She checked the barrel of her Glock. Jessie couldn't remember the last time she'd fired her gun, but she was sure to use it this time. She eyed her bulletproof vest on the chair and, without hesitation, slipped her arms through the loops and sealed the Velcro, stopping only to dial Gerard's number. He answered on the first ring.

"Changed your mind already?"

"I need backup stat," she said out of breath. "Another note, two vases of dead black roses on my balcony, and two calls: one with evil laughter, the other the wail of a cat. I'm on my way outside. Meet me there." Without waiting for Gerard's response, Jessie slapped her phone shut and took the stairs two at a time. Reaching the bottom floor, she knocked on the building manager's door.

"What's up Jess?" he asked.

"I need to check the building; please contact the neighbors and ask them to remain in their apartments." He began to ask a question when she held her hand up. "I'll tell you later." He nodded and shut the door.

Jessie ran the length of the building, checking the hallway and back entrance. The hallway was clear. Unlocking the back door, she pushed on it and scanned the area to see if anyone was around. Once outside, she checked all the logical places someone could hide. Satisfied there was nothing out there, she rerouted through the hallway and out to the front of the building.

A throng of passersby crowded the sidewalk. Flashing her badge, she motioned for them to leave. They took off like a shot down the street, but a few curious bystanders stopped mid-way to see what was happening.

Screeching sirens got closer, and she knew Gerard would be there within seconds and it wasn't long before he barreled out of the car and over to her.

"Are you okay?"

"Yes, I've checked the back; you guys take the sides of the building," she instructed the four officers, who separated in different directions to surround the building. The sound of mocking laughter continued to echo in her ears. She cringed, wondering if she was overreacting. Despite her slow tempo, her heart throbbed in her chest. The pair moved closer to the building, their backs against the wall, easing closer to the fire escape. The streetlights from the adjoining neighborhood silhouetted its massive structure.

Hearing the evil laughter, she noticed a dark object sitting on the back steps—the laughter loud and clear now. She used her T-shirt to remove the recorder to avoid damaging evidence.

"What is that?" Gerard said, coming up behind.

"The culprit. Sickening canned laughter."

Gerard shoved his hands inside rubber gloves, reached for the recorder, and instructed the team to perform a canvas of the neighbors to question everyone.

"I need to tell my neighbors everything is okay first."

"These guys will take care of it."

"No. I need to see Mrs. Curly. She's an older woman who's probably scared out of her mind. I want to tell her myself. The guys can tell the others." He smiled, obviously warmed by her compassion.

"Okay, but afterward, it's back in this car. You got that?"

"No, Gerard, I have to work on the investigation."

"Oh, no, you're not. Get your sweet little buns in that car," he said, pointing to his vehicle. She nodded, knowing he was right.

"I'll get in the car after I talk to Mrs. Curly."

When she returned to the car, Gerard returned down the stairs from her apartment. One of the investigators carried a bag, and she had no doubt it contained the roses. Her eyes filled with water, trying to rid her mind of the cat's scream. She leaned her back against the seat and closed her eyes so her partner wouldn't see her crying.

She jumped when the car door opened on the passenger's side. "Everything all right now?" Jackson's husky voice rang out. She looked at him and then over to Gerard, who had entered the car simultaneously.

Jessie's hand slapped against her heart. "Oh my god, you scared the crap out of me."

"I'm sorry, Jess," Jackson said. "I just wanted to make sure you were all right."

"I am. Thank you."

"What are you doing here, Jackson?" Gerard asked.

"I heard the call and was concerned about Jessie." He gave Gerard a sharp look. "Is that okay with you, Gerard?"

CHAPTER 22

*M*ax parked his bike in the driveway and ran up the steps, expecting to walk inside the house without using his key. The door was locked. He sighed, pulled his backpack off his shoulders, and unzipped the front pocket where he kept the house keys. He thought his mother might be in the basement doing laundry. He called out to her, but there was no answer. The silence was deafening. It gave him an eerie feeling.

Max tried to remember if she'd told him she would be out but soon realized she hadn't. He rolled his eyes, annoyed she wasn't there to greet him when he walked into the house, but that wasn't anything new. She was rarely home these days.

He dropped his backpack on the floor, opened the dishwasher to remove a clean glass, and balked when he realized he hadn't run the washer the night before. By avoiding his parents, his father in particular, he'd neglected to complete his chores. The truth, their constant bickering was driving him crazy, especially hearing his mother's accusations toward his father. Initially, he'd been on her side, but now he was beginning to understand how his father felt. He was a good man, and it made him feel sick every time she started in on him.

He exhaled, grateful he had his little world behind the closed door of his bedroom so he could play detective.

He checked the clock on the wall and noticed it was 3:20 p.m. If he ran the dishwasher now, they'd be clean in plenty of time for dinner, and then he could put them away in the cupboard before he got chastised. Otherwise, he'd have to wash them by hand, which wasn't happening.

Max reached under the sink, removed a detergent packet, and shoved it into the soap dispenser when he noticed another freshly baked cherry pie on the counter. His mouth salivated, especially after touching the warm plate. These days, her cherry pie was all he had to look forward to at home.

He leaned on the counter and retrieved a plate from the cabinet. The smell of the cherries and buttery crust made his stomach growl. He quickly pulled the drawer open for a knife and cut a colossal wedge. The cherries oozed out the sides when he transferred the pie to his plate. Unable to contain his urge, he licked the thick red syrup from the edge of his plate and headed upstairs to his bedroom, shoving the fork through the crust.

He rubbed his stomach when he finished, contemplating a run back downstairs for another slice but quickly talked himself out of it, knowing his mother would only go off on him if he didn't eat dinner. Max huffed out a disgusted breath and entered his room when he suddenly remembered his father had brought the surveillance equipment home last night to review some evidence. Max's heart raced excitedly at the prospect of listening to what he'd recorded in the confessional. Rushing to his closet, Max reached for the hidden cassette, checked the clock, then galloped down the stairs to the basement, hoping the recorder was still there, and smiled when he saw it on the table. He shoved the cassette inside the recorder, adjusted the headset on his ears, and pressed the play button.

The cassette began to spin. He listened as someone cleared their throat, then the muffled sound of a vacuum in the background and a woman speaking in Spanish to someone else. "Oh, no. Don't tell me I didn't get anything." He released a hefty sigh. "Cripes. I lied to Dad about having the cassette when all I have is a vacuum cleaner?" He wasn't sure he'd share that bit of information with Ritchie, especially after the way his friend had mocked his covert operation. Eyeing the large circle of recorded tape, he knew he had to have something else recorded. He'd give it a few more minutes just to be sure. His pulse quickened when he heard the familiar sound of the shuttered window sliding across the aluminum track. Now, he was getting somewhere.

He closed his eyes to visualize the darkened room containing only a kneeling bench in front of the window where the priest sat, and for a second, he felt as though he was in the booth confessing his sins. A long delay ensued, and all he heard was someone breathing heavily. Thoughts raced through his mind until he heard a man's voice reciting the customary phrase used by Catholics before confessing their sins.

Bless me, Father, for I have sinned," the man said, releasing a heavy sigh.

How can I help you, my son?

I killed my wife.

There was a noticeable silence. Max's eyes were wide, with fear waiting for the details. He heard a knock and jumped thinking it was someone at the basement door, until he realized it was on the recording.

Are you listening to me, Father? More silence. *Why aren't you speaking?* The man growled. *"Is this a ploy of yours to trick me?*

No. I'm trying to absorb the magnitude of what you've just told me. Why would you do such a horrific thing?

She wouldn't give me what I wanted.

And what was that?"

"It doesn't matter now. She wouldn't give it to me; because of it, she's forced my hand, and now she's paid the price. He laughed. You should have seen how scared she was when she ran and jumped into a car in the middle of the road, but I tricked her because I was right behind. And you know what that stupid bitch did? She drove right into Central Park. The park was closed, and that's when I nailed her up against Bow Bridge. The way I rammed into

the back of the car she'd stolen . . . let's say it's over for her. Talk about a lucky break. Good riddance, bitch, was all I could say before I pulled away."

Max checked the time, removed the cassette from the recorder, and rushed upstairs to see if anyone was home. Noting the coast was clear, he knew the cassette was something he could no longer hide from his father. If only he'd listened to the recording sooner. Now, because of his stupidity, a woman was dead and a killer was walking around the streets of New York. He shoved the cassette into his pocket and took the stairs two at a time.

When he reached his bedroom, the man's voice replayed in his mind and he suddenly remembered where he's heard it. This was the same man whose face was on a few billboards in town and his commercials on television advertising the cars from his Mercedes Benz dealership. Max's pulse raced faster when he realized this was Gabi Sawyer's father. He wondered if the man had hurt Gabi too.

Reaching for his backpack; he removed the cassette from his pocket and shoved it into the zippered compartment for safe keeping, then hustled back down the stairs just as his mother entered the house. "Hi, Mom," he said, bolting for the door.

"And where do you think you're going?"

"I'll be back later," he said, running out the door. Ginny stood with her hand on her hip, but he couldn't worry about her; he'd already wasted too much time. He ran as fast as his legs would carry him to the train station, hanging onto his backpack tightly, worried the cassette would disappear before he reached his father.

CHAPTER 23

"Where are you taking me?" Jessie demanded.

"To my place for the night," Gerard said, never looking in her direction.

"Thank you."

He turned his head in her direction. "Thank you?"

"Yes, thank you for caring about what happens to me." This time, she was the one reaching for his hand.

Gerard willingly reached out and gave her hand a tight squeeze. "Finally," he said with a wide grin.

She smiled back. "I know. I've been brushing you off far too long, but I'd be a fool to deny my feelings anymore. One of us will have to transfer to another precinct, and that's fine. I've got to stop pretending that you don't matter. My heart is having a tug of war with my head, and my heart is winning."

"Well, it sure as hell took you long enough."

"I know. Please understand this isn't a forever commitment but a start. You have to know I'm afraid of you breaking my heart, so if I'm a little distant, you'll understand why. Okay?"

"I understand, and I promise you, I won't play with your heart. Maybe your body, but not your heart." The excitement of hearing her say those magical words had his adrenaline pumping blood through his veins.

"You know I'm crazy about you, don't you?" he said with a glint in his eye.

"I think I do know that, but I need to be sure it's not sympathy for my situation or . . ."

"Absolutely not," he barked. "I was crazy about you long before I knew about the notes. I won't lie and tell you I'm not concerned because I am, but we'll get to the bottom of this."

Gerard pulled up in front of his place and became distracted by his cell phone ringing. He checked the caller ID. "Crap," he rolled his eyes, "Harwell," he said, looking at her. "What do you think? Should we blow him off?"

"Are you kidding? If he's calling at night, you know it's important."

"Damn." He made a face, then clicked the speaker so they could both listen. "Gerard here."

"We've got him, Detective!" Harwell announced.

"Who?"

"Sawyer."

"For the missing wife and Lenny's death?" Gerard asked while watching Jessie's face light up.

"Yes, sir. For the two murders."

"And how do you know this?"

"I have a cassette with Sawyer's confession on it, but I'll fill in the rest when you get here."

"Sounds like we hit the jackpot, Lieutenant." Gerard grinned. "We're on our way."

CHAPTER 24

$\mathcal{M}$ax took the train and two subways to get to the precinct. He prayed his father was in his office because he was going to explode if he didn't tell him soon. Running up the subway stairs, he ran down the block and inside headquarters, where the desk sergeant was finishing up a call.

"Max?" Sergeant Thompson's face froze in a frown when he looked at the clock. "Hey bud, what are you doing here at this hour?"

"I need to see my dad," Max said, trying to hold his composure together to avoid alerting anyone other than his dad about what he'd done. He didn't know what his dad would do about it, but as a lieutenant's son, hurting his father's reputation wasn't in anyone's best interest.

Thompson chuckled. "Is this on official police business, or are you here for money?" he teased.

"For the money," Max said, trying his luck at humor.

"It's always about the money with you, darn kids," Thompson said, shaking his head. He keyed in Pauline's number.

"Pauline, Sgt. Thompson. Max Harwell is standing at my desk and says he needs to see the Lieutenant." Thompson winked at Max while nodding in response to whatever Pauline was saying. When he finished the call, he turned to the boy. "Max, your dad is out playing bad cop this evening. Pauline said you should wait in his office. She thinks he should be back soon."

"Okay, Sarge. Thanks." Max forced himself to stroll toward his father's office instead of running like he wanted. Although he knew he was in for big trouble this evening, he felt relieved to be one step closer to ridding himself of his burden. When he reached the door, Pauline was waiting.

"Hi, Max." She hugged him, then flipped on the light in the Lieutenant's office. "It's late for you to be traveling by yourself. Is your mom with you?" she inquired.

"No. I'm here alone."

Pauline gave him a puzzled look. "Is everything okay? Is there something I can do for you?"

"Nah. This is dad business," he said, his foot tapping nervously on the floor.

"It must be if you came down here by yourself. Okay, the Lieutenant should be here shortly." She shut the door, leaving Max alone with his thoughts.

Anxiety had him pacing back and forth. He glanced at his father's wall of commendations, remembering how he'd vowed to work hard to have more awards than him after becoming a police officer. Though, right now, his future was questionable. What he'd done was like driving a car without a license—only worse. Withholding information was a serious offense. He sat down on the sofa and sighed, wringing his hands together and trying to remain calm, but his nerves got the best of him, and he stood. When the door opened, he was startled until he realized it was only Pauline. He blew out a breath.

"Did I scare you?" she asked.

"Only a little." He released a low laugh.

"Sorry." Max noticed her curious expression. She was dying to know why he was there, but he didn't explain. "Are you sure you're alright?"

"Yes. I'm just anxious to see my dad."

"Is your mom okay?"

"Yeah," he nodded, "she's fine. Can you call him?"

"I did, sweetheart. He's on his way back. Want a soda while you wait?" she asked.

"Yes, please." Max watched her walk away. He'd always liked Pauline. She was like the grandmother he'd never known.

A few minutes later, she returned with a can of soda and a bag of chips and handed them to him. "Let me know if you need anything else. I'll be in my office."

"Thanks." Max popped the tab and took a long swig. He hadn't realized he was so thirsty and managed to guzzle down the contents of the can within minutes. Now that he was in his father's office, he needed to figure out how to approach the subject. He questioned whether he should blurt it out and come clean or gently explain the situation. He knew using the wrong opening line could be problematic because of his father's lack of patience and tendency to blow up. Max filled his cheeks with air and blew it out swiftly. He knew nothing would relieve the gut-wrenching ache playing havoc in his stomach until he bared his soul. The anticipation of his father walking through the door was killing him. He'd repeatedly told himself that having regrets was a waste of time. It was way too late for that. He was going to take his punishment like a grown-up.

***

Harwell entered the building to a loud commotion that was taking place at the far end of the precinct. A line-up of hookers were being escorted to a communal cell, waiting for their pimps to show up and bail them out. One of the ladies, a woman of color, was shouting at the officer in charge.

"I ain't making no damn money wasting time in this place, Charlie. I got a kid to feed, you know."

"Yeah, I know all about it. And, just for the record, Lola, I'm Officer Gertz to you, not Charlie."

"What's the matter, handsome? Am I turning you on or something?" she said in a sexy voice.

"Not a chance, sweetheart. Why would I need a hooker when I have the crown jewels at home?"

Harwell grinned and headed past the women when the desk sergeant called out to him. "Hey, Lieutenant, did anyone tell you Max is here?" he asked.

"Yes, Pauline mentioned it when she called," he said with a frown. "Is he with his mother?"

The sergeant shrugged. "No. He's by himself."

Harwell's brows rose. "I wonder how he got here."

"I didn't ask."

"Where is he?"

"In your office," Thompson said, then made an about-face and walked toward the kitchen.

"Lieutenant," Detective Santori called out to him. Harwell stopped in his tracks. "The lab put a rush on the DNA sample from Jane Doe's dress and that bloody piece of flesh, and it's a ninety-seven percent match to the Milligan's."

"Superb! Did you tell Jess and Gerard?"

"I spoke to Gerard a while ago." He started to walk away. "Oh, and the neighbor to the right of the Sawyers—they did have a security camera, but the damn streetlight must have blown because we can't see a thing."

Harwell snickered. "Glad to hear about the DNA, but we can't seem to catch a break with this case." Harwell waved and entered his office. Max was still pacing back and forth.

"Max? Hey."

"Oh, Dad," Max said, nervous tension strumming through his veins.

"What are you doing here at dinnertime? And, more importantly, how did you get here?"

Max ignored his questions, anxious to get the ordeal over. "Dad, I have something important to tell you."

"What is it, son? You look scared."

"I know you're going to be mad at me, and I don't blame you, but this is more important than being punished. And I'll take any punishment you want to give me."

"Okay, go ahead." Harwell's eyebrows rose, but he held his

patience. "Tell me what's on your mind." He pulled a chair close to the sofa and urged Max to sit beside him. Max didn't answer right away. "It's okay, Max. Talk to me."

"I . . . I've been lying to you."

"Uh-huh. About what?"

"I did use your equipment. I was playing detective. I was celebrating being finished with summer school and having two weeks to myself to hang out with my friends. . and so . . . I used the surveillance equipment and planted it in the confessional at St. Catherine's—just for fun, though," he added as an afterthought.

"Geez, Max," Harwell's eyes opened wide. "I thought I raised you better than that. What the hell's the matter with you, son?"

"I know, Dad. It wasn't very nice." Max lowered his head and watched his feet tap the floor.

"Okay, go ahead," his father said, shaking his head. "Tell me the rest."

Max could hear his heart pounding in his ears. His anxiety had nothing to do with what kind of punishment he was going to get. It was about his irresponsible disregard for another person's life who was probably somewhere rotting away.

Harwell looked his son square in the eyes. "Max, take a deep breath. I'm not going to discipline you here. We'll discuss that later. Now, go ahead and tell me. Whatever it is that you came to say sounds important."

"Well, I think I aided and abetted."

Harwell held back a snicker. "You did, huh? Okay, so tell me what you did."

"I did record a confession, but it wasn't what I thought I'd get," his voice became more fragile and shaken. "Some man killed his wife."

"What?" Harwell's head jerked forward.

Max nodded. "Uh . . . if only I'd listened to the tape sooner," he diverted his eyes again. "I'm sorry, Dad."

"For God's sake, Max," Harwell's palm rose. "Is this the missing cassette you said you didn't have?" He gave Max a clipped side glance.

"Yes," Max said in a low voice, "but this confession is Gabi's father," he said raising his voice and no longer remorseful but proud he'd solved his first case.

"Who's Gabi's father?"

"Gabi Sawyer. She goes to my school."

"You're kidding." Jack's head jerked back. "You mean Patrick Sawyer?"

"Yes, I guess that's his name. He's the man who showed up at the police picnic and was shouting at you. I've also seen his face on the billboards in town selling cars."

"Really? Do you have the cassette with you?" Harwell asked anxiously.

"Yes, Dad. And Dad," he said with excitement, "I removed the plastic tab to preserve the integrity of the tape just like you taught me." He grinned with pride as he reached for his backpack sitting on the floor, unzipped the pocket, and handed the cassette over to his father.

Harwell chuckled. "You did, huh?" He walked behind his desk and called someone. "Would you bring a recorder to my office?" He hung up and looked at his son. "Okay, go on."

"The reason I didn't give it—"

Harwell rolled his eyes. "Max, give me the important information now. We can discuss the details later. Okay?"

"Okay." Max took a deep breath, his hands visibly shaking.

Harwell gave his son a startled look. "You took one hell of a risk, young man. You know that?"

"Yes, sir, but I didn't think of it then. Does this mean you're not mad at me?"

"Ooh," Harwell released a snicker, "I wouldn't go that far."

The office door opened, and Ryan entered with a recorder. "Thanks, Ryan. Max is going to need a ride home in a little while. Would you mind driving him?"

"Not at all, sir."

Harwell nodded toward the door. "I'll call you when he's ready to leave."

"Oh, sure," he said and exited the office.

THE LAST WITNESS - BOOK 1

Excited, Harwell rushed over, inserted the cassette, and pushed the play button. When he heard the vacuum cleaner, he rolled his eyes. "What is this, Max?"

"Just hang on, Dad." Seeing the expression on his father's face, he added, "The good stuff is coming."

When Father McKinley's voice echoed through the recorder, Harwell commented. "I'd recognize that Irish brogue anywhere." Sitting down at his desk, Harwell listened intently to the entire recording. When the recording finished, he blew out a whistle.

"And I was right about it being Mr. Sawyer?"

Harwell nodded and made a mad dash for the door. "Max, I'm going to call the detectives working this case. Let's keep this between us, okay? Do you understand?"

"Yes, I do, Dad."

"What about Ritchie? Does he know you recorded this?"

"He was with me when I set up the covert operation," Max said in a rush of words, "but he doesn't know what I got."

"Okay, let's keep it that way." Harwell blew out a hefty breath of air. "If anyone," Harwell stressed, "finds out you've recorded this confession, we're both in trouble. You because you invaded someone's privacy, and me because it will look like I told you to record it."

"Don't worry, Dad. I won't. I was even careful when I talked to Sgt. Thompson, and I didn't tell Pauline anything either."

"All right, you sit tight and don't move a muscle," he said. "I'll be back in a little while." Fumbling for his phone on his belt, he removed it and tossed it to Max. "Call your mother and tell her where you are before she has a coronary."

Max nodded. "Okay, Dad." He smiled when his father left the room, feeling so much better. The heavy burden was finally out in the open and he could relax a little. He obediently called his mother's cell phone, knowing she didn't care that he was gone. She'd probably left again right after he did.

***

Harwell walked out of his office. He was happy to have the evidence, but he'd just told his son to lie. What kind of father was he?

He tried to justify it in his mind. He'd be solving the Sawyer woman's disappearance and Lenny's death, and with Vito's testimony about the chop shop, he'd be able to close it down and maybe learn who the mole was in his department. Now, all he had to do was figure out a way to explain how he got the cassette.

CHAPTER 25

"*R*yan," Harwell said from the hallway, "Max is ready."

Max was standing next to his father by the opened door.

"Are you ready, champ?" Ryan asked.

Max nodded, unsure of his current status with his father. All he knew was he felt better. He bent over to pick up his backpack and carried it out of the office. Queasiness waved through his stomach. On the one hand, he could see the excitement on his father's face when he'd listened to the recording, but he was still worried about the victim. Either way, though, he knew he did the right thing.

Max followed Ryan out into the hallway. His father had walked out of the office and was now conversing with two people he assumed worked for his father when he saw firearms on their hips.

"Thanks for stopping by, Maxie, and don't forget what I told you," Harwell said to him.

"I won't, Dad."

The Lieutenant winked at his detectives, a slight grin on his face. "The kid took the train over here without his mother's permission. Not that I mind the visit, but it's pretty late for him to be doing such a gutsy thing." He watched Max push his arms through the straps of his backpack. "Before you leave, Max, I'd like you to meet Detectives Kensington and Gerard." He pointed to Jessie. "We call her Jessie James."

Jessie laughed and extended her hand. "I'm delighted to meet you. I've heard so much about you from your dad."

"Me too, buddy," Gerard said, also extending his hand. Max nodded.

"Okay, son." Harwell patted Max on the back. "Thanks for seeing him home, Ryan."

"You're welcome, sir."

The detectives hurried into the Lieutenant's office.

"What's on the recording?"

"The answer to our prayers, Gerard . . . The answer to our prayers. Wait until you hear what I've got." Harwell chuckled as he pushed down the button on the recorder. "Of course, we're going to have one hell of a time entering this into evidence, but that's the DA's problem."

Jessie sat mesmerized, listening to Patrick Sawyer's confession about killing his wife. When the recording finished, her mouth was agape. "Wow," she blurted out. "We've got the bastard. But unless we find Amanda Sawyer, we must prove his guilt without a body." She shrugged. "This should be interesting. It sounds like our Jane Doe was Amanda Sawyer." Jessie's expression changed when she thought of the Sawyer woman. "Holy cow, I think our Jane Doe *was* trying to tell me her name when I questioned her that night. A man, a man certainly sounds like A-man-da."

"That might have had a double meaning that it was a man who'd done that to her," Gerard said. "It makes perfect sense. He must have gone back to the hospital for her. We need to find her body. Will he even admit to going back to get her?" Gerard gave a sympathetic shake of his head. "Probably not, but we just have to ensure we've dotted all the 'i's' and crossed all the 't's.'"

"Most likely," Harwell said, "he won't admit to anything. But the good news is we have enough for a warrant." Harwell stood. "Go get him."

"Where did you get this cassette, Lieutenant?" Jessie asked before exiting the room.

"I don't know where it came from," Harwell shrugged, suddenly coming up with a response. "All I know is, it was in my mail in a manila envelope. There were no notes, return address, or nothing except this beautiful little recording." He held up the envelope.

* * *

Distracted by her phone ringing, Jessie quickly moved to the side and noticed Jane Clayton's name flash on the screen. She covered her ear with her hand to block out the conversation between Harwell and Gerard regarding a trip to the ADA's office. When the call concluded, she turned to the men. "And the good news just keeps on comin' in, gentlemen."

"Do tell," Gerard said.

"That was Jane Clayton letting us know Gabi Sawyer called Marti again, and this time, Gabi's airing her father's dirty linens—literally. Maria Alexander is her father's lover."

* * *

Assistant District Attorney Samantha Richards sat behind an enormous mahogany desk, talking on the telephone. She was the consummate professional who walked the talk, dressed for success, and when she strolled down the hallway, people sat up and took notice. Today, Samantha wore a black tailored suit with a simple white blouse. Her blonde hair pulled back into a tight bun accented with black horn-rimmed glasses, was the perfect ensemble for someone so confident.

"Detectives," she smiled, "And to what do I owe the pleasure of this visit?"

"We need an arrest warrant for Patrick Sawyer."

"Okay. Talk to me."

"Double homicide, staging a burglary, money laundering . . . shall I go on?" Gerard said, his hands resting on his hips.

"Alright. Show me your evidence."

Detective Kensington opened her file and slid the photographs from the crime scene in Central Park, the Sawyer residence, photos of Lenny and Tony, the CIs, and Vito, the manager of the chop shop.

Samantha examined the images. "You said a double homicide. Do you have another photo of the second homicide? There's only one body in this photo? Where is the other victim?"

"She was taken to the hospital and then went missing."

"So, she's alive?"

"She was when we came to the crime scene, but then she went missing from the hospital, and we haven't been able to find her."

"Where did she go?"

Jessie shrugged. "We believe Mr. Sawyer found out she was still alive and went to the hospital to finish the job."

"That's speculative, Detective. Do you have any proof the husband removed her from the hospital? Surveillance tapes?" Samantha looked from one to the other, waiting for a response.

"There were no surveillance tapes from the hospital. They were installing a new system that day, but we also believe the scene at the Sawyer residence was staged."

The attorney viewed the photos more closely. "Staged? Tell me how you know that?"

"Because it was too perfect. Other than the Sawyer family's prints, there were no others, no forced entry into the house. We found some blood on the bedroom carpet and near the fireplace in the living room, which was Mrs. Sawyer's." Jessie offered.

"But that doesn't prove Sawyer killed anyone. She could have cut herself shaving her legs to account for the blood in the bedroom . . . but I am concerned about the victim's blood being in the living room."

Gerard added to the conversation. "We've had this guy on the radar for a long time when we suspected he was the owner of a chop shop on 117th Street, which is where the money laundering comes in. He has a struggling Mercedes dealership. We had two confidential informants in the shop, but Sawyer killed one." Samantha viewed the crime scene photo again. "Where's your second CI?"

"Tony was questioned but left for parts unknown. He was scared to death—fearful of what Sawyer would do to him if he found out he came to the precinct."

"That doesn't help me if I don't have his testimony to prove it. What else do you have for me?"

"We do have Vito Lorenzo, the manager of the chop shop, who will testify if we give him a deal and Witness Protection," Gerard said. Jessie smiled, knowing they'd done their job. "We've caught Sawyer in several lies. This guy's scum." Jessie stopped and stared at Samantha as she jotted down something on paper. "Lies about timeframes, his whereabouts, you name it." Jessie stopped and stared at Samantha as she jotted down something on paper. "And we also have Vito confirming Sawyer owns the shop under the assumed name of Sonny Alexander. Vito also revealed that on the night Lenny's dead body was found, Mr. Sawyer called him in the middle of the night and told him to get over to the chop shop immediately with a crew; he needed a grill replacement on his SUV."

"That seems a little odd," Samantha frowned. "He couldn't wait until morning to have his grill replaced?"

"Precisely," Gerard said.

"We met with Vito a few nights ago, and he told us when Lenny inquired about how the accident happened, Sawyer told him he'd hit a deer. When Lenny heard that, he teased Sawyer about hitting a 'blue' deer, which turns out to be the same color as the Volvo Mrs. Sawyer was driving," Jess said.

"Vito said when they couldn't fix the grill, Sawyer ordered Lenny to drive him to the dealership but must have changed his mind at the last minute and went to Central Park instead . . . maybe his sick mind wanted to see his dead wife again."

Samantha shook her head, "But why would he have killed this Lenny?"

"According to Vito, Sawyer didn't like Lenny asking him so many questions. When Sawyer ultimately told Vito he wanted Lenny to drive him, Vito knew right away what he would do to Lenny. He even begged Sawyer not to. Sawyer told him he just wanted to get to know Lenny better, and then, of course, Lenny ended up shot in the back of the head."

"And," Jessie added, "We have a taped confession of Sawyer telling a priest he committed the crimes."

"Now, Detectives, I don't have to tell you any decent attorney will fight to keep that out. I wouldn't count on getting that into evidence."

"We know," Gerard acknowledged. "At least we know for sure he's guilty, and all our instincts about him were on the mark."

"Yes, but you knowing he's guilty and me proving it in court are two very different things. It sounds like you have a personal vendetta against Sawyer Detective Gerard. Did you record this confession?"

"Absolutely not," Gerard responded with force. "We have no idea how or who recorded this session. Our Lieutenant got it in the mail in a manila folder."

"I'm not sure I believe you, Detective." Samantha studied his face for a while. "I don't think I have to tell you what happens if you commit perjury."

"No, ma'am. I'm well aware of the law."

Okay, give me a minute." Samantha pushed back from her desk and walked down the hall.

"Whoa," Jessie said wide-eyed. "For a minute, I thought Samantha was going to charge us."

"She's just doing her job." Gerard shook his head.

Let's face it; everyone knows Harwell's feelings about Sawyer." Gerard stopped talking when Samantha returned.

"Okay, Detectives. Pick him up," she said, handing the warrant to Jessie.

* * *

When Gabi Sawyer answered the door at Maria Alexander's house, she looked like she hadn't slept in days.

"Hi, Gabi," Detective Kensington said, the tightness constricted in her chest at the sight of this young child's expression.

"Did you find my mommy yet?"

"We're working hard to find her, sweetheart," she answered. Gabi lowered her head. Anger made Jessie's stomach sick, and she quickly turned around to take a deep breath of fresh air. Her hand went to her midriff, and she inhaled deeply.

"Is your dad here?" Detective Gerard took the lead.

Gabi backed away from the open door and called out to her father, her voice barely audible. "Dad."

Sawyer rushed down the stairs, looked sternly at his daughter, and chastised her. "Did you see who was outside before you opened the door, young lady?"

Gabi remained silent.

"What's up, Detectives?" he asked in an upbeat tone. "Do you have news about my wife?"

"Sir, would you ask your daughter to leave the room?"

"Gabi, go into the kitchen. The detectives have something they want to discuss with me." Gabi meandered toward the kitchen.

"What's wrong?" Sawyer asked.

"Patrick Sawyer," Detective Kensington said. "You are under arrest for the murder of your wife, Amanda Sawyer, the murder of Lenny Scerbo, using a chop shop for money laundering, and staging a break-in into your own home."

"What?" he shouted, bolting for the door, ready to run outside. The two officers behind Jessie lurched forward, lowered him to the floor, and held him down while the other one slapped the cuffs around his wrists. "Are you out of your mind? You prove it."

Gabi must have heard the scuffle because she charged into the living room with Maria in tow and released a blood-curdling scream. "What did you do, Daddy? I knew you were going to hurt Mommy."

Maria gasped, her hand clutched to her chest as she stood frozen in space, unable to move.

"Get Gabi out of here," Sawyer shouted.

"You have the right to remain silent; you have the right to an attorney, you—" Jessie's voice faded into the background when Maria gasped again and wrapped her arms around Gabi, who wrangled free from her grip.

"Keep your hands off me," she shouted at Maria and turned to her father. "This is all your fault, Daddy. I hate you."

"Gabi, you don't mean that."

"Yes, I do."

"Maria, please take care of Gabi until I return."

"That won't be necessary, Mr. Sawyer. You won't be coming back." Jessie said. "And you don't need to worry about Gabi either because Child Services is here to escort your daughter to her grandparents' home."

"You're going to pay for this, you bastards," Sawyer shouted.

"Thank you, Mr. Sawyer," Jessie quipped. "Now, we have two more charges to add to your growing list of offenses. Assault and Battery, and threatening an officer."

"Keep it up, you two-bit whore," he shouted at Detective Kensington. "I know you're screwing Harwell."

Everyone turned to look at Jessie. A blush of red crimson rushed up to her cheeks. Sawyer continued to taunt her, apparently dissatisfied with her reaction. "Did you hear what I said, bitch?"

"I definitely did, Mr. Sawyer," she answered sweetly, then fashioned a smirk.

Sawyer's anger escalated. "My attorney will have all your asses on the unemployment line."

"How about that, Jessie," Gerard said, "we're finally going to get a vacation." Twisting Sawyer's cuffs, he watched the man grimace. "Oh, I'm so sorry, Mr. Sawyer," Gerard sneered.

"That's police brutality."

"Mr. Sawyer," Jessie said sternly, "Is this really how you'd like your daughter to remember you?" She nodded for the officers to take Sawyer out of the residence. He glanced over his shoulder to look directly at Detective Gerard. "Maria, call Alan Gerard, my attorney."

Sawyer's intentional sting aimed toward Gerard's relationship with his father sent a jolting stab to his stomach. Sawyer's knowledge of their personal lives confirmed there was only one place he could have gotten that information—someone in the department was on the take.

In that brief second, Gerard vowed to see Sawyer and whoever was helping him behind bars. It was clear that Sawyer was trying to intimidate him by hiring his father. Sawyer didn't know that he'd leave nothing to chance, no stone unturned, and he would show his father he was just as good a detective as his father was an attorney.

Sawyer cocked his head to the side. With his eyes shut tight, he released a disdained snort on his way out the door and shouted to the two detectives. "You sons of bitches. You can add whatever charges you want, but I'm telling you, you won't get away with this. You're looking for a scapegoat, and I won't be your patsy."

CHAPTER 26

"Docket number 08-N-629-014," the Court Clerk bellowed in a strong New York accent, "People of the State of New York versus Patrick J. Sawyer."

Assistant District Attorney Stephen Barringer watched Patrick Sawyer hobble across the floor toward the defendant's stand. For Sawyer's arraignment, Stephen was filling in for ADA Samantha Richards to present the State's case against Sawyer. Standing in front of the Honorable Adam Kohl for the first time made him nervous because the judge was known for chewing up and spitting out rookie attorneys just for the sport of it.

Dressed in a prison-issued orange jumpsuit, Sawyer's leg irons and wrist manacles attached to a belly chain around his mid-section jiggled like coins brushing against a metal surface. A guard on each side of him led him to the defendant's stand, where his attorney, Alan Gerard, gave a nod of acknowledgment.

Stephen nervously adjusted his eyeglasses for the umpteenth time and sighed heavily. He was diagnosed at a young age with nystagmus, an involuntary eye movement he couldn't control; it seemed to be more accentuated when he was nervous, causing those looking at him to turn the other way because they didn't know which eye to watch.

Couple that with being overweight, tight kinky curls covering his head, and thick eyeglasses that magnified the size of his eyes. And that was why he'd studied so hard. It was vital for him to impress his mentor, ADA Samantha Richards, who was next in line to be DA, because a recommendation from her would help him get a job in a well-respected law firm.

Seeing Stephen, Sawyer's face flushed with anger, his words loud and precise, catching everyone's attention. "You get me the fuck out of here."

Judge Kohl looked up from the file he was reviewing. His quick movement jarred the small framed reading glasses he wore to slide further down the bridge of his nose. "Counsel, kindly remind your client he is in a court of law. Any more outbursts and I'll make my decision commensurate with his behavior."

"I'm sorry, Your Honor." Alan shot a stern look toward his client. "It won't happen again."

Sawyer twisted his mouth to one side and gave Alan a daggered look. Alan elbowed his client and leaned over to warn him. "I'd keep my mouth shut if I were you," he said. "The more you challenge the judge, especially this one, the worse it will be for you. Let me do my job."

The judge lowered his eyes and resumed his review of the file. A few minutes later, he addressed Counsel. "Okay, let's get this show on the road. Will the attorneys introduce themselves to the court?"

"Stephen Barringer, for the State of New York."

"Alan Gerard, for the defense."

The Bridge Officer stood in the well of the courtroom, directly in front of the judge's bench. "Will the defendant state his name for the record?"

"Patrick James Sawyer," he said, shifting from one leg to another.

"Do you waive the reading of the rights and charges, Mr. Sawyer?" he asked.

"Yes, we do," Alan said.

"What do you mean?" Sawyer's volume escalated. "I'm giving up my rights?"

"No, Mr. Sawyer," Alan said through gritted teeth. "I'll explain it later."

"I might have understood the process if you had come to see me before —"

"How do you plead, Mr. Sawyer?" Judge Kohl interrupted impatiently.

"Not guilty, Your Highness."

Judge Kohl's mouth tightened in a thin line; his bushy eyebrows rose in a warning. "Mr. Sawyer, I don't know who you think you are, but I own this courtroom, and what I say here is law. Do you understand?" Patrick glared back defiantly but remained silent. "That's what I thought." The judge turned his attention to Stephen. "Mr. Barringer, you may proceed."

Stephen stepped forward. "Your Honor, the State is filing a Seven-Ten-Thirty-One-A—the defendant has made statements on several occasions that support this arrest."

Judge Kohl looked over the rim of his glasses again and smiled, apparently amused by Stephen's description. "I should hope so, Mr. Barringer. And by the way, I know what the notice means."

Stephen shoved his shaking hands inside his pockets. "I meant no disrespect, sir . . . I mean, Your Honor," he stammered.

"Duly noted. Mr. Barringer, would you like to make a statement regarding bail?"

"I would, Your Honor. The State asks the court to remand the defendant until a court date is on the calendar. We believe Mr. Sawyer is a threat to society, and the State sees him as a flight risk." Stephen breathed a sigh of relief, grateful Kohl had taken pity on him by not embarrassing him in court.

The judge nodded. "Defense counsel?"

"Thank you, Your Honor," Alan said. "Mr. Sawyer is an upstanding citizen in this city. He owns a large car dealership on Broadway a home on W 87th Street. Mr. Sawyer is also very involved in his church and passionate about helping the less fortunate by making large contributions and donating used cars to the Catholic Charities organization. He has no prior criminal record, so I ask the court to reconsider the prosecution's request."

Judge Kohl pursed his lips and glared at the defendant, then slammed his gavel onto the wooden block. "I hereby remand the defendant be held without bail in the City jail until the trial date." He hammered his gavel against the sound block. "Next case."

"A fucking good job, counselor," Sawyer said as the guards escorted him away.

"Docket number 08-N-341-924, People v. Fernando Rodriquez," the Court Clerk bellowed.

* * *

Alan Gerard stormed out of the courtroom, unhappy with his client. Entering the jail to see Sawyer, he braced himself for the meeting. An officer escorted him to a conference room. The room hadn't changed much since Alan had last visited the jail many years ago when he was a hungry young attorney. The chipped Formica tabletop looked as bad as he had remembered it. The two vinyl-covered chairs, one on each side, were in dire need of repair. He chose the chair with the least damage to avoid ruining his silk Versace suit and pulled Sawyer's file from his briefcase. He placed the file folder on the table before him and waited for his client to arrive. Outraged by Patrick's disrespectful behavior, he increased his fees. The buzzer sounded, and Sawyer entered, free of restraints.

"Oh, really nice job for a hotshot attorney," Sawyer hissed.

The muscles in Alan's jaw flexed. "Let's get one thing straight, Mr. Sawyer. I have neither the time nor the patience for your outlandish behavior. You called me for represent—"

Sawyer interrupted the man. "Exactly, Mr. Gerard, but you couldn't be bothered coming to see me before my arraignment, and I don't have a clue as to what went on in that courtroom this morning," his words seethed with arrogance.

The attorney picked up the file folder, shoved it inside his briefcase, and headed for the door, pressing the button to alert the guard the meeting had ended. "Find yourself another attorney, Mr. Sawyer," he said over his shoulder.

Sawyer huffed out a deep sigh. "No, wait – Alan, please — don't go." Alan stopped and faced him. "I'm sorry," he said, lowering his head to his hands. "I didn't mean to be so arrogant. This whole thing has me reeling with disbelief. Please don't leave. I need your help."

"Fine, Mr. Sawyer. It will be on my terms, or not at all." Alan waited for Sawyer to agree. "Do we have a deal?"

"Yes. We have a deal." Patrick shook his head. "I'll do whatever you say."

"Good, then here are my terms. I want a retainer of fifteen thousand dollars up front, and my fees are two thousand an hour. There will be no more outbursts -- not with me, nor in the courtroom. Is that understood?"

"Yes. But I can't promise I won't get upset."

"There are no *buts*, Mr. Sawyer. I do not represent two-bit criminals off the street. Either you agree, or we don't have a deal. You know my reputation; otherwise, you wouldn't have called me." He paused. "Or did you hire me to get back at my son for arresting you?"

"No," Sawyer lied. "I know you're the best."

"Do we have an agreement?"

"I'll do my best."

"No. You need to do better than that."

"Yes, for chrissake," Patrick flung his hand in the air. "Yes, we have an agreement," he said with resignation.

"Good, sign your name on the dotted line, and let's get down to business."

CHAPTER 27

*L*ieutenant Harwell walked down the hall and greeted his two detectives. Jessie gave a casual wave and crossed the room to her desk.

"Chalk one up for the prosecution," Gerard said, catching up with his boss, his face covered in a wide grin.

"I heard," Harwell said, returning the grin. "Josh Galveston, from the New York Recorder, called a while ago and filled in the details while asking for my comments." Harwell shook his head. "Sawyer's taken his arrogance as far as it can go."

"Did Vito show?" Harwell asked.

"Yes, sir." Jessie had a wide grin on her face. "He gave us everything we need to put Sawyer away."

"Good job, Detectives. Thank you," Harwell said, heading for the door. The minute he was outside, his shoulders relaxed, relieved to be going home. During the cab ride, Jack had rehearsed what he would say to Max. Although he was more than grateful Max had saved the day, the boy needed to understand there were consequences for his actions, just like the criminals. He worried his excitement over the recording may have sent the boy the wrong message. Yet disciplining him too harshly might stifle his desire to become part of law enforcement. That was the last thing he wanted.

Unlocking the front door to his home, he entered. The house was dark except for the glow of lights shining down the stairwell from Max's room. He flipped on the light switch and called out to his wife. "Ginny, I'm home." There was no answer.

Max barreled down the stairs. "Hey, Dad. Is Mom with you?"

"No, son." He raised his brows. "I guess that means she's not here."

"Nope. But that's no big surprise."

Harwell's stomach tightened. "What do you mean it's no big surprise?"

"I mean, Mom's hardly ever home when I get here. But she's late tonight. Did she tell you she was going somewhere?"

"No. But mom must have left a note, son." He placed his briefcase on the counter, removed his jacket, and laid it over the back of the chair.

"No. I checked everywhere." Max shrugged. "She used to leave notes but stopped a while ago," he said, shuffling through the refrigerator.

"What do you mean?" Jack asked.

He shrugged again. "Mom doesn't care about us anymore."

"Don't say that, Max. That's not true. Your mother loves you." He watched Max pull a cold piece of fried chicken from the refrigerator and bite into it. "Your mother will be upset if you spoil your appetite."

Max strode toward the steps; his expression resigned. "Okay," he said, taking another bite and mounted the steps.

"Whoa, not so fast, young man. We have a little matter that needs addressing." Jack motioned to the sofa. "Have a seat, son."

Max plopped down on the sofa next to his father. "I'm sorry, Dad, but helping you catch the killer . . . that was a good thing, wasn't it?" he said with anticipation in his voice.

"That's a matter of opinion. If you're going to be a police officer, Max, you need to be accountable for your actions, and lying is a grievous offense." Jack looked directly into Max's eyes. "And I'm even more disappointed that you disobeyed me. Regardless of whether you helped us capture a killer, your disregard for someone's privacy is the issue. Lying and breaking the rules has consequences." Jack paused. "What do you have to say for yourself?"

"You're right, Dad. I'm sorry. It won't happen again."

"Okay, apology accepted. Now, you get to choose your punishment."

"Dad, is the wife dead?"

"Max, your punishment!"

Max sighed. "No television for a month?"

"You need to do better than that, Max. You don't watch much television." Jack said. "Son, I don't think you understand the seriousness of your behavior. You risked your life and Ritchie's by recording a killer's confession. You lied to me and disobeyed a direct order."

"Yeah, but I didn't know what I had recorded . . . not until I listened to it today."

"You're missing the point here."

Max sighed again and lowered his head. "All right, Dad, take my computer away for a month. I probably deserve worse than that."

"I'm very proud of your decision, Max. Taking your computer away is a major step in the right direction. I'd like you to go upstairs now and disconnect the cables. Call me when ready, and I'll help you bring it to my office." Jack's heart ached for Max, but he was proud the boy gave up something he loved. "I will be locking it away until you've completed your punishment. Do you understand?"

"Yes, Dad."

"Okay, son, you're excused."

Max mounted the steps slowly, his head down, shoulders sagging like he was going to the guillotine. Jack forced himself to remain objective. He checked the clock on the wall and noted it was six-thirty. Upset but trying to think positively, he keyed in Ginny's cell phone number and left a message when she didn't answer. Maybe she'd been in an accident and didn't have identification. The thought made him shudder. Indeed, he would have heard something by now. He walked to the refrigerator and pulled out a container of turkey soup. He removed a pot from the lower cabinet, emptied the box's contents, and placed the pot on the stove to heat.

Walking around the kitchen, Harwell rummaged on the counter, looking for a note, thinking Max may have been too hasty when he searched. It was unusual for her not to leave a message. Had he been so caught up in his little world that he hadn't realized she'd been going out regularly? Maybe she'd found a boyfriend. He shook off the thought. Was Ginny's lack of attention to Max the catalyst that drove the boy to seek revenge by disobeying?

He turned the dial to heat the oven, tossed a loaf of bread from the freezer, and set the table while the Grandfather clock chimed seven times. A knot formed in his stomach, tightening like a noose around his intestines. His mind reviewed the list of friends Ginny might be with until he suddenly realized she hadn't mentioned any of her friends lately. It was no secret that Ginny was difficult to get along with, always starting fights because of her insecurities. Maybe her friends had abandoned her. How had he ignored that?

A torrent of nervous energy made him feel panicked. He removed the personal phone directory from the drawer and called Nancy Stone, a friend of Ginny's.

"Hi, Nancy," he said when she answered. "Jack Harwell. How are you doing?"

"I'm doing great, Jack. How about you?"

"Mostly, I'm doing fine but concerned about my wife. Is Ginny with you?"

"No, Jack. I guess you haven't heard."

His heart pounded inside his chest. "What haven't I heard?"

"Ginny and I haven't seen each other in months."

"No. I didn't know that, Nancy. I'm very sorry to hear that. Dare I ask what happened?"

"Well . . ." Nancy's heavy sigh told him she wasn't sure how much she should say to him.

"Please, tell me."

"I don't want to rehash it, but Ginny's been acting odd these last few months. I tried to help her by suggesting she seek medical attention or counseling, but she became upset and told me she didn't need help."

"Oh, Nancy. I had no idea. I'm sorry."

"Do you want me to call around for you?"

"No, thanks. I'm probably overreacting. You know, it's my law enforcement mentality working overtime. She's probably out shopping and just forgot to leave a note." He chuckled and placed the phone back on the cradle when he heard Nancy's voice.

"Jack," she shouted.

"Yes?"

"Please let me know -- discreetly, of course, when she returns home. Even though we don't see each other, I'm still very concerned about her."

"Will do, Nancy. Thanks." Jack walked back into the kitchen, pulled two salad bowls from the cabinet, and filled them with the precut lettuce from the plastic container in the refrigerator. He'd been so self-absorbed about his own needs he'd neglected to notice his wife was struggling. How had he allowed himself to get so caught up trying to impress his superiors that he hadn't seen she was crying out for help? The frequent arguments between them should have told him something, but he viewed them as Ginny's problem. Regret filled him. He exhaled a breath of frustration and promised himself as soon as she walked through the door, he'd sit down with a glass of wine and have a discussion—just the two of them.

Max walked back down the stairs carrying the monitor from his computer, the cables draped over his shoulder. "What's wrong, Dad," he asked, apparently noticing his father's discord.

"I'm worried about your mother, son."

"Why?" he asked, placing the monitor and cables on the floor next to the stairs. "Do you think something happened to her?"

"I don't know, Max. Come sit down at the table, have some soup."

Max walked around to the opposite side of the table and sat down. The smoke alarm went off, and he jumped. Rushing to grab two towels, he called out to his father. "Dad, something's burning in the oven." Max pulled the door of the oven down in one swift motion.

Smoke billowed out like a dust storm. He fanned the air with the towel until his father rushed over.

"Oh, crap, the bread is in flames," he said, "I've got this, Max," moving him to the side. "Open the windows and door. Dammit, I forgot the bread was in the oven." He shook his head from side to side, reached over and shut the oven off, switched on the exhaust fan, and waited for the flames to die. Once the bread cooled down, he tossed it into the sink and turned on the faucet. Max stood at the back door and swung it back and forth, trying to redirect the smoke outside.

"Nice mess I've made," Jack said. "Okay, start eating; I need to call the precinct."

"About Mom?"

"No," Jack lied. He didn't want Max to worry but reconsidered since he'd just punished his son for lying. "I'm sorry, Max. I just lied to you, and there's no excuse for that. I am calling the station house to put them on the alert." He noticed the frightened expression on Max's face. "Son, please don't worry. If something happened, we would have heard about it by now."

"You think so?"

"Yes, Max. I think so."

After making the call, Jack returned to the table and sat across from Max. He pushed his bowl to the side, no longer hungry, and reached to pat Max's hand. "They're on the lookout for Mom's car. They promised to call me later, but Mom will probably be home anyway, and all this worry will have been for nothing." He lowered his head to look into Max's eyes. "Are you okay?"

"Yeah, Dad. I'm okay. Mom's going to be fine," Max reassured.

When Max finished his dinner, Jack stood to clean the kitchen. "Have you finished your homework?"

"No."

"Okay, go upstairs and get it done." He listened as Max bounded the stairs and continued to scan the kitchen for a note. When he finished, he draped the dishtowel over the oven handle and headed for the living room. Deciding he needed a distraction, Jack walked to the wicker basket, pulled a magazine from the pile, and leafed through it when he noticed a page caught on something. He opened the page and saw a block had been cut out. Figuring Ginny had cut out a coupon, he put the magazine down and picked up another when he noticed the same thing. Blocks on several pages had been cut out.

"Oh, dear God," he gasped, his heart racing out of control like a plane at takeoff. "Please tell me what I'm thinking is crazy."

CHAPTER 28

*J*essie unlocked the door to her apartment and sashayed across the room, struggling to get to the table with the heavy bag of groceries. It felt good to be home. Gerard had been wonderful to let her stay at his house, but she didn't feel right about him sleeping on the sofa while she slept in his bed. So, tonight, she was going to hang out in her apartment and enjoy the silence without any outside influences.

A glance around the apartment, and she shook her head in disgust. It hadn't cleaned itself while she was gone, and the only difference to the room was the folded pile of clothing on the chair had dwindled, and she was running out of things to wear. Jessie placed the bag on the table, dropping the pile of mail and keys from her hand next to it. Right now, the only thought on her mind was a glass of Pinot from the bottle sitting on the counter. Exhausted, she strolled toward the cupboard, grabbed a wine glass, filled it to the brim, and sipped it.

The red wine was just what the doctor had ordered. She slowly made her way across the room to the overstuffed, comfy armchair. She never liked the chair with its loud floral print, but it was all she had left of her mother.

Setting the drink down on the end table, she removed her shoulder holster and belt, hanging them on the corner of the chair, then kicked off her shoes. Flopping down on the chair, she propped her feet up on the coffee table and reached for the glass. "What a day," she said aloud, releasing a heavy sigh, and tipped the glass to her lips, allowing the wine to linger on her tongue awhile.

A yawn escaped her mouth, and she closed her eyes, resting her head against the cushion to quiet her over-active mind. She was tired and didn't want to think about anything, but it wasn't easy to shut down after the kind of day she'd had. At least she was alone in her apartment without the daily pandemonium on her job, drinking wine and sitting in a comfy chair.

Her thoughts returned to Patrick Sawyer's upcoming trial. How much more evidence did they need to collect before Sawyer's fate was sealed? They could prove Sawyer's guilt even though they'd never found Amanda's body. Thank God for Vito's testimony. Knowing Alan Gerard's reputation meant ADA Samantha Richards needed all the ammunition she could get, and it was their job to see that she had it. But was Samantha good enough to win against Alan? He had a lot more experience than she, and from the articles Jessie had read, Alan Gerard was brilliant. Word had it that he was a master of diversion. Samantha had to know his reputation, and she'd have to make sure she was just as prepared.

Jessie scrubbed a hand over her face. Why did she always put so much pressure on herself? Because she needed to be perfect—that's why. Thinking about the scuttlebutt in the office, she found it hard to believe her peers thought Harwell was treating her better than he did them. And then, for them to think she was the kind of woman who would date a married man made her crazy. She had her standards, and that was the last thing she'd ever do. Of course, they didn't know that, but still . . . . She blew out a breath. She had to stop thinking about this nonsense and focus on the evidence against Sawyer.

A tinge of insecurities crept through her mind, and she worried they wouldn't be able to pull it off. Sure, Vito had come forward, but would he survive long enough to testify? Was the safe house secure

K. T. ROBERTS

enough? Her stomach recoiled, and she sucked in air, blowing it out in a steady stream to calm her nerves.

Christ, if she was this nervous, what was Gerard going through knowing his father was the opposing attorney? Considering the stature of Alan's reputation, there was little chance he'd treat Sawyer's case any differently than all the others. If anything, the competition that was about to take place between father and son would be interesting. Based on what Gerard had told her about Alan, there was little doubt he would shoot holes in all the evidence they'd collected. That was his job. And what about the taped confession? Jessie forced herself to stop, relaxed her shoulders, and twisted her body to lay kitty-corner across the chair, her long legs draped over the mound of the armrest. Maybe she should consider passing on dinner and go straight to bed. No, it was too early. She forced herself to sit upright.

Out of the corner of her eye, she thought she saw the drape move. Jessie frowned, wondering if she'd left the window open after burning her toast the other night. She smiled to herself, concluding the wine was affecting her judgment. Leaving a window open is the last thing she'd do. Too tired to check, she convinced herself if someone were to come in, she was a gun-toting law enforcer. They wouldn't get very far. She resumed drinking her wine, convinced it was the wind blowing through the cracks of the old window frame. She made a mental note to ask the superintendent to caulk the cracks and resumed her thoughts about the case.

Amanda Sawyer's DNA was an undeniable match to that of the Milligans. Would the murder charge stick even though they hadn't found her body? For sure, Lenny's murder was a given with Vito's testimony, but that wouldn't put Sawyer behind bars long enough.

Maybe she was just paranoid. But if she relaxed too much, they might overlook something significant.

Minutes later, the drape moved again. This time, Jessie stood and strolled over to the window and pushed the curtain aside. Her hand no sooner touched the fabric than she realized someone was hiding behind it.

The intruder leaped out to the side, wielding a gun. Jessie gasped, her heart pounding ferociously against her rib cage.

"Surprise, surprise, bitch," she said. "This isn't exactly how I'd planned to surprise you, but this works." The woman stepped closer, her firearm now aimed at Jessie's chest.

"How did you get in here?" Jessie shouted, the blood rushing through her veins while she feigned composure.

"The old lady downstairs let me in," she snickered. "She thinks I'm your sister."

Dread crept through Jessie for having given Mrs. Curly her apartment key so she could call her daughter on Jessie's house phone. "What do you want?"

"What you've taken from me, bitch."

What had she taken from this woman? The woman's anger intensified, and she brandished the gun insecurely. Jessie edged closer.

"You must think I'm an idiot, Detective." She aimed the firearm at Jessie's forehead. "Don't you move another inch," she demanded in a firm voice.

"Whatever you think I took from you, ma'am, was decided by a jury, not me. I only did my job."

"You still don't get it, do you?" The woman shook her head. "That's what's wrong with you sluts. Now, get your fucking hands up where I can see them."

Jessie could see the woman was stressed. Still holding her wine glass, she obeyed the woman's instructions but quickly took control by tossing the wine into the woman's eyes. The woman staggered back against the bookcase, and before she could retake control, Jessie used one swift karate kick and managed to knock the gun from the woman's hands, landing on the carpet in a thud. Jessie grabbed the woman's wrists, twisting them behind her back, then dragged her toward the overstuffed chair for the handcuffs.

The woman's shoulders slumped, and she sucked deep breaths. Jessie tightened the cuffs, leaving little room for movement. The woman cried out in pain.

"Lady, you're in a lot of trouble," Jessie said, forcibly pushing the woman down onto the upholstered chair and grabbing her gun from the holster. The woman lowered her head and wept.

"Hasn't anyone ever told you pointing a gun at an officer of the law is illegal?" Jessie shook her head in disgust. "Did you think you could overpower a cop?" With her firearm pointed at the woman, Jessie squatted down to retrieve the gun from the floor. A tiny spot of orange peeked through the black tip, signaling the Glock was a fake.

"You stupid asshole," Jessie barked. "You break into my apartment with a fake gun?" The woman continued to sob. "Are you out of your fucking mind? I could have killed you." Jessie's skin pebbled from the chill, skirting down her spine. "Who the hell are you?"

The words were no sooner out of Jessie's mouth when someone pounded on her door. Assuming it was one of her neighbors who'd heard the commotion, Jessie checked the peephole first, and when she saw Harwell, she knew the identity of the woman. Slowly pulling the door open, she gave him access to the view.

"Oh, Ginny," Harwell said, his voice cracking as he rushed over to her. "For the love of God, what have you done?" The woman hung her head and continued to sob.

A lump formed in Jessie's throat as she watched Harwell's tender moment with his wife. "What's going on, Jack?"

Harwell took a deep breath. "Ginny thinks we're having an affair." He exhaled with exasperation.

"What?" She turned to him. "You can't be serious?"

"I'm afraid so. Tonight, while I was waiting for her to come home, I was looking through some magazines and found several pages with cutouts."

"That doesn't mean anything," Jessie offered. "She could have been cutting out coupons for all you know."

"No," his voice lowered, "Ginny spends a lot of time in the attic. She has a trunk up there with what she calls her treasures. I went to the attic and looked inside." He nodded in confirmation. "There were several more magazines with cutouts. Ginny's the one . . ."

"Lieutenant," Jessie said with a sigh, her hand in a stop gesture, "you don't have to explain." She shook her head. "Just take her home."

"I can't." He turned toward his cuffed wife. "Ginny," his voice wobbled, "I have to arrest you."

"No, you don't," Jessie said firmly. She walked behind Ginny and removed the cuffs from her wrists. "She needs help, Jack, not jail time."

"I have to do what is right, Jessie. Everything is on record."

"Your wife is volatile right now—counseling, Jack. That's what she needs."

"I'm so sorry, Jessie. I had no idea."

"Jack," she said, exasperated. "Please . . . just take her home."

Harwell nodded his head in agreement. "Thank you. I can't tell you how sorry I am."

"I know, Jack. Stop worrying about what happened and take care of her. She's your top priority."

Jack nodded again. "C'mon, Ginny, let's go home." The lieutenant and his wife brushed past Jessie on the way through the door. "You have to write an incident report."

"What incident, Lieutenant?"

Harwell patted Jessie's arm as he eased past her. Jessie watched as they walked away. Halfway down the hall, Jack turned to look back at Jessie and mouthed his regret. She blew out a breath of air, grateful the fiasco was over.

CHAPTER 29

"You look tired, Jess," Gerard said. "What's wrong? Aren't you sleeping?"

"Nothing's wrong." She focused on the hustle-bustle of the crowd on the sidewalk to avoid letting him get another glance at her. Ever since the episode with Harwell's wife, she'd kept to herself, afraid of letting on about what happened. She didn't owe Harwell anything, but she didn't want him to lose his job either. Harwell had worked hard to get his promotion. If he lost his career, he wouldn't have health insurance to care for his family. She shrugged without turning her head to face him. "Nope, life is good."

"Oh? Then why are you looking out the window instead of talking to me?"

"Oh," she lied, "a fat woman is walking down the street wearing a tight chartreuse skirt and orange shoes. A large crowd has gathered around her, but I can't figure out why."

"That's bullshit! What's going on?" he said firmly. "Did you receive another letter?" He pointed his finger at her. "And don't you lie to me?" She didn't respond. "Jess?" Maybe telling him would make her feel better. "Jess. Talk to me. Get out whatever is causing this depression."

"I'm not depressed."

"Well, something's wrong. Tell me." When she didn't respond, he turned down a side street and stopped the car. "Okay, spill your beans . . . right now."

Jessie forced the air from her lungs. "Okay, okay. I know who's been harassing me."

"Good. Who is it?"

"Harwell's wife."

"What? How do you know that?"

"She was hiding out in my apartment a few days ago."

"Holy shit! Why?"

"She was jealous and thought we were having an affair. She just lost it, I guess."

Gerard shook his head in disbelief. "You're filing charges, aren't you?"

"No. Of course not!"

He reached for her. "Are you sure?"

"Absolutely. Jack's got a ten-year-old son. Who do you think will care for him while the wife's in prison and Jack's at work?"

"Family?"

Jess shook her head. "No. I know I don't owe Jack anything, but his kid deserves as normal a life as he can."

"I'm so sorry, sweetheart. Are you okay?"

"I will be. Can we just let this go and not discuss it again? I want to forget the whole thing ever happened."

"Absolutely." He watched her for a few minutes. "I'm so sorry." He patted her hand, put the car in gear, and continued down the street. They drove in silence until she finally spoke.

"I'm feeling pretty good about the evidence we're collecting against Sawyer," she said, "and I'm praying Father McKinley will talk to us."

"That's wishful thinking. Haven't you ever heard of the *vow of silence*?"

"Yeah, but that's all for a show, right?"

"Are you kidding me? When a priest hears a confession, regardless of what he's told, he can never repeat one word. Compare it to the attorney-client privilege."

"Surely, God wouldn't send him to hell for cooperating with the police by telling what he knows." She frowned. "Would he?"

"Well, maybe not God, but it warrants ex-communication from the church." Gerard parked the car in the parking lot at St. Catherine's. A light rain misted the windshield. He looked upward. "I think we'd better make a run for the door. It looks like the sky is about to open up."

"The *vow of silence* sounds like a silly rule to me."

"If your attorney told the court something you confessed to him, how would you feel about it?"

"I'd be pretty pissed, that's how I'd feel."

"Okay, then, I rest my case. Why expect anything less from a priest? We're dealing with a court of law versus the church's laws. It's the same thing."

"Okay. Point taken. So why are we going to see Father McKinley?"

"I thought it was worth a try. I want to confirm Patrick being here and get whatever else we can." They ran across the parking lot, the gravel crunching beneath their feet. Inside the church, Gerard dipped his finger into the holy water and blessed himself.

"You know, I've always wondered why Catholics do that," Jessie whispered.

"I'm purifying myself before I walk down the aisle to the altar." He grinned.

"Does that mean you're never going to sin again?" she asked in a low voice.

"Only while I'm in here."

"That's kind of what I thought." She grinned and followed close behind, watching him genuflect before the altar. She'd never seen this side of Gerard before. She liked watching the formalities that was so automatic to Catholics when they entered their house of worship.

The smell of musty old wood was suddenly noticeable, and the creaking of the floorboards beneath her feet caused her to tiptoe so she wouldn't disturb parishioners kneeling in the pews. Candles flickered in red votive cups before statues in the various niches dedicated to patron saints. She inhaled the smell of the incense and felt a surprising calm come over her. She didn't remember the last time she'd been inside a church.

Although she wasn't Catholic, she'd spent time with her childhood friends while they confessed their sins, never entirely understanding why they had to admit them to an actual person. To her, talking to God and confessing sins in the privacy of your mind seemed the most logical and least embarrassing.

Jessie noticed the confessional booth up against the wall. It had one center door and smaller doors on each side. She wondered which side Patrick Sawyer had used to confess his sins. Gerard made a right turn.

"Is Father McKinley expecting us?" she asked.

"Yes. Father is vesting in the Sanctuary," he pointed.

Suddenly aware they both had guns strapped to their hips in a house of God, Jessie felt awkward, as though she was defying the church's laws. "Should we be in here with our firearms, Gerard?"

"It's okay. We're cops, remember? It's not like we're planning to use them."

Father McKinley walked to the door and greeted them. "You must be Detectives Gerard and Kensington," he said in his deep Irish brogue. Two altar boys and a young priest, preparing for Mass, gave a curious glance.

"Yes, Father." Gerard handed the elderly priest his card. "As I mentioned on the telephone, we're from the two-one precinct. Is there somewhere we can speak privately?"

"We can go to my office. Father Gabriel is saying Mass tonight."

"I'm sorry, Father. I didn't mean to take you away from your duties."

"That's fine, Detective. He's a newly ordained priest. He can use the practice."

Jessie figured Father McKinley to be in his late seventies. His smile and gentle manner gave her a warm, comfortable feeling and reminded her of her Irish grandmother. She watched the priest limp down the hallway and wondered if he was in pain.

"Tell me, Detectives," the priest said, glancing over his shoulder, "Are you Catholic?"

"I am, Father," Gerard said, a prideful expression on his face.

"I'm not, Father," she said. "But I attended Mass with my friends occasionally during childhood."

"And did you learn anything from it?"

"Yes," she chuckled. "I guess I did."

"And what would that be, my dear?"

"Be more patient with my friends who were always in trouble with the nuns."

"I've seen a few of those in my day." He stopped and faced Gerard. "Did you attend Mass on Sunday?"

"No, Father, I was working." Gerard shifted around uncomfortably while Jessie enjoyed watching him squirm. He'd just lied to the priest unless he had a second job she didn't know about. She snickered quietly. So much for cleansing his soul before entering the nave, but she wouldn't give him away.

"Well, as soon as we finish here," the priest offered, "you're welcome to attend the five-thirty Mass—then you won't have to worry about making another excuse to me about why you didn't attend this week." The priest grinned, exposing his coffee-stained teeth.

Jessie gave Gerard a playful pinch on his forearm and watched his ears turn a crimson red.

The smell of roast beef baking in the oven wafted into the office, inciting hunger pangs. Jessie inhaled the comfort food, enjoying the familiar aroma.

"Have a seat," he gestured. "Can I get you a soda or something?" he asked.

"No, thanks, Father."

The priest scanned through his telephone messages as though he was alone.

He pushed the pink call sheets to the side when he realized they were staring at him. "Oh, I'm sorry. Okay, you wanted to talk to me. What would you like to talk about—pre-Cana?"

Jessie snorted when she saw the surprised expression on Gerard's face. "Oh, no, Father," she answered, a giggle escaping in between, "You'll give this man a coronary at the very use of that word. We're here on official police business."

"Too bad. You look like such a loving couple. Okay. What business?"

"We'd like to talk to you about Patrick Sawyer."

"What about him?" He shook his head disgustedly.

"Father," Gerard cleared his throat, "we have a recording of Sawyer's confession to you. Can you tell me anything about him?"

The priest swallowed hard. "A recording?" He jerked his head back. "How is something like that even possible?"

"Someone's pretty clever, Father, but it could be a mischievous prank."

"I hope you find out who this so-called clever person is and ensure they never do anything like that again."

"Someone sent it to the precinct in an unmarked package."

Father McKinley sat motionless momentarily; a horrified expression crossed his face. "If you are a Catholic, then you know about the Laws of the Church. There is no way I would break my *vow of silence.*"

"Relax, Father, I'm not asking you to tell me anything about the confession. We already have that information. We're asking if you'll come to the precinct and identify his voice."

"I'm sorry. But I cannot do that. What transpires between a confessor and his priest is confidential."

"Can you tell us if Patrick Sawyer is a parishioner?"

"You'll have to call my secretary on Monday. Her name is Mrs. Vickers. I don't keep track of that information." Father McKinley's voice became impatient. He rose from behind his desk. "I'm sorry I can't be of more help. Now, if you'll excuse me, my dinner is waiting."

"I know about the *vow of silence*, Father," Gerard said in a rush of words, "but we need your help to put this man behind bars."

"If you know, Detective, you can understand why I can't reveal what I've heard. I'm afraid you'll have to find someone else to help you. I can't." He turned on his heels and left them standing in the room, surprised by his abrupt exit.

CHAPTER 30

*N*ovember 2008

Gerard scanned the crowded hallway with his eyes watching for the Milligans to arrive at the courthouse. When he spotted Charles Milligan standing in line at the security check, he waved to let them know he was there.

"We're a wreck," Charles spewed in a rush of words when they caught up to Gerard. "Why did the judge throw Patrick's recorded confession out?"

"Because it was recorded without his knowledge. And quite frankly, there's no way the padre would have confirmed the contact due to his *vow of silence*." Gerard shrugged.

Gerard had expected Joyce and Sara Milligan to be hyper, but he hadn't counted on Charles' composure slipping. "Hey, we knew it most likely would be ruled out, but don't worry, there's no doubt in my mind that Sawyer's going down. We've done our homework. I don't see how the jury can return with anything other than a guilty verdict." He watched a blaze of emotions cross Charles' face.

"Okay," Joyce argued, "but it could happen if his attorney is smarter than the DA. Couldn't it?"

"Of course, but it's doubtful." Gerard knew giving them false hope wasn't the best approach for encouragement, but he was confident he was more than ready to meet his father head-on.

"You said the DNA proved it was her, but how do you explain that when you don't have a body?" Charles asked. "Will the judge throw the murder charge out, too?"

"Look, why don't we let the attorneys do their job? Samantha Richards is sharp, and I feel more confident with her pleading this case than anyone else from the DA's office."

"We need closure," Joyce insisted, tears brimming on her lashes. "And we need to know Patrick will suffer for the rest of his life."

"I agree, Mrs. Milligan, and we'll do whatever we can to help that along."

"The newspaper said Patrick's attorney is your father," Charles said wearily. "Is that true, Detective?"

"Yes, sir. Alan Gerard is my father."

A piercing pain erupted in the pit of Gerard's stomach. Being in his father's presence always made him tense and insecure, wishing he didn't have to speak to the man. But this time, he had no choice. And this time, he wanted his father to eat the thunderous, painful words he'd launched at him all those years ago about being a detective. Gerard felt a surge of confidence charge through him until his father passed by with his entourage of attorneys. He thought Alan would have given him a nod or at least looked in his direction, but that didn't happen. Gerard fought to maintain his confidence, but like it or not, his father had a firm hold on him that temporarily shook his resolve. Gerard inhaled a deep breath, determined not to let the man's presence deter him from his course of action. Charles interrupted his thoughts.

"How will that work then?" Charles asked.

"The same way it does in any other trial." He shrugged and motioned toward the courtroom door when he noticed the bailiff walking toward them. "Please try to relax." He placed his hand on the small of Joyce Milligan's back and guided her toward the double doors. "Let's go inside and watch Patrick Sawyer squirm." Gerard sucked in a deep calming breath as he made his way down to the end of the row.

Gerard watched his father leaf through papers in a file, preparing for trial—a sight he'd seen many times during his growing years in the replica courtroom set up in their family home. A wave of trepidation skittered through him at the thought of his impending testimony.

"I imagine he'll be pretty hard on you?" Charles suggested, sitting down in the seat next to Gerard.

"Yes, sir, but that's okay. I'm ready."

Charles exhaled. "Forgive us, Detective. It's hard to release the stress we've felt for so long. I'm unsure how to get through this ordeal or if I can stand in the same room with him. I could never imagine what Amanda saw in the man when they married." He paused as if deep in thought. "I guess he fooled her too."

Seeing the Milligans shocked expressions when a large crowd filed into the courtroom and rushed to the few remaining vacant seats. It was apparent they had not witnessed a trial before. Five minutes later, Patrick Sawyer was escorted into the courtroom, dressed in an expensive suit, a red tie with a matching hanky in his breast pocket; he appeared to be the consummate professional who could do no wrong. Gerard watched as Alan introduced his client to the other staff members and drew the jury's attention.

"All rise for the Honorable Jamie Cooper," the bailiff bellowed. A hush of silence fell over the room, shutting down any chatter. The judge, better known as The Hawk because of his sharp aquiline nose and hawk-like features, had no difficulty in living up to the moniker given to him by distinguishing himself from the more reasonable judges. He was a favorite in the DA's office because he was known for being fair, yet he was a hard-nosed officer of the court who took control of his courtroom, and no one dared to cross him. His reputation preceded him from the many high-profile cases he'd presided over.

"Docket number 08-N-629-014, in the matter of the State of New York City versus Patrick James Sawyer. The Defendant is charged with Two Counts of Murder, One Count of Money Laundering, Two

Counts of Documentation Fraud, and One Count of Threatening Law Enforcement."

Judge Cooper rapped his gavel and addressed the District Attorney.

"Miss Richards, you may proceed with your opening statement."

"Thank you, Your Honor." Samantha walked from behind the prosecutorial table and crossed the room to the jury box to speak directly to the twelve members deciding Patrick Sawyer's fate. Today, Samantha wore a brown tailored suit accented by a pale rust-colored blouse that cast a warm bronze glow on her cheeks. She was the personification of success. One juror, a good-looking man with piercing blue eyes, focused his attention on her face, a half-smile raising the corner of his mouth. She moved to the other side of the box.

"Ladies and gentlemen of the jury, let me give you the facts of this case." She stopped in the center to address them. "On August 23, 2007, the defendant, Patrick J. Sawyer," she said, pointing to him, "murdered his wife, Amanda Sawyer . . . The mother of his ten-year-old daughter. The People will show that he killed her because she wouldn't give him a divorce and custody of their only child. We will prove that he blamed his wife for the six miscarriages she had throughout their twelve-year marriage. We will also prove that his anger turned him into a raging bull after each miscarriage. And as if that wasn't hard enough on Amanda Sawyer, he beat her because she'd ruined his promise to his mother to have a house filled with children."

The audience gasped. The jurors' reaction told her she'd driven her point home, boosting her ego. Gerard turned to see the family's response. Mrs. Milligan and Sara were crying softly, each on opposite sides of Mr. Milligan, whose arms were wrapped around each of their shoulders. His jaw flickered with anger.

"This man," Samantha pointed to the Defendant, "abused his wife's body, mind, and soul to get what he wanted. He didn't marry his wife for love, ladies and gentlemen; he married her as his baby factory."

Samantha paced back and forth; all eyes focused on her. Excitement surged through her veins. The sound of her heart echoing in her ears was invigorating, and she loved the high. The enthusiasm kept her going and helped her drive her points even harder. "And that's not all of it, ladies and gentlemen; the State will prove Mr. Sawyer killed Lenny Scerbo, an employee from his chop shop because he knew too much. The State will further prove Mr. Sawyer and his accomplices stole vehicles, changed the VINs, and sold them from his car dealership lot to unsuspecting customers. Instead of going to the bank for a loan like a normal businessman would, he found what he thought was a foolproof way to defraud unsuspecting customers by opening a chop shop to offset his dealership's financial shortfall. A chop shop, ladies and gentlemen -- that's right," Samantha's voice rose a few octaves, "under the alias of Sonny Alexander—the last name of his lover, Maria Alexander, a former employee from his dealership. Those poor unsuspecting customers thought they were buying a legitimate car with a warranty." She paused to allow her words to sink in.

"These are the facts of the case, ladies and gentlemen, but defense counsel will try to tip the scales of justice by dissuading you into believing we have no case. The defense counsel will try to convince you that because we have not located Mrs. Sawyer's body, we have no proof of her death. But ladies and gentlemen, make no mistake, we have enough physical evidence to prove them wrong." Samantha turned and walked back to the prosecution's table.

She inhaled the musty smell of old mahogany wood on her way back. The beauty of this courtroom, with its majestic, old-world charm, made her feel stately, like she should be wearing a black robe and wig. She'd argued many cases in this courtroom, and the magic of being in this historic room where many famous criminals met with their fate never waned. The raised heavy wooden panels and sculptured trim couldn't have been any more beautiful than if Leonardo De Vinci had used his creative hands to craft this splendor. Her eyes scanned the room. She wasn't surprised to see standing room only.

"Mr. Gerard, do you wish to make an opening statement?" Judge Cooper called out.

Alan Gerard stood, pushed his chair underneath the table, and buttoned the top button of his suit jacket before making his way around. The suit, a grey pinstripe, offset by his matching gray hair and deep blue eyes, gave him a striking appearance as he made his way over to the jury. He stopped in front of the box and moved his head from left to right, making sure he obtained eye contact with each juror.

"Ladies and gentlemen of the jury. I have a news bulletin for you. Amanda Sawyer is not dead." The audience released another gasp. "If she's dead, where's her body? For all we know, she could be off somewhere with a lover."

Charles Milligan stood and shouted. "He's lying."

Judge Cooper hammered the wooden block. "Another outburst like that from the audience, and I'll clear the courtroom." The defense attorney grinned, apparently pleased he'd gotten a reaction.

Gerard's lips tightened in a thin line. Mr. Milligan eased himself back down onto his seat. He was shaking from the inference. Sara and her mother continued to cry, holding hands across the father's lap.

"Even her parents," Alan pointed toward Sawyer's inlaws, "can't fathom that their daughter would do such a thing. You heard her father's outburst, ladies and gentlemen. The morning Amanda Sawyer left, she willingly gave up her only child -- for a fistful of money."

Charles rushed from the courtroom.

"You see what I mean, ladies and gentlemen," his hand gestured toward Mr. Milligan's back, "the truth hurts. No, ladies and gentlemen, this case is not about the disappearance of Amanda Sawyer. It's not about the death of Lenny Scerbo, the money laundering, the documentation alterations, staging a break-in, or any other bogus charge." He stepped closer toward the jury box. "No, no, no," his finger wagged back and forth. "This case is about vendettas: Amanda Sawyer's and the personal vendetta of Lieutenant Jack Harwell, a newly appointed officer in the NYPD. And you know why? Two years ago, the lieutenant's good friend and former lieutenant of the two-one Precinct was accidentally killed in my client's garage at his car dealership when a mechanic, who hadn't noticed the lieutenant standing under the car lift, retracted it." Expressions of horror capped the faces of the jurors.

Alan pointed toward Sawyer. "You see this man, ladies and gentlemen? This kind, generous man is trying to make an honest living in a car dealership." Alan walked back to the jury box. "There's no doubt business is bad. It isn't good for anyone in this day and age. But a chop shop?" Alan shook his head in disgust. "Our district attorney has a creative mind. She's trying to make you believe my client is a tyrant, but that's not so."

Alan cocked his head to the side and gave a slight smile. "Ladies and gentlemen, the Patrick Sawyer I know is an upstanding citizen who has donated his money to more charities throughout this city than most people. He's even worked in soup kitchens, helping plate food for people experiencing homelessness. But that wasn't enough for him. He had to take it one step further. Do you know what he did? He bought beds because he couldn't bear the thought of someone being turned away from the shelter. After all, they were out of beds." Alan paused, making eye contact again with each juror.

"Now, I ask you. Does this sound like the same person the DA has described? Certainly not! And when this case is ready for your deliberations, there will be no doubt about my client's innocence. And yes, my client's insurance company paid a hefty fee to the family. I'm not suggesting money can negate the loss of human life, but Lieutenant Harwell has made it his mission to put Mr. Sawyer away. We can certainly understand the lieutenant's grief, but it was an accident, nothing more, nothing less." Alan walked back behind Patrick at the defense table and rested his hands on his client's shoulders. Patrick flashed a weak smile to the jurors.

Alan turned and walked back to the defense table.

"Thank you," the judge said. "Let's take a fifteen-minute break before we begin the trial." He squinted his eyes to see the clock on the wall. "Court will resume at ten-thirty, at which time, the prosecution will call its first witness."

CHAPTER 31

"*I*s the state ready to call its first witness?" Judge Cooper asked.

"Yes, Your Honor," Samantha announced. "The People call Detective Zachary Gerard."

Gerard's stomach tightened, knowing he would testify before his father.

The court clerk approached. "Do you swear to tell the truth, the whole truth, and nothing but the truth, so help you, God?"

"I do."

"State your full name and occupation for the record."

"Zachary Alan Gerard, detective first-class, 21st Precinct, NYPD."

"You have the same last name as the defendant's attorney," the District Attorney announced. "Is Alan Gerard any relation to you?"

"Yes. Mr. Gerard is my father."

Samantha walked to the center of the room and stood before Gerard. "Detective, have you discussed this case with your father?"

"No, ma'am, I have not."

She smiled and walked away, then turned to speak to Gerard.

"Detective, were you the arresting officer of the defendant, Patrick Sawyer?"

"My partner and I were the arresting officers."

"Is the accused in this courtroom today?"

"Yes."

"Can you show us where he's sitting?"

Gerard nodded his head toward Patrick. "He's at the defense table with the red tie." Everyone turned to look at Sawyer.

"Detective, will you tell the court the events that led to the arrest?"

"On August 23, 2007, at approximately 3:50 AM, my partner and I were called to a crime scene at Bow Bridge in Central Park." Gerard looked directly at Patrick Sawyer, ready to describe the scene to watch the expression on his face. "When we arrived, two paramedics were carrying the only survivor of an automobile crash on a stretcher to their vehicle. She was unconscious then but eventually awoke and was disoriented and tired."

Gerard savored Sawyer's reaction as he watched his body tense and his fingers curl into a ball. Alan jotted something on his pad.

"My partner stayed with the woman until the EMS vehicle drove away while I headed to the scene at Bow Bridge."

"Is that where the vehicle the victim drove was located?"

"Yes, ma'am."

"I direct your attention to Peoples one through five," Samantha announced to the jury. Twelve heads turned to view the slide on the screen. "Will you describe these pictures for us?"

"Yes." Pointing to the first picture, he said, "This, is the front-end view of the vehicle Mrs. Sawyer was driving. As you can see, the front of the car is pushed tightly against one of the pillars of the bridge." Samantha clicked the remote and nodded to Gerard. "This second picture is the rear view of Mrs. Sawyer's vehicle where you can see by the deep dents, the defendant's vehicle rammed into the car several times."

"And how do you know it was the defendant's vehicle that rammed his car into the victim's vehicle?"

Samantha pointed to the marks on the vehicle on the screen. "Detective, what are we looking at here?"

"Those are traces of black paint from the defendant's vehicle."

"Were you able to determine what type of vehicle hit this car from behind?"

"Yes."

"What was that vehicle?"

"From the location of the dents on the Volvo, we determined it to be an SUV."

"Were there any other markings that confirmed your suspicion?"

"Yes, the plaster mold we made from the tire tracks leading up to the Volvo."

Samantha nodded to the bailiff who stepped in front of the jury box, holding a mangled grill.

"Detective, is this the grill from the perpetrator's vehicle?"

"Yes."

The bailiff returned the item to the table and picked up another piece. "How about this mangled bumper?"

"Yes. It came from the same vehicle."

Samantha moved closer to the bailiff and pointed to markings on the bumper. "Detective, can you tell the court what these marks are on the bumper?"

"Blue paint."

"Will you tell the court the color of the mangled Volvo, the vehicle the victim was driving?"

"Blue."

Samantha walked to the jury box and leaned against it. "Detective Gerard, will you also tell the court what type of vehicle the defendant drove before August 23, 2007?"

Gerard looked directly at the jurors when he answered his question. "A black Mercedes SUV."

Samantha turned slowly and headed back to the stand in front of Gerard. "With so many black Mercedes SUVs out there, Detective, how did you determine these items to be from the defendant's vehicle?"

"We obtained this evidence that was believed, and later confirmed, to be a chop shop owned by Mr. Sawyer."

"And what did you find in that pile on the premises?"

"We didn't find it, the manager, Vito Lorenzano, provided the damaged car parts."

"And why would Mr. Lorenzano hold onto these parts? Is that normal procedure?"

"I don't know if it's normal procedure, but Mr. Lorenzano kept them as proof."

Patrick's fists tightened into another ball. Alan Gerard leaned over and whispered something to his client, who quickly shoved his hands under the table and then shifted uneasily in his seat.

"Okay, Detective Gerard. Was there anything else at the crime scene?"

"Yes. Fifty feet to the vehicle's right was the body of Lenny Scerbo, a new employee at the chop shop operated by Mr. Sawyer who was our Confidential Informant, that we'd planted at the shop to find out the owner's identity. Mr. Scerbo died from a close-range gunshot wound to the back of his head." Samantha clicked on a remote to show Lenny Scerbo's wound.

"Is this Mr. Scerbo's wound, Detective?"

"Yes, it is."

"What kind of gun was used?"

"It was a .45 caliber."

"Was such a gun registered to Mr. Sawyer?"

"No, it was not."

"Is there anyone related to this case with such a firearm?"

"There is a .45 caliber firearm registered to Sonny Alexander."

"And did you ask Mr. Sawyer to confirm this was, in fact, his firearm?"

"As I mentioned earlier in my testimony, Sonny Alexander was the assumed name Mr. Sawyer used in his chop shop."

"How do you know this?"

"His daughter confirmed he was known as Sonny by his girlfriend, Maria Alexander."

"Okay, Detective. Let's get back to the woman at the crime scene." Samantha rested her hand on the railing of the jury box. "Was the woman's body found inside the vehicle?"

"No, Jane Doe, as she was called until we had a positive ID, was found unconscious at the edge of the bedrock platform in the Ramble."

Samantha flipped the chart to show the map of Central Park. "Can you tell the court the location of the Ramble and its proximity to the crime scene?"

Gerard turned his body toward the easel and pointed his finger at the map. "As you can see, the bridge is west of Bethesda Terrace, which connects Cherry Hill and the Ramble, about mid-Park at 74th Street."

Samantha placed the pointer on the diagram. "Is this the location, Detective?"

"Yes. As you can see from the map, the Ramble is a heavily wooded area, with a long drop from the bedrock platform where the victim was found to the lake below. If the victim had walked further, she might have fallen down the hill and into the water.

"Yes."

"Did your victim have any personal identification on her?"

"No. And there was nothing on the victim or in the vehicle that told us who she was. Fortunately, we found her fingerprints on the steering wheel."

"How did you know the prints you found were hers? Does she have a record?"

"No, she does not have a record. When her daughter had her fingerprints taken in school as a precautionary measure, Mrs. Sawyer also decided to have hers taken."

"Where did you get the prints to compare?"

"Mrs. Sawyer's parents kept them for safe-keeping."

"Did you ever find out why Mrs. Sawyer had her prints taken?"

"Most likely because she feared something like this might happen to her."

"Objection, Your Honor," Alan said in a rush of words, "Ms. Richards is leading her witness whose response is speculative."

"I agree, Ms. Richards," Judge Cooper said. "The jury will please disregard the exchange of words?"

"My apologies, Your Honor." Turning back to Gerard, she continued with a slight smile that only those who knew her understood.

"So, you're saying she didn't even have a registration in the car to identify her?"

"No. There was no registration, but after tracing the VIN, we found that the vehicle did not belong to her. We ultimately traced it to John Graham, who told us he saw Mrs. Sawyer run from behind a house on West 87th Street and jump right into his car, which had been double-parked, and left with the motor running while he walked his date to the door. Shortly after, the black SUV backed out of a driveway and raced to catch up to the Volvo."

"Is it your opinion the woman was running from something?" Samantha asked.

"Objection, Your Honor," Alan said. "Ms. Richards is leading the witness."

The judge scowled. "I agree, counselor. More questioning like this, Ms. Richards, and I will hold you in contempt of court."

"Sorry, Your Honor."

"The court stenographer will strike Ms. Richards' last question from the trial transcript," Judge Cooper ordered

Samantha cleared her throat. "Did Mr. Graham know the woman who stole his vehicle?"

"No."

"Did his date know the woman?"

"No. Mr. Graham's date was from out of state, visiting her aunt, who does live on West 87th Street."

"Is West 87th Street the same street where the Sawyers live?"

"Yes."

"Okay," Samantha continued. "Can you tell the court what happened to the woman you've described as Jane Doe while at Lenox Hill Hospital?"

"Detective Bradshaw, from our precinct, was already at the hospital and stayed with the woman while we finished our investigation at the crime scene."

"Then what happened? Did you ever go to the hospital to see her?"

"We received a call a few hours afterward that she was missing from the hospital."

"What went through your mind, Detective, when you received that call?"

"That the assailant had returned."

Alan Gerard stood his finger in the air. "Your Honor, Ms. Richards is taking tremendous liberties here. Once again, she's asking her witness to speculate."

"Approach the bench," Judge Cooper said, his voice vibrating impatiently. The two attorneys stepped forward. "Ms. Richards," he said in a deep timbre voice, his hand covering the microphone. "Your behavior is out of order. This is your last warning. I will not tolerate this nonsense in my courtroom. The next time, I'll slap you with a contempt charge and throw you in jail. Do I make myself clear?"

"Yes, Your Honor. I apologize."

"You may proceed," he said with a nod.

Samantha walked back to the prosecutor's table and checked her notes.

"Tell me, Detective, did the hospital have a security camera?"

"They did, but it was out of order that day."

"Did the hospital perform any blood tests on the woman?"

"No. On this particular day, the victims of a massive bus accident at the downtown Brown and Lowe Insurance Building took precedence. After the initial cleanup of Jane Doe's facial and arm lacerations, her injuries were deemed minor by comparison, and she was left in the hallway with other patients until the staff had control of the situation."

"Detective, let's fast-forward now. How did you ultimately learn this victim was Amanda Sawyer?"

"We had a piece of flesh we'd found on the broken window of the vehicle Mrs. Sawyer had driven that was determined to be hers when she'd ultimately exited from the vehicle she'd stolen, and a torn piece of fabric from her dress."

"Can you tell the court what happened to the dress Jane Doe wore to the hospital?"

"It went missing along with Jane Doe."

"You mean she wore that torn dress when she left the hospital?"

"It's believed that Jane Doe left the hospital in a pair of scrubs taken from the rolling rack used by the staff."

"Then what happened to the dress? Did the hospital staff discard the dress?"

"No. Standard ER practice is removing the victim's clothing and keeping it in a brown paper bag, which is given to the police as evidence. That bag went missing right along with the victim."

Samantha paced back and forth in front of the jury box. "Tell us, Detective. Did a lab perform a DNA sampling on those two items, and were they a match to her parents and daughter?"

"Yes. A ninety-seven percent match."

Samantha stopped and faced the jury's reaction. "Was there anything else unusual on that piece of fabric . . . besides blood?"

"Yes, there was a foreign mucus of some sort, which turned out to be the DNA of the defendant after testing."

"Did you have the defendant's DNA?"

"Not at first. Mr. Sawyer refused to give us a sample until we obtained a court order."

"Did you searched the defendant's residence?"

"Yes, we did."

"What prompted you to go to the Sawyer household?"

"The Milligans, the parents of Mrs. Sawyer, came to the precinct to file a Missing Person Report after receiving a call from their youngest daughter, who'd first alerted them that she thought Amanda was missing. "

"Did they visit the Sawyer house and see it in disarray?

"Yes."

"Did they have a key to the residence?"

"Yes."

"Did they give you the key to the residence, or did you obtain a warrant?"

"We first obtained a search warrant, then used the Milligan's key to gain entry into the residence."

"Detective Gerard, is this a photo of the residence?"

"Yes," Gerard said, pleased with his performance. "As you can see, it was a mess. Upon entering the residence, expensive statues were shoved over and broken, the pieces scattered over the floor in the circular foyer. It looked as though there'd been a scuffle of some sort in the living room. The kitchen counter was a mess, with items such as a box of cereal on its side, the contents strewn all over the counter, half-eaten bowls of cereal sitting in curdled milk, and a half-gallon container of curdled milk."

"Do you know if it was unusual for the victim to leave the home in such a state?"

"From everyone we've spoken to, including the defendant, the wife was constantly cleaning."

"To your knowledge, was anything stolen from the residence?"

"Not that we could tell."

"Was an insurance claim ever filed by the defendant?"

"We have nothing on record stating he filed a claim."

Samantha paced back and forth, the frown lines on her forehead wrinkled in thought. She stopped in front of Gerard. "Detective, did you ever find out how the burglars entered the residence?"

"There was no forced entry anywhere in the residence."

"No forced entry, no claim filed from the defendant . . . did that seem odd to you?"

"Yes. After the investigation, based on evidence, it was determined to be a staged break-in."

"Did you tell Mr. Sawyer this was your conclusion?" Samantha asked, walking to the front of the defense table. She gave Sawyer a cold stare. Gerard paused and watched Samantha. He sensed her strategy was to tempt the defendant's lack of self-control for the jurors to see. Gerard watched Sawyer with interest, waiting to see whether he'd bite. When Patrick's nostrils flared, Alan scribbled something on a piece of paper and shoved it over to his client.

Patrick's demeanor changed. He squared his shoulders and shoved back in his chair.

"Detective?" Samantha queried.

"Yes . . . we did inform the defendant of our conclusion."

"What was his reaction?"

"First, he laughed, then he became angry and suggested we were looking for a scapegoat."

Samantha clicked the remote, but nothing happened. She clicked it several times in succession, and still, nothing happened. Her mouth twisted to the side. "It appears our slide projector has decided to take a break." She walked back to the table and took the stack of photos her assistant held in his outstretched hand, then turned and made her way across the room to stand in front of Gerard.

"Detective, will you look at these photos?" She handed them over and spoke while Gerard viewed them. "Is this the Sawyer residence you referred to earlier?"

"Yes." When he finished viewing them, he handed them back to her. She walked to the jury box and gave the photos to the foreperson for viewing.

She returned and handed him two more photos. "Detective, tell me what you see in these two photos?"

"The first photo is a spot of blood on the carpet in the master bedroom, and the second photo is a picture of blood on the living room carpet."

"What did the lab results reveal?"

"Both spots were the victim's blood."

"By victim, who do you mean?"

"Amanda Sawyer, the defendant's wife."

"How about fingerprints inside the residence?"

"The only prints were those of the Sawyer family."

"No other prints?"

"None."

"Is that how you arrived at your conclusion . . . that the break-in was staged?"

"Yes."

"Did you try to contact the defendant?"

"Yes, we'd made several attempts to locate Mr. Sawyer. We went to his dealership to find him. His secretary said he and his family were on a cruise, but she didn't know on which cruise line. After checking the logs of every cruise line, we did not find the Sawyer's name on any of the logs. Even his travel agent, whose name he'd provided, did not know of any cruise plans."

"Was there anyone else who thought the Sawyers were on a cruise?"

"Yes. Mrs. Simon, the school secretary at St. Catherine's Catholic school, where the defendant's daughter attends. The secretary told us Mr. Sawyer had contacted her to say the family was going on a three-week cruise, and the daughter would miss the first week of school."

"So, how did you ultimately contact him?"

"After a canvas of the neighbors in the West 87th neighborhood, where the Sawyers live, we found a witness who had spoken to Mr. Sawyer's daughter, Gabrielle, on the telephone. She told her friend they were staying with Mr. Sawyer's cousin, a woman named Maria Alexander. Through various methods available to law enforcement, we were able to track him down at Ms. Alexander's residence."

"Can you tell the court about your first meeting with Ms. Alexander?"

"When Ms. Alexander opened the door, we asked if Mr. Sawyer was there. She adamantly denied he was, except Gabrielle Sawyer was present, and immediately corrected Ms. Alexander by telling us that her father had gone to the grocery store."

"What was Ms. Alexander's reaction to the Sawyer child's correction?"

"She appeared embarrassed and explained she was guarding Mr. Sawyer's privacy."

"Then what happened?"

"The child ran down the stairs and asked if we were there because something had happened to her mother."

"Did she explain why she asked if you had information about her mother?"

"Yes. Gabi Sawyer said she hadn't heard from her mother and was concerned. Shortly after, Mr. Sawyer walked into the house."

"Detective Gerard, please tell us about your conversation with Mr. Sawyer."

"We told him the Milligans, Mrs. Sawyer's parents, had filed a Missing Persons' report after seeing the condition of the residence."

"What was his reaction?"

"He was furious and said Mrs. Sawyer wasn't missing at all; she was in Ohio with her girlfriends on a shopping spree."

"At any point during this and future conversations with Mr. Sawyer, had he ever mentioned that his wife ran away?"

"No."

"One last question, Detective. Has it ever been confirmed that Maria Alexander is Mr. Sawyer's cousin?"

"No. Ms. Alexander is Mr. Sawyer's lover."

"Objection, Your Honor," Alan's voice rang out. "That's speculation on the part of the witness."

"Objection is overruled. The witness may continue."

"Detective Gerard, can you tell the court how you know this to be true?"

"The defendant's daughter told us she'd heard them in the bedroom."

Alan Gerard leaned over to say something to his client, who had now lowered his head in his hands and began rocking back and forth. Alan's expression tensed.

"One more question, Detective. You told us this earlier, but I'd like to hear you repeat it. Can you tell the court what name Ms. Alexander used when she addressed Mr. Sawyer?"

"She called him Sonny."

"Did you hear Ms. Alexander calling him Sonny?"

"No, his daughter, Gabrielle Sawyer, told us this was the name Ms. Alexander called him when we asked if she knew a Sonny Alexander."

"Since Mr. Sawyer went under the assumed name of Sonny Alexander, is it fair to say Ms. Alexander may have been a partner in this chop shop or that he may have married her illegally?" Samantha shook her head and directed her attention to the court reporter. "Strike that."

"Your Honor," Alan Gerard said, "Ms. Richards is way out of line. Ms. Alexander is not on trial here."

"I agree, counselor." Judge Cooper gave Samantha a stern look and turned his attention to the jurors. "Members of the jury, please disregard Ms. Richards' reference to Ms. Alexander."

"My apologies to the court, Your Honor." Samantha turned her attention back to Gerard. "Thank you, Detective Gerard. I have no further questions for this witness."

CHAPTER 32

*G*erard's body tensed, sir as he readied himself to face his father. He inhaled slowly, coaxing the knot in the pit of his stomach to ease up. Out of the corner of his eye, Gerard noticed his father huddled with his three associates. When the conversation concluded, one of the associates stood and buttoned his suit jacket, walking around the front of the table.

A sense of relief washed over Gerard, like air releasing from a balloon, knowing someone other than his father would question him. It wasn't as though he was afraid of his father—Gerard wanted to make his father eat the words he'd repeatedly replayed in his mind whenever he thought of him. The associate, a young man probably in his early thirties, paused before Alan and leaned toward the senior attorney, who drew him into a discussion. When the debate ended, the young attorney stood erect, his face seared into a disparaging expression, turned, and went back to his seat. Curious, Gerard watched with interest.

"Is there a problem?" Judge Cooper asked.

"Sorry, Your Honor. Just a changing of the guards," Alan said.

"Well, hurry it along."

Alan Gerard shoved his chair back and stood, buttoned the top button of his suit jacket, and confidently strode across the floor toward Gerard.

Gerard sucked in his breath and steeled himself for his father's usual degradation, refusing to allow the man to rattle him. How could he have forgotten Alan's customary attempt to psyche out the prosecution's first witness? The muscles in Gerard's back tensed with every step his father took toward the witness stand. Fleeting thoughts of his growing years passed through his mind. Since he was a young boy, he knew all too well the rules of argument Alan Gerard used. In the few seconds it took his father to approach the witness stand, Gerard forced himself to focus on the points he'd been practicing for weeks in preparation for this occasion. His mind blanked. Sheer fright swept through him as he struggled to remember. A trickle of sweat ran down his chest under his dress shirt. His father approached. Gerard cleared his throat and grabbed the glass of water to buy time. Jessie walked in through the double doors just as he set the glass down. She smiled at him, and his confidence returned.

"Good morning, Detective Gerard," his father said.

Gerard nodded his acknowledgment and watched his father's body language.

Alan crossed his arms and rested them against his chest, his legs spread apart in a power stance. He stared at Gerard without blinking. "I have a real problem with your testimony, Detective." Alan paused, no doubt for effect. "Tell me, Detective. Do you think you're good at your job?"

"Yes, sir, I do."

"Have you ever made mistakes on the job . . . you know, with evidence?"

"No, sir, I have not."

"You mean you've never tampered with evidence to sway the jurors' votes?"

Samantha jumped to her feet. "Your Honor, Mr. Gerard, is badgering the witness."

Judge Cooper held up his hand. "I'll allow it. The witness will answer the question."

"No, sir. I have never tampered with evidence. Not now, not ever," Gerard answered with conviction.

"Isn't it a fact that certain officers in your precinct have mishandled evidence? Isn't that a fact, Detective Gerard?"

"Yes."

Alan returned to the defense table, picked up a stack of papers, and waved them in the air for the jury to see. "I hold in my hand complaints lodged against Sgt. Thomas "Tip" Jackson, a member of the same precinct in the NYPD, tampered with evidence for one of his officers caught sleeping with a prostitute while on duty. Do you remember this incident, Detective?"

"Yes, I do."

Samantha jumped to her feet again. "Your Honor, I fail to see how this questioning is relevant to the matters before the court, not to mention that Sgt. Jackson is not on trial here; Patrick Sawyer is."

"Mr. Gerard," Judge Cooper said, "make your point."

"Yes, Your Honor." Alan casually slipped his hand into his pocket, sashayed across the floor to the jury box, and stood in front. "So then, Detective Gerard, you're confirming that evidence was tampered with in your precinct?"

"Sir," Gerard said, raising his voice. "That can happen anywhere, but—"

Alan cut him off. "Is that what you did with the front end of Mr. Sawyer's vehicle, Detective? Didn't you conspire to make it appear that my client is the guilty party here on the orders of your superior and with the help of the State's witness, Vito Lorenzano, a known felon?" Alan turned to the jurors. The two females in the front row stared at him wide-eyed.

Gerard felt his pulse increase again but resisted the urge to be drawn into his father's game. He stared back at him without answering and glanced over at Patrick Sawyer, who was grinning from ear to ear as though Alan's questioning was a sign of victory. The expression on Alan's face brought it all back, and the "rules" echoed through his mind.

Rule Number One: Divert the focus away from the defendant.

"The witness will answer the question," Judge Cooper demanded.

"No, Mr. Gerard," the detective said.

"You testified earlier that Mr. Sawyer never mentioned his wife had run off when, in fact, he wept during the ride to the precinct for questioning and discussed it with you then. Isn't that true, Detective?"

"Mr. Sawyer never said anything about his wife running off, nor had he cried. My partner and I discouraged communication while in the vehicle with Mr. Sawyer. It was for his protection, and we suggested he wait until we were in an interrogation room to record his statements for the record."

"Detective, isn't it true that your superior, Lieutenant Jack Harwell, directed you and your partner to make it happen . . . do what was necessary to put him behind bars?"

"No. Lieutenant Harwell does his job."

"Of manipulating his team of detectives to arrest an innocent man and tamper with the evidence to satisfy his own needs. Isn't that correct, Detective?"

Gerard forced himself back into composure as Alan's Rule Number Two rushed through his mind.

Get the witness on the defensive, and you've won your case. Gerard opened his mouth to speak just as Alan took his parting shot.

"I have no further questions for this witness at this time." Alan marched back to the defense table.

Samantha stood, "Redirect, Your Honor?"

* * *

Jessie and Gerard walked down the stairs of the courthouse and headed toward the parking lot in silence. The outside temperature had warmed up since the early morning chill. Jessie inhaled the smell of roasted chestnuts from a vendor's carts.

"You did a good job in there, Gerard. You held your own and were one up on him after Samantha's redirect."

Gerard remained silent, deep in thought.

"Your father is one tough hombre," she said.

"Mmm." He continued to stare into space, deep in thought.

"But you did grea—" Jessie stopped talking when her cell phone played its musical ring tone pulling her from the conversation. "Detective Kensington here." She stopped short. "What?" she said panicked. "What do you mean he's gone?" She shot Gerard a look. "Did you check the grounds -- the basement -- the attic?" She held her hand over the receiver. "Vito's gone."

"Dammit," Gerard said, his hand bouncing off the fender of a parked vehicle. "One friggin' step forward, two steps back."

"Call in a team," she said and snapped her phone shut. "Can you believe this shit?" She stopped and placed her hands on her hips. "Okay, this is for the birds. Harwell needs to step up the investigation to find out who's on the take."

"How did this happen?"

"After breakfast this morning, Vito and Rory played cards for a while, then watched a little television. Rory Dodd . . . I think that's his name. Anyway, he fell asleep, and when he woke, Vito was gone."

"Where the hell was the second guard?"

"He went to a local store to buy coffee." She sighed and continued to walk.

"What? The coffee at the house wasn't good enough?"

She rolled her eyes. "He went to purchase ground coffee, Gerard. They were out of it."

"Oh."

"Besides the two guards and Harwell," she said, turning to her partner, "they were the only ones who knew where Vito was hidden. Right?"

"Correct," he said with a huff. He grumbled and increased his stride.

"Oh my God." Jessie gasped. Her hand slapped against her chest. "Holy shit! I just remembered this guy Dodd . . . works for Jackson."

Gerard pulled his phone out. "Lieutenant. Vito's gone."

Harwell's rage echoed through the receiver. "And guess who was guarding him?" he said.

"Rory Dodd," Gerard spewed. "Dodd works for Jackson. I think we just found our mole." Gerard licked his lips. "Good. Kensington and I were saying the same thing. Okay," his head nodded. "Yep, yep. Yeah, on our way back to the precinct."

"Harwell's going out to the safe house to confront Dodd. He's hiring Bradshaw to put a tail on him and Jackson. Let's see if they're smart enough to figure this out." He looked down on the ground as if in thought. "You're pretty damn smart."

"Why? Because I remembered Dodd works for Jackson?"

"Well, that, and many other reasons. See, that's why I love you so much." Her head jerked toward him. "Technically speaking, that is," he added.

"Oh. Right, right, right. Me too, you -- technically speaking," Jessie said, returning the comment. She gave him a once over when he wasn't watching and decided he looked pretty damn hot today with those broad shoulders of his tucked inside his perfectly fitted jacket. Goosebumps pebbled her flesh and caused her to shudder.

"Are you okay?" he asked.

"Yeah, why?"

"Do you need an arm around you to keep warm?"

She laughed. "No." She would have liked nothing better but to change the subject instead. "This Sawyer case is beginning to bug the crap right out of me. When are we going to catch a break?"

"Hey," he said, "I just thought of something. The rash of burglaries in the borough--isn't Rory in charge of security for the residents on vacation?"

"Yes, he is."

"Has anyone checked the records of the break-ins to see who's on the roster for those daily checks?"

"That's a good question, Gerard."

CHAPTER 33

ew York City Supreme Court - December 5, 2008

Jessie and Gerard huddled with Samantha Richards before the start of the proceedings. Both were looking rather grim.

"Do you think Sawyer could walk away from all of this?" Jessie asked.

Samantha could see the frustration etched on the detectives' faces and had trouble hiding her disappointment with how things had turned out. Losing Vito had severely damaged their case.

"Well, probably not on all of the charges, but it's doubtful we'll get a conviction on the murders. We don't have the murder weapon in the case of Lenny, and not knowing what happened to Amanda is a real stretch for a jury to convict. We've established that Sawyer is evil, but that's hardly enough compared to what he deserves."

"I know I shouldn't feel this way," Jessie admitted. "Lenny was hardly a positive contributor to society, but not getting justice for Amanda will haunt me for the rest of my life." The trio walked to their seats.

"All rise for the Honorable Jamie Cooper."

Judge Cooper walked from his chambers, mounted the steps to his seat, and eased himself into the chair.

"Mr. Gerard? You may call your next witness."

"Thank you, Your Honor. The defense rests at this time."

"Thank you." He turned to the District Attorney. "Miss Richards?"

"The prosecution res—" She stopped mid-sentence when a law clerk from her office rushed into the courtroom, waving a piece of paper. Samantha sensed the judge's impatience. "Excuse me, Your Honor." She read the note. Her mouth creased into a smile. She looked into the audience and noticed the two detectives staring at her quizzically. Turning back to face the judge, she spoke. "Your Honor, it appears I have one last witness."

"Your Honor," Alan Gerard rushed to his feet, a frown on his face. "I wasn't notified there was another witness or even the possibility of one."

"Sidebar," the judge bellowed. Both attorneys made their way toward the judge's bench. "What's going on, Ms. Richards?"

"I'm as shocked as you are, Your Honor. You saw my clerk rush into the court. I'm just finding this out myself."

"That's convenient, Samantha," Alan said with contempt. "One last shot at sneaking in through the back door to save your case. What did you do? Stay up all night trying to drum up a witness after Vito Lorenzano skipped out on you?"

"I swear, Alan," she turned to face him, "I had no idea." She passed the note to the judge.

"Hmm." The judge shook his head from side to side. "This ought to be interesting. All right, Miss Richards," Judge Cooper said, "I'm sorry, Mr. Gerard. I have to allow this witness's testimony. But," he spoke directly to Samantha, his index finger in the air, "if I find out you knew anything at all. Even the slightest hint about this witness appearing, I'll have you disbarred. Do I make myself clear?"

"Crystal, Your Honor. I swear to you," she appealed, her hand held in the swearing position.

"All right, you may proceed."

When he returned to his table, Alan leaned aside and informed Sawyer of the witness's identity. Unable to hide his anger, Sawyer's face flushed.

"The state calls Father Joseph McKinley to the witness stand," the bailiff announced. A surprised buzz hummed over the courtroom as the bystanders watched Sawyer's expression change when the elderly priest made his way to the stand. Sawyer's face contorted into a furious rage, ready to take on the world. The priest no sooner walked up the steps than Patrick jumped to his feet, his two hands balled into fists.

"You lousy sonofabitch," he shouted. His attorney tried to talk him down, but Sawyer continued his tirade.

Judge Cooper pounded his gavel against the block and roared his voice. "Remove the defendant from my courtroom." There was a hush of silence.

Within seconds, Sawyer's eyes took on a daunting expression, and in one quick movement, he propelled his body over the table. His foot caught on the table's edge, causing it to topple onto its side. Bystanders gasped as Sawyer's balled fist was within inches of Father McKinley's jaw, but the bailiff's quick action knocked him to the floor. With the help of two security guards, Sawyer's wrists were cuffed behind his back with two more security guards standing close by ready to yank him to an upright position. Sawyer lurched back and forth like a caged lion, trying to free himself to no avail. His rage continued unabated as he shouted obscenities over his shoulder, the tears rushing down his cheeks. "You can't tell . . . you can't." His head slumped forward, and he sobbed uncontrollably.

When the commotion ended, Judge Cooper exhaled to calm down and hammered his gavel on the block. "Okay, folks, sit down and be quiet. Let's listen to the testimony of this last witness."

Relief rushed through Gerard when the old priest placed his hand on the bible and swore to tell the truth. He turned to Jessie and winked. She got his message.

"Are you all right, Father?" Samantha asked, rushing over to him.

"I'm fine, my dear. How about you?"

Samantha sucked in a deep breath and blew it out. "I must admit, Father, I was scared for you."

He smiled and looked toward the ceiling. "I had someone watching over me, Miss Richards."

"So you did, Father." She sighed. "Father, would you like to take a break before I begin questioning you?"

"No. I'm fine. Please go ahead."

"Thank you, Father." She stopped in front of the stand. "Are you an ordained priest in the Roman Catholic Church?"

"Yes."

"And, what is the name of your parish?"

"St. Catherine's."

"Father, would you tell this court what the *vow of silence* means to the Catholic Church?"

"Certainly," he responded. "Quite simply, it requires a priest to maintain complete silence when it involves a confession of sins."

"You took that oath when you became a priest. Is that correct?"

"I did."

"Then, how is it that you are here today to testify against the defendant?"

"For two reasons. The first is I've recently learned I am dying. The second reason is about what I've read in the newspapers about the disappointments our police department has endured with this case and I refuse to keep this secret any longer." He paused. "I can't go to my grave knowing what I do. I've had a good life, and I'm certain God will forgive me."

Samantha turned to see the jurors' faces and continued her questioning. "Father, I'm sorry to hear of your illness." He nodded. "Do your superiors know you are here today?"

"They do."

"They can't be pleased about this appearance?"

"No, they are not." He lowered his head. "I'm not very proud of it either, but I'm doing God's will."

"By testifying today, Father, have you been given an ultimatum?"

"Yes." He made the sign of the cross. "I've been told if I do, I will be excommunicated from the Catholic Church."

"Does that also mean you will lose your pension?"

"Yes, it does, but I have enough money to get me through until I go home to my Father."

"Then you must have an awful lot to tell us, Father."

"I do."

CHAPTER 34

 ecember 16, 2008

The bailiff walked into the center of the courtroom. "All rise for The Honorable James W. Cooper of the County of New York."

The judge took his seat. "Has the jury reached a verdict in the matter of State of New York City v. Patrick James Sawyer?"

"We have, Your Honor."

The families of the deceased sat silently; their eyes focused on the jury in anticipation of the verdict. Gerard leaned over to Jessie, "Are you ready, Jess?" A pang of uncertainty rushed through his body.

"You bet."

The bailiff went to the jury box, where the foreperson handed him a paper containing the jury's verdict and then delivered it to the judge.

Judge Cooper's face remained emotionless as he read the note. "Will the defendant please rise?" Sawyer and his attorneys stood erect. Alan folded his hands in the front of his body.

Judge Cooper's attention turned to the foreperson. "On the first charge of two counts of murder in the first degree, how do you find?"

"We, the jury, find the defendant, Patrick James Sawyer, guilty."

The smirk on Sawyer's face turned stone cold, and his shoulders slumped. Maria Alexander, who sat directly behind him, sobbed out of control. Her hand touched his arm, but a court officer stood in front of her.

Jessie glanced over at Gerard, who had a wide grin. She gave him the thumbs-up and then leaned over toward him. "What a special day this has turned out to be."

"On the second charge of two counts of money laundering and documentation fraud, how do you find?"

"We, the jury, find the defendant, Patrick James Sawyer, guilty."

"On the third charge of one count of threatening law enforcement, how do you find?"

"We, the jury, find the defendant, Patrick James Sawyer, guilty."

Reporters ran from the courtroom, cell phones glued to their ears, anxious to report the verdict to the media. A grim-faced Alan Gerard addressed the judge. "Your Honor, may we poll the jury?"

"Yes, counselor." Judge Cooper faced the jurors again and asked each member if they agreed with the guilty verdict. When all twelve voiced their agreement, he immediately moved on to the final phase of the hearing. "After careful consideration of the facts of this case, the evidence presented, and the jury's verdicts," he said, "sentencing will resume in my courtroom thirty days from this date. Mr. Gerard, please see the court clerk for the date." The judge's gavel hit the block with a resounding bang.

Tears ran down Sawyer's cheeks. Alan Gerard patted his shoulder and whispered something to his client. Patrick jerked away from his touch.

"Bailiff, take the prisoner into custody." Three court officers swiftly led Patrick Sawyer out of the courtroom. The judge continued. "I'd like to thank the jury for their time and commitment to the community. You are now free to leave." Raising his gavel, he brought it down one last time. "This Court is adjourned."

The two detectives rushed over to Samantha and hugged her. "I can't believe the jury bought our entire case," Jessie said.

Samantha shook her head, more than a little amazed herself. "That's the thing with juries. You never know what little thing will push them in either direction. Once Father McKinley told his story, the jury had no problem believing that the charges against Sawyer were highly probable. Sawyer's outrage helped our case even more. Good job, detectives."

* * *

"We did it, hotshot," Jessie squealed with delight as they walked down the court building steps.

"We certainly did. I'm just happy the families have closure." Gerard reached for her hand. She pulled it back, concerned the others might see. "What's wrong, Jess?"

"I have to tell you something."

"Uh-oh, this sounds ominous. Okay, shoot."

"I'm leaving the department and moving over to Missing Persons."

Gerard stopped dead in his tracks and stared at her. "Why, Jess?" His brows knitted together. "Have I been coming on too strong?"

"No. Not at all."

"Then, why are you leaving?"

"Because I can't continue to be your partner and date you at the same time."

Gerard reached out and pulled her into his arms, and kissed her tenderly. "Do you know what this means to me?"

"I'm sure as much as it means to me."

CHAPTER 35

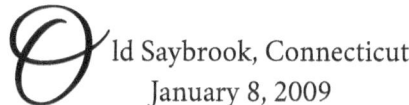ld Saybrook, Connecticut
        January 8, 2009

Gabi Sawyer pulled the collar of her wool coat tightly against her neck to block out the wind whipping around her body. Winter seemed much worse in this sleepy little town of Old Saybrook, Connecticut, than when she lived in Manhattan—no tall buildings to block the ravages of the weather. Already a foot deep, the snow was still falling from the sky like an angry avalanche.

Gabi shivered and pulled her scarf up to cover her mouth and nose. The quick movement caused the straps from her backpack to slip off her shoulder. She hitched the straps higher, her mittens getting caught underneath. Annoyed, she released an exasperated sigh, pulled her gloves out from under the straps, and quickly slipped her hands back inside to avoid frostbite from the frigid weather.

Despite the winters, she did like living in Connecticut. But leaving her friends hadn't been easy. Neither was knowing her father would spend the rest of his life in prison with no chance of parole. Tears welled in her eyes. She couldn't believe how drastically her life had changed at the hands of her father. Thoughts of the trial entered her mind and the day her grandparents returned from court.

Though Gabi had begged them to let her go to court, they refused her request. At the time, she was upset because it was the last time she would ever see her father. Now, in hindsight, Gabi was glad she hadn't, especially after learning the truth about the man she'd adored at one time. Neither grandparent was savvy on the computer or had an inkling of what was published for the world to read, but that's where Gabi learned the truth about the father she'd once adored. Thinking back on the verdict day, her grandparents returned with a ridiculous story about her father's conviction to spare her feelings. Gabi knew they meant well. She'd never tell them she knew the truth, but ever since then, she'd often cried herself to sleep.

Her mind clouded in confusion about what her father had done. The continuous dull ache in her heart was more cumbersome than carrying her backpack. Tears splashed her cheeks, the wind stinging them like they were on fire. She shut her eyes and used the tail end of her scarf to dry her tears. Her mind drifted back to the online article reporting the things her father had done. None of it made any sense to her and she would never understood his reason for doing what he did. He killed her mother because she could not give him more children? The hatred welled inside her. Her pace slowed in concert with the heaviness she carried in her heart. Parents weren't supposed to do such awful things. She angrily kicked the snow with the toe of her boot — God, how she missed her mother.

Moving away from the city with her grandparents and aunt after her father's conviction had been a blessing. At least, that's what her grandmother said. She missed her friends—especially Marti. But now that she had a cell phone, they kept in touch regularly, and Marti planned to spend time with her during the summer months.

She didn't understand everything that had happened, but she knew once the government had taken the house and the dealership, whatever was left over was put into a trust for her. She didn't care about the money. She didn't care about anything. All she wanted was a quiet family life with two parents.

The smell of wood burning filled the air and spiraled up her nose. She inhaled the sweet scent of pine as she passed an evergreen tree. This year, Christmas had come and gone. She tried to feel the excitement she usually did, but the holidays would never be the same without her parents. She had her father to thank for that.

Shuffling down Main Street, Gabi glanced at the snow-covered brick Georgian structures and odd-shaped saltbox houses. It reminded her of a scene from the Charles Dickens' story, *A Christmas Carol*. The wind picked up and knocked the crusted ice from the trees in a spray-like glass shattering from a window. Gabi ducked to avoid getting hit and couldn't wait to get home. She could hardly wait to warm up in front of the fireplace. Just as she was about to mount the steps, her aunt exited the house.

"Aww, Gabi, you poor thing." Her Aunt Sara rushed down the stairs to help her. "You must feel like a popsicle," she said, pulling the backpack off Gabi's shoulders. Sara's brows quirked together in confusion. "Hey, what are you doing home so early? I thought you were supposed to be dismissed at one o'clock?"

"The lights went out at school, so they told us to go home." She shivered.

"Why didn't you call."

"I left my phone at home." She shivered. "I'm freezing, Aunt Sara," she said, jumping up and down to warm her body.

"Well, let's get you inside." Sara wrapped her arm around Gabi's waist and helped her up the stairs.

Joyce Milligan rushed into the living room, carrying a blanket. "My God," she said, cupping Gabi's cheeks with her hands, "let's get you out of these wet clothes." Disrobed down to her underwear, Joyce wrapped the warm blanket around Gabi.

"Mmm, Gram," she said, snuggling inside the blanket, "this feels so good." She smiled at her grandmother. "You're the best Gram in the whole world."

Joyce cradled Gabi in her arms. "I like you a lot, too," she said, her voice cracking. Gabi could tell she was crying and hugged her even tighter. When they stopped hugging, Joyce turned around and headed for the kitchen.

"Here, Gab," Sara said, guiding her closer to the fireplace, "stand in front of the fire for a few minutes. Keep turning around slowly to warm that little body of yours."

"You mean like the rotisserie chickens in the supermarket?" Gabi teased as she turned around in a circle.

"Exactly. But we're not going to eat you, silly," Sara gave a gentle poke to her ribs. Gabi jerked back and giggled, pulling the blanket tighter; she continued to rotate in a slow circle.

Sara bent down and gathered Gabi's wet clothes off the floor. "I'll put these in the dryer for a few minutes."

"And I'll bring your hot chocolate out here so you can drink it by the fire," Joyce said by the kitchen door. As she walked in the opposite direction, the phone rang. Joyce stopped mid-step.

"I'll get it, Gram." Gabi said and scrambled to the end table to answer the call.

"Hello." No one answered. "Hello?" she repeated.

"Gabi? Gabi? Is that you?" the familiar voice echoed through the receiver.

"Mommy?"

ABOUT THE AUTHOR

Internationally recognized, K. T. Roberts writes romantic suspense and cozy mysteries with sass and brass.

Missing her roots, this Jersey Girl recently returned home with her real-life hero, Bob, and like Dorothy in the Wizard of Oz says, "'there's no place like home.'"

They have four children. As a professional chef, on those rare occasions when she's not writing, she loves to whip up gastronomic treats for family and friends!

$\sim$

K. T. has memberships in Romance Writers of America, Valley of the Sun Romance Writers and Sisters in Crime.

For more information about her books, visit her website at http://ktrobertsmysteries.com, and while you're at it, drop her a note. She loves to hear from her readers.

Sign-up for her monthly newsletter titled Jersey Girl's Musings where you'll be the first to receive exciting news about releases and noteworthy events. Don't miss out on the fun! https://ktrobertsmysteries.com

One of the greatest gifts you can give to an author is a review for their work. If you enjoyed this as much as she enjoyed writing it, please leave a review. Thank you!

www.ingramcontent.com/pod-product-compliance
Lightning Source LLC
Chambersburg PA
CBHW020340180626
46812CB00001B/277